LIGHT BEFORE DAY

LIGHT BEFORE DAY

CHRISTOPHER RICE

miramax books

HYPERION

NEW YORK

Copyright © 2005 Christopher Rice

ISBN 0-7394-5747-0

IN MEMORY OF MY FATHER

Behold the door.
The lock's alive.
—STAN RICE

With one finger he traced designs on the wooden table. He made a
circle out of a lake; he formed two rivers from the
circle; he flooded and destroyed an island, creating a sea. There were
so many things that could be done with
whiskey and water on a table.
—GORE VIDAL, *The City and the Pillar*

Such was the popular superstition—that California's interior was the
province of beastly condors and giant dragonflies
and Satan himself—that not a single Spanish land grant
was ever sought or given inside the valley.
—MARK ARAX AND RICK WARTMAN, *The King of California:
J. G. Boswell and the Making of a Secret American Empire*

Avenal, California

Several weeks after her husband's death, Janice Hughes packed what remained of her belongings into her Toyota Camry, left her daughter's apartment in Berkeley, and drove east into California's Great Central Valley, where the knee-high carpets of tule grass make the low, rolling hills look like sand dunes, and the California Aqueduct, with its rippling surface and wide concrete banks, flows south alongside Interstate 5. From there, Janice somehow ended up in the tiny town of Avenal, teaching seventh and eighth graders at Boswell Junior High.

Avenal sits in the narrow valley between the tule-blanketed Kettleman Hills and the first rounded peaks of California's Coast Ranges. Its main street is just several blocks long, and city hall could easily be mistaken for a doctor's office. No one could see what such a small town had to offer a longtime San Franciscan like Janice Hughes.

To her fellow teachers, Janice mentioned a daughter who never came to visit. She wore her steel-colored hair in a pageboy cut and had a fondness for Native American jewelry, which gave birth to rumors that she was a lesbian. People suspected that when she wasn't working, she didn't spend much time in their town at all. But to her neighbors and colleagues, none of these speculations would have merited anything more than a passing mention if Janice had not become so dangerously obsessed with a thirteen-year-old boy named Caden McCormick.

* * *

A few days after Janice died, her colleague at Boswell Junior High, fifty-one-year-old Glenda Marsh, told a reporter for the *Bakersfield Californian* that Janice had come to her the week before, asking about a new student named Caden McCormick. There were trails of dirt around the boy's ears, and other students had started to make fun of his bad smell. It was clear the kid wasn't bathing. Glenda Marsh knew the real story. Most of the other teachers at Boswell knew how to spot the child of methamphetamine addicts from a mile away.

But in Glenda's opinion, Janice was getting a "little too worked up" about the boy, so she gave the woman only half of the story. Tonya McCormick and her boyfriend Kyle Purcell had moved to town recently and lived in a trailer park that sat north of town, close to Highway 33. There were rumors that Tonya had spent time in prison. Glenda assumed that these details would be enough to satisfy Janice: parents who moved their kids from town to town as if they were cars, a family history of trouble with law enforcement. She was trying to convince Janice that her concern for the boy could never make a difference. She failed.

In the journal discovered by the Kings County Sheriff's Department in her house, Janice described how one May afternoon she followed Caden home from school. The boy walked for almost a half hour north on Highway 33 before he came to a small trailer park with only six plots and a massive dried-out date palm in its center. Hidden from sight in her car, Janice watched the boy spend several minutes standing outside a high chain-link fence topped with coils of razor wire that surrounded a trailer with blackout curtains inside its windows and plywood sheets nailed over the rips in its walls. A pickup truck sat on blocks next to the trailer, its hood propped open and the contents of its engine spilled over the dirt, as if someone had been called away in the middle of ripping out its innards.

Caden wouldn't touch the gate in the fence. A few seconds later, Janice saw why. A pit bull vaulted from the rear of the trailer, its barks crazed and ferocious and its head twisting in the air, as if it were chewing on something. Caden McCormick took a few steps back from the fence and watched the dog plow headfirst into the chain link. Then Janice heard a sound like the snap of a giant guitar string—and suddenly the dog was sprawled out on the dirt on its back, yelping in pain, its head flailing and its legs jerking in quick spasms.

The man who emerged from the trailer wore a backward baseball cap. Red welts covered his bony arms and spindly legs. His long face was wasting into sharp angles, and in his right hand he carried something long and metallic. He threw open the gate without getting shocked, and Caden ran through it and toward the trailer.

Just as the pit bull rolled squirming onto its back, the man raised the metal stick in his hand and Janice saw a blue tongue flicker at its tip.

"A Taser," she wrote in her journal. "The kind they use on lunatics and inmates, and this man uses it on the family pet. And who knows who else."

On the afternoon of her death, Janice Hughes instructed her class of eighth graders to make family trees. No one could remember her giving such an assignment before. She passed out photocopies of possible formats, construction paper, and scissors and instructed the class to get to work.

Janice Hughes's students claimed she never took her eyes off of Caden McCormick, who sat in the third row. The boy did not use the construction paper or scissors Janice had given him. He sketched steadily, bent low over his desk to hide his work from the kids around him.

At one point, Janice walked up behind the boy, placed both hands on his back, and peered over his shoulder. Several students would tell the *Bakersfield Californian* that their teacher went pale when she saw Caden McCormick's work.

"What is that, Caden?" she asked.

The boy gave her a blank look and went back to work.

Deputy Amy Stahl was on patrol when a call came in from dispatch about an open 911 line in Avenal. Amy recognized the name of the caller. She had visited Janice Hughes one night when the woman had phoned to report a prowler. A search of Janice's property had turned up nothing. Janice had been embarrassed and had offered the deputy coffee, then asked Amy questions about her life without offering up a single piece of information about her own. Amy had heard the rumor that Janice was a lesbian. She never worked up the courage to ask Janice if the rumor was true. Now Janice had called the Kings County Sheriff's Department in a panic, screaming something about how thirteen-year-old Caden McCormick was in danger. Amy was fairly sure Janice had been given the runaround, which is why the woman had bolted out of her home without bothering to terminate the call. Or perhaps Janice thought the best way to get the police's attention was to get them to come after her.

"She kept saying something about 'get the boy,'" the dispatcher said, slipping out of policespeak.

Amy heard another deputy call in to say that he was en route to Janice's home, so Amy flashed her lights and blew through the town of Avenal. She was heading north on Highway 33 in the direction of the trailer park Janice had mentioned to dispatch when a flash of white lit up the northern horizon. It strobed the metal power poles in the distance and flashed across the flanks of the Kettleman Hills.

Blinded, Amy slammed on her brakes. When she opened her eyes, she saw pieces of a double-wide trailer tumbling back down to earth on a pond of fire that burned so white it looked like someone had spilled a piece of heaven. Amy grabbed the radio. She went lights and sirens and slammed her foot on the gas.

When she arrived on the scene, she almost ran into Janice's Toyota Camry. It was lying on its roof in a bed of shattered glass that shimmered with the reflection of white flames. Janice was not inside it. Amy found her across the road from the trailer's flaming crater, lying facedown on a torn piece of chain link. Most of the hair had been burned off her head and her burned lips were trying to form words.

Her eyes smarting from the flame's noxious fumes, Amy gripped one of Janice's hands and brought her ear to the woman's lips. She was whispering something about a dog but it was lost in the wail of approaching sirens. Janice Hughes died several minutes after she was loaded into the ambulance.

Later that night, Amy Stahl was the first sheriff's deputy to enter Janice's home. A muted television still flickered in the corner of a small, immaculate living room. A hanging pendant chandelier sent a harsh corona of light down onto the dining room table, where a river of red wine wound its way around a stack of papers.

Amy leafed through them and saw the family trees Janice had instructed her students to make earlier that day. One family tree lay off to the side, facedown. When Amy turned it over, her breath caught. It was a detailed pencil sketch of a trailer just like the one that had blown sky-high earlier that night. The trailer was surrounded by a chain-link fence topped with razor wire. Behind it, Tonya McCormick's pit bull had been turned into a grotesque monster, its gaping jaws twice the size of the rest of its body. In the expanse of open field behind the trailer, there was a small dark figure without a face, its head rounded slightly as if it were wearing a helmet of some kind.

Amy turned the drawing back over and saw what had propelled Janice to call 911 and dash out of her house to the trailer. There was a message written on the back in small block letters. It was the answer to the question Janice Hughes had asked Caden McCormick in class that afternoon:

He's a demon. He comes every night now.

CHAPTER 1

Three days before I quit drinking, Emilio Vargas met me at a giant Starbucks on Santa Monica Boulevard. He had a long, pocked face with high cheekbones and a sunken jaw. His springy black hair had been pulled back into a small ponytail. He wore Coke-bottle glasses and his left eye couldn't focus on anything higher than his nose. Emilio was a bartender at a hole-in-the-wall club in West Hollywood's east end that catered to male hustlers and hard-core crystal meth addicts. A week earlier, he had re-arranged the faces of two Latino gangbangers who had tried to gay-bash him as he walked to his car after a grueling Saturday night shift.

According to the LA County Sheriff's Department, Emilio's would-be assailants had spent the earlier part of the night walking the Sunset Strip, charming drunken bachelorette party attendees into giving them their phone numbers. Like most of the gangbangers who visited the city of West Hollywood each weekend, they had decided to spice up the long walk back to their car by breaking a gay man's jaw. One of them had carried a bicycle chain, the other a switchblade. If the two guys had simply cut to the chase, instead of calling Emilio the same names his mother called him when she shoved him out the back door of their house after discovering a gay porn magazine under his bed, they might have made off with Emilio's wallet and a chunk of his pride. Instead, they were still recovering from their injuries a week later.

No one in the local press had picked on Emilio's story. If it hadn't been for a deputy at the West Hollywood Sheriff's Station who had taken me on a ride-along a few months earlier for a piece I was trying to put to-gether, I wouldn't have heard about Emilio's seemingly impossible act of self-defense either.

Two hours after we sat down together, my microcassette recorder was almost out of tape and I had Emilio Vargas's entire life story. June Gloom had brought veils of sun-lanced haze to the main thoroughfare of America's premier gay strip mall, and the rainbow flags tied to the lampposts rose and fell in a persistent breeze. The tables on the sidewalk around us were crowded with tank-top-clad men, their mops of windblown hair dyed the color of egg yolk and crow's feathers. They pretended to have conversations while they watched the parade of muscles heading into the 24 Hour Fitness across the street.

For the past year, I had been a glorified office assistant at a gay men's lifestyle magazine called *Glitz*. My editor, Tommy Banks, was convinced that a gay man's lifestyle didn't include much beyond his pecs and his underwear. Recently Tommy had agreed to let me start pursuing what I defined as real stories. That meant no more profiles of pretentious queens who owned their own specialty boutiques and became breathless with anger when I told them the magazine couldn't afford to hire a stylist for their twenty-minute photo shoot. Emilio Vargas was anything but a retail queen.

"You're too pretty to be a reporter," he said. "And too young," he told me when we finished the interview.

I thought I looked like a British orphan with a better haircut, but I accepted Emilio's compliment with a smile. We stood and I extended my hand. Instead of accepting it, Emilio reached for my face and brushed the chapped skin beneath my nostrils with one fingertip. I felt the rest of my face flush with embarrassment.

"You stay away from that stuff," he said. "It's no good. All the time I got boys coming to my bar. Sad boys doing sad things."

I mumbled something about how his was an inspiring story and I looked forward to telling it. He gave me a brusque nod and a shake of the head and walked off.

I didn't tell him that I hadn't done a line of cocaine in over a week. In my current state, that was a triumph. I didn't tell him that I spent most of my days wondering just who it was I should be grieving: a drunken mother who had stumbled in front of a speeding taxicab or a boyfriend who had forcibly attempted to change my life over the course of three weeks and left me stunned and scarred.

Maybe Emilio was right. I was a sad boy who did sad things. I wondered if I was more addicted to being sad than I was to bourbon or cocaine.

* * *

Glitz magazine kept an office in a 1980s glass and steel building on Hollywood Boulevard, just steps from Mann's Chinese Theatre. What was referred to on the magazine's masthead as Glitz Worldwide Headquarters consisted of a central area crammed with two desks, along with separate offices for the editor and advertising sales director. The walls were framed with blowups of past covers. Every other day a deliveryman asked me if we were running an underwear catalog.

It was four-thirty when I got to the office the Wednesday of my interview with Emilio Vargas, but Jason, the new receptionist, was still out to lunch. He had made it clear he thought I had an attitude problem. Considering that he had been given a brand-new PowerBook G5 with stereo-surround speakers to assist him in the task of answering the phones, I thought he had a blowing-the-boss-in-the-bathroom problem.

I found Tommy Banks in his office, staring down at a mess of papers with both hands pressed lightly to the sides of his face as if he were assessing himself for a face-lift. The floor around his desk was piled with advance reader's editions of gay-themed novels that had been released months earlier and stacks of promo CDs from disc jockeys who had remixed Top 40 hits with the sounds of revving engines and what seemed to be bronzed sneakers tumbling inside a dryer. Tommy was long and lean with a blond-highlighted bouffant hairdo and a bushy mustache dyed to match. I had never seen him wear anything other than a white T-shirt and form-fitting Diesel jeans. When Tommy didn't ask me how the interview had gone, my heart sank and my fists tightened. He gave me a narrow look and held up a copy of the *West Hollywood Informant*. It was a pencil-thin local that covered new construction projects, purse snatchings, and local residents possessed of notable stamp collections. On the cover was a photograph of Emilio Vargas in all his sulking glory.

"Are you kidding me with this shit?" Tommy asked. "This guy looks like he should be walking in a Day of the Dead parade."

"Then don't put him on the cover," I said.

"I won't," he said. He pursed his lips, as if he didn't want to say what he would say next. "Oh, for Christ's sake, Adam."

"Bury it, Tommy. Don't kill it. I worked too hard on this one."

"Yeah, well, take it up with all your gay brothers out there who won't shell out for anything other than a hot boy in briefs. It's not going in, Adam. I'm sorry."

I took a step toward his desk, which made him slouch back in his chair.

"It took five voice messages to get Emilio even to call me back. After that, I had to pay three visits to his bar before he agreed to talk to me."

"Since when is visiting a bar a problem for you?"

I ignored the jab. "This is crap, Tommy. This isn't about ad sales. This is about you not doing a story that doesn't involve a guy you're trying to sleep with."

Tommy's eyes went wide and he gave me a long slow nod, as if one of his dire suspicions about me had just been confirmed. "Adam Murphy. For the past six years, I have dragged this magazine along on an editorial budget that barely covers our phone bill. I'll fuck the janitor on my desk if I want to. And I won't answer to you about it." He cast his eyes back to the cover shot of Emilio Vargas. "Take the rest of the day off."

I willed myself to leave the office, but my feet didn't go along with the plan.

"Come on, Adam," Tommy muttered, "go drink something. Get laid. We all know that when you took time off last month, it wasn't to help your sister move. It was about your mother, wasn't it?" I had made the mistake of confiding in Tommy about my mother's progressive and fatal alcoholic condition right after I had started working for the magazine. "How is she?" Tommy demanded.

I saw my mother as she had appeared in the crime scene photos I had forced myself to look at. She was lying facedown in the middle of Dumaine Street in the French Quarter. Her platinum hair was fanned forward from her head, and her right arm was extended as if she was pointing in the direction of the cab that had run her down at forty-five miles an hour.

"Or are you still caught up with your stud from the car wash? What's his name?" Tommy asked.

"Corey."

I could see Corey Howard so sharply he might as well have been looming over Tommy's shoulder. He was six-foot-four, with briskly combed jet-black hair and hard plates of muscle armoring his chest, shoulders, and arms. Everything about the man was unyielding until you got to his dark eyes, deeply set beneath the hard line of his brow. I felt the man's breath in my ear, felt one of his hands pinning me to my mattress by my bare chest, urging me to relax. Tommy could read my face. "I guess it didn't end well."

I didn't answer. "Emilio Vargas didn't want to do the interview because he was afraid of disgracing his mother's name. The same mother who threw him out when he was sixteen because he was a fag. She went to her grave without saying another word to him. That's what I had to talk him through to get him to sit down with me today, Tommy. Any idea what I should say to him now?"

"Yeah," Tommy said. "Tell him to get a stylist."

I shut my eyes briefly and reminded myself why I worked at *Glitz* magazine. My position allowed me to avoid doing the legwork required to become a real journalist. I just had to find a subject who looked like an Abercrombie & Fitch model.

I was almost out the door when Tommy called out to me. He was standing over his desk. He handed me a computer printout of a *Los Angeles Times* article that I saw was almost two years old. The headline read: GAY COMMUNITY BELIEVES SERIAL KILLER IS BEHIND DISAP-PEARANCES.

I scanned the article as Tommy stood over me, but it didn't tell me anything I didn't already know. Some twenty-two months earlier, three model-perfect gay guys had vanished without a trace from West Holly-wood. Local activists with too much time on their hands had become convinced that a serial killer was at work, even though there wasn't a shred of forensic evidence to support such a theory. Since then, the Slasher had become a punch line to an old joke.

Shortly after I moved to LA, I attended a Halloween party where one of the guests had come dressed in a black ski mask and a black sweater. He carried a bottle of Cristal champagne by the neck, its shattered base smeared with fake blood. He had pinned pictures of the three alleged victims to the back of his sweater. The real Ann Coulter would have received a warmer reception from the other guests.

"The West Hollywood Slasher?" I asked in disbelief.

"The guys who disappeared," Tommy said. "They call them the Vanished Three. Have you seen their pictures? They look like God's gift to the Undergear catalog. There's some little memorial to them online. I can give you the web address if you want it." I didn't respond. "Anyway, they're superhot. I'd put all three of them on the cover. Twice."

"That's the only reason anyone cared when they went missing," I said. "Guys vanish from West Hollywood all the time and nobody pays attention."

"So I guess you're not interested?" Tommy asked.

"It's ancient history, Tommy. These guys went home with the wrong guy and there was never any evidence that it was the same one. Why don't I just try out Bigfoot instead?"

Tommy let out an exasperated sigh and sank down into his desk chair. I folded up the article and shoved it in my pocket.

"I'll see you at nine tomorrow," Tommy said. "I need you to stuff boxes for that promotion we're doing in P-Town." I turned on my heel. "And leave the hangover at home this time, please."

My apartment building sat a block below the Sunset Strip. It had stucco walls painted dark gray and one story of south-facing units above a row of driveways. Every night, the city of West Hollywood raised three concrete columns in the middle of my street to keep the traffic on the Strip from spilling over into the residential blocks below.

The liquor store several blocks away was made famous when an Oscar-winner-to-be slammed her car into its side wall. I stopped off there on my way home from the office and left with a bottle of Crown Royal, a six-pack of Diet Coke, and two bottles of cheap Chardonnay that I managed to convince myself were for guests. I had never hosted more than one guest in my tiny studio.

My bed was a mattress that sat on a short platform next to the living area, and I had placed a love seat in front of the television because I wanted room for an Ikea desk station I had never finished putting together. The vertical blinds were so old and tattered that I had purchased an Oriental screen to block out the morning sunlight. It was heavy, and on most nights I didn't feel like dragging it across the pseudo-shag carpet, so it rested on the wall just inside my front door, and I would awake in the morning squinting. From my tiny balcony, I could see all the way to that grounded UFO called downtown LA.

Before I poured my first drink, I shoved the *LA Times* article on the West Hollywood Slasher into my desk drawer and pushed my desk chair out onto my balcony. Across the cascade of rooftops, a police helicopter circled lazily above Santa Monica Boulevard, its searchlight stabbing the lingering haze.

Instead of calling Emilio Vasquez and breaking the news about the failed feature, I left a message for my friend Rod Peters. I didn't tell him what was wrong. Rod was an assistant to a celebrity manager and on the fast track to getting his own desk, which meant he didn't have the time for the kind of self-obsession and drug use that I did. The last time we had seen each other, Rod had come to pick me up from a gas station in Silverlake after I emerged from a brownout with a dim memory of being tossed from some guy's pickup truck because I had made fun of his Daisy Dukes. I told myself that if he called me back within twenty minutes, I would fix myself one bourbon and Coke, then pour the rest of the bottle down the sink.

Rod didn't call. I remember pouring my first drink. I remember hearing the police helicopter I had watched earlier fly so low over my apartment building that it rattled my sliding glass door against its frame.

I remember composing part of a letter to my sister, Candace, a letter that thanked her for asking me to be in the room during her C-section and allowing me to witness my niece's first breath. A letter that tried to explain that I hadn't called her in the weeks since our mother's death because when our parents had divorced, she had picked the parent who didn't call you screaming in the middle of the night because the nightmares were back and you were in every single one of them. She had picked the right side, the side that had lived, but I still thought I deserved a medal for sticking with the side that had withered and died.

I remember balling up the letter and tossing it in the wastebasket.

To this day, I do not remember anything else about the night of Wednesday, June 2.

The next morning I woke up staring at a geisha's gold-leaf face. The Oriental screen I rarely touched had been opened and placed next to the bed. I was tucked neatly under the covers in boxers and a T-shirt, and the top sheet had been folded back over my comforter. It was seven A.M. and I still had two hours to get to work.

When I got to my feet, my butt knocked the screen and it went over. I heard a crash and saw pieces of the Crown Royal bottle dance out from under my coffee table. The vertical blinds were closed. To avoid cutting my bare feet, I walked the screen like a plank and then hopped to the carpet on the other side. It was a huge mistake. My stomach rose into my throat and my ass hit the floor. For a long while, I just sat there, fighting down bile, gazing dully at the poster for the Krewe of Dionysus on the wall above my love seat. It was one of the larger and more popular New Orleans Mardi Gras parade organizations, and my father had been a riding member since before I was born. If my mother had not given it to me as a housewarming present, I never would have hung it on my wall. My father and I had barely exchanged a word since their divorce. The poster featured a cartoon rendering of the god of wine lifting a golden goblet full of plastic Mardi Gras beads toward his leering mouth. I figured it was time to replace him with a picture of Bill W.

When I was a senior in high school, my parents had purchased a condo on Florida's Gulf Coast, just a few hours' drive from where I grew up in the Lakefront area of New Orleans. On our first trip there, my mother threw a drink at my father because he refused to leave four days earlier than we had planned. This single act effectively ended a marriage that had been dead for years. On my mother's orders, I had helped pack all of his belongings before we left. I'm still not sure if she wanted him to follow us in pursuit of his shorts and polo shirts or if she just wanted to punish him for not giving in to her demands, as I had done. A few hours later, I was following my mother east on I-10, through a pelting rainstorm, when my father called her cell phone to tell her that their marriage was over.

Later, my mother and I were eating dinner at a Cracker Barrel in Mississippi when she came out of her daze to give me her opinion on the day's events. "I hope you never know what it's like to have a life you can only get rid of," she told me.

Now, as I sat paralyzed by nausea on the floor of my apartment, I realized that my mother's hope had been dashed. I was a twenty-six-year-old blackout drunk. I had grown accustomed to checking my Jeep for dents and bloodstains every other morning, studying the call log on my cell phone to see if I had given anyone a piece of my alcohol-soaked mind the night before.

I had a life that I could only get rid of.

I spent an hour throwing up, then another hour trying to slide into clothes that didn't put too much pressure on my abdomen. I made it to the office right on time. Tommy was at his desk looking through photo proofs of fashion models. He took one look at me and his nose wrinkled.

"I'm quitting drinking," I said.

"Fabulous," he mumbled, then went back to work.

Later that day, after the nausea had abated and the overwhelming sense of self-hatred had turned into a slight dizzy feeling, I was grateful for the fact that I hadn't told my boss just when I was going to quit drinking. I had just told him that it was in the cards.

The next night, Friday, I was sitting in a bar sipping a cosmo on the rocks. My date for the evening was supposed to be a handsome TV weatherman named Dave Bolter. He had a nice house in the Norma Triangle section of West Hollywood and an ass that could stop a war. I had called to tell him that while I had decided to quit drinking, I was tapering off slowly. This seemed to intrigue him. He sounded interested in spending a night with me that didn't feature hours of cocaine and pornography, as our previous two get-togethers had. Tonight he was already an hour and a half late.

People in West Hollywood still talk about the days when The Abbey was just a coffee shop. It used to be the place to go if you wanted to pick up on fresh-faced young men who didn't have the fake IDs to get into the clubs along Santa Monica Boulevard. Several years and a liquor license later, it is West Hollywood's most popular gay bar. Several griffins guard the entrance, and a statue of Saint Francis stares out at the crowd like a closeted missionary who has grown too comfortable with his potential converts. At ten P.M., the Friday-night crowd was swelling. It already featured a surprising number of men who had appeared on popular reality television shows.

A hand slid under my leather jacket and tweaked my right nipple. "Cool jacket," a vaguely familiar voice whispered into my ear.

Nate Bain gave me a broad smile that revealed teeth even as piano keys. The last time I had laid eyes on the guy, I had been sitting on the couch in my apartment with my pants around my ankles, wilting from the realization that once again I had inadvertently rented a porn film with someone I knew in it. Nate had a short, broad-shouldered body, and his white tank top set off his sculpted arms. A U.S. Marine Corps baseball cap concealed a spiky crop of jet-black hair. I had encountered him at various parties over the last year, where his sheen of sweat and nonstop conversation told me that he was amped up on something stronger than cocaine.

Now Nate's cheeks looked sunken, and his wide eyes were bloodshot. A welter of red dots disfigured his right arm, which told me he had spent some time picking at the skin. June Gloom had brought chill to the night air, but he looked feverish. He saw me notice these things and his smile waned.

"Where'd you get it?" he asked.

"The jacket?" I asked.

He nodded, his eyes darting past me as if he thought he had been followed. "I ordered it from the J. Crew catalog back when I was in high school." I heard the slight slur in my voice and steadied myself with a deep breath. "Back then, ordering anything leather seemed like an act of rebellion. My first boyfriend always said it smelled like vitamins."

"What was he like?" Nate asked.

"He was a patrol cop in Jefferson Parish," I said. "He almost succeeded in keeping his wife and me from finding out about each other."

"Where's Jefferson Parish?"

"Outside New Orleans. Where I'm from. Is there something I can help you with, Nate?"

The bite in my voice made him flinch. "I need to talk to you," Nate said in a low voice. His smile had vanished and his tone was suddenly so serious I thought he was about to tell me I had three hours to live.

"Can it wait?" I asked. "I'm on a date."

"The weatherman?" he asked. "He dates everyone. You can do better, Adam."

Just then, Nate's eyes darted past my shoulder. I turned, expecting Dave Bolter to give me the kind of smile that made television viewers across the Southland fall in love with terms like *marine layer* and *offshore flow.*

I found myself eye to eye with a barrel-chested guy in an Abercrombie & Fitch tank top. He had sprayed his bangs straight up and moisturized himself back into his thirties. The glassy sheen in his round eyes reminded me of old heavy metal album covers. He smacked his gum as if he were working his way to a piece of solid gold in the middle.

"I want my shirt," he said.

"Excuse me?"

"You don't even remember me, do you?" he asked.

"We were having a conversation," Nate chimed in, sounding like an irate third grader.

Our new companion gave Nate a dull stare. "Love your work," he said. Then to me he said, "Seriously. I want my shirt. It's Prada."

"You better cut those bangs before you catch a bird," I said. I tried to return my attention to Nate, but the guy grabbed my shoulder and spun me around.

"Let me refresh your memory. You made me drive you to Silverlake to see my dealer, then you spilled all my fucking cocaine, then you were too busy crying about your drunk mother to do any of the things you'd promised to do on the ride back to your place." He let this sit for a few seconds. "I want my fucking shirt."

"This is bullshit," I heard myself whisper. But I wasn't talking to the man in front of me. I was talking to myself.

Nate seized my elbow and pulled me away from the bar. Some reflex led me to pick up my pint glass and take a slug from it as Nate dragged me into the crowd.

"What the fuck is your problem, dude?" the guy shouted after us. "Did your mom get loaded and mistake you for your dad?"

My feet turned to concrete blocks. Nate said my name in a low voice that he hoped sounded authoritative. I turned. The guy was standing several feet away, his fists balled at his sides. Several heads had already swiveled to stare at us.

The next thing I knew, my pint glass was sailing through the air in front of me at a speed that didn't seem possible. I heard screams that were too loud to be mistaken for drunken laughter. The guy hit the deck on all fours and the glass smashed into a rack of tea candles on the wall behind him.

Nate swore, grabbed my shoulder, and pulled me into the throng of men. The two of us were halfway across the patio before two muscular arms grabbed me. One bouncer pushed Nate off to the side while the other gripped the back of my neck, forcing my head into a bowed position. I saw the crowd before us parting like the Red Sea gone pink, and then I hit the sidewalk in front of the entrance on all fours.

"What was that shit?" one of the bouncers barked.

I thought if I got to my feet we might have West Hollywood's version of a Rodney King moment, which meant they would flog me with Glosticks. Nate started to explain in a frantic high-pitched voice, but one of the bouncers silenced him.

"Domestic dispute," I groaned.

"Let me take him home," Nate pleaded.

There was a silence from above and I could feel a thousand sets of eyes on me through the patio's front gate. Shame misted my eyes and clogged my throat. One of the bouncers told Nate that I was forever banned from The Abbey, then shouted the same thing down in my direction just to be clear.

Nate pulled me to my feet and suddenly we were walking against the tide of pedestrians toward Santa Monica Boulevard. "It's over," I said.

"What?" Nate asked.

"Nothing."

"Where do you live?"

I pointed uphill. In the low fog, the lights of the Sunset Strip were a milky mist that obscured the foothills, turning the lights of their terraced houses into dusty floating pearls. Nate took my hand and tried to pull me onto the sidewalk.

"This hasn't been my night, Nate."

"Just come with me, Adam. Please." I averted my eyes from his. They were still moist. "Come on! I just saved your ass from a night at the sheriff's station."

"Thanks."

A silence fell.

"I hear you're a real reporter now," he said. I didn't refute this charge. "I've got a story for you."

CHAPTER 2

As soon as Nate and I got back to my apartment, I went into the bathroom and washed my face. I avoided looking at myself in the mirror. Nate was waiting for me on the love seat with a cup of instant coffee. I was surprised to hear myself thank him. Humiliation was sobering, and with sobriety came better manners. I took a seat on the love seat next to him as he channel-surfed.

"You still work for that magazine?" Nate asked.

"Are you angling for an interview? We don't usually cover porn stars, but I guess it's not that much of a stretch."

"I'm not a porn *star*, Adam," he said. "There have only been, like, two gay porn stars in history and they don't exactly have houses in the Hollywood Hills, all right?"

I just stared at him. He grabbed the remote, found an eleven o'clock news broadcast, gave me a grave look, and raised the volume. The two of us sat there as an eighty-one-year-old woman described what it was like to have her arms ripped off by her nephew's pit bull. When the reporter asked her what the worst part of her experience had been, the woman replied, "Losing my arms."

I squawked with laughter, but suddenly Nate grabbed my knee. He raised the volume even more, and I found myself staring at a rolling patch of black ocean pierced by the searchlights of Coast Guard cutters. A reporter's voiceover informed me that a UH-1 Huey helicopter had gone down that afternoon without warning during a training exercise, ten miles off the coast of Oceanside. Four members of a Marine Light Attack Helicopter Squadron had been on board, all of whom were only a few months home from Iraq. A search and rescue mission was under way, but the prospects looked grim.

They showed a photograph of the pilot in full dress. His name was Daniel Brady, and the first thing I noticed about him was that he and I had the same eyes: big, blue, and widely spaced, the kind that make someone look surprised even when he's not. We were the same age, twenty-six, with the other resemblances between us more subtle: the rounded chin, the baby-fat padded cheeks. Brady had sharper versions of each.

"Hot, right?" Nate asked.

If I agreed, I would be flattering myself. I watched as Brady's distraught wife was led away from a duplex apartment building by a tall, big-boned Hispanic woman whose furious expression didn't dim in the lens flare of the surrounding cameras. The most I could see of Melissa Brady was her tangled honey blond hair as she sobbed against her friend's shoulder.

When the story ended, Nate killed the volume and said, "Daniel Brady was in West Hollywood this week."

I pondered this for a second. My head was starting to hurt as the aftereffects of the alcohol kicked in. "Start at the beginning," I said.

He took a deep breath and got to his feet. "It was Wednesday night. Around midnight. I went on a walk, just to get some air, you know?" I didn't believe that any gay man in his twenties who took a walk in West Hollywood at midnight was out just to get some air. But I kept my mouth shut. "I was right down on Santa Monica and San Vicente when this black BMW X5 pulled to the curb beside me. Scott Koffler was driving."

He let this name hang. In the rarified social scene of West Hollywood, Scott Koffler was notorious for bringing barely legal pretty boys to the most exclusive pool parties. In fact I was fairly sure his young charges weren't legal at all, so I stayed the hell away from him. He seemed to have no actual profession aside from high-class pimp, and even though he was in his early thirties, he always dressed the part of the college undergrad, in university sweatshirts and backward baseball caps. He and I had never exchanged anything aside from a thin smile.

"So anyway," Nate continued, "Koffler asks me to get in, so I do. I mean, he's not my favorite guy or anything, but he's kinda cool." I didn't ask him how a jailbait supplier could be considered cool. "So I climb in the backseat, and guess who's in there with me?"

"Daniel Brady."

He nodded. "Brady was nice enough at first. Kinda antsy. Freaked out. I figured he was closeted, but I didn't have any idea he was a marine."

"Or married," I said.

"He's hot, though," Nate said, as if this dismissed the fact I had just given him. "I almost thought he was you. You guys have the same build and everything."

He gave me a slight smile, and I wondered if he was buttering me up in anticipation of how this story of his was going to end. I didn't smile back.

"Suddenly Koffler's asking me if I would like to do stuff. You know, like, mess around. With Brady." Nate didn't see what he wanted to in my face. "So I started following Scott's instructions. The whole setup. I don't know. It turned me on." His voice lacked conviction, which told me there was another layer to the story he was leaving out. His hollow cheeks and the welts on his arms gave me some idea what it might be.

"For a second, I thought Brady was going to go along with it," Nate said. "Then he just flipped out. He slammed my head into the side of the door, and the next thing I knew the motherfucker had thrown me out into the street and I was lying there watching them speed off. I almost got run over."

I gave him a moment to catch his breath, and then I said, "Sorry, Nate. I'm not buying it."

"What?" he barked. He turned his back to me and peeled the back of his tank top up over a skid mark that covered the right half of his lower back. His skin had been turned to ribbons over a bruise that looked like a giant ink stain. "What about this?" he cried.

"Why'd you really get in the car, Nate?" I asked. "Come on. You've got no shortage of willing sex partners, not in your line of work. Brady's hot, but he's not that hot. Why agree to go down on a guy who doesn't seem interested?"

I watched the fight go out of him. "I was high," he whispered.

"On what?" He didn't answer. "You asked me if I was a real reporter, Nate. These are the kinds of questions real reporters ask."

Slowly he reached inside the front of his shorts and removed something. Holding it in his fist, he sank to his knees on the carpet and laid a plastic bag of small white rocks and a glass pipe on the table. Even though this was one of the few drugs I had never done before, I knew what the rocks were the minute I saw them.

"You ever done Tina?" he asked as he loaded the pipe.

"No. I value my HIV-negative status."

"Some of us play safe," he said.

He extended the pipe toward me with a slight smile. I took it, turned it over, and tapped the rock out onto my coffee table.

"Koffler promised you some crystal meth if you screwed around with Brady. You agreed and they humiliated you. Put your life in danger, even."

He shoved the bag and pipe back into his crotch, made a snorting sound in his throat, and started for the door with his eyes on the carpet.

"Do you want me to write this story or not, Nate?" I asked.

Nate whirled around. "The *story* is that some closet-case Marine thought he could come up to WeHo and fuck with some fags and it didn't go so well. A couple days later, the helicopter he happens to be flying makes a nosedive right into the ocean. Does that sound like a coincidence to you, Adam?"

"No, it doesn't," I said. "And I didn't say they had a right to humiliate you, Nate."

"What *were* you saying?"

"I don't get kicked to the curb when I'm not drinking," I said. "And you might not get thrown out of speeding cars if you're not tweaking."

His level stare told me my words had affected him. I needed to hear them as much as he did. I wanted to tell him a story in the *LA Times* wouldn't erase the shame of being thrown out of a car like a piece of meat, but I figured that if I played this story right, the *LA Times* might be where I would end up.

"I'll see what I can do, Nate."

His face softened and he took several steps toward the sofa. "Seriously?"

"Seriously. Did either one of them say where they were headed that night?"

"No," he said. "Koffler talked the whole time, but just to me. To . . . urge me on."

"Can you ask around for me?" I said. "See if anyone else saw them?"

Nate nodded emphatically, and for a second I thought he might hug me. If Brady had made many additional appearances that night, mouths would be flapping all over West Hollywood, and a real reporter would be on the story before I had time to blink. If this story was going to be my ticket out of *Glitz*, I would have to move fast.

"Thank you, Adam," he said breathily.

"Don't thank me yet," I said.

I got to my feet and waited for him to leave. He didn't. Instead, he chewed his lower lip and fiddled with the right leg of his shorts. After a painful moment he met my eyes and said, "How's Corey?"

At first I was too startled to say anything. The people close to me knew better than to ask me about a man named Corey Howard unless, like Tommy Banks, they enjoyed gouging my scabs.

"I wouldn't know," I said.

"You guys aren't seeing each other anymore, right?" he asked. "At least that's what I heard."

I just nodded, hoping whatever expression was on my face would scare him off the topic.

Nate sensed my anger but decided to ignore it. "Can I have his number?" He kept his eyes on the carpet. Instead of hurling him off my balcony, I went to my desk and wrote Corey's phone number on a note card. When I handed it to Nate, he stared down at it. "Just one number?"

"You're pushing it, Nate."

Nate turned red at the sound of my voice.

"There's no future for the two of you," I said. "Trust me. Corey Howard gives new meaning to the word *sobriety*."

Nate didn't seem as disappointed as I expected him to be. He returned his attention to the note card.

"Corey only has a cell phone," I said. "My guess is whoever's paying his rent and whoever bought him that nice new pickup truck didn't feel like getting him a land line."

"No shit," Nate whispered. "Corey has a sugar daddy?"

"Ask Corey," I said. "See if you get a better answer than I did."

Nate gave me a brusque nod and a weak smile. Then he left.

If there was anyone I knew in West Hollywood who might have some good dirt on Scott Koffler, it was my friend Rod Peters. The next day he met me for lunch at a restaurant on Santa Monica Boulevard where the waiters looked like Tom of Finland drawings and served steaks the size of puppies.

As I told him Nate Bain's story, Rod listened with his hands clasped against his lips. We were sitting at a table on the restaurant's sidewalk patio, and I kept my voice low so we wouldn't be overheard by the transgendered matron who held a squirming pug on her lap. Rod's eyes were hidden behind gas-station sunglasses, and his hair was a mess of dirty blond spikes. As usual, he was wearing an outfit that would be more suited to his native South Carolina than the sleeveless sidewalks of West Hollywood: khaki shorts and a green-and-white-striped polo. "Koffler's connected, Adam. You really want to go after him?"

"What does 'connected' mean?" I asked.

"If I tell you, it's only going to make you want to go after him."

I gave him a slight smile. He let out a hiss.

"Koffler's boys aren't legal," Rod said. "He meets them online and then he promises them Hollywood gold if they do his bidding."

"What's his bidding?" I asked.

"You're asking if he sleeps with them?" Rod asked. I nodded. "I don't know for sure, but I wouldn't be surprised. I do know he gives them a fake ID and a different name they're supposed to use when they're in West Hollywood. He also promises to set them up with acting jobs and film careers."

"Does he make good on those promises?"

Rod asked me if I remembered a certain teen heartthrob who had almost risen to stardom the year before. I did. "He was one of Scott's kids," Rod said. "No acting experience, not even an acting class. Just a couple pool parties in the Hollywood Hills with Scott, and suddenly he's got supporting roles in two features."

"How do you know all this?" I asked.

"I met a recovering Scott's kid after I first moved here," he said. "Things didn't go so well for him. He told me Scott took him under his wing like he was his best pal. Then the threats started. Scott would tell the guy that he needed someone to watch out for him—because what if someone back at his high school found out what he was doing every weekend? That kind of thing."

"What happened to this friend of yours?" I asked.

"You're really serious about this, Adam?" he asked. "Christ, I don't know who you should be more afraid of—Koffler or all the powerful men he's servicing."

"I'm not looking for a job on the studio lot."

Rod flashed me his palms and sank back into his chair. "The guy's name was Jim," he said. "He moved back to Biloxi or wherever last year. I can try to find him, but I'm not promising anything. He did tell me that Koffler lives with his mother out in Palmdale. That's where he brings the boys first."

"His mother doesn't object?"

"Jim said Koffler has her wrapped around his finger."

Why would a closeted marine come to LA's gay ghetto in the company of a pimp who specialized in underage twinks and used threats and intimidation to get what he wanted? The early news reports I had collected that morning online all hinted that the crash was a result of pilot error. Daniel Brady's error. I didn't want to get ahead of myself, but I thought it was possible that Daniel Brady had chosen to take his life and those of his three crewmates because Scott Koffler had made one threat too many.

For me, the result of my investigation would be a story that made a bloody statement about the military's "Don't ask, don't tell" policy, to say nothing of the fact that it would expose a devious bastard who used the fears and insecurities of self-hating teenagers to line his pockets. I thought of myself at sixteen and how I might have reacted if Scott Koffler had taken me to a party where all the gorgeous men seemed eternally twenty-five and I was the hot new thing. If Koffler had whisked me from being despised in the locker room to being worshipped poolside in just a day's time, I might have sold him my soul as well.

Even though his eyes were hidden behind sunglasses, I could tell that Rod was giving me one of his unnerving stares. If he knew about my ouster from The Abbey the night before, he wouldn't mention it.

"There's something else, Rod," I said. "I think I'm going to quit drinking."

I expected him to scoff, to make some remark about how every gay man gives up alcohol a thousand times, but instead he lowered his hands to his lap. His lips parted, but nothing came out, and for a while the two of us stared at each other as traffic chugged past us on the boulevard. "I hope you're serious," he finally said.

I was too startled by his reaction to say anything. He sat forward and closed one hand over mine. "Please be serious, Adam."

When I gave him a nod, he withdrew his hand and inhaled deeply. "Will you still be my friend if I tell you I've started praying for you every night? And I'm not a big prayer person."

My eyes misted suddenly, and I felt my face go tense as I shifted my attention to the street. Neither one of us said anything for a while. "A friend of mine just started going to AA," Rod finally said. "I can give you his number if—"

"I'm not going to do the AA thing," I said. "I'm not a fan of folding chairs, and if I drink any more coffee my heart will explode."

*   *   *

The drive to Palmdale took me farther outside the city limits than I had ever ventured. I was one of those West Side boys who thought the San Fernando Valley started at Laurel Canyon and extended to San Francisco.

Interstate 5 brought me to the 14 freeway, which threaded through the foothills of the San Gabriel Mountains. I drove past rolling grasslands marked by the occasional farmhouse and a few unfinished subdivisions with freshly laid streets terracing the sandblasted hillsides. The freeway made a sudden descent, and the Antelope Valley opened up before me, the westernmost corner of the Mojave Desert. The city of Palmdale is a small grid tucked against the base of the hills, with its own small reservoir. The map told me that Edwards Air Force Base was due north, but all I could see was an expanse of desert enveloped by haze.

After I had said goodbye to Rod, I had gone home and found a Palmdale listing for an Edina Koffler. I had also made a few calls to social acquaintances and found out that the night before, Scott Koffler had failed to show up at a barbecue hosted by a gay investment analyst. He and his product had been sorely missed.

I was counting on the fact that I was the last person Scott Koffler would expect to come asking him about a marine named Daniel Brady. The most Scott knew about me was that I wore a leather motocross jacket everywhere I went. In the year that I had lived in LA, I had been a social guy merely because it afforded me the chance to drink other people's alcohol. I was hoping that when I asked him about Daniel Brady, Koffler would give me either an outright denial I could disprove or a bogus cover story that I could go back to West Hollywood and unspin thread by thread.

Edina Koffler lived on a curved street lined with split-level stucco houses that looked exactly like her own. Each one had a mini–cathedral window above the front door and a willow tree out front, its branches thin and dry from too many buffetings by the desert winds. At the front door, I heard furious bass beats rattling a stereo that was blasting into the backyard, followed by a young man's peal of laughter. I rang the doorbell three times and got no answer.

A service alley the width of a garbage truck ran behind the house. As I made my way toward Edina Koffler's back gate, I could make out Britney Spears cursing the fact that her latest love interest was, in her opinion, toxic. I reached over the top of the gate, found the latch, and cracked it by a few inches.

Two boys sat in a gurgling Jacuzzi positioned against the back wall of the house's garage. It was impossible for me to determine the ages of the boys from their appearance alone; they had the smooth limbs and defined muscles of the average twenty-something party boy. They slugged awkwardly from beer bottles as they watched Scott Koffler perform a gyrating parody of Miss Spears's music-video dance down the aisle of a jet plane. Koffler wore his ubiquitous backward baseball cap and an unbuttoned short-sleeved blue shirt, revealing his sagging chest and swell of belly. Both were shaved smooth. The boys' laughter had more derision than enjoyment in it, and I couldn't tell if Koffler's gyrations were truly a burlesque of the pop diva or his own sexuality.

When the song finished, I shut the gate and pounded on it with my fist. I heard several splashes; then the stereo died, and Scott Koffler opened the gate. His eyes were tiny black dots above long and sunburned cheeks, and his weak chin was frosted with brown stubble. He looked like he'd been hiding out at his mother's house for a few days now—maybe ever since the night he drove Daniel Brady around West Hollywood.

"Adam Murphy is at my house," he said in a soft and breathy voice that gave the illusion of Zen-like calm. "What could this mean?"

"I had a little incident at The Abbey last night," I said. "I'm tracking down everyone who might have been there and giving them a personal apology."

"I wasn't at The Abbey last night," he said with the obligatory flicker of a smile.

"That's a relief," I answered.

He gestured me inside the yard. The Jacuzzi was empty but ringed with beer bottles. A Chiminea sat next to a parched willow tree that had a rope swing dangling from one of its branches. A picture window gave me a view into the living room, where a huge flat-screen television presided over an assemblage of black leather furniture that would have looked more at home in a drug runner's South Beach pied-à-terre. It looked like Koffler's mother benefitted from her son's operations.

There was a loud crash from inside. I saw one of the kids pressed up against the house's glass back door. He had an explosion of Q-tip-colored hair, miniature plates of muscle, and a towel wrapped loosely around his waist. He mouthed an apology and vanished.

Scott stared at me with a tense set to his mouth, his nostrils flaring.

"Kids," I said with false sympathy.

"That's Josh," he answered. "Some jocks decided to stuff him in a trash can and tape the lid shut. A teacher found him three hours later, but he was afraid to tell her anything because he thought they might do something worse. I'm sure you're aware of the kinds of things that type of abuse can do to a kid."

"I wear as much polyurethane as possible," I said. "That way no one can get a grip."

Scott crossed to the Jacuzzi and started collecting the empty beer bottles. "I try to do the best I can for these guys, but sometimes I worry that they look up to me too much. Like I'm their guardian angel." He didn't make this sound like a burden. "Prom. Homecoming. Sweet Sixteen. All of it's designed to shut out kids like Josh, and it doesn't have to—"

"What's the other one's name?" I asked.

He took a moment to realize that I had seen more than he thought I had. "I remember what it was like for me the first time I went to a party in West Hollywood," he said in the same concerned social-worker voice. "I kept wondering why everyone had kept this whole world a secret from me. I would have had a much easier time if I had known. I guess I could be bitter about it. Or I can give something back."

"Maybe guys like us should wait a while before we hit the booze and the drugs," I said.

"I'm talking about parties, Adam," he said with a thin smile. "Not bars. Just parties." I nodded as if this made sense to me. "Can I get you a beer?" he asked.

"I've decided to lay off for a while," I said.

This announcement seemed to please him. "Let me know how it goes," he said with an arch smile.

I told him I would add him to the list. Then I took out my wallet and handed him a photograph of Daniel Brady. He took it, eyebrows raised; then his face settled into something firm and unreadable as he studied it. The picture was a candid shot of Daniel Brady out of uniform, not the one that had been all over TV for almost a day. I had found it illustrating an article in the *North Coast Times*.

"Who is this?" he asked.

He handed the picture back to me without taking his eyes off me. "He's a marine helicopter pilot," I said. "He died last night. There's a rumor going around that he was in West Hollywood last week, so I've been asking people about him. Mostly guys who frequent the scene. Like yourself."

He grunted in his throat but nothing on his face moved. The calculated placidity that had settled over him made me nervous, suggested that I had cut to the chase too quickly.

"How did he die?" Scott asked.

"His helicopter crashed," I said. "He was the pilot, and everyone's saying it was pilot error. If this guy was having some issues with his sexuality, you can't blame me for thinking this might make for a good story."

He pursed his lips and nodded. "Don't you get people water for a living?" he asked.

"I don't think I've ever told you what I do, Scott." My sharp tone seemed to startle him. I held the picture out to him and said, "Do me a favor and pass this around if you can. Maybe someone in your circle saw him."

His arms remained crossed over his chest. For a while we listened to a motorcycle revving nearby and the caws of the crows that had been frightened by it.

"Let this one go, Adam," he finally said.

"Excuse me?"

"For your own sake."

"For my own sake?" I asked him, to see if he would confirm the fact that he had just threatened me. He gave me a small nod and studied my face intently.

Then, as if he had just given me the time, he strode to a recycling bin and dumped the empty beer bottles into them. I remembered Rod Peters's warning from earlier that day and wondered if Koffler's threat was one of those signs from the universe that I stupidly ignored, like the fact that when a guy didn't return my calls it meant we probably wouldn't end up living together. Then I remembered the ink-stain bruise and shredded skin on Nate Bain's lower back and decided that being threatened was just another stepping-stone on the road to journalistic glory.

When he saw that I hadn't moved, Koffler gave me a bemused smile. "Do you see much of Matt Ryder?" he asked. "Oh, sorry. That's his professional name. I think his real name is Nate Bain. Cute kid. But real messed up. I ran into him at a party once and he was apologizing to everyone for the Homeland Security helicopter that chased him up the hill. You can't blame me for thinking he's been doing a lot of dancing with the White Lady, Miss Tina."

Not only was Scott telling me that he knew who my source was, but he was informing me my source was a crazed drug addict. Nate had seemed pretty coherent the night before, but the bag of white rocks he had dumped on my coffee table had looked full. Maybe when Nate indulged, things changed—things like eyewitness accounts and the truth.

"I don't see much of Nate these days," I said. But Koffler's wry grin told me I had just blown the interview. "I'll see you later, Scott."

I was at the back gate when he called after me. "I worry about that kid. I really do."

"Well," I said, "maybe if you had gotten to him when he was sixteen, he might have turned out a little better."

"Who says I couldn't get to him now?" he asked.

The blank look on his face reminded me of what I had read about the everyday passivity of serial killers.

"You do that and you're handing me a story on a silver platter," I said.

I saw a brief flare of anger in his eyes, and his lips parted slightly. I gave him the broadest smile I could and left.

That evening, the *LA Times* posted on its website a full story on the crash, which summarized a press conference the Marine Corps had held outside the gates of Camp Pendleton at the time I was questioning Scott Koffler. A female lieutenant gave a brief nod to the stellar service records of all four men aboard the helicopter. She didn't mention Brady's name specifically and her words had about as much passion as those at a shotgun wedding. Then her statement turned into a rundown of the Huey's near-perfect safety record, followed by an elaborate description of the near-perfect weather it had gone down in, including descriptions of wind patterns, cloud cover, and ocean currents. Even though the Marine Corps was launching a full investigation, it was clear that Daniel Brady was being assigned blame for the crash.

Daniel Brady had been a juvenile delinquent shuffled between foster homes throughout Wisconsin before enlisting at the age of eighteen, the article said. His service record was spotless, and he had been married to his wife Melissa for three years. But there was no quote from her, and no mention of the big-boned Hispanic woman I had seen leading her away from her apartment on the eleven o'clock news.

Since that morning, I had consumed two pots of coffee, three iced venti lattes, and a six-pack of Diet Coke, which had induced something close to the edginess of several lines of coke but without the feeling of general well-being. I had left three messages for Nate that he hadn't returned, and I couldn't stop obsessing over the fact that I had revealed him as my source. I told myself that Nate was relatively safe. I couldn't see how Koffler could effectively use sexual blackmail on a gay porn star who was open about his crystal use.

There was also the possibility that Nate had managed to snag my old flame Corey Howard; the thought of it made me want to drop the story altogether.

Unlike most other Saturday nights, I did not spend the first part of the evening in the shower scrubbing myself with bath products that gave my skin the glow and smoothness of a cartoon character. Before I came up with any more theories about Daniel Brady's visit to West Hollywood I needed to establish if he had been seen by anyone besides Nate. I had gone almost twenty-four hours without thinking about a drink. I told myself the trend would continue simply because I had work to do.

CHAPTER 3

None of the usual suspects I talked to in the bars on Santa Monica Boulevard recognized Daniel Brady from anything besides the evening news, and after two hours of blank stares and apologies, the throb of bass beats had quickened my heartbeat and greased my palms with sweat. I was hovering too close to the flame. I walked into the Norma Triangle, a leafy neighborhood that sits just east of West Hollywood's border with Beverly Hills. It resembles any upscale suburb until you notice that the houses are actually glorified bungalows and the lighting in their front yards is about drama and not security.

This last Wednesday night, just blocks from here at Santa Monica and San Vicente, Koffler had been acting as Daniel Brady's chauffeur, allowing Brady to sit in the backseat behind the protection of tinted windows. Brady's trip to West Hollywood was supposed to be a secret, and I was pretty sure they were on the way to meet one of Koffler's wealthy clients, probably a guy who had more of an interest in marines than underage boys. Picking Nate up off a street corner seemed like a stupid move, but the more I thought about it, the more it seemed like the stunt had been Koffler's attempt to impress his passenger—to show Brady that he could get any random boy in West Hollywood to do his bidding. But the stunt had backfired and Nate had ended up rolling down Santa Monica Boulevard. I wondered if the two men had even made it to their destination that night.

A pair of headlights shaped like a serpent's eyes turned the corner in front of me. An ice-blue Lexus SC430 pulled to the curb. Billy Hatfill was behind the wheel. Thanks to a sugar daddy who had skipped town after his dot-com went belly-up, Billy was one of the wealthiest gay men in Los Angeles, at an age when most guys were graduating from college. His fine blond hair was parted on the side, and his full lips and button nose made him look sixteen. He wore a powder-blue oxford with a squared-off collar and a pair of tight khaki pants that made his long legs look shapely and feminine.

There wasn't a gay man in West Hollywood who hadn't attended at least one party at the glass and steel hilltop mansion his sugar daddy had signed over to him before he disappeared. I had attended several of those parties, but I tried to steer clear of the host because I thought he mistook pretense for style. Billy had not returned the favor. Whenever he wasn't actually trailing me, his eyes were. My friend Rod Peters was convinced that Billy had a crush on me, probably because the guy had given me his cell phone number more times than I could count, always acting as if the two of us could do beautiful business together. I still hadn't entered his number into my phone.

"How are you doing tonight, Adam?" he asked me, as if he already knew the answer and was afraid to hear it come out of my mouth.

"Fine. Heading home."

"I've heard you've had a rough few months," he said. "Actually, I've seen it with my own two eyes. I was at The Abbey last night." I just nodded. "Seriously. How are you, Adam?"

"I'll make it," I said.

"Are you sure?" he asked. "Get in," he said. "I'll give you a ride."

When it became clear that I wasn't going to comply, he pursed his lips and shook his head as if I were a recalcitrant child. Then he hit his flashers, killed the engine, and stepped out of the car. He sat down on the hood, pulled a pack of Dunhill Lights from his jeans, and lit one. "Still doing the reporter thing?" he asked.

"Trying," I said.

"Write a story about me," he said with a slight smile. "Poor pretty boy snags a lecherous millionaire with a penchant for scamming Hollywood moguls out of their millions. After Daddy skips town, little Billy Hatfill is left with nothing better to do than open up a home that isn't even his, so that a bunch of aspiring model-slash-actors can feel like they've *arrived* before they all go back to their jobs in retail."

His sudden scathing self-awareness startled me. Billy Hatfill seemed determined to get my attention any way he could. I wasn't sure I agreed with my friend Rod Peters. I thought Billy could sense my distaste for him and his lifestyle and had set out to change my opinion of him as if I were a potential investor. That had less to do with me and more to do with Billy's ego. He held my stare, oblivious to the slow curl of smoke that divided his youthful face. "My parties are just another drug, aren't they? The views, the pool, the boys. They all just make a bunch of drug dealers and club kids feel less like sodomites. That's a pretty accurate assessment, don't you think?"

I thought it was only too accurate. Billy Hatfill had either read my mind or heard me repeat these sentiments to someone else. He wanted me to see him as a victim of his sugar daddy's bad business dealings and his own materialism. I wasn't buying it.

Billy's sugar daddy had been a charismatic dot-com darling named Joseph Spinotta. When it became clear that his much-hyped website was not going to revolutionize the entertainment industry as he had promised it would, Spinotta had fled in the night with all of the venture capital, but not before signing over most of his physical assets to the twenty-year-old the *LA Times* had uncomfortably referred to as his young companion. I was willing to believe that Billy Hatfill had some abandonment issues, but I also thought a ten-million-dollar mansion was one heck of a consolation prize.

"I hear you weren't that poor before you met Joseph," I said. "Didn't you go to Rappaport?"

He shot me a surprised look at the name of the private school he had attended on New York's Upper East Side. "I'm impressed that you remembered, Adam."

"A couple of your classmates ended up in my freshman class at Tulane," I said. "Considering your high school's a feeder for the Ivy League, they weren't too happy to be in New Orleans."

"Bitches," he whispered. "Did they mention the guy who slept with his English teacher?"

"They didn't," I said. "You want me to include that in the article?"

"Absolutely not," he said. "I have no hard feelings at all about the relationship."

"You had something to tell me, Billy."

He exhaled a long drag through his nostrils. "We're friends, right, Adam?" I gave him a noncommittal nod. He laughed at it. "Do you remember the night we met?"

"Has someone written a song about it?"

"Not that I know of," he answered with a smile. "You came to one of my parties right after you moved here. You were with that jabber-jaw manager's assistant you call your best friend, probably because he does all the talking so you can do all the sulking. You were the only guy I met that night who didn't compliment me on my taste in luminaries or the way I had the grass cut. You were unimpressed, to say the least. My first thought was 'Well, here's this little southern yokel, just off the bus from wherever, and he's already looking down his nose at everybody 'cause he's too high to realize he's got a little coke on it.'"

"I didn't take the bus here."

"Don't get offended, Adam. I'm not finished."

"I drove."

"Congratulations," he said firmly. "But then the more I thought about it, the more I thought about you. I started to wonder if you had seen something in my life that merited a closer look. Something rotten, if you will."

He gave me a level stare. He hadn't noticed that his cigarette was a smoldering butt between two of his fingers. I pointed to it and he tossed it to the pavement and stepped on it with one chunky black shoe.

"Which gets back to my original question, Adam. Are we friends? Because your ex-boyfriend certainly thinks we are," Billy said.

"Corey?" I asked. Billy nodded gravely and crossed his arms over his chest. "What are you saying?" I asked.

"Corey came to one of my parties two weeks ago," he said. "I was surprised to see him, to say the least. I had heard he was pretty straitlaced. I also heard your relationship didn't exactly take off for that very reason. At first, when I saw him walk in, I thought he was looking for you."

"Was he?" I heard myself ask.

"No," Billy said. "He wanted to talk to me about you." He let this sit. "He wanted to warn me about you is more like it. He said your drinking was out of control and I shouldn't have you over to my house anymore. I could tell he was very angry about how the relationship ended. Even though he didn't tell me just how it ended."

Billy waited for me to brief him on the brutal details of my split with Corey. I didn't. I was too sidelined by the story he was giving me. The idea of Corey Howard setting foot inside Billy Hatfill's mansion seemed, on the face of it, absurd. When I had suggested to him that we attend one of Billy's parties, Corey told me that he had heard of Billy and thought the guy was a waste of space and cash. In the three weeks we spent together, Corey had practically kept me housebound and away from all forms of alcohol and drugs. Now he had gone to one of my regular hangouts and tried to poison the waters. He was still trying to save me from myself.

"Look, I know it's none of my business, Adam. But you might want to have a talk with him. He's incredibly angry, and the things he said—"

"Like what?"

Billy inhaled sharply, his nostrils flaring, and stared down at the pavement. "He said your mother died. He said if that didn't teach you a lesson, nothing would. I'm sorry, Adam. Maybe I shouldn't have said anything. But I thought you should know. It was . . . scary, to say the least."

"Scary?"

"Yes," he said flatly. "Adam, anyone who has ever met you can tell that you only go for guys who look like they can and will beat you up. Corey sounded pretty determined to teach you a lesson. Talk to him. Apologize to him, even if you don't mean it. Maybe that will be enough to cool him off."

"Have a nice night, Billy," I said.

Billy nodded and straightened up, brushing invisible lint from the front of his pants. "Are you sure I can't drive you home?" I gave him a distracted wave and he paused at the driver's-side door. "I didn't mean to upset you."

"For some reason I just don't believe that."

His cheeks colored and his arm went rigid as he rested his fingers on the door handle. "You believe a lot of things about me. Whenever I try to tell you otherwise, you don't return my calls."

I waited for him to get in the car. He didn't. "Do you still think about Paul?" he asked.

Paul Martinez, one of the first friends I had made after moving to LA, had died of a drug overdose two months ago. Given all that had happened since then, I hadn't thought about him much. Paul had been a fixture at just about every party in West Hollywood, probably because he encouraged the illusion that drug addicts were all bright spirits with a genuine love for each and every party guest. He had been proof that an overweight guy with a mouth like a Pez dispenser could run in a world of absurd physical beauty, as long as he always met the challenge of delivering the perfect one-liner.

"I was at the funeral, too," Billy said. "I saw you walk out."

"He died of a drug overdose in a bathhouse," I said. "Suddenly all of his friends are standing in front of his family talking about how the party won't be the same without Paul—"

"With a martini in one hand and a cigarette in the other," Billy finished for me. "I know. I stayed for the whole thing." He met my stare. "The way you walked out—that took guts, Adam. Actually, I'm not sure if it was guts or just *nerve*. There's a difference between the two, don't you think?"

I shrugged.

"You made a lot of people angry," he said. It sounded like he was one of those people. I wasn't about to apologize to him.

"So I'll see you at the next party?" he said.

"No you won't," I said. "I'm laying off for a while."

He made a small sound in his throat. "Sounds like Corey got his wish after all." He got in his car and drove off. As soon as his taillights disappeared, my thoughts drifted back to an afternoon in late April.

The April day when Rod called to tell me that Paul Martinez's body had been discovered that morning by a cleaning crew up at a gay bathhouse in Hollywood, I was planning to take my Jeep into the car wash. Three days later, after I walked out of his funeral in a righteous rage, I decided to pick up where I had left off.

By the time I pulled into the Twin Palms Car Wash on Sunset Boulevard, I had managed to lighten my limbs and put the world in soft focus, thanks to the nickel-plated flask my mother had given me for Christmas. I didn't notice the attendant taking orders until he stepped back from the BMW in front of me.

He was over six feet tall, with a tight helmet of jet-black hair, long dark eyes deeply set beneath the hard line of his brow, and a Roman nose that looked prominent only in profile. His broad shoulders stretched the back of his white button-up, and everything about him looked hard and unyielding until you got to his full lips and sleepy eyes.

I rolled my window down and he placed a hand on the edge that was so heavily veined it looked sculpted. "Your left brake light is out," he said in a deep voice that matched with the fantasies his body inspired. "If you get pulled over, they'll put points on your license. When you leave here, you should go to an auto body place and have them take care of it."

I tried to speak and failed.

"You could also stop at Koontz Hardware down the street. They might have the right fuse. We don't do that kind of work. That's why I'm telling you all of this."

"Sorry," I mumbled.

"Uh-huh," he answered quietly, his eyes locked on mine. "You might also want to get some breath mints and get rid of that flask that's on the floor of your passenger seat."

"I just came from a funeral," I managed. "How about giving me a break?"

The hard look in his eyes didn't change, but his top teeth hooked his lower lip in a gesture that wasn't nearly as determined and masculine as the rest of him. Suddenly he jerked back from my window and asked for my order.

I pulled forward to the vacuum station, wondering if the words *new car smell* would be the last I would ever say to one of the most attractive men I had ever encountered. I caught him staring at me as I walked toward the car wash's main building as if he thought I was about to hold the place up and was prepared to take action.

In the men's room, I splashed my face with water and succumbed to the vision I had been trying to avoid for several days. I saw Paul Martinez walking down a dark and narrow corridor, his stubby limbs lacquered with detox sweat and his towel slipping from his round waist. The walls pounded with piped-in techno that did little to cover the cries of drugged lust coming from the stalls around him. He tried to pull various men into a slow and swaying embrace until each of them realized he was waltzing to the beat of Paul's fading heart and pulled away with the naked disgust you find only inside this kind of meat market.

By the time the men's room door opened, I was blinking back tears. When my vision cleared, I saw that my flask sat on the counter in front of me, and the attendant was resting his butt against the edge next to it.

"Who died?" he asked me.

"A friend of mine," I said.

He nodded gravely. I noticed that the top three buttons of his shirt were undone, revealing the scoop of a white tank top underneath and a small gold chain that disappeared under it. "I forgot to mention something out there," he said. "Your mouth may smell like a bar at three A.M., but the rest of you smells good. Real good." He was trying his best, but I could tell he had never hit on a guy in a men's room before and it put a slight dent in his rigid demeanor. "Don't drink so much," he said, lapsing back into brigadier general mode. "I've seen what it does to people's eyes. I like your eyes."

He walked out of the bathroom with a straight back and a determined gait that would have parted an army. When I went back outside, I saw that he had been replaced by another attendant, and when I asked the cashier where he had gone she told me that he got off at two P.M. She also told me his name. Corey.

Although Tommy Banks had given me the day off for Paul's funeral, he forbade me from having a lunch break that took me any farther than the coffee shop in our building's lobby. I visited the car wash several times over the next few weeks hoping to catch him again, but I didn't, and I was too embarrassed to press the other staff for information about him.

On the last Saturday in April, Rod dragged me to a party down in Laguna Beach, hosted by an entertainment attorney we had never met who owned a two-story white clapboard house that sat perched on stilts above a slice of craggy beach. The balcony was crowded with goggle-eyed, gum-smacking muscle boys in tank tops and cargo shorts. My stomach dropped when I saw Corey leaning against the rail.

He was gripping a water bottle in one fist, and the swells of his chest strained against his white T-shirt. He was wearing the thin gold chain I had noticed at the car wash, and I could see a tiny medallion at the end of it. As I approached him, I saw what held his attention. In a Jacuzzi gurgling several yards away, a lanky older man in a blond beehive wig and a bikini stuffed with socks lip-synched to the pounding dance track. Every few seconds he lost his footing, and all you could see was the top of the beehive sticking out of the bubbles.

"You know that guy?" Corey asked me.

"The drag queen?" I asked.

He shook his head and pointed a finger at Scott Koffler. Koffler was standing on the other side of the Jacuzzi, his arms around two ruddy-faced adolescents whose wide-eyed stares suggested that the last party they had attended had faculty monitors and a crepe-paper-strewn dance floor. "I hear those boys he's with are too young," Corey said.

"Me too," I answered, hoping he would change subjects.

"I hear the guy's basically a pimp," Corey continued, with what sounded to me like a mix of fascination and disdain. "He brings those kids to parties and sets them up with rich guys."

"I stay away from Scott Koffler," I said. I figured he was probing me to see what kind of guys I ran with, and whether a creep like Scott Koffler was one of them.

Now I had his full attention. "Who did you come with?" I asked.

"No one," he said. "Some guy who came into the car wash the other day invited me. He said I'd be a big hit." He didn't smile or act bashful about what he had said; he was not bragging but flatly communicating a fact. "But I only came 'cause I thought you'd be here." His voice lacked guile and his expression remained impassive. "I forgot to tell you something the other day."

"What?" I asked.

"I'm sorry about your friend."

"You drove all the way down to Laguna to tell me that?"

"No," he said. He placed his hands on my cheeks and brought our faces together until our noses were touching. He took a deep breath and made a soft sound in his throat. "I came to get you before you drank too much."

He backed me up against a nearby wall. His mouth met mine and his hands traveled up under my shirt, where he took both of my nipples between his thumb and forefinger and applied just enough pressure to make my back arch. He cocked his head to one side and kissed me with enough open-mouthed passion to bring my hands to the sides of his face.

He studied my face for a few seconds. "Let's go, Adam Murphy," he said, even though I hadn't told him my name. "I don't want my good luck to run out now."

He drove a red Dodge Ram, and as we sped through Orange County on the 405 Freeway, he rested his hand on my knee and didn't make any attempt at conversation. For the first time in my life, I traveled out of my body without the aid of a chemical. I saw us from above as we traversed a glittering island at the bottom-left-hand corner of the country, separated from its neighbors by miles of black desert. The rest of the country had already given up on the night, but soon the last midnight on earth would sweep across the two of us. (Unless you counted Alaska or some pissant island in the Pacific, which I did not.)

We didn't exchange a word during the long drive home. Corey stared at the road the entire time, as if what awaited us back at my apartment was a fate not worthy of excitement or anticipation, probably because it was a fate he had designed.

I had left the desk lamp in my apartment on and it threw a dull halo across the Krewe of Dionysus poster hanging above my love seat.

I babbled about myself for a good twenty minutes. Part of me was hoping he would return the favor, and another part of me was trying to delay sex as long as possible so I could see if that was all he was interested in. I told him about my mother and my parents' divorce, my sister's C-section, and the enduring radio silence between me and my father. I couldn't tell if he was listening.

"Your mother's a drunk, isn't she?" he finally asked.

If anyone else had asked me that question, anyone who didn't have the body of a Greek god and hadn't driven two hours just to find me, I would have asked him to leave my apartment. Instead I said, "Yes. And I think she's going to die soon."

His eyes flared with some emotion I couldn't identify, and suddenly my words felt like a betrayal of the woman who had tried to teach me that I was different from everyone else, that the answers to life would elude me if I strayed too far from her path. Years earlier, I had hung my moon on a sinking ship, and I wasn't quite sure how to avoid going down with it.

I crossed to the kitchen counter so he couldn't see my face. I was about to offer him some water when I felt his mouth open against my neck. He unbuttoned my jeans and tugged several times to get them past my hips. I slid my hands out in front of me to get my balance as the cool air hit my butt. The knowledge that I was half naked and he was not sent a small shudder through me. I rocked back against him and stifled the sound that wanted to come out of me, because it was too desperate and pained.

He pushed the back of my shirt up until it was bunched behind my neck. He used three fingers to apply pressure to the opening in my body that had never felt sexual until that moment; then he pulled my shirt up over my head, lifted me up onto the counter, and took me in his mouth, his eyes locked on mine as if my every breath would determine his next move.

He was still fully dressed and I was completely naked, which seemed absurd given how much I had already explored his body through my gaze alone.

In bed, he pressed one hand against my chest, pinning me to the mattress as he guided himself into me. His gold chain brushed against my bare chest and I glimpsed a tiny scorpion embossed in the medallion.

Everything inside of me coiled. He sensed it and waited patiently.

I did my best to draw deep breaths, then I felt my ankles go lax against his lower back, and suddenly the words coming out of my mouth were so desperate and profane that if you played a recording of them for me now, I would have to leave the room. Over the next few hours, I traveled the arc from shame to bliss, a short but irreversible journey.

Some time in the night I awoke to a strange rustling sound. The vertical blinds turned the streetlight outside into a series of orange bars that fell across Corey's naked back as he studied my bookshelves. I blinked and saw that he was taking books off the shelf and flipping through their pages without reading a single word.

He pulled out the Merriam-Webster's dictionary and opened it. The center of the pages had been hollowed out, and inside were two tabs of ecstasy, an ounce of cocaine, and five two-milligram pills of Xanax. He closed them all in his fist, put the book back on the shelf, and disappeared inside the bathroom. A few seconds later, the toilet flushed.

When he slid back under the covers, I expected him to turn his back to me and then leave before I woke in the morning. Instead he wrapped an arm around me and pulled my back against his chest so tightly I could feel each breath he took. Later I awakened to him making breakfast in the kitchen. When he saw that my eyes were open, he asked me how I wanted to spend the day.

On Sunday morning at nine A.M., as I lay in bed pondering the death of Daniel Brady, the phone rang. It was my boss, Tommy Banks. He had never called me on a Sunday morning before.

"Heard you had a little incident at The Abbey the other night," he said without saying hello. "Is it true you almost killed someone?"

"Sort of."

"What happened to quitting drinking?"

"It's a definite now."

"Were you aware that we're doing a promotion at The Abbey with GLAAD next month?"

"No."

My feet hit the floor as I struggled to come up with a good cover story.

"There are two thousand AA meetings a week in this city," he said. "I suggest you find one of them."

"I'll think about it," I said.

Tommy groaned as if he had called me from the toilet. "I'm sorry, Adam. I just can't take this anymore."

"What are you talking about, Tommy? The only time I've missed a day of work in the past year is when I went home last month." Since he'd figured out that I had gone home to bury my mother, I thought this might shut him up.

"Enough, Adam."

I let a silence fall and waited for him to fire me explicitly. He couldn't. Finally I said, "There's no promotion at The Abbey on the calendar. I keep the calendar, remember?"

"You know, Adam," he began in a calmer voice, "some people like being a big fish in a small pond. You like being a piranha in an aquarium. This magazine is never going to go in the direction you want it to, so there's no point in your staying—"

"Who called you?" I asked. He didn't answer. "Did Scott Koffler call you himself, or did he get one of his rich friends to do it?"

"You have a key to the office, Adam. Go in and clean out your desk this afternoon."

"I don't have a desk. You gave it to the intern you're fucking." The next thing I knew, my portable phone was lying on the other side of the room and the vertical blinds were tossing as if a sudden wind had torn through my apartment.

I spent the next few hours listening to a Dido CD. I called Rod's cell phone and left him a message telling him that I had been fired. I ate a pint of Ben & Jerry's ice cream and watched a few hours of professional bowling. Somewhere along the way I came to terms with the fact that the Daniel Brady story was too big for *Glitz* magazine anyway.

By noon I had managed to convince myself that getting fired was the best thing that had ever happened to me. I wasn't giving up on Daniel Brady's foray out of the closet and into the Pacific. I had to take stock of what I had. If I was going to take the story somewhere else, it was time for Nate Bain to officially go on the record.

Nate Bain's apartment building was a four-story stucco palace with balconies that ran the length of each unit and a line of tall hedges flanking the entry door. I was half a block away when I saw a half-naked blur come flying down the front steps. When I shouted his name, Nate whirled and almost dropped the dishrag he was holding against his left temple.

He was shirtless and barefoot. His plaid pajama pants were stained down both legs, and he reeked of body odor and lubricant. His eyes were cue balls and his black hair was matted with something that looked thicker than sweat. "Can you take me to the hospital?" he gasped. "See, I've got this oscillating fan and it's been blowing spores all over the place. One of them went behind my eye. I can totally feel it moving around—"

"Let's go back inside, Nate."

"I tried to get it out," he went on, "but I don't think I . . ." He pulled the dishrag from his temple, revealing a welter of oozing scratches that looked like they had been incised with a fork. A car flew by and I watched the male passenger crane his head to stare at us, his mouth an O.

Several streams of dark blood slid down the left side of Nate's face. He scratched at them as he looked at me with jerking pupils. He had obviously been awake since Friday night and he was about to come in for a crash landing. My facial expression must have pierced his paranoid frenzy. His jaw quivered, his eyes dropped to the pavement, and he started shaking his head back and forth as if I had just told him that his mother had died.

I suppressed my gag reflex and put an arm around his back. I led him inside the building and through a maze of brightly lit stale-smelling hallways. When I asked him where his apartment was, he pointed toward a door that was pounding with bass beats.

I asked him who was inside and he put his forehead against his closed fists. I wondered if the pose was a method for keeping the drugs in his brain.

When I opened the unlocked door, I was hit by a stronger version of the stench that came from Nate. Towels and blankets had been nailed over the apartment's windows. The only light in the room came from a porn film playing on a tiny television set in the corner. The sole piece of furniture was an overstuffed sofa, and there were four naked guys on it. Two older men with stripes of bristle down their lean torsos lowered a rail-thin blond kid onto the condomless erection of the man who sat below him. The kid's flaccid penis spilled from his cock ring like an elephant's tail. It took me a second to realize that the red spots on it were the result of extreme chafing.

"Party's over, guys!" I announced. "I hate to tell you guys this, but I've been watching everything on the camera inside that smoke detector, and I had to call the FBI. They'll be here in five minutes."

The men scrambled to get out. Three of them made for the front door. "Get dressed first!" I barked. Each one of them had shed his clothes in a different part of the apartment, but they were dressed and out the front door in the blink of an eye, which shouldn't have surprised me considering they were speed freaks. Once they were gone, I looked up and saw that Nate was one step ahead of me: the smoke detector had been covered with newspaper.

I walked Nate into the bedroom and dropped him onto the mattress on the floor. The sheet was so badly stained it looked like it had been lifted from an auto body shop, and the piles of dirty laundry gave off a smell like rank water poured over cut grass. It took me a second to realize that the piles were sorted by color. In the tiny bathroom, I found three bottles of Viagra in the medicine cabinet. Crystal meth lights a fire under some men's sex drives, but it also turns their equipment to mush. But there was also a bottle of Xanax, just as I had expected there would be. Two-milligram pills. The good stuff.

I dumped several into my palm and asked Nate if he could swallow without water. He just stared at his laundry. In the kitchen I opened the cabinets and discovered that Nate had smashed through the back of them with a hammer, pulled coils of wiring through, and taped the individual strands to the shelves in a pattern that made sense only to him. I found a dirty glass and scrubbed it as if I'd retrieved it from a sewer pipe.

Once the pills were in him, Nate rolled onto his back, his eyes wide and his chest red and heaving, and started picking at the skin on his left arm. I asked him to stop and he told me he would as soon as he could feel his arm again.

For a while, I just stared down at him. My Daniel Brady story was dying on the vine. I had just been fired from the only media outlet I had access to, and my only source was a speed freak who believed that an organism had taken up residence behind his eye and that the Department of Homeland Security was having him tailed. I did believe that Nate had seen Daniel Brady in West Hollywood, but I didn't think there was a chance in hell I could make anyone else believe it too.

I wanted to hurt him as much as he was hurting himself. That's when I realized that pursuing Daniel Brady and Scott Koffler had been nothing more than an attempt to escape from myself, and I felt a sudden surge of guilt that kept me from shaking the gasping deranged wreck of a young man before me.

The look in Nate's eyes told me that he was seeing eight of me or none at all. I leaned against the wall until his eyes started to drift shut; then I went into the living room where I pulled the blankets and towels from the windows and stacked them next to the sofa. Screw Nate's privacy. If he got any more privacy, it would probably kill him.

I checked on him again and saw that he lay limp and twisted on the mattress, as if he had been dropped from the Emser Tile building. I put one hand to his bare chest to make sure he was still breathing.

Out in the hallway, Nate's neighbor was standing in the open door to his apartment. He was tall and lean, with a shiny bald dome and sympathetic eyes behind invisible-framed glasses. "You guys finished yet?" he asked in a soft, high-pitched voice.

"I wasn't with that crew," I said.

"I've talked to that kid," he whispered. "Back in my day, the drugs were about the search for the soul. That drug is about getting rid of it."

"Are you sober?" I asked.

"Twenty years," he said. "You?"

"Forty-eight hours."

He disappeared inside his apartment. When he returned, he handed me a business card printed with his first name and last initial, along with his home and mobile numbers. The guy was obviously a member of Alcoholics Anonymous. "Your generation," he said quietly. "You die too quickly to get anyone's attention."

After he went back inside his apartment, I turned and slid the card under Nate's door, even though I knew that I was the one the man had tried to reach out to.

Rod Peters had left three messages for me expressing his condolences and asking me to meet him for dinner. He made no mention of Jim, the former Scott's kid he had been trying to locate. I figured he had assumed I had dropped the story.

The six o'clock news had just started when I heard a harsh knock on my door. I thought it might be one of my neighbors, but when I opened the door, Scott Koffler brushed past me before I had time to collect myself.

"How'd you get in?" I asked him.

"Your neighbor's nice," he said.

I leaned against the edge of the open door as he studied the Krewe of Dionysus poster above my love seat. He was wearing a backward baseball cap and a USC Trojans football jersey. I still couldn't tell if his costume was a device for earning the trust of his young charges or if the guy genuinely lived in a state of perpetual adolescence.

"How's not drinking going?" he asked, giving me his full attention. "I hear you had a rough day."

"You need to leave, Scott."

He raised his eyebrows and pursed his lips. "I thought you were a southern gentleman. You're not even going to offer me anything to drink?"

"There's a sink right behind you."

His silent laugh shook his shoulders. "Does the name Dale Dupré ring a bell?" he asked.

It didn't, but I had a feeling Koffler was going to ring it for me.

"Dale's from your hometown. I knew him when he lived out here. He wanted to be an actor, did some porn, ran back home—same old story. Anyway, he's a bartender at this club down in the French Quarter now. I understand it's one of your old haunts. Dale says you visited his bar after your mother's funeral. You remember?"

I didn't. I couldn't remember anything about the night of my mother's funeral except calling my sister from a French Quarter pay phone because I couldn't find my rental car.

"Dale says you told him that there were witnesses to the accident that killed your mother, and they claim that your mother was fighting with her boyfriend just before it happened. Apparently the boyfriend came to the funeral and sobbed to everyone about how he hadn't pushed her."

My pulse sounded like a tribal drumbeat in my temples.

"But the next thing you told Dale . . ." Scott shook his head. "Dale says he'll never forget it. Do you remember, Adam?"

"Get out, Scott."

"You said if the guy had pushed her, you would understand."

His eyes went wide and then his head snapped sideways on his neck. I felt the impact in my fist as I retracted it.

He hit the floor like a sack of dirt and made a sound like a window unit in August. I grabbed the back of his belt and hoisted him up on all fours.

He hit the door across the hall from mine hard enough to shake the wall. He rolled over onto his back, and I saw that his nostrils were bubbling and his lips were smeared red. His dead eyes met mine. "You're too easy," he breathed.

He sat up, wiped blood from his face, then stared down at his red palm. "You're just too fucking easy," he croaked.

I heard a door down the hall open just as I closed mine. One of my neighbors was calling after Scott as he walked down the hallway. I leaned against my door until the hallway was silent and the only sounds I could hear were Scott's car pulling off down the street and my own breaths whistling through my nostrils.

When I reached the Strip, a sheriff's cruiser was parked in the median across from Keyclub, where a line of Goth kids waited to gain admittance to see some band whose name kept flashing on the Jumbotron above the entrance. I had never heard of them. I heard a squeal of brakes and saw the crime scene photograph that depicted my mother's death pose. Now her outstretched arm was not pointing in the direction of the cab that had run her down at forty miles an hour. She was telling me to walk past her fate. In life, my mother had never been so direct or so caring. In death, she had no choice but to become everything I chose to endow her with.

I felt as if my mind were encased in steel and every thought inside my head had tried to escape a few seconds too late, clanging the walls of their prison until my ears screamed. The next thing I knew, I had turned my back on the Sunset Strip, a river of bass beats and heterosexual aggression, and was walking into the tree-shaded blocks that sloped downhill.

At the door to Nate Bain's building, I studied the call box and determined the apartment number for the sober neighbor who had given me the card I had left for Nate. I don't remember what I said when he answered his buzzer. The neighbor opened his door for me without asking me what I was doing there. I sat at his small dining room table as he fixed a pot of tea.

"There's blood on your shirt," he finally remarked. I didn't respond, which didn't seem to bother him. He handed me a cup of tea and sat down across from me. The overhead light bounced off his glasses, hiding his eyes, and gave a moist sheen to one side of his bald head.

He sipped his tea and allowed a long silence to pass between us. "You're going to stay here until two A.M.," he said gently. "You can watch TV with me. You can sit right there and stare into your own head. You can even go in my bedroom and entertain yourself with the Men of Falcon. But you don't leave this apartment until two A.M. Deal?"

Two A.M. was when the bars and liquor stores closed. I nodded. "What do you guys talk about at your meetings?" I heard myself ask.

"Everything." He sipped his tea. "There's a midnight meeting I know of over in Hollywood. You want to go?"

When I didn't respond, he smiled slightly and rose from the table.

"I don't want to die like my mother."

I heard his footsteps stop behind me and realized I had given voice to the thought.

"You won't, honey," he said gently. "You'll die just like you."

A few seconds later, he raised the volume on the television. The apartment filled with the sound of enervated British people discussing petty trifles as if they were of global consequence. The longer I listened, the less petty their trifles seemed. After a while, I joined my strange companion on the sofa. Eventually I nodded off, and when I awoke, my guardian was tugging gently on my shoulder. It was ten after two, and he was telling me that I had made it through another day.

He closed the door behind me before I could thank him or ask him his name. As I walked back to my apartment, I cried for my mother for the first time since she died. My tears didn't last as long as I had feared they would.

In 1891, the Southern Pacific Railroad Company established
the small town of Coalinga at the northern end of the narrow valley that
lies between the Coast Ranges and the Kettleman Hills. It was named for
the coal discovered under its soil, and today it is the only mining boom-
town in California to have survived into the twenty-first century. Over the
years, it had subsisted off what was once the largest oil field in California,
the cattle ranches that lie in the hills to the west, and one of the only small-
town medical centers to be constructed with a federal grant in recent
memory.

At night, the sodium vapor lights of Avenal State Prison throw an orange glow across the tule-blanketed hills to the south. Highway 198 marks
the town's southern border before it travels into the rolling landscape of
grassy plateaus and rounded hills that make up the Inner Coast Ranges.
Lucy Vernon was the only clerk on duty when a young woman named Caroline Hughes pulled her silver Chevy Tahoe into the service station's parking lot, bypassed the gas pumps, and slid into the parking spot next to
Mike Harberson's pickup. For the past hour, Mike and his partner in
crime, Joey Murdoch, had been sitting at one of the tables next to the coffee machines, shouting things about how the Ding Dongs didn't look fresh
and how it must have been a bad season for Twinkies. Lucy wasn't responding, and they had returned to snickering like *South Park* characters

and taking sips from squeeze bottles that smelled like they were full of Drakkar Noir.

When Caroline entered the gas station, Lucy recognized the spray of freckles across the woman's nose and forehead and the pupils that reminded her of frozen amber. There had been a picture of the woman on the front page of the *Coalinga Record* a few weeks earlier, taken just as Caroline Hughes emerged from the Kings County sheriff's station after identifying her mother's burned corpse.

Lucy figured the woman's expression must have been what her grandfather referred to as a thousand-yard stare. Caroline pulled a basket from the stack without acknowledging anyone else inside the service station and disappeared into the racks.

"Whatsa matter, Luce?" Mike Harberson called out. "You see a ghost?"

Lucy returned her attention to the copy of *US Weekly* she had been flipping through and listened to Mike's shuffling footsteps. He leaned on the counter with both elbows. His eyes were red-rimmed, and his latest attempt at a beard looked like a swarm of fleas clinging to his chin. Mike was a nice enough guy when you got him alone. He had an almost childish affection for the nearby foothills and he liked to share it with women like Lucy, women who saw him for the jackass he was and forgave him for it.

"Or maybe it was your special friend?" Mike whispered.

"Your breath's gonna make me throw up," Lucy said.

Her sharp tone brought a flash of pain to his eyes. "Hey. Look, Luce. I know I wasn't supposed to tell anyone about your—"

He saw her glaring at him and stopped talking. For a second Lucy thought he might not mention the story she had told him a few days earlier, after he had plied her with Strawberry Boone's and lured her into his F-150 for a drive out 198 West. The sex itself had been fine. Lucy wished she had been able to keep her mouth shut once it was over with.

Instead she had told Mike a story she had promised never to tell anyone, a story her father had repeated to her through a haze of morphine years before. It scared Mike so badly he hadn't said much for the rest of the evening. Now he was going to use it to make fun of her in some way, just so he could get it out of his head.

"Hey, Joey!" Mike called over one shoulder. "Remember that story I was telling you about? Shit! What was his name again, Luce? El Mariachi or something."

"El Maricón," Joey answered. "It's Spanish for fag."

"Right," Mike said. "But this ain't no redecoratin', *Queer Eye for the Straight Guy* kinda fag now, is it, Lucy? This guy is badass, right?" He laughed nervously.

Lucy glanced up to see Caroline looking at cleaning products, then tried to focus on an *US Weekly* photo of an emaciated former child star who had just been carted off to rehab. Mike returned his attention to his buddy. "He rides around the hills on some hog, blowin' up shit right and left. He wears a black motorcycle helmet so no one knows who he is, right? And according to Lucy here, he carries a machete on his back. You know, like, in a holster, so he can just reach up . . ."

Mike reached up into the space behind his back, then whipped his hand forward. ". . . and whack your fucking head off like X-Men or something!" His head twitched.

"I heard of him before, dumbass," Joey said. "The guy's just a fairy tale."

Joey's comment stabbed Lucy in the gut. The story her father had told her had been far too specific and gruesome to be dismissed so easily.

"So what do you think, Luce?" Mike asked. "You think your homo hero had anything to do with what happened down in Avenal?"

"Shut up, Mike," Lucy said.

Mike turned to see Caroline Hughes standing several feet behind him. She had pulled her lustrous red hair back into a ponytail and her white tank top revealed broad shoulders and biceps that were as big as a woman could make them without looking like a freak. A strange light had come into her eyes and the sight of it was enough to silence Mike Harberson where he stood.

"I want to know what you're talking about," Caroline Hughes said. Her voice was low and hoarse. Lucy thought it might be a smoker's voice, but the woman's face was taut and unblemished, save for the gold freckles that gave it an almost muddy sheen.

"I asked you a question," Caroline Hughes said.

"No, you didn't," Mike answered. "You gave me an order. Bull dykes don't give orders around here. This ain't San Francisco."

Caroline closed her eyes briefly, gave Mike a brief nod, and turned on one heel. Lucy was about to take a breath when the woman spun and landed Mike with a sucker punch that sent him stumbling backward into a rack of sunglasses.

Before Lucy or Joey could make a sound, Caroline was on her knees, holding the back of Mike's head against her breasts with a grip so tight it looked like she would pull his stringy hair out by the roots. The knife she held to his throat had a six-inch blade and a five-fingered rubber grip on the handle.

Tears spit from Mike's slitted eyes. Lucy almost felt sorry for him until she remembered what Caroline Hughes had been through—her mother burned to death just because she had gone to visit one of her students in trouble. Maybe Mike Harberson was finally getting the ass-kicking he deserved.

"You've got a story to tell me," Caroline Hughes said. "Tell it."

"You heard it," Mike groaned.

"I want to hear all of it," she said.

"Fuck you," he spat.

"You're an asshole, Mike. Not a dangerous asshole. Just a third-rate white-trash small-town asshole who hangs around gas stations threatening every sixteen-year-old who crosses your path. You want to know something, Mike? Not even sixteen-year-olds are afraid of guys who hang out at gas stations."

"I told him the story!" Lucy snapped. "He was just repeating stuff I told him." Caroline didn't lift her gaze from the top of Mike's head. "You're right. He's an asshole. But that's all he is. Let him go and we can talk."

"Tell me now," Caroline said without looking at Lucy.

"Maybe you need to know," Lucy answered. "But they don't."

"They already do," Caroline answered.

"Not all of it!" Lucy shouted, panic flaring in her voice.

Caroline met Lucy's eyes, and the intensity of her stare lit up hairs on the back of Lucy's neck. "Joey can go first," Lucy said. "Then you let Mike go and I lock the doors."

"And what if I call the cops?" Joey Murdoch shouted.

"Then I tell them you've been hitting the glass pipe just like your brother!" Lucy told him. Joey paled and sank back down into his chair.

Caroline gave Lucy a slight nod. Lucy jerked one thumb at the front doors and Joey bolted. Caroline lifted Mike to his feet, walked him to the door, then kicked him square in the ass. The two men scrambled into their pickup and peeled off into the night.

Lucy locked the doors. Then she went behind the counter to turn off the sign outside. When she turned, Caroline Hughes was standing right behind her, watching her every move. She still held the long-bladed knife in one fist. Several locks of hair draped her face and her eyes were red-rimmed, her breaths rapid and shallow.

Lucy told her everything because she thought she didn't have a choice.

She included the bloodiest and most baffling details, the ones she had kept from Mike because she had wanted the guy to believe her.

Caroline Hughes listened intently to the story of El Maricón, a man who haunted the Great Central Valley in search of a vengeance that was as gruesome as it was ambitious. She didn't flinch and she didn't ask questions. After Lucy finished, Caroline was silent.

"Who told your father this?" she finally asked.

"Dad was a foreman for a cotton-picking crew over in Corcoran," Lucy answered. "One of his guys was missing work all the time, so he went to find him. The guy was drunk off his ass, probably high too. Who knows? Maybe he was making it up."

"Do you know his name?" Caroline Hughes asked.

After a long silence, Lucy gave Caroline Hughes the name of the young man who had given her father a nightmare that had plagued him until he died. Lucy had thought about locating the young man herself over the years. Part of her thought she might be putting the guy in danger. But Lucy Vernon had the strange feeling that the woman standing in front of her was the only one who could give the story an ending.

CHAPTER 4

I slept until noon, and then I spent the afternoon on the sofa eating Ben & Jerry's and watching an intensely homoerotic movie about a group of young boys who go on a sailing excursion in the Caribbean with a taciturn but compassionate captain. When the ship sank with several underwear-clad heartthrobs inside, I got tears in my eyes.

Around six, I thought about getting some dinner the way some people think about buying a vacation home. Rod Peters called around seven. He was on his way home from work. That's when I remembered it was Monday. The excitement in Rod's voice made me nervous.

"Don't freak out," Rod said. "But I've been talking to someone about this story of yours. In total confidence, of course."

"Who?" I asked, feeling like I should care but lacking the energy.

"A writer," he said. "It sounds like he wants to help."

"Who, Rod?"

"James Wilton."

I had heard of him, but that was all. His novels took up an entire shelf at Book Soup, and I had never read a word of them. Their covers featured segments of beautiful women's faces overlaid with chalk outlines and glistening gun barrels. I figured they were the kind of hard-boiled, embarrassingly heterosexual stuff in which all the pretty prostitutes talk in precious metaphors right up until they get their throats slashed.

"You're kidding, right?" I asked. I had sworn Rod to secrecy about the story to avoid the risk of getting scooped by a reporter with a real desk. Now he had spilled the beans to a world-famous novelist. I hoped he had a good reason. Rod was the last person I wanted to be angry at that day. The list was already long and I was at the top.

"No, I'm not," Rod said. "Listen, I didn't tell him everything. Just that you were working on something big, too big for the magazine you worked for. I also mentioned that it involved the Marine Corps. But that's all. I swear."

"Wasn't Wilton in the news recently?" I asked.

Rod let out a sigh that told me whatever information he was about to reveal might discourage me from meeting with Wilton. "A year ago, he published a novel called *Last Daughter*. It was based on a real case. This porn actress named Jenna Hartt was found murdered in her apartment in Malibu, but the sheriff's department never caught the guy. Wilton did, in a manner of speaking."

"I'm listening," I said.

"In Wilton's novel, the woman was murdered by her Christian fundamentalist brother. Turns out Jenna Hart actually *had* a Christian fundamentalist brother—and he wasn't too happy about how he was portrayed. He broke into Wilton's house in the middle of the night and went to work on him with a tire iron."

"Obviously the guy didn't work hard enough."

"I wouldn't say that," Rod answered. "Wilton's wife came home early and shot him five times. Killed him."

"And this guy wants to meet with *me*?"

"Of course he does. You two have similar interests," Rod said, as if James Wilton and I shared an interest in rare diseases. "Come on, Adam. What could it hurt?"

"That's what my first drug dealer said."

I heard Rod shift his cell phone from one ear to the other. Then he lowered the volume on his car stereo. "I heard you had an interesting night last night," he said.

"Jesus," I said. "Can't I beat the shit out of anyone in this town without everyone finding out about it?"

"I don't know, Adam," he said. "You've never beaten the shit out of anyone before." It wasn't a joke. I realized that Rod thought I needed help on other levels as well. For some reason, he thought that help would come from a best-selling novelist with a gunslinging wife and a penchant for plagiarizing real life.

I agreed to meet with James Wilton, and Rod happily agreed to call me back with a time and a place.

A shotgun blast exploded in the center of my computer screen. James Wilton appeared inside the splintered hole. His round, suntanned face had just enough weight on it to smooth out the lines of age, and his full salt-and-pepper hair was brushed back from his forehead in several loose waves. He looked to be in his late fifties, but his elfin features didn't support the glower he had affected for the camera.

A file cabinet appeared, each drawer labeled with the title of one of Wilton's novels. Then a quote bloomed at the top right corner of the screen in blood-red text: "Wilton is the poet laureate of crime fiction . . ." said a midwestern newspaper I had never heard of. I was curious to know what lay on the other side of the dots.

I clicked on his bio.

James Wilton is widely regarded as one of America's leading crime writers. His first novel, *Diamonds at the Gate*, was published when the author was twenty-six years old. Inspired in part by the author's brief but highly public marriage to seventies film star Vicky Malden, *Diamonds at the Gate* was an overnight best seller and became a television mini-series.

Since then, Wilton has authored sixteen consecutive *New York Times* best sellers, including the nine novels in his wildly popular series featuring LA Sheriff's Department homicide detective Joe Ring, and the fact-based *Blood and Flowers*, based on the real-life murder of Baton Rouge high school teacher Patricia Landry. *Blood and Flowers* won the Edgar Award and was adapted into an Oscar-nominated film in 1998. His most recent novel, *Last Daughter*, almost cost him his life.

Wilton's childhood was divided between Texas and San Francisco, and he moved to Hollywood after obtaining a master's in political science from San Francisco State University. He lives in the Hollywood Hills with his wife.

The rest of the site was devoted to cover images and plot descriptions of his novels, so I logged on to Amazon.com to find out whether the critics had had any say in James Wilton's being proclaimed one of America's leading crime writers.

It became clear that Wilton had no friends at the vaunted *New York Times Book Review*. On *Ring Makes Good*, the newspaper of record wrote, "Reading a James Wilton novel is like being beaten with baseball bats by a gang of five-year-olds. His prose is as terse as a voter registration card and his characters so sullen you wonder if they're secretly bemoaning the fact that they were born too late to earn inclusion in a narrative penned by one of the author's far superior predecessors." *Publishers Weekly* described *Ring Runs Out* as "short on real suspense and high on grotesque explosions of improbable violence."

But a quote from the *Washington Post's* review of *Last Daughter* shed a different light on the previous reviews:

> If critics had gotten their way, James Wilton would have stuck to the kind of exhaustive and atmospheric reporting that marked his true-crime best seller *Blood and Flowers*, but Wilton's over-the-top fiction has earned him commercial success and legions of devoted fans, if not critical acclaim. *Last Daughter*, however, is not the work of a writer trapped in a successful formula. Indeed, the critical opprobrium Wilton endures has turned him into one of our more fearless and inventive crime writers. The fictionalized tale of murdered porn starlet Jenna Hartt is a riveting and disturbing read that takes the reader smack into the dark heart of LA's porn industry, but without the condescension or hollow sermonizing one would expect from Wilton's contemporaries in the genre.

I turned up some more reviews and articles about *Blood and Flowers* and learned that the departure into fact-based crime had been a major risk for the best-selling novelist. Four publishers had rejected it, including his usual one. Wilton couldn't work at the speed of the sensationalist hacks who had stitched together news articles on Patricia Landry's murder to create instant paperbacks.

But Wilton had gone ahead with the book anyway. It had taken him three years, three years without the hefty advances and royalty checks he would have earned from churning out three more Joe Ring novels, three years in which the case became a distant memory and the book lost its major publicity angle.

The result had brought the author things he had never seen before: widespread critical acclaim, a literary award, and a screen adaptation that didn't have commercials in it. Wilton had gone right back to his formula soon after. But *Last Daughter*, a novel based on a real-life case, suggested that Wilton was seeking to get his feet wet in the world of fact-based crime once again.

Now he was interested in meeting with me about Daniel Brady. I was eager to see whether that would involve helping me out, as Rod had said.

I thought it was a great deal more likely that Wilton was looking to steal my story.

On Tuesday morning, I drove up into the hills to James Wilton's house, beneath a sky that shade of blue you can find only on an ocean in an atlas. Some desert thunderstorms had blown the smog out to sea without spilling a drop of rain on the city. Laurel Canyon is a treacherous mountain pass that the city tries to pass off as a major thoroughfare. It's lined with driveways and steep walls of bedrock festooned with tinderbox brush.

At Wilton's house on Mulholland Drive, there was a three-foot shoulder near the front gate for me to park on. As I rang the call box, a black Lincoln Navigator flew around the sharp bend in the road and swerved to avoid me. I had noticed the same SUV on Laurel Canyon a few minutes earlier and couldn't help but wonder if one of Scott Koffler's little charges might be behind the wheel.

I gave my name to the security guard, and the spiked black gate in front of me rolled smoothly to one side. I drove up a long gravel road leading through a forest of eucalyptus trees. Their branches did a lazy dance, offering me brief glimpses of the two-story Spanish Mission revival house that sat on a bluff overlooking the San Fernando Valley. The thick concrete walls were painted the color of a fresh mud puddle, and a short tower with a rounded roof anchored the L-shaped wings. The front door had a Moorish arch and a wood carving that depicted Montezuma's last stand against the Spanish invaders.

I rolled my window down and found myself staring at the security guard's slight beer belly and silver belt buckle. I reminded myself that the property had seen both an attempted murder and a real one, so I decided not to stick my head out the window.

"Jimmy wants you to fill this out," the guard said. He thrust a clipboard through the open window. The document on the clipboard did not have a heading, but there was a pen shoved through the clip.

The Black Dahlia is . . .
   a) a discontinued brand of Johnnie Walker
   b) methamphetamine in pill form
   c) Mayor Hahn's drag persona
   d) an unsolved LA homicide that no one in his right mind will
      ever write a single word about again

I circled D.

The greatest high-profile murder case of the last ten years is . . .
  a) the murder of Nicole Simpson
  b) the murder of Laci Peterson
  c) the attempted murder of yours truly
  d) 9/11

I bypassed the opportunity for brownnosing and circled D.

The greatest mystery writer of all time is . . .
  a) Ross McDonald
  b) Sidney Sheldon
  c) Raymond Fucking Chandler
  d) I'm a pretentious navel-gazing windbag who lives in a manu-
      factured version of reality where murder is to be leered at
      with passing interest, and all those who explore its ramifica-
      tions are to be dismissed as arrested adolescents and gutter
      punks. I enjoy poring over self-indulgent and monotonous
      explorations of what pompous grad students think of dis-
      gruntled academics, nuclear families, and their dead parents.
  (If you circled D, please leave.)

I circled Raymond Chandler just because I had read him. I handed
the clipboard to the guard, and he departed. A few minutes later, he returned and gestured me to follow him down the side of the house.

A tide of perfectly tended lawn swept toward a view of the San Fernando Valley that stretched from the mirrored skyscrapers of Universal
City to the dusty flanks of the San Gabriel Mountains on the northern
horizon. The swimming pool had a black bottom, and the water glistened
like Coca-Cola in a glass bottle. An expansive flagstone terrace sat between the house's two wings, and it was packed with enough patio furniture to host a small wedding party.

The guard escorted me down a flagstone path lined with waist-high
hedges that had smatterings of pink blossoms. At the end of it, an expansive pool house was laced with the sun shadows of live-oak branches.
The guard gestured for me to step through one of the French doors, and
I did.

The pool house was James Wilton's office. It had a ten-foot-high vaulted ceiling and a wrought iron chandelier with seven pillar candles stuck in it. An ancient-looking computer sat in the crook of an L-shaped desk, its screen glowing black and red with the text of some word processing program from the 1980s. The only other items on the desk were a copy of that day's *LA Times*, some empty file holders, and my pop quiz. The sweep of corkboard on the wall above was empty. Just as I had suspected, James Wilton was between projects.

The guard asked me if I wanted anything to drink. I declined. He left me to study the wall of bookshelves. Wilton's novels were not on prominent display. Instead I found texts on criminal profiling, practical guides to homicide investigation, and probably every piece of true-crime writing ever published.

A toilet flushed. I heard a strange scraping sound against the carpet.

The bird that waddled out of the bathroom stood about half a foot off the carpet. Its white feathers were stained yellow at the tips, and there was a metal band around its right leg. The bird and I stared at each other for a few seconds; then it raised its crown of pink feathers and let out a scream that curled the hair on my ass.

James Wilton emerged from the bathroom without glancing in my direction. His mahogany cane was topped with a chunky silver stallion's head. He transferred it from one hand to the other and finished zipping up his khaki shorts. He wore a dark blue Hawaiian shirt with dancing red fish all over it, and his chicken legs were dusted with wiry brown hair. His picture had rendered him accurately, except for the moist sheen in his big blue eyes and the scars that clung to the inside of his right leg like strands of wet toilet paper.

"This is Archer," he said, his eyes on the bird. "Don't get any screwy ideas. I can't shake the son of a bitch. You Adam Murphy?"

I nodded, just so he would have to make eye contact.

"You're homosexual," he said flatly.

"How could you tell?"

"Your skin looks like margarine, and your pants are so tight I feel like congratulating the blood that can get to your ass." He eased himself down into his desk chair and gestured for me to do the same in one of the Eames chairs in front of the wall of books. "You're a good writer," he said.

"How could you tell?"

He opened a desk drawer and dropped several back issues of *Glitz* magazine on his desk. "Shit," I whispered.

"I especially liked the one about the cologne that's supposedly made from real bull testosterone. You made me believe it for a second. That's talent. A lot of great journalists can't write advertising copy."

I just stared at him. He slouched back in his chair, pursed his lips, and studied me.

"Who died?" he asked.

"Excuse me?"

"You're wearing your grief, little man. You just don't know it. Your jaw's so tight it looks like you're about to take a bite out of the wall. Any sudden movement and your eyes turn to saucers."

"What am I doing here, Mr. Wilton?"

"Beats me," he said. "Maybe you're sick of trying to spin four hundred words out of a new brand of men's underwear that has a zipper on the side."

"And maybe you're looking for another *Blood and Flowers.*"

His eyes widened slightly. I had scored a direct hit. "You are here, Mr. Murphy, because your friend Rod Peters says you're onto something big and you're painfully out of your depth. Evidenced by the fact that last night you beat the shit out of your primary subject." He saw that I was sitting very still. "He also said that in barely twenty-four hours' time you uncovered something significant enough to get you fired. Feel like telling me what it was?"

"No."

He gave me a slight smile and pulled at the skin on his chin with his thumb and forefinger. "Why? You think I'm going to steal it?"

"Like I said, I think you're looking for another *Blood and Flowers.*"

"How'd you learn how to protect yourself so well?" he asked.

"I was raised by a drunk."

"Is that so?" he asked. "Who won?"

"I think you invited me up here because you thought I would be starstruck," I said quickly. "When you saw that wasn't the case, you tried to goad me with some homophobic remarks so I would try to prove myself by telling you what I've found out."

"That's a fairly damning accusation, son," he said, as if it were anything but.

"Is it true?"

"Are you calling my genuine concern for your circulation homophobia?"

I glared at him. He smiled back at me for a few seconds, then cleared his throat. "Your friend Rod Peters said that if it wasn't for your dipshit boss at *Glitz*, you would have broken three major investigative stories by now and would probably be a staff writer at a better magazine.

He said when you're onto something, you stay on it until it socks you in the jaw."

Rod had never said these words to me. I felt my face flush and I broke eye contact with Wilton for the first time since I had sat down.

"Sounds like things got a little scary on this one, though," Wilton said. "You ready to chicken out?"

"I haven't decided yet."

"Tough shit," he said evenly. "Your temper made that decision for you when you beat the shit out of this guy who got you fired. You're part of the story now, and that means you've got no choice but to drop it."

"So you can pick it up?" I asked.

"I'm starting to get the feeling that you don't trust an older man unless he wants to sleep with you," he said. "This has been a job interview, little man. To be honest, I'm not quite sure how it's going."

"A job doing what?"

"I need an assistant," he said. "Based on what Rod told me, I thought hiring you would be like hiring a fashion designer to do my laundry. Now I'm not so sure." He saw the look of surprise on my face and allowed me a wan smile. "You're mouthy. Mouthy and defiant. That's not the same thing as confident and adult. You stick around here, and that will be just one of the distinctions I'll remind you of every day."

"What would your assistant have to do?" I asked meekly.

"Who cares?" he snapped. "I'm a best-selling novelist. People get arrested trying to climb over my front gate. You're real low on gratitude, hot pants."

"Last week a marine helicopter pilot named Daniel Brady came to West Hollywood in the company of a man named Scott Koffler. Koffler furnishes underage boys with fake names and fake IDs and then sets them up with wealthy men. Sometimes the boy gets a supporting role in a feature out of the deal."

Jimmy's face lost some of its rosy color.

"How much?" I asked.

"Excuse me?" he asked.

"How much do you plan on paying your assistant?"

He cleared his throat and straightened. "Twenty-five dollars an hour. Six days a week. Nine to seven. I'm aware that's high, so don't launch into a Gloria Gaynor song when I ask you to get me my shoes."

"I accept," I said. "Can I see something in writing?"

He opened a desk drawer and removed a folded piece of paper. I unfolded it and saw the words CONFIDENTIALITY AGREEMENT written across the top. Below, there was a single line of text: "I promise to keep my big fat mouth shut about all the crazy shit that goes on at James Wilton's house. Signed: _____." I signed my name and handed it back to him.

He studied my signature, then gestured for me to continue with my story.

"While they were riding around West Hollywood, Koffler tried to get Brady to have sex with a friend of mine in the backseat of his car. Brady flipped out and tossed the guy into the middle of the street. On Friday afternoon, it looks like Brady flipped out a second time and flew his helicopter right into the Pacific Ocean. He had been married for three years."

Jimmy sat forward, picked up a pen, and began jotting notes down on the side of my pop quiz. I waited patiently for his response.

"You hungry?" he asked me.

Jimmy's car was a black Cadillac Seville with windows tinted the color of midnight at sea. He told me he was able to drive, but he would have to use his left foot, so I took the keys out of his hand and got behind the wheel. The car had so much leather upholstery it could have doubled as a padded cell.

At Beverly Glen Canyon, he directed me into a strip mall that sat right at the spot where the canyon road became a twisting water slide shooting motorists down into Beverly Hills. The mall was a secluded town square for the residents of the hills above the West Side, and its parking lot was full of expensive SUVs and luxury sedans.

At a small Italian restaurant, the hostess seated us on a patio fenced in by hedges. Our fellow diners were all white women dressed in white drinking white wine.

"The food's good here," Wilton remarked.

"It's romantic, too."

"Shut up."

When I tried to order an iced tea, Jimmy demanded I get something that had sugar in it so that I would stop glowering at everything that made a sound. I gave the waitress a broad smile and said, "You should see what he's like when I don't have dinner ready on time."

Jimmy glowered at me as the waitress laughed all the way back to the kitchen. He instructed me to start at the beginning and I did. I omitted the specific words Koffler had used to send me over the edge.

"Your working theory was that one of Koffler's clients requested an au-

dience with a hot marine, right?" he asked. I said yes. "You didn't like Koffler very much when you started, did you?" he asked. "It sounds like you
don't like any of his wealthy clients very much either. Let me guess. You
think moral bankruptcy is the price they pay for financial success and
swimming pools full of cute young things."

"Something like that," I answered.

He nodded. "Is any of what I'm saying the reason you didn't stop to assume that maybe Daniel Brady was the client?"

"You think Daniel Brady wanted to sleep with one of Scott's kids?" I
asked.

"I think that's where you should have started," he said. "The stunt with
your buddy Nate—it sounds like Koffler had something to prove to this guy
Brady. That he was powerful. That he could manipulate pretty boys into doing his bidding. That implies that Koffler was supposed to give Brady a lot
more than a nice drive." He let me absorb this. When I didn't speak up, he
continued. "You had the guts to peel back the layers of the world you live in,
and I admire that, little man. The problem was, you picked your hero and
your villain from the get-go. Brady was the victimized closet case, Koffler
the devious pedophile. I'm a little surprised, to be frank."

"Why?"

"Daniel Brady threw your friend into the middle of traffic," he said.
"Not Scott Koffler."

I felt my face get hot. He had exposed my bias and laid it on the table
between us.

"Brady was stationed at Pendleton, right?" I nodded. "You should
have gone after him first. You were dealing with a closeted marine prone
to violent outbursts around his sexuality. You should have hit the bars
down in San Diego. Maybe Brady made a similar appearance there and
left some wreckage. If he had, you could have given it to Scott Koffler."

"Why on earth would I *give* it to Scott Koffler?"

"Because then you allow Koffler the chance to play the victim," he
said. "You tell him that you've been made aware he was traveling in the
company of a violent, self-hating closet case. You express concern for his
well-being. And you give him the chance to clear the air about a guy who
probably ruined his night."

Every defensive bone in my body went dry. He saw how much his
analysis had affected me and continued. "Now let's look at what you *did* do.
You went out to Scott Koffler's house and found him with two underage
boys. But you didn't pay one whit of attention to either one of them, and

when Koffler offered you a drink you didn't accept. Instead, you opened the interview by shoving a picture of Daniel Brady in his face."

He picked up his fork and tapped it on the table to accentuate each point. "You accept the drink. You ask Koffler to join you. He tells you he's a guardian angel to those boys, and you express nothing but admiration for his charity work. You ask him how he does it and how he finds the time. You ask to meet the boys, and you play the perfect gentleman. If need be, you give the subtle impression that you're interested in getting to know one of them on a more intimate basis.

"That gets Koffler talking about what you'd have to do to sleep with them. Privately you give those boys your phone number in case one of them needs a ride home—in case one of them happens to be around when Koffler throws a fit because his buddy Brady offed himself and the kid needs someone to talk to about it."

He let his words sink in. "*This* is investigative journalism, little man. You had a huge advantage going for you and you blew it. A guy you knew socially might have been involved in the deaths of four marines. You could have been the guy's friend and walked away with something before he even knew he'd given it to you. Instead, you started a pissing contest that got you fired."

"In an article I couldn't use something Koffler told me in confidence," I protested.

"Of course not," he countered. "But it opens the door for something you can use. This was a huge story, little man, and you went after it like you were going to file the next day."

The waitress came to take our orders and I heard myself ask for the veal. Jimmy ordered without taking his eyes off me, and I wondered if he was waiting for me to fall apart under pressure.

"You still here?" he asked in a low voice.

"I'm trying to remind myself of something," I said.

"What?"

"That being humbled isn't the same thing as being humiliated," I said. "Maybe if I let myself get humbled a little more often, I won't end up being humiliated so much."

His expression softened, but I got the sense that he was sitting on a smart remark. "You want to really be humbled?" he asked. "Let me put your buddy Nate in touch with a friend at the *LA Times*."

My stomach went cold. He smiled a little. "No thanks," I said.

"Fine," he said. "But you won't be working on this one while you're on my watch. The Marine Corps will be launching an investigation of its own, which means if you go back to doing what you were doing, you'll probably end up in a military prison. That might be a fantasy of yours, but I need someone to get me coffee."

I was already well aware that I would have to let go of the Daniel Brady story, but I still didn't like hearing someone else say it. When I didn't protest, I realized that James Wilton and I might have some kind of future together.

"One more thing," he said softly. "What hooked you into this? Are you sleeping with this Nate kid?" I shook my head. "Do you and Koffler have some kind of history together aside from what you've told me?"

"No," I said tightly.

"What then?"

I could tell he wasn't going to give up.

"I had a relationship that ended badly," I finally said. "I'm tired of thinking about it. I wanted a distraction."

"Your mother wasn't enough?"

"No," I answered flatly.

"What happened with this guy? The one you were in a relationship with?"

I stared down at the table. "He wanted me to stop drinking."

"So it is a family disease after all," he said.

I expected to see some judgment or revulsion in his expression, but I didn't. Still, his frank and open stare did little to convince me that I wasn't about to lose the job that had just fallen into my lap. "Maybe he wanted you to quit some other stuff, too?" he asked.

"I've changed my ways since then," I said. "I just wasn't willing to change for him."

"Makes sense," he said. "What happened?"

"I've been humbled."

"What happened with *him*, little man?"

"I want this job, Mr. Wilton. You're right. I haven't been very good at showing my gratitude." I tried to keep my voice steady, but my words came out sounding like a plea.

"And now you're showing your gratitude by stonewalling me?" he asked with a devilish smirk.

I took a deep breath. The waitress delivered our entrées. I waited for her to leave.

"I had a dealer," I said. "This big fat guy who always used to grab my ass and pretend like I would have to put out to get what I wanted out of him. I used to pretend that was the reason I hated visiting his apartment. It was easier than admitting I had a problem. Corey and I spent three weeks together. Every night, every minute of every day—"

"Christ," Jimmy mumbled. "I hope the sex was good. I don't want to talk about it, but I hope it was good."

"Anyway, after three weeks, I felt like I needed some space." The dishonesty of this statement struck me the minute I voiced it. That afternoon I had wanted a lot more than space. I had wanted a total release from the nagging voices convincing me that I was not worthy of a man as strong, confident, and beautiful as Corey Howard. That, or I didn't want to admit that I was having trouble living with a guy who tucked in my shirts for me, cleared my coffee cups before they were empty, and responded to my every honest emotion with a grave and distant expression that suggested he would spend the rest of our lives trying to talk me out of feeling differently than he did.

"As soon as Corey left my place to go to work that day, I went to my dealer's apartment. He didn't have anything for me, but he told me to come back in a few hours. When I left, I thought I saw Corey's truck outside, but I told myself I was just being paranoid." I had Wilton's full attention and I wasn't sure I wanted it. "When I came back, my dealer didn't answer his buzzer. I waited for someone to go through the entry door, and I went in behind them. The door to the apartment was unlocked and Sa— my dealer was lying facedown on the floor. He was covered in blood. At first I thought he had been stabbed. He hadn't been. Someone had beaten the shit out of him and spread his stash all over the apartment. Practically every drug you could think of. It was everywhere."

"So you couldn't call the police," Jimmy said.

I shook my head. Wilton hadn't touched his food and neither had I.

"What did you do?" he asked.

"I called an ambulance and left."

"Did you clean up the drugs?"

"No."

He raised his eyebrows, but his stare was steady and unblinking. "I take it you didn't mind the thought of your dealer spending some time out of town. Maybe you thought it would help you on the road to recovery."

"I knew Corey had done it. I also knew that he couldn't afford a brand-new pickup truck and a three-bedroom apartment in West Hollywood on a car wash attendant's salary. He was getting checks from somewhere and didn't tell me where. At the end of three weeks, I barely knew anything about him, but he knew almost everything about me."

"Is that what you said to him?"

"Yes," I answered. "Then I told him I knew what he had done, and if he didn't stay out of my life, I was going to call the police."

Jimmy was visibly surprised by the story's ending. Maybe he thought that I had been dumped. I picked up my fork and knife and cut off a piece of veal I didn't have the stomach for.

"Did he?" he finally asked. "Stay out of your life, I mean."

I remembered the visit Corey had paid to Billy Hatfill, the warning he had given Billy about me and my dangerous addictions, a blatant attempt to deprive me of one of my more glamorous sources of free liquor. "Sort of," I answered.

He gave me some time to recover, and the two of us started eating our lunch. He took big bites that required him to work his jaw. I ate pieces so small a strong wind could have blown them off my fork.

"Where do you think Corey's checks were coming from?"

"I don't know."

"Guess."

"I know he was a Scorpio because he always wore this gold chain around his neck that had a scorpion on the medallion." I remembered how the medallion would brush up against my bare chest. "I know he didn't come from a rich family. I know he could barely remember his father, and he didn't want to talk about his mother. At one point, he mentioned tule grass—"

"Tule grass?" Jimmy asked.

"You can find it all over the Central Valley," I said. "From Bakersfield to Redding. It looks like wheat in the summer, and the Yokut Indians used it to make huts. He told me that someplace where he used to play when he was a kid was covered in the stuff. When I asked him where this place was, he changed the subject.

"There's no way a guy like Corey wasn't making money off his looks. Not in this city. I checked every listing of male escorts I could find, but I didn't see him. The guys who black out their faces in their ads are usually shirtless or naked, and none of them had Corey's body. That leaves a sugar daddy. I don't know—maybe this guy's closeted."

"Like the guys Scott Koffler pimps for," Jimmy said.

My eyes shot to his and he gave me a small, satisfied smile. Even though we had drifted far from the topic, he had just exposed one of my major motives for going after the Daniel Brady story, and with almost no help from me. James Wilton was not a mind reader, but he certainly subscribed to the belief that human beings were more basic and petty than most of them would like to admit. I wasn't sure which bothered me more: James Wilton's insight or the fact that I was just another human being.

"I'm still not sure why you hired me, Mr. Wilton," I said.

"Neither am I," he said. "But I think you'll answer that question for me in due time." We ate in silence for a few minutes, and when he spoke again, it sounded like he was continuing a conversation he had carried on in his own head.

"You're right," he said. "I want another *Blood and Flowers* and I want you to help me find it and research it. Preferably some case that hasn't been splashed all over CNN. It doesn't matter if it's closed or not. I want something everybody else overlooked."

I nodded, even though I wasn't sure why he needed me to help him in this endeavor.

"The downside of being a best-selling author is that I can't be the fly on the wall the way I was when I wrote *Blood and Flowers*. I was a success then, but as I've learned, there's no fame like the fame that comes after someone tries to bash your head in with a tire iron."

I thought his fame had more to do with the fact that his wife shot the guy. I realized we had been together a good two hours and he hadn't mentioned his wife once.

"What?" he asked.

"What does your wife do?"

"She's a nurse. Why?"

"Is she ever around?" I asked.

"We're still together, if that's what you're asking."

"Okay."

An uneasy few seconds passed between us. "Why do you ask?"

"No reason."

"Horseshit!" I saw realization in his eyes. "Oh, for Christ's sake," he said, dropping his fork. "You really think I hired you because I wanted to sleep with you?"

"It's a valid concern."

"For you? Why? Because you're so young and impressionable? Please. Strip off all that lycra and leather and you've probably got the shine of an old shoe." He shook his head at his plate. "Never fear, Lolita. I didn't even try that stuff in college. I can't even see how you—"

"How I what?"

"How you guys . . . *do* that," he said.

"It starts with a wheelbarrow full of Aveda products and a Fleet Enema," I said. "After that, it's mostly deep breathing."

James Wilton glared at me. The waitress came and asked him how our food was. He didn't acknowledge her, so she left. "You're fired," he whispered.

CHAPTER 5

Nate Bain called me as soon as I pulled out of James Wilton's front gate. It was two o'clock, and I had strict instructions to be there at nine the next morning, after having discovered and researched several potential candidates for his next true crime masterpiece. Even though Jimmy had warned me off the Daniel Brady story, I agreed to meet Nate at the corner of Santa Monica and San Vicente Boulevard, the same place where Scott Koffler had picked him up.

He was standing on the corner when I got there, watching the sheriff's department helicopter descend out of the clear blue sky as it came in for a landing on the roof of the brown brick substation across the street. Nate was getting his fair share of looks from passersby, but he was too busy watching the helicopter's landing, like an ineffectual dictator about to be forcibly removed from his island country.

He wore a light blue polo shirt that had bleach spots on it and a pair of navy running pants with a white side stripe. He had cleaned up well. His face had a moisturized shine to it that almost distracted me from his etched cheekbones. But his eyes were glassy and his face frozen in the first threat of a scowl, and he held himself as if he had just been sucker-punched.

Nate saw me coming, slid his backpack off one shoulder, and unzipped it. I expected him to produce some piece of evidence about his meeting with Daniel Brady and I had already mentally prepared a brief statement about why I couldn't work the story anymore. I was startled when he plucked a blue hardcover book out of his backpack, the words *Alcoholics Anonymous* on the spine. He pulled an envelope from the book's pages and handed it to me.

I tore the envelope open and removed the greeting card inside. There was a Maxfield Parrish print on the front, and inside Nate had written the words "Thank you" in a chicken scratch that reminded me of the time I wrote my rent check on the morning after a long weekend.

"You didn't have to do this," I said.

"My sponsor says people stay sober by doing estimable acts," he said.

"AA?" I asked.

He nodded and looked at the traffic surging through the intersection.

"That's great, Nate. Who's your sponsor?"

"I can't tell you. It's an anonymous program."

I tucked the card in my pants pocket.

"I've already been to two meetings today," he said quickly. "It's all right, I guess. The speaker at the second meeting, she talked about how she got drunk and shot her husband and how today they're, like, best friends. You've probably heard of her. She was in that—"

"It's an anonymous program, Nate."

"Right," he whispered. "Sorry. My brain . . ."

I smiled. Two Hispanic boys with swollen chests and enormous sunglasses walked by. One of them whistled at Nate, and then once they were several feet past us, the other turned around and cried, "Love your work!"

Nate stared after them with what I assumed was anger. "My sponsor has me on this whole celibacy thing right now," he said in a low voice, and I realized his anger was actually desire. The fact that anger felt like desire to Nate might have played a role in his little meth problem.

"Try not to bite off more than you can chew," I said. "So I guess the porn's out?"

"No," Nate answered. "He said porn is a job. Just as long as I don't try to convince myself I'm in love with any of my costars."

The logic of this was beyond me. "Thanks for the card."

"I didn't want you to see me like that, Adam."

"You don't want anyone to see you like that. That's why you're getting sober, right?"

He reacted to my parental tone with a wounded look, then said yes unconvincingly.

"Look, I don't mean to sound like an asshole, but I'm kind of speaking from experience here," I said. Forty-eight hours of experience, I thought, but what the hell. "Be proud of yourself. My mother couldn't do it and she died."

His eyes widened slightly and a line appeared across the bridge of his nose. "Maybe you could come to a meeting with me sometime."

"Maybe," I muttered, even though I knew I wouldn't.

"The guys are hot, Adam. Trust me. They're, like, hot and conscious."

I chuckled, but when I saw that Nate's smile looked almost genuine, I got the sense that he didn't care whether the men in AA were good looking or not. He wanted me to stay sober, which meant he cared for me, in a way that probably felt as new to him as it did to me.

"I'll think about it," I said. "Listen, Nate. I dropped the story. I don't want to go into too much detail, but let's just say I wasn't the man for the job."

His eyes fell to the pavement. "It doesn't matter, Adam," he said. "My sponsor said the same thing you did."

"What did I say?" I asked.

"I don't get thrown out of speeding cars when I'm not tweaking."

He was more willing to let the story go than I was. I wondered if he would revisit it with fresh anger once the reality of sober living began to set in. Nate stepped forward and gave me a quick peck on the cheek.

"Why don't you call me?" I asked him. "Every day. Just to check in." I was thinking of the threat Scott Koffler had made against him, but I thought if I told him about it, I might be endangering his newfound sobriety. He smiled and said sure.

He was about to step in the crosswalk when he turned and called my name. "That number you gave me for Corey doesn't work anymore," he shouted.

I gave him a little wave as if I was grateful for this information, even as I told myself to get rid of it. As soon as I was back in my Jeep, I dialed Corey's cell phone. An automated message informed me that he was no longer a subscriber.

I told myself to let it go. I told myself that he had probably changed services. Then I told myself that if there was even the smallest chance that Corey had left West Hollywood, I had to know for sure. I told myself it might give me the closure I needed.

Corey lived in a salmon-colored duplex that sat in the shadow of a condo high-rise, just a block south of Sunset Boulevard. I had visited his apartment only twice, in his company, so that he could get a change of clothes before heading back to my place.

His second-floor apartment had a porte cochere that extended over the building's driveway; an exterior stairway led to his front door. There was a small drift of fast food menus on the other side of the wrought iron gate on the first floor. The lone palm tree out front had shed dried fronds across the building's front lawn. The accumulated debris was peculiar. Corey had made my bed so tightly you could bounce a quarter off it. I didn't see his truck anywhere, and I knew it was too big for the small garages in back.

At the Twin Palms Car Wash on Sunset Boulevard, I gave the cashier a description of Corey that left her wide-eyed and winded. She went to get her manager, who told me that Corey worked Saturdays through Thursdays, and they hadn't seen him since Thursday. When I pointed out that this meant Corey had missed four days of work, the guy stiffened as if I had accused him of a crime. Evidently, employees at the Twin Palms Car Wash came and went without fanfare.

I returned to Corey's duplex and rang the doorbell for the downstairs apartment. The guy who answered was in his early thirties, with shoulder-length brown hair and a thin beard. When I expressed my concern about his upstairs neighbor, he asked me to wait while he went to get a key for the apartment. He let me through the wrought iron gate and knocked on Corey's front door.

As we waited, I managed to learn from him that Corey had lived there for only six months and the neighbors rarely saw him. After a few more knocks met by silence, the neighbor unlocked the front door. A foul stench hit us, and I saw my first thought register in the neighbor's eyes: we were about to walk in on a corpse.

I stepped in ahead of him and brought one hand to my nose and mouth. I recognized the smell for what it was: sour milk. I followed the scent down on a long hallway that traversed the depth of the apartment. On the kitchen counter, I found an open container of milk. Corey's wallet and keys rested several feet away. Fear ran its fingernails down my arms, and I felt a sudden tension in my lower back. I wondered if the sour milk stench was masking a more dire stench from somewhere else in the apartment. I called out to Corey and heard a squeak of sneakers behind me. The neighbor stumbled back into the fridge, his eyes wide and his mouth curled in something that looked like a snarl.

"Should I call the police?" he breathed. I told him to stay where he was.

The massive living room had a large fireplace and a hardwood floor. It was the kind of room in the sort of apartment an upwardly mobile gay man would have covered with throw rugs and fine art. Yet the only pieces of furniture in the living room were an overstuffed sofa and an entertainment center.

The bedroom door was halfway open. The gray comforter on the queen-size bed was thrown back as if Corey had awakened several minutes before. A wall of sliding mirrored doors reflected Century City on the near horizon. I pushed back one door; Corey had hung his T-shirts and blue jeans on individual hangers.

The bathroom's black and white tile work had probably raised the rent by a hundred dollars. Next to the basin sat an open bottle of shaving gel, its cap, and Corey's cell phone. A rumpled towel rested on the tile floor several feet away from the sink. I clearly saw Corey dropping the towel from around his waist as he reached for the cell phone. My heartbeat turned into the kind of pitter-patter most people associate with children's feet.

I was still frozen in the bathroom door when I heard a loud metallic whine outside. I called out to the neighbor. When he responded, I followed the sound of his voice into one of the back bedrooms. It was empty save for a beanbag chair and a desk lamp on the floor next to it, with wine crates stacked as bookshelves, stuffed with paperbacks.

I joined the neighbor at the back window and saw what he was staring at. He had opened a garage door. Corey's Dodge Ram sat inside one of the garages, with barely an inch of clearance on either side.

"He never parks in the garage," the neighbor whispered. "He can barely fit."

After asking the neighbor to stay where he was, I went out the back door in the kitchen and descended a set of steps to another wrought iron gate. I couldn't fit inside the garage to get a good look inside Corey's truck. Coming back upstairs, I turned the inside lock on the wrought iron gate and did the same on the back door in the kitchen. I planned on making a second visit, and I didn't want company.

The neighbor was pouring the spoiled milk into the sink. When he saw me, he dropped the carton and balled his hand to a fist. "Shit," he whispered. "I guess I shouldn't be touching anything."

"How long has it been since you've heard him up here?"

"Hard to say," he answered. "I've barely heard him since he moved in."

"Any visitors recently?"

"No," he answered. "He'd go to work pretty early and then he'd be home only for a while in the afternoon. He's got surround speakers in there. Sometimes I'd hear those, but that's about it. You going to call the police?"

"Let's give him twenty-four hours," I said.

He looked to the floor. I could tell he was trying to disengage. "Never thought I'd get so freaked out by sour milk."

At the front door, I gave him my cell number and asked him to call me if Corey came back. He gravely agreed, as if I had enlisted him in a matter of national security.

It was already clear that Corey Howard had been missing for at least four days. I knew of someone who had a rather strange meeting with Corey two weeks earlier and tracked me down to warn me about it.

The gate to the house that Joseph Spinotta built was a ten-foot-high wall of brushed steel that sat at the end of a cul-de-sac just below Mulholland Drive. A door opened in the middle of the gate as soon as I pulled up. The guy who stepped through it looked like Calvin Klein's idea of a cherub. His hair was a cap of sandy blond bristle, and his big blue eyes looked as if they could both use their own pool man. Except for his manly jawline and the serious muscle visible through his white T-shirt, his face gave no evidence that he had ever to shave more than his upper lip.

He offered his hand and introduced himself as Everett. I smiled instead of returning the favor. "You're Adam Murphy," he said with a vague smile. "Billy likes you."

"He does?"

"He says you're angry, and anger is the new integrity. It's a post nine-eleven thing." I laughed, which seemed to please him. The silver bicycle chain around his neck was so shiny it looked as if his mother had polished it with the Thanksgiving silver.

"Is Billy home?" I asked, even though I knew he was. I had called on my way there, without telling him why I wanted to visit, and he'd readily agreed to see me, almost as if he had been waiting for my call.

"He is," Everett answered. Then he tongued his upper lip briefly and gave me a once-over. "I'll take you to him. But you have to make me a promise first."

I didn't respond.

"Don't do anything to him that you won't do to me. Twice."

"Does your mother know you're hanging out at Billy Hatfill's place?"

A dark cloud passed over his face that made him look a lot older than a teenager. His eyes went heavy and he jutted his lower lip. I had hurt his feelings, and in his world that was a crime.

I followed him through the gate. A set of slate steps descended through terraced beds of cacti and rocks. The house was a one-story U with walls of glass and a flat roof that seemed to hover above the sage-green lawn. It sat in the middle of a miniature plateau that looked as if it had been sand-blasted out of the hillside. The Sierra Tower rose at the base of the hill, in fourteen stories of concrete I-beams and glass walls. It was a vertical re-tirement community for wealthy celebrities who had abandoned their mansions in the hills, and also the lighthouse that marked the western end of the Sunset Strip. A low cloud cover was moving in off the ocean on the western horizon.

Billy's foyer was the size of Jimmy's office, but the only thing in it was a glass-topped dining table that could have seated six, back when it had chairs to go with it. Today it held a vase of Casablanca lilies and the latest issue of *Vanity Fair*. The house had rolling dividers made of blond wood instead of doors and silver automatic shades that could be lowered over each wall of glass.

I had never seen the place without at least three hundred other gay men in it, and I was struck by how vast and empty it seemed. Rod Peters had once joked that the house had been designed with only three things in mind: huge parties, group sex, and cocaine. That explained the absence of furni-ture, the plush sweep of carpet in every room, and a glass surface topping anything that stood still long enough.

Billy called out my name from somewhere in the house's east wing. Everett rested his butt against the back of the sofa and gave me a blank look. I took his casual stance to mean that I was now on my own. I passed through a dining room and into a kitchen with miles of white marble coun-tertop and blond wood cabinets.

Billy sat at a glass plate of a coffee table supported by a giant chrome X. He was flipping through the recent issue of *Glitz* magazine. His hair was damp and he wore a white T-shirt and gym shorts. He flipped several pages in his magazine without glancing in my direction.

"Everett's pretty interesting."

Billy dropped the cover of his magazine and met my eyes. "Interest-ing," he repeated, his tone a mocking echo of mine. "I guess he hit on you. That's part of the reason I've decided to take him under my wing. He could use a little grooming, don't you think?"

"What are you grooming him for?" I asked. "A house like this? A man like Joseph?"

He seemed to hear the undertone of disdain in my voice. He gave me a wry smile, but I noticed the flash of anger in his big blue eyes. "I take it that means you think I have something to offer a guy like Everett," he said, giving my little dig a positive spin. "It can be tough for a guy like Everett to make a life for himself out here. Have you ever noticed something about my parties? A few months go by and it's a completely different set of faces. A whole new crop of overly exfoliated, bright-eyed, twenty-something faces."

"The turnover rate is pretty high all over this city," I said.

"Maybe," he said. "But the shelf life for these West Hollywood boys is shorter. The acting gig doesn't work out. The porn doesn't pay enough. The drugs are too strong. Within less than a year, they're either in rehab or on a bus back to Des Moines. Or in a coffin." I worked to keep my face neutral. Corey wasn't your typical West Hollywood party boy, but after what I had just discovered, Billy's comments packed a punch.

"I'm just saying—I know I sold my soul to the devil, Adam. But sometimes the way I did it is the only way to do it. It's the only way a guy like Everett can keep himself from turning into a party flaw."

"You're a regular Scott Koffler," I said.

Billy's eyes went flat. "I'm going to try to forget that you compared me to that fat fuck." He shot to his feet.

He opened the fridge and poured himself a glass of Gerolsteiner without offering me one. "Scott Koffler is a white-trash pimp, and those boys of his are hardly little innocents. He's also banned from this house. A few months ago, I caught one of his kids going through my nightstand drawer, and when I said something to the little prick, he called me a candy ass poseur."

"I was kidding, Billy."

He took a twenty-five-dollar slug of his mineral water. "I'm trying to keep Everett from making the same mistakes I did. Where's the crime in that?"

"I didn't say there was one."

"What life would you pick for Everett? Mine? I doubt that. We already know how you feel about mine."

"Take a Xanax, Billy. You're hearing things I haven't said." The words were out of my mouth before I could stop them, and they had an immediate effect on the man across from me. He closed his eyes gently and cocked his head to one side, as if he were conversing with his chi on how best to deal with me.

"You bleed judgments, Adam. You leave a trail of them wherever you go. You're going to drown in them someday." He said these words gently, as if he thought they were a strange kind of compliment. "I thought you came here to apologize?"

"For what?"

"For acting like a bitch just because I warned you about Corey Howard," he said, his eyes roaming the length of my body as if he thought the mention of Corey's name would send me lunging for his throat.

"I don't need any warnings about Corey," I said.

His eyebrows jerked, and his tongue made a lump under his upper lip. I thought my words would be enough to focus him on the topic of Corey's strange visit to his house. But he crossed to a glass door that opened onto the pool deck, which seemed like my cue to leave.

"I wish you could have met Joseph. Maybe you would have figured him out before I did. But the real question is, would you have warned me about him or just let me go along for the ride?"

"The ride was that bad, huh?" I asked.

"I guess that's a no."

Billy opened the glass door to the pool deck and took a step through it. "Corey's missing, Billy," I said in a firm voice. My words stopped him. "He's been missing at least four days."

He stepped back inside and crossed his arms over his chest. The door drifted shut behind him. "Missing?" he asked.

"Yes," I said. "How long ago did he come here? Two weeks? He wasn't the most social animal on the planet. You might have been one of the last people to talk to him. Did he say anything about leaving town?"

"No," he said. "He was too busy talking about you. I told you what he said, Adam."

"Did Corey mention anything else when he talked to you? Anything about his job, his apartment?"

"Have you talked to his uncle?" Billy asked me quickly, as if the thought had just occurred to him.

An uncle. I shook my head, trying to act as if I'd somehow misplaced the phone number of a man I hadn't known existed. Corey had barely told me anything about his family aside from the fact that he had run away from home when he was sixteen. I had guessed that he met up with his mysterious sugar daddy somewhere around that time.

"I take it you didn't know," Billy said.

"Know what?"

"Corey's uncle is a man named Martin Cale," he said. "He's a real estate developer. He also happens to be an old friend of Joseph's. Martin Cale is actually the reason that Joseph and I moved here from San Francisco. Cale's firm was doing a subdivision out in the Inland Empire and he wanted Joseph to install a wireless Internet system for the entire property. It didn't happen. The technology wasn't quite there yet, but he and Joseph hit it off. Cale even invested in Broadband Access Media."

I blinked. Billy had given me a big chunk of information, the implications of which I'd have to work to understand, but he had skipped over the most important details. "How long have you known this man was Corey's uncle?" I asked.

"Two weeks," he said. "Joseph never mentioned Corey. Neither did Martin Cale. Corey told me the night he came here. It was his entrée, if you will. I have to say, I was surprised. I don't mean to sound like a snob, but I didn't think Corey Howard came from money."

Corey Howard had not come from money; he had run to it at the age of sixteen. The sugar daddy I had always suspected him of having was actually a wealthy uncle with connections to white-collar criminals and their trophy boys.

"What's Cale like?" I asked, with what I hoped appeared to be just casual interest.

Billy rolled his eyes. "Let me put it this way. Cale's wife died last year. In New York. Where she had been living for ten years while her husband did business out here. He and Joseph were primarily business associates, but every now and then Martin Cale would come to one of our parties here and leer at every young thing that crossed his path like it had a For Sale sign on its ass."

"Were these young things male or female?" I asked.

"Guess," he said.

"Martin Cale is a closet case?" I asked.

"And a recluse," he said. "He lives on his yacht and rarely comes to shore. I might be able to set up a meeting, though, if you're interested."

Once again I had to hide my surprise. Why was Billy offering to connect me with Martin Cale? "Cale invested in Joseph's website? And he still talks to you, even though Joseph skipped town with his money?"

Billy stared down at the floor, as if his next line were written on the marble in front of my feet. I had cornered him, even though I wasn't quite sure how. "He's fond of Everett," he finally said.

"Martin Cale?" I asked carefully.

"Martin doesn't have a lot of connections to the gay world," Billy finally said. "He managed to get over his hard feelings about Joseph's departure rather quickly."

"I'd like to meet him," I said.

Billy nodded distantly. "I'll call you as soon as I talk to him," he said.

"I appreciate it."

He just nodded. He had been the one to suggest that I meet with Martin Cale in the first place, and now he seemed to regret his offer. Billy had already done a good job of telling me bad things about Corey; maybe he thought Corey's uncle would do more of the same, even if the man had presumably set Corey up with his apartment and car. But there was also the possibility that Martin Cale might have some unflattering things to say about the man standing across from me.

I told Billy goodbye before he could retract his offer.

I made my way out to my Jeep through the falling dark. I took out my keys, and suddenly I was eye to eye with Everett and his hand was on my crotch. He was standing with his back against the driver's-side door. He started kneading me, slow and hard, and got an instant response. His smile was genuine, without the sneering insolence of porn stars. He brought his lips to mine and I felt a sudden chill that told me my equipment was exposed and in the heat of his hand.

"We can pretend like we're brothers," he said, manipulating me with unnervingly practiced efficiency. "It's okay for brothers 'cause they can't have kids."

The boy was too many fantasies all at once, and they all belonged to someone else. I seized his hand and pulled it from my cock. His eyes flared and his mouth set into a defiant line. I held his hand in the air as I tucked myself back inside my jeans.

"Seduction is a lost art, Everett. Why don't you go look for it?"

I released his hand. His face went into neutral and he reached for the silver bicycle chain around his neck. I saw that the spokes were too chunky and strangely shaped to have come off a bicycle. Then a voice I didn't recognize shouted the boy's name. Billy was standing in the open gate, a faceless silhouette backlit by the glow from the house. He had called out to the boy with a depth of anger I didn't think he possessed. Everett rushed around the nose of my Jeep, then ran past Billy down the steps toward the house.

I expected Billy to step forward and offer some explanation for the boy's behavior. I couldn't see the expression on his face. Instead he turned and pulled the gate shut behind him. Billy's plan for Everett was to deliver the boy to a life as opulent as his own, but I was more curious to know where the boy had come from. It was obviously a place where it was acceptable for brothers to have sex, a place where hand jobs were the preferred method for greeting guys you had just met.

By the time I got back to my apartment, my head was spinning. I wanted to wait until at least after midnight before I made a second visit to Corey's apartment. That gave me a lot of time to try to sort through everything Billy Hatfill had told me that afternoon.

The Corey Howard I had known presented himself as a loner disdaining the West Hollywood social scene. Now I knew that he was the nephew of a wealthy closet case with connections to the shining stars of that very social scene. Even after I had offended him by comparing him to Scott Koffler, Billy had offered to set up a meeting with Martin Cale, a reclusive closet case that I would have had a hard time getting to on my own.

I picked up the phone and called my new boss. I gave Jimmy a rundown of everything I had learned that afternoon. He didn't interrupt. I couldn't tell if he was bored or intrigued.

"Are you just asking for my opinion here because you're worried about your old boyfriend?" he asked. "Or do you think this has the makings of a good book?"

"That's your decision," I said.

"Joseph Spinotta," he said distantly. "I read about that guy. I saw that disaster coming from a mile away." I waited for him to say more. "This is interesting, Adam. This is very interesting."

I kept my mouth shut. The prospect of James Wilton paying me to investigate Corey Howard's disappearance excited me a great deal more than I wanted it to.

"Two nights ago, Billy picks you up off the street and tells you that Corey paid a strange visit to his house," he recited. "He warns you about Corey, says Corey seems determined to teach you a lesson."

"Right," I said.

"All bullshit," Jimmy said. "It was a cover story. Billy knew you would find out that Corey paid a visit to his home, so he tracked you down and fed you his line. He also made it personal, said they talked about your drinking, which was just another attempt to distract you from how much this strange meeting stinks to high heaven. Play it out in your head: Corey drops in on Billy out of the blue and in the middle of a large party at Billy's home. Why would you intrude on someone's party like that if you had never met the person?"

"If I wanted to surprise him. Catch him off guard."

"Right. Especially if you had bad news and you didn't want him to react poorly in front of people. It sounds like parties are Billy Hatfill's life, and you offend the shit out of him because you're not sold on the image he's trying to project. Corey wanted to catch this guy at his most vulnerable."

"What are you saying, Jimmy?"

"I'm saying Corey was running some kind of game on your friend Billy Hatfill," he said. "And I think he was using some dirt he got from his uncle to do it. My first guess would be that Corey learned something about Billy's former sugar daddy and he used that information to get something out of Billy."

"Like what?"

"Money," Jimmy answered. "Maybe Billy paid him off and that's why Corey left town."

"Then why did he leave behind his truck, his wallet, his keys, and his cell phone?" I asked. "Not to mention a container of milk out on the counter that's going to stink up the whole building in a few days? And Corey's got a wealthy uncle who's probably supporting him. Why does he need to extort money out of Billy Hatfill, who he's never met before?"

"Fine," Jimmy said. "Maybe it wasn't money Corey wanted."

"What, then?"

"That's a very good question," he said. "You feel like finding out the answer?"

"Do you?" I asked.

Jimmy didn't answer directly. "Tomorrow morning, let's pay another visit to Corey's apartment. If the neighbor's not home, we can poke around for a bit."

"Cool." A pulse was beating above the bridge of my nose, and it didn't respond to the pressure of my thumb and forefinger. The only parts of Corey Howard I was familiar with were his naked body and his swift and controlling reactions to my every move. Was Jimmy indulging in the same paranoid fantasies he made his living off of?

"You think I'm an overimaginative lunatic, don't you?" he asked. "Trust me, little man. Even the wildest conspiracy theory cuts a path through woods that bears further exploration. And I've given you a good working theory. Whatever Corey and Billy actually talked about two weeks ago is the reason Corey's no longer around."

"Fine," I said. "But that doesn't explain Billy's behavior toward me. If Corey got dirt on Billy from his uncle, why is Billy giving me a meeting with his uncle? Martin Cale doesn't even live on dry land. I'd have had a hard time rowing out to his yacht."

"Meet with Martin Cale and find out."

He told me to pick him up at his house the next morning at nine A.M. and we said our goodbyes. I lay down on my bed and stared up at the room's Oriental screen, its painted landscape impossibly calm. Two weeks ago, Corey Howard had paid Billy Hatfill a strange visit. Barely a week and a half later, Corey had missed his first day of work. It was almost impossible not to believe that the two events were connected, even if I wasn't totally sold on Jimmy's explanation.

Another possibility hit me so hard I felt a spasm of panic. I scrambled up and pulled open my desk drawer. Inside was a folded piece of paper. I took it out and found myself staring at the two-year-old *Los Angeles Times* article that Tommy Banks handed me the previous week. This time, instead of scanning it, I read every single word.

Gay Community Believes Serial Killer Is Behind Disappearances
by Linda Walsh, *Times* staff writer

The unexplained disappearance of a West Hollywood gay male prostitute has spurred anxiety that a serial killer may be on the prowl, according to some city residents, who claim the LA County Sheriff's Department is ignoring their concern over this and two other missing-persons cases.

Ben Clamp, 23, was reported missing two weeks ago and is the third in a series of recent missing-persons cases in West Hollywood that suggest a killer is at work in the gay community, gay activists say. Clamp, who went by the name of P. J. Carter and whose business cards told people he was a physical trainer, had appeared in fifteen gay adult videos over the last year and had been featured in a local gay magazine advertising gay male "escorts." In January, 22-year-old Terrance Davidson, a chemistry major at Duke University who dropped out of school to pursue his acting ambitions, was also reported missing. Two months later, friends reported that Roger

Vasquez, 24, a Sacramento native and a graduate of USC film school, had disappeared.

"Three young, handsome men just vanish without a trace from our neighborhood, and the cops just ignore the links among them," said Sal Garcia of the Greater Los Angeles Gay and Lesbian Antiviolence Project. "It's getting so that people are afraid to go out at night. And they are getting very, very angry at the nonchalance of our police department in the face of this danger."

A spokeswoman for the Sheriff's Department, Bernice Evans, said the police are taking the cases seriously, but they have no evidence that the three incidents are connected. "The LA County Sheriff's Department investigates all missing-persons cases as potential homicides," Evans said in a written statement. "We are keenly attuned to the concerns of the community, but the detectives handling these active investigations do not believe that they are connected and have no reason to suspect criminal activity."

In spite of police denials, Garcia claims many West Hollywood residents believe a serial killer in Los Angeles is targeting young gay men. The killer has even been given a moniker. "They're calling him The West Hollywood Slasher," Garcia says.

Tensions between activists and the Sheriff's Department escalated after Clamp was reported missing by Leo Bodwell, 56, the owner of the West Hollywood eatery that bears his first name, who told police that Clamp had lived with him since the younger man's arrival in Los Angeles two years earlier. When police questioned Bodwell at his restaurant, activists alerted reporters, and television cameras captured a dozen people protesting what they called official reluctance to name Bodwell a suspect in the case.

Leo Bodwell declined to be interviewed for this article, but after being questioned by police, he issued a detailed statement to reporters in which he insisted that he and Clamp did not have a sexual relationship and he knew nothing of the missing man's whereabouts. According to Bodwell, the two met online in a popular gay chat room when Clamp was still living with his parents in Knoxville, Tennessee. Bodwell declared he took Clamp in after his parents learned he was gay and ejected him from the house. Clamp stayed in his guesthouse, Bodwell said. "Our relationship was distant but cordial," he said in his statement, saying that Clamp grew distant when the older man expressed concerns about his work in the sex industry.

For many West Hollywood residents, the strange case of Ben Clamp seems eerily similar to the mysterious disappearances of two other young gay men whose faces never appeared on the evening news.

Six months before Clamp's June disappearance, Terrance Davidson failed to meet a group of his friends at Rage, a popular West Hollywood nightclub. After more than a week of unreturned phone calls, those same friends contacted Davidson's parents in West Virginia and learned that there had been no contact between the young man and his family after he disclosed his sexuality to his parents on Christmas Eve. A missing persons report was filed, and friends posted flyers bearing Davidson's picture on telephone poles and in storefront windows along Santa Monica Boulevard.

After his disappearance in March, friends of Roger Vasquez described him as ambitious, driven, and dead set on being a Hollywood talent agent. In the year and a half since his graduation from USC film school, Vasquez worked in the mailroom of American Talent Artists, one of the largest talent agencies on the West Coast.

When Vasquez missed two days of work without contacting his employer, a co-worker visited his West Hollywood apartment building, where he and the landlord found Vasquez's apartment intact but seemingly abandoned. They also found his wallet, keys, and cell phone. His Toyota Camry was parked in the building's garage.

Sheriff's investigations of the other two missing persons cases showed that personal items such as wallets and keys were also found in the homes of Davidson and Clamp, along with their cars—details that continue to haunt both outraged West Hollywood residents and perplexed city officials.

"It's bizarre," says West Hollywood mayor pro tem John Quinn. "I know that missing-persons cases are more common than most of us like to believe. But if these young men weren't driving off somewhere themselves, that implies they were in the company of another person. It's very difficult not to believe that whoever these young men were with is the reason they didn't come home."

But Quinn does not believe that there is a serial killer at work in his small and relatively crime-free city. "It's an unfortunate

truth, but we see a lot of young men go missing from West Hollywood on an annual basis. There's a party atmosphere here for some
people that leads them to make some dangerous choices."

But for some people, public reassurances do not seem to be
enough. For them, Leo Bodwell has become a possible face for a
serial killer who had gone undetected until Clamp's disappearance.

Business at Leo's, Bodwell's restaurant, has plummeted, and
employees resist any mention of the West Hollywood Slasher. At
Bodwell's Spanish-style home in the West Hollywood flats, neighbors say several carloads of young men broke the front windows
with rocks and beer bottles Saturday night. On Monday, a For Sale
sign was placed on the house's front lawn.

Yesterday, a new flyer appeared on telephone poles along
Santa Monica Boulevard. It bears the faces of Terrance Davidson,
Roger Vasquez, and Ben Clamp, beneath the words YOU ARE NOT
FORGOTTEN.

CHAPTER 6

Wednesday morning brought another marine layer over the city, and the light inside Corey Howard's apartment had the quality of dawn below the surface of a cove. The stench of sour milk still lingered, and Corey's wallet and keys still rested on the counter. The downstairs neighbor hadn't responded to his doorbell, so Jimmy and I had entered through the back door I had left unlocked the day before.

Jimmy and I stood across from each other in the kitchen as he read the *LA Times* article on the West Hollywood Slasher. I had waited until we were in the apartment to give it to him. I wanted him to see firsthand the similarities between Corey's disappearance and those of the three young men my community referred to as the Vanished Three.

"You think a serial killer murdered Corey?" he asked when he was finished. "That shoots my theory about his meeting with Billy Hatfill to hell, doesn't it?"

"Not necessarily," I said.

I was still bowled over by the deductions Jimmy had made the day before and I wanted to hear his response to the *LA Times* piece before I gave mine. The night before, I had located a "Memorial to the Vanished Three" website online and managed to print out relatively good copies of their photographs and the snippets of biographical information that accompanied them. I handed this page to Jimmy.

Terrance Davidson had short but curly blond hair, round cheeks, and a creamy complexion. His photograph was a professionally done head shot, his big blue eyes electrified by the studio lighting and his pouting lips glistening as if they had been slathered with lip balm. He had disappeared two and a half years ago, and the last time he had been seen alive was one January afternoon at a Gelson's grocery store on Santa Monica Boulevard.

Roger Vasquez stood posed confidently on a windswept beach, dressed in a wool skullcap and a heavy denim jacket that was unbuttoned over a white wife-beater. He had mahogany skin and a black goatee on his jutting chin. His ice-melting smile turned his cheeks into hard knots and his eyes into small slashes on either side of his button nose. He had disappeared two years ago last March. The last place he had been seen alive was Master Beat, a music store on Santa Monica Boulevard that specialized in dance music.

The picture of Ben Clamp stole my breath. The resemblance to Corey was striking. The young man whose disappearance had given birth to the legend of the West Hollywood Slasher had a smooth, statuesque torso and arms so ridged with muscle it looked like he couldn't straighten them. A small tattoo was barely visible above the navel on his flat stomach, and his biographical information told me that it depicted a crucifix wrapped in barbed wire. He wore a backward baseball cap and a leer, and his arms were outstretched as if he were inviting the photographer to take a crack at his chest. His leer revealed teeth that were too white and perfectly spaced for an aspiring auto mechanic who had been thrown out of his family's trailer by Bible-thumping parents. The memorial site's webmaster noted that it was impossible to determine the last place Clamp had been seen alive, because Leo Bodwell, the last person who claimed to have seen him in one piece, was also the only suspect in his disappearance.

Jimmy handed both sheets of paper back to me without comment and walked off into the apartment. I followed him into the back bedroom, where a beanbag chair rested on the floor next to a desk lamp. Jimmy opened a large walk-in closet. It was virtually empty.

"How long did Corey live here?" he asked.

"About six months," I said. "He didn't tell me where he lived before then."

"There's not even six months of life in this place," Jimmy said. "Either he wasn't spending much time here or this place has been cleaned out."

He backed away from the closet door and turned to face me. His Hawaiian shirt had saddlebags and his face was flushed. "This whole apartment—everything about it looks staged. The towel on the floor of the bathroom. The bed unmade just so. And there's nothing too personal here that Corey might not want anyone to see. Then there's the sour milk on the counter, which was going to lure someone up here eventually." He grimaced. "So where does that leave your West Hollywood Slasher?"

"Corey's sending a message," I said. "He's saying the reason he left town has some connection to the Vanished Three. The personal belongings left out in the open are the most obvious connection. Then there's the fact that Corey's about the right age and the right physical makeup. Anyone who plugged the words *gay, West Hollywood,* and *disappearances* into a search engine would have hit on this right away."

Jimmy extended his hand and I gave him the *LA Times* piece and the pictures of the Vanished Three.

"I know this woman," he said.

"Who?"

"Linda Walsh," he answered. "The one who wrote the article. Like everyone else who's worked at the *LA Times,* she's a fairly successful mystery novelist now." He gave me a bright smile. "We should go talk to her."

"Should we call first?" I asked.

"No. We shouldn't."

"Should I file a missing-persons report?" I asked.

He shook his head, folded up the papers I had given him, and shoved them in his back pocket. "That sounds like a request for the family to make. Ask Corey's uncle to do it when you meet with him. See how he responds. It should tell you something about their relationship."

The high shelf inside the closet wasn't as empty as it looked. I reached up and pulled out a large sketch pad. Jimmy came up behind me as I opened it.

Neither one of us said anything for a long while. I had been rendered by a skilled and steady hand that had captured every curve in my upper body. I slept with one cheek pressed against the pillow and my lips puffed open, the covers riding back over one bare shoulder. Above my sleeping form a row of steel windmills receded into an implied horizon as if they were the contents of my dream.

"Corey drew this?" Jimmy asked.

"If he did, he never showed it to me," I told him. Jimmy heard something in my voice that made him straighten up. "The windmills," I said. "That's Banning Pass. On the way into Palm Springs. We spent a weekend there." Jimmy's face was still blank. "I told him about how the first time I drove into LA I thought they were, like, magical."

"*Like* magical?" he asked.

"I told him I thought they were a sign that I was entering a new world,"

I said, my voice shaky with embarrassment. "Where human failures were blown away before they could take root."

"That's good. Were you drunk?"

"No."

"Can I use it?"

"*No*," I said. I flipped through the sketch pad. The frayed binding told me that there had been other drawings inside the pad but they had been ripped out. Jimmy read my mind. "Maybe Corey wasn't just sending a message to anyone. He was sending it to you."

He gave me a second to absorb this. Then I was listening to his footsteps shuffle off down the apartment's main center hallway. I had no idea that Corey Howard could draw. It was just one of many things I didn't know about the man. If Corey had left the pad out for me to find, that meant he wanted me to discover that he had used his secret talent to render a flattering depiction of me. Maybe the picture was a goodbye letter, or maybe it was a sign that he wanted me to finally make my way into the parts of his life he had guarded so vigilantly during the three weeks we had lived together.

Jimmy was already heading down the back steps when I entered the kitchen. I picked Corey's keys up off the counter and shoved them in my back pocket.

Linda Walsh lived just north of Santa Monica's border with Venice, where the blocks rose and fell like ocean waves. Her house was a one-story concrete box with a line of clerestory windows below the lip of the flat roof.

She came to the door with a slobbering two-year-old on her hip. Her hair was dyed honey blond and held in a pile on her head by two wooden sticks. Her long face was bronze and deeply lined, and her small brown eyes had a perpetual squint.

The two-year-old gave me a lazy once-over and reinserted his action figure into his mouth, legs first. Linda saw Jimmy standing next to me and her polite smile dropped from her face like a married father's pants in a rural rest stop.

"Get off my property," she said.

"Morning, Linda!" Jimmy boomed. "This here's Adam, my new assistant. He has some questions to ask you about a piece you wrote for the *Times* a few years back."

"Seriously," she said. "Get off my property."

I introduced myself and gave her my hand. She shook it and gave me a glazed stare. "Why do you work for him?" she asked me.

"It was either Jimmy's or Denny's," I said.

"Fair enough," she said. "You can come in. Tell your boss to wait in the backyard. If he gets bored, he can walk my dog."

Inside, the weak gray light gave the blond wood a dull glare. The living room furniture was so spare it looked like a strong wind could blow it away, and the floor was covered with toys that looked like they might make ghastly music if I stepped on them.

Jimmy slipped in behind me and pushed the door shut. Linda sank down onto the black velour sofa and regarded me dispassionately. On the wall behind her there was a framed blowup of the cover of one of her novels. The words *Blood Circus* dripped over an image of the LA skyline visible through the open flaps of a big-top tent.

"Why, thank you, Linda!" Jimmy said. "I'll have a gin gimlet."

Linda Walsh popped a piece of nicotine gum into her mouth and clearly decided to say nothing. Jimmy broke the tense silence. "Linda and I sat on a panel together at Left Coast Crime a few years back. I gave her a hard time, and apparently she's still sore about it."

Linda Walsh cracked her gum. "The moderator asked me a question about how I come up with my characters. Jimmy started to answer. When the moderator stopped him, he apologized and said he thought the question had been directed at someone who actually created characters."

"Oh, come on!" Jimmy burst out. "You weren't the only one I gave it to that day. One of the other authors on the panel introduced himself as a writer of *literary* thrillers, so I asked him if that meant he took a break from the action to describe how a tree was a metaphor for human evil."

"I think it's safe to say that Jimmy charmed the pants off of everyone at Left Coast Crime that year," Linda remarked.

Jimmy turned to me. "Linda writes novels about a saucy but determined female reporter who's willing to break a high heel to get a good story. Check your local listings soon."

Linda said, "And Jimmy writes novels about loser vigilantes in which all of the female characters are either prostitutes or his mother. Check your local drunk tank soon."

"I'm happy to say I've never had an alcohol problem," Jimmy said. "Now, Adam, on the other hand—"

"Shut up, Jimmy!" I snapped.

After this, the conversation predictably stalled. Linda's son slid off her lap, surveyed the living room, and decided he didn't like his options. Jimmy strolled across the room with a bowed head and started poking at a Tickle Me Elmo with the tip of his cane.

"Well, this has been a real treat," Linda announced. She got to her feet. "Will I see you at Bouchercon, Jimmy?"

"Tell us about the West Hollywood Slasher, Linda," Jimmy said.

Sharp lines appeared at the corners of Linda Walsh's mouth. She hoisted her son onto her lap and put one arm tightly around his back as if trying to shield herself with his body.

"Why?" she asked in a small, tight voice. The mention of the Slasher pained her and I was curious to know why.

"Adam here thinks the guy might have nabbed his boyfriend," Jimmy said. It was basically a lie, but I could tell that Linda Walsh wasn't about to give us any information unless the stakes were high and personal.

She put her son's head on her shoulder. "People usually go missing when they're driving from one place to another," she began. "These guys vanished out of thin air. All of them had barely been in LA for a year, and according to their friends they were the type of West Hollywood guys who thought they would catch fire if they went east of Fairfax or west of Doheny. None of them took any long road trips. None of them were driving on any isolated highways.

"We're also talking about type A guys who worked out at the gym five times a week. You don't abduct someone like that off a street corner without someone noticing. West Hollywood is *the* most densely populated area of the Southland, and even after pictures of these guys were flashed all over the news, no one came forward to report anything suspicious. No one saw them leaving a bar with a strange guy. No one saw them, *period.*"

"Was there any evidence these guys visited chat rooms?" I asked. "It's a popular way to meet people in my part of town."

"That's a good theory," she said. "So you think they were lured out of their apartments by someone they met online, then the guy drove back to their places and put their personal items out for anyone to see?" I still thought a chat room might have been the Vanished Three's portal to oblivion, but I didn't believe they had met up with one individual. I nodded anyway, just to keep her talking. "Too bad none of them had Internet access."

"You're kidding," I said.

"Terrance Davidson had an America Online account he canceled a few months before he disappeared," she responded. "He also didn't have cable TV. Out of the three, he was habitually unemployed, so it made sense that he wasn't willing to pay for it. But Roger Vasquez had steady employment and he never subscribed to any service. I thought for sure that Ben Clamp would have taken out an escort advertisement online, but it turned out he ran ads in the back of a couple of gay magazines with his beeper number and that was it."

"Leo Bodwell," I said quietly. "The man Ben Clamp was living with."

Linda gave me an unblinking stare. I saw a slight pulse beating in the side of her neck. "What about him?"

"What did you think of him?"

"He didn't deserve what happened to him. At all."

I glanced at Jimmy and saw that he was staring at Linda with one eyebrow slightly raised. His eyes flicked to mine and he gave me a small nod.

"I'd like to talk to him," I said.

"You can't. He's dead." She put her son down and walked quickly into the kitchen, her child waddling after her. "He died of an aneurysm last year. He moved to Arcadia after I wrote my story and ended up managing an Olive Garden."

"Kind of a long fall from owning your own restaurant," Jimmy noted.

She bristled and took a slug of water. I got the sense that she was having an argument with herself.

"So it wasn't Leo Bodwell's arrest that got you on the story?" Jimmy asked. "It was your brother." Linda gave Jimmy a piercing look. "How's he doing, by the way?" Jimmy asked.

"He committed suicide," she said quietly. She held her water bottle halfway to her mouth. "All those wonder drugs weren't working for him, and he'd seen what happened to his friends at the end."

"AIDS?" I asked.

Linda looked like she was about to pounce on Jimmy and wring his neck. I thought that was our cue to leave. Jimmy didn't. "What got you so invested in this, Linda?" he asked. "Were you just acting out of obligation to your brother?"

Jimmy had an agenda here. I wasn't sure what it was, so I kept my mouth shut. "You created the story, didn't you?" he asked. "Your brother called you about these disappearances, and you went to the West Hollywood Sheriff's Station and convinced them they would have a riot in the middle of Santa Monica Boulevard if they didn't storm Leo Bodwell's restaurant."

"No! And I don't use my novels to accuse men of murders they might not have committed!"

Jimmy's lips set into a thin line. I knew she was referring to the man who had broken into Jimmy's house in the middle of the night with a tire iron. She turned to me. "I was looking out for your community! I was trying to keep those men from being turned into a statistic!"

Linda reddened and wilted slightly in the same instant. She turned her back to us and tapped the edge of the doorframe with the side of a clenched fist. "I knew somebody would come asking about this someday," she said. "But I sure as hell didn't expect it to be you, Jimmy. Are you writing a book about this?"

Jimmy just kept his mouth tight. "A name came up," she said haltingly. "A name that I didn't think I could use because I thought if I did, this man would find a way to kill the story."

I tried to affect a sympathetic look.

"A man named Joseph Spinotta," she said quietly.

I was grateful that her back was turned. Jimmy did a lousy job of hiding his reaction; he sputtered before he shut up. Our two theories had just converged. Corey's strange meeting with Billy Hatfill, as well as the specifics of his disappearance, both pointed to a connection with Billy and his missing sugar daddy.

Linda turned around. "Spinotta was still one of the biggest names in town. Everyone thought that website of his was going to make television obsolete. Leo Bodwell told Sheriff that Ben Clamp had started attending parties at Spinotta's home. A-list-only affairs—not that many gay boys on the guest list. The beeper Ben left behind didn't turn up that many clients, but his hourly rate was steep. I figured Spinotta's place was where he did most of his business. But I couldn't find anyone willing to talk about what went on up there, so I couldn't pursue it."

"What about Terrance Davidson and Roger Vasquez? Were either of them connected to Spinotta?"

"Terrance Davidson waited tables at a restaurant in Beverly Hills," she said. "His manager fired him for being late. The manager claimed that she received several threatening phone calls from an older man protesting Terrance's termination. This man kept using a certain phrase that stuck with her. He said that Terrance was *not quality material.*"

She met my heavy stare. "It was one of Spinotta's catch phrases. He would say it in meetings all the time. He would write it on project proposals that he thought were dated or out of step with the nation's youth. He even turned it into an acronym, NQM. To be sure, I even tape-recorded an interview Spinotta did with KCRW and played it back for the manager. She said the voice was the same."

"And Roger Vasquez?" I asked.

"I didn't find anything on him," she said quietly. "But by then I wasn't looking anymore. I was just going to run with what I had."

"Why didn't you mention their parents, their families?" I asked.

"None of them gave a shit," she said. "Even after my article ran, none of them lifted a finger to find their son. I finally called Roger Vasquez's mother. She told me her son was with the angels and she hoped the angels weren't pissed." Her anger over this was palpable. Given that she had taken up the cause of the Vanished Three even after their parents had turned their backs on them, I almost forgave Linda for what she had buried.

"I'll make a deal with you two," she said. "You keep my name out of this, and I'll give you my file. If you ever mention me, I'll say you broke into my office."

I drove west on Pico Boulevard as Jimmy leafed through Linda's file. It was not nearly as thick as I had hoped it would be. "Unbelievable," Jimmy finally said. "She sat on all that even after Spinotta became one of the most notorious white-collar criminals in this city. And she's still got the nerve to lecture you on what she did for your community."

"You think Spinotta could have killed the story?" I asked.

"Hell no," he said. "She was afraid of something else."

"What?"

He gave me a long look, which told me he was measuring his words carefully. "If Linda dug too deep into Spinotta's social world, she was going to find out those three guys were doing something that didn't fit with her image of them as innocent victims. That wasn't exactly *Little House on the Prairie* up there."

"She had no trouble reporting that Clamp was a male prostitute," I countered.

"Clamp's disappearance made the evening news before her story ran. She didn't have a choice." He gave me a few seconds to absorb this. "We need to find out what those three guys were doing up at Spinotta's place."

"Partying, probably."

"I don't think so. Does it strike you in the least bit that these guys all left town over the months leading up to Joseph Spinotta's big exodus?"

I felt foolish for not having noticed it sooner. He continued. "Linda said Spinotta's parties were A-list-only affairs. Not that many gay boys on the guest list. So what were these three guys doing up there? I bet it was a lot more than drugs and skinny-dipping."

"They were eye candy, Jimmy."

"I doubt that's all they were," he said. "I'd bet these guys were in Spinotta's inner circle. Your job is to find out what they were doing in there."

"You want me to ask Billy Hatfill?"

"Not yet," he said. "Not until you get your meeting with Corey's uncle. Ask Billy about this now, and he'll probably leave town himself."

Neither one of us said anything for a while. Jimmy broke the silence. "Terrance Davidson canceled his dial-up service. Roger Vasquez never bothered to get any, even though he could have afforded it. Ben Clamp didn't advertise his services as well as he could have in this new cyber-age. What does that sound like to you?"

"Three guys who were new to the city and struggling to maintain?" I asked.

"Or three guys who didn't plan to stay here for very long."

"Linda said the sheriff's department went through Ben Clamp's beeper and didn't turn up that many clients," I said. "She assumed he was doing most of his business at Spinotta's house."

"Or he was slowing down before he skipped town," he said.

"All right," I said. "So where does that lead?"

"If you ask me, these boys were planning some sort of escape," he said.

"You think they were running from something?"

"Nope," he said, "I think they were Spinotta's advance team. I think Spinotta figured out he was going to have to skip town and he sent these three guys to prepare the new residence."

I waited for him to add to this theory, but he didn't, leaving me to imagine the everlasting party Spinotta and his Vanished Three might have created on a private island in the South Pacific, where drugs and alcohol flowed unabated and each morning saw the departure of another piece of reality on the retreating tide. It sounded inviting. Too inviting. I forced myself back to the present.

"So before they leave town, these guys leave their personal belongings out for anyone to find? You would think an advance team would be a little more subtle."

"It's just like Corey's apartment," he said. "It's a message."

"What kind of message?"

"They were turning their backs on their old lives," he said. "Shedding all vestiges of their former selves."

"So you think Joseph Spinotta and the Vanished Three are all living in a Franciscan monastery somewhere?"

Jimmy brayed with laughter.

"Seriously, Jimmy."

"I don't know what the hell they were doing," he said. "But I think they were doing it together. I pulled together a file on Joseph Spinotta last night. It's interesting. I want you to read it."

When we passed under the 405 Freeway, the fog lifted slightly and the sun looked like a runny soft-boiled egg through the high, milky clouds.

"Where does this leave Corey?" I asked.

"Same place he was this morning," he said. "I think he's trying to point the finger at these three men."

"And Billy Hatfill and Joseph Spinotta," I added.

"Yep."

"You think that two weeks ago, Corey got some dirt on Billy and used it to get something out of him," I said. "You think this was it? You think it's got something to do with Spinotta and the Vanished Three? Maybe he knows where they are."

Jimmy just smiled.

"What?" I asked him.

"You should write fiction, too."

CHAPTER 7

We pulled over at a hamburger stand on Santa Monica Boule-
vard just west of Crescent Heights. The place had a warren of tables and
chairs under a rippling plastic tarp, and the neighboring businesses were
small bars with patrons who remembered what it was like when the most
dangerous STD you could get was hepatitis.

Jimmy walked out onto the sidewalk to make a phone call. I wondered
if he was phoning his mysterious wife to tell her that his adversary Linda
Walsh had not shot him. I was left with a chiliburger and a file on Joseph
Spinotta that was as thick as a novel. Jimmy had used his LexisNexis account to print out everything that had ever been written about the man.
He also located a photograph of the guy online. I studied it, trying to see
what Billy Hatfill had seen in him besides dollar signs. Spinotta had a
thatch of black hair and a long, angular face. His black eyes were mostly
iris, and his high cheekbones and dimpled chin looked constructed by a
surgeon.

When Spinotta first arrived in Los Angeles with his big idea to trans-
form entertainment by bringing it to the web, it seemed as if most of the
reporters who profiled him were convinced they were covering the first
wave of a revolution. Spinotta abetted them, making extravagant prophe-
cies of a new world. *Wired* quoted him as saying, "When you consider the
limitations of television and film and then when you look at the strangle-
hold they have on all forms of creative media, you have the kind of situation that led the French to leave their lattes and start building barricades
in the streets."

But the irony behind Spinotta's rhetoric wasn't lost on most of the reporters who profiled him. He was securing gobs of investment money

from the very media tyrants he was assailing in the press. At the time, Silicon Valley's billions were starting to make the Hollywood Hills look like a third-rate suburb. Joseph Spinotta promised to link the two in the interest of making the entertainment industry more cutting-edge, and allowing Hollywood moguls to co-opt and quash any industry that was more profitable than their own.

The early articles mentioned neither Spinotta's sexuality nor his young companion, Billy Hatfill, but as his venture capital mounted and Broadband Access Media neared its vaunted launch, another element crept into Spinotta's public comments. "Young people are tired of being condescended to," he told the *Wired* website. "Every horror movie geared toward the young audience tries to teach them that their sex drives are evil. One of the great advantages of BAM is that we won't be hamstrung by a set of outdated Puritan values that alienate our nation's young people."

It was a brazen misstep for a man who had been so good at propagandizing his vision. Spinotta's musings on outdated Puritan values elicited fiery responses from several conservative columnists. Some commentators went so far as to accuse Spinotta of seeking to sexualize the nation's children for the delectation of the cabal of gay men who secretly ran Hollywood. A few even blamed him for the massacre at Columbine High. Spinotta responded to his critics by inviting all of them to become columnists for Broadband Access Media.

Amid all the hype, it was difficult to find any concrete biographical information on the man leading the charge. An early BAM press release made mention of the fact that he had "been part of the innovative tech firm that conducted the first test of a satellite-based phone system." But if you read between the lines, it was clear that the words *first test* meant the test had failed, and the fact that Spinotta's specific role in the project wasn't mentioned meant it was possible he was working in the company's mailroom at the time.

None of the profiles mentioned any degree from Yale Business School, a detail I had picked up through word of mouth, and I wondered if it was merely a rumor started by the man himself. There was a mention of the project that had first brought Spinotta to Southern California. In early 2000, Spinotta had been hired as an independent contractor by the real estate firm of Cale & Faulkner, which was well known for the massive cookie-cutter subdivisions it had laid out all over Southern California. I realized that the Cale in the company's title was Martin Cale, Corey's uncle.

Meadow Oaks was the name of the project Billy Hatfill had mentioned to me, the one that had first brought Spinotta to Southern California.

Spinotta's quick rise ended thanks to one small detail: the website itself. Rumors had surfaced that the site was running behind schedule in producing its promised original dramatic programming and was probably not going to make its much-touted launch date. Stories surfaced of a massive but badly run office in a Culver City warehouse where employees fresh out of high school flitted around on scooters, neglected to return people's calls, and kept A-list actors and directors waiting for up to an hour.

Then the site debuted, a slick page with four links to pages that were still under construction and four original movies that required high-speed connections that most users outside of major cities didn't have yet or couldn't afford—especially the kids who were Spinotta's targets.

The press turned on the mogul as quickly as it had embraced him. Within a week of the site's inauspicious launch, a middle manager fired all of the forty-five Culver City employees, and when reporters attempted to contact Spinotta at his home, they were told that he was unavailable.

A few days later, it became clear that Spinotta and most of the venture capital had gone with the wind.

Those BAM investors who didn't support gay marriage probably had an about-face on the spot. Even though Billy Hatfill had regularly attended meetings with Spinotta, he was not listed as having any stake in the company itself. Spinotta's Sunset Strip mansion had been fully paid for and placed in Billy Hatfill's name before BAM's incorporation. There was no bridge the angry investors could cross to collect on their investment from the young man Joseph had left behind.

The press framed Spinotta's exit from town as a shameful exodus. My impression was different. The media interpreted his big talk and bluster as symptoms of a shameless self-promoter painfully out of his depth. I heard a scam artist who was playing on the sensitivities and fears of his wealthy investors.

There had barely been a week between the site's disastrous launch and Spinotta's flight. Wouldn't a man with Spinotta's ego have held on a little longer? Spinotta had also taken pains to make sure that Billy Hatfill would be protected after he left. I filed these details alongside the facts that Terrance Davidson had canceled his dial-up service and that Ben Clamp's beeper had yielded a sparse client list.

* * *

"Speak," Jimmy said, taking a seat across from me. The tables around us were now mostly empty.

"I don't think Spinotta had any interest in creating a website," I said. "I think the whole thing was a scam."

"There are easier scams out there," Jimmy said, but I could tell he was just playing devil's advocate.

"Not the kind that yield tens of millions in venture capital. He made sure Billy was taken care of, months before he left. He skipped town right after the site's debut. He didn't hang in there and fight, didn't try to stonewall the press with talk about how BAM had just hit some bumps in the road." I now had Jimmy's full attention. "I think he was planning to leave the whole time."

Jimmy's thoughtful frown told me he was impressed. His eyes cut past me to the sidewalk. The man approaching our table was over six feet tall and almost two hundred pounds. His head was a bald dome with a neat fringe of red hair, and his dark green polo shirt strained against his beer belly's weight. He studied me with beady eyes nearly buried in the folds of his face.

"Adam, this is Dwight Zachary. He's a homicide detective for the LA County Sheriff's Department—"

"Jimmy!" the man named Dwight barked.

"He also doesn't want you to know that," Jimmy added. "See, Dwight and I have what you might call a special relationship."

"Who's the bottom?" I asked.

Neither man got it.

"Dwight is the real Joe Ring," Jimmy announced.

He saw my confused stare and his face went red. "Joe Ring. My series character. The reason I can afford an office that's detached from the main house and a view of every mini-mall from Burbank to Panorama City." I still didn't say anything. "Jesus Christ. You haven't read a word I've written, have you?"

"I've been busy."

"Your whole life?"

"Drunk mom, remember?"

Dwight Zachary took a seat and regarded me with dubious interest.

"Dwight has something to share with us," Jimmy said.

"I have something to share with *you*, Jimmy," he said.

"I sent Dwight on a little fishing expedition and it looks like he caught something," Jimmy said to me.

"What was he fishing for?" I asked.

"Joseph Spinotta," Jimmy said.

Dwight looked from me to Jimmy and then back again, with his cheeks puffed and his lower lip jutting out like a sad baby's. "Your boss doesn't have much faith in law enforcement," he said. "He's barely told me what you guys are up to, and already he's phoning me like I'm his errand boy. But Jimmy and I are friends. And he says you two might be onto something big. I figured I would help out. That way, if Jimmy gets ready to throw shit at a fan, I can step in and unplug the fan first."

And land a high-profile arrest, I thought, and maybe get himself written about in another installment of the Joe Ring series. I had an automatic respect for most cops, but I didn't see their desire for fame as any more noble or interesting than that of the pretty Starbucks employee who screws up your order because she's too busy reading Tony Barr's *Acting for the Camera*. I managed to keep my mouth shut.

"A friend of mine's at the Santa Clarita Station," he continued. I noted that he didn't give us the friend's rank because he didn't want us to identify the person. "She used to be over at the West Hollywood station before she put in for a transfer. I asked her if the name Joseph Spinotta meant anything to her, and it was like I had told her what day she was going to die."

"Memories from West Hollywood?" I asked.

"Nope," he answered. "A little over three years ago, a girl came into the station in Santa Clarita, scared out of her mind, said she had to talk to a woman. The only woman there was my friend, so she agreed to see her, just to calm her down. The girl said a friend of hers had been raped at one of Spinotta's parties."

"A male friend?" I asked.

He nodded, and my chest knotted as I asked the next question, "How old?"

"Fifteen," he said quietly. I saw Jimmy's eyes light on me and was grateful that mine were hidden behind sunglasses.

"He identified Spinotta?" I asked, my voice reedy.

"He told the girl it was Spinotta," he answered. "Technically he never identified anyone. The boy wouldn't come in. Didn't think it was a big deal supposedly. I doubt that. If it wasn't a big deal, why'd he tell his best girlfriend about it? Maybe all he needed was some convincing."

"Did anyone try?" I asked.

"The only person in a position to do that was the girl," he said. "My friend suggested she try to talk to the kid's mother about it."

"Did she?" I asked.

He met my eyes. "She said she would," he told me. "And she never came back to the station. A few months later the boy got shipped off to boarding school. No one ever said which one."

"Dwight, what was the boy's name?" Jimmy asked him.

"You didn't get it from me," he said in a low voice. "As in, if you're hanging off the side of a cliff in Angeles Crest with a blade against your throat and a shotgun up against your ass, you still didn't get it from me. My friend even had a problem giving it over, but I told her it was related to a case of mine. She couldn't pursue Spinotta without a statement from the alleged victim, so I had to convince her to break personal ethics, not department regulations. Not to mention the fact that the girl didn't even give the boy's name. My friend did a little digging to figure out who the boy was." Dwight Zachary glared at both of us. He was the kind of guy who could attach an ultimatum to his every trip to the bathroom.

"Fine," Jimmy said.

But it was obvious that I was the one Dwight Zachary had a problem with. He gave me a narrow stare. "Jimmy and I have a deal," he said. "That means you two don't put a word to paper until law enforcement has their say. I don't care if you turn up something I need to deal with, LAPD needs to deal with. FBI. NSA. Not a word, you understand me."

"Fine," I said.

Dwight reached into his pants pocket and removed a crumpled Post-it note. "Brian Ferrin," he said. "Lives on Coldwater Canyon Avenue in Studio City. Drives a blue Acura Integra."

Jimmy reached for the crumpled Post-it note and picked it up without opening it. "Thanks, Dwight."

Dwight eyed me. "You don't look so good."

"It's Wednesday," I said. "I hate Wednesdays. Middle of the week and all that."

He cocked one eyebrow and gave me a slow, patronizing nod. He was goading me. "Come on. You must have something to say about all this. I thought guys like you stuck up for your own kind. Do you think Joseph Spinotta's innocent or not?"

"Rushing to conclusions sounds like your job, Detective."

Jimmy's stifled laughter came out as a series of hacking coughs. Dwight reddened, braced both of his elbows on the table, and gave me a furious glare that must have worked for him in the past. "Sometimes you people act like cops have never done anything for you," he said. "But you know damn well that the West Hollywood Station has to hold a press conference every time some guy's scented candle doesn't smell right."

I leaned forward, my face close to his chin. "For decades, *your* people went into every gay bar you could find, beat the shit out of most of the people inside, and then published their pictures in the paper so you could ruin their lives," I said. "If you're genuinely interested in working on this relationship, Detective, you might want to start with some better manners."

Without taking his eyes off mine, Dwight said, "You going to let him talk to me like that, Jimmy?"

"Yes."

Dwight got to his feet and forced an official smile onto his face. "Stay out of trouble," he said.

I waited until Dwight was gone. Then I said, "He's an asshole."

"Of course he is," Jimmy answered. "Who else would agree to help me? The same might be said for you, little man. And I've got a feeling your bad mood has more to do with the fact that Joseph Spinotta might have raped a fifteen-year-old."

I felt put on the spot and ended up verbalizing an emotion I had not yet fully articulated even to myself. "There's a gay kid in Wisconsin who's fingering a box of razor blades right now. You write a book about a bunch of wealthy gay ephebophiles assaulting fifteen-year-olds, and you're giving ammunition to the assholes who shove him in a locker each day."

Jimmy bristled. Without meaning to, I had made my words sound like an accusation, and I wished I could take them back.

"Are you willing to deny the existence of criminals simply because they conform to a hateful stereotype?" he asked.

"No."

"Good." He got to his feet and gestured for me to do the same. "Don't worry about Dwight. I own his soul and he knows it."

"How's that?" I asked.

"Just trust me," he said.

Jimmy had introduced Dwight as the real Joe Ring, but he had said nothing about whether the detective had been involved in the murder of a porn star named Jenna Hartt and the subsequent novel that had almost cost Jimmy his life.

"I want you to talk to this Brian Ferrin kid," Jimmy said. "It's been a few years since what went down at the Spinotta house. Maybe he's ready to spill the beans. Especially to a charming and handsome young man like yourself who is going to do everything in his power to put him at ease."

"Any reason Dwight didn't meet us back at your house?"

Jimmy paused next to the Cadillac's passenger door. He rested both hands on top of his cane and twisted his lips as if he were cleaning a sticky film from his front teeth. "Yes. And if you haven't noticed, I've put off introducing the two of you as long as possible."

He didn't have to tell me he was referring to his wife.

As soon as we got back to the Wilton house, I called Brian Ferrin. He shared an answering machine with a female roommate whose greeting message was so curt it made me feel like a busboy who had interrupted a heated dinnertime conversation. I didn't leave a message. I cut the photographs of the Vanished Three from the computer printout I had showed Jimmy that morning and stuffed them in my wallet.

The San Fernando Valley has a greenbelt of affluent communities that hug the base of the foothills. Their names have become the punch lines of jokes, but they still typify suburban perfection on television sets around the globe. Ventura Boulevard is the artery that connects them all, and it's lined with enough retail chain stores to keep Middle America stocked up on Gap jeans and venti lattes for centuries to come.

Brian Ferrin and his easily inconvenienced roommate resided in a low-rise stucco palace a few blocks south of the 101 Freeway. A sign on the front lawn assured me that they enjoyed luxury living. Reading closely, I learned that luxury living was defined as having wall-to-wall carpet and air-conditioning and tolerating other people's pets. According to the call box, the roommate's last name was Martin. I wondered if she was the concerned friend who had visited the Santa Clarita Sheriff's Station almost three years earlier.

I slipped in the entrance door behind someone else. The girl who opened the door to unit 204 had a tiny face with a pageboy cut she had dyed coal. She gave me a resigned look, telling me that guys my age often came to her apartment for reasons that had nothing to do with her.

I smiled and held up a Visa envelope that had the word URGENT stamped in red on it. Thanks to Jimmy, I would be mailing my delinquent payment at the end of the week. I had typed Brian Ferrin's name and address on a piece of paper and taped it inside the address window. "This was in my box by mistake," I said.

She reached for it and I pulled it away. "Would *you* want everyone to know *your* credit history?"

Her eyes narrowed a little.

"I'm on my way out," I said. "Does he work nearby? Maybe I could—"

"I don't read other people's mail!"

"How am I supposed to know that?" I asked with a bright smile.

"You're not," she said. "You don't need to."

I just smiled, hoping she would hear her own anger. "Looks like we've both got Brian's best interests at heart."

The apartment behind her was dorm-room chic: an array of Ikea furniture, a plain brown sofa that looked like a rental, and an entertainment center that one of their parents had sprung for. "You're not supposed to date people who live in your building," the girl said flatly. "It's like dating someone at work."

"Where'd you hear that?"

"Just intuition," she said. "So you want me to tell you where he is so you can stalk him? What's got *you* hooked? Is it his puppy-dog eyes or the fact that he doesn't give up the goods after five minutes like the rest of his friends?"

"You're protective of him," I said. "That's sweet."

She rolled her eyes and leaned against the edge of the door. "Yeah, I guess." I gave her time to elaborate. Instead she said, "Can you, like, do something violent so I have an excuse to call the police?"

I pretended to consider this. Then I lifted the Visa envelope in both hands as if I was going to tear it down the middle. She gave me the name of a record store in Sherman Oaks, called me a jerk, and slammed the door.

The record store was on Ventura Boulevard, right next to a mini-mall that housed a Starbucks with a gaggle of aspiring screenwriters sitting out front, pecking away on laptops and talking into their cell phones at the same time. If any of them were actually studio-employed, I figured we had cellular technology to blame for the sorry state of mainstream cinema.

Back Beats was a narrow corridor with a high ceiling and famished shelves that told me the place was bleeding business to the Virgin Megastore. The minute I stepped through the front door, I was hit by a blast of whiny frat rock reminding me that straight white guys still think they've got it worse than anyone else. I told myself I shouldn't judge; my gay brothers appropriate the vocal stylings of black women because they're under the impression that not getting a call back from the drunk straight guy who used you for a night of release can crush your soul as surely as separate water fountains for whites and coloreds.

There was only one male employee, shelving CDs in the soundtrack section. He was about five-six, with a slender, broad-shouldered body, brown curls, and a ruddy complexion. When he glanced my way, I saw his big brown eyes and baby-fat-padded face. At eighteen, he looked sixteen, which meant I didn't want to think about how old he had looked when he had attended one of Joseph Spinotta's blowouts.

I cruised past him toward the dance section, the gay Grand Central at any record store anywhere across the country. I scanned the racks of CDs with psychedelic covers gone digital, then picked one up as if I were considering buying it.

A voice behind me said, "It's new."

Brian Ferrin had dragged his pushcart over, and when I smiled at him, he started shelving into the racks next to mine. There were still stacks of soundtracks on the top shelf of his cart, but apparently he had decided to switch sections.

"This?" I asked, holding up the CD.

"No, the section," he said as he worked. "I finally convinced my manager to start stocking this stuff. It's not like it's as good as Virgin or anything. But it's a start, right? So what are you into? We've got all the basics, like Junior and Paul Oakenfold. Personally, I like more vocals."

"Me too," I said. "I'm more of an ambient guy."

"Like Moby?" he asked, shooting me a smile. "Or as I like to say, Moby who never performs without the obligatory swaying black women in the background."

I didn't have to fake my laugh.

The phone at the front counter rang. The cashier put down her copy of *High Times* and answered it. "Brian!" the cashier shouted. "It's for you."

"Who is it?" he called without turning.

I knew exactly who it was, so I said, "I'm more of a compilation guy. That way, I don't have to commit myself to a certain DJ—"

"It's your roommate," the cashier shouted. "She says watch out for the guy with the baby face."

The cashier giggled and hung up. Brian raised one eyebrow and placed a hand on his hip. He was trying to remain playful, but the warning had rattled him.

"I kind of snuck my way into your building this morning," I said sheepishly. I took out the Visa envelope and showed it to him. "See. You're past due." His eyes moved from the envelope to my face. "I live a couple blocks from you."

"Uh-huh," he finally said.

I let out a pained breath and shook my head like a little boy shamed. "I got dumped a few weeks ago. Hard. Bad relationship, bad breakup, that kind of thing. A friend of mine told me if I wanted things to change, I had to be more assertive. Looks like I overshot the mark. Sorry."

I could see that he was trying to overcome his trepidation, that he wanted to believe my story, and it made me feel dirty. I told myself that I would make my real intentions clear to him as soon as I got him over the hump. I wasn't sure what the hump was and when it would flatten out, but it was a good enough rationalization for now.

He returned to his work. "How long?"

"I'm sorry?"

"This relationship," he said. "How long did it last?"

"Too long," I answered.

"Was he cute?" he asked.

"Too cute," I said, my eyes locked on his face to tell him he fit the same bill. "It's my weakness."

"Isn't that, like, everyone's weakness?" he asked with a sideways glance, but he was blushing. The clerk behind the counter announced to everyone and no one that she was going on break and walked out the front door with her pack of cigarettes in hand.

I held up the CD and said, "I'm going to buy this."

Brian followed me to the counter, where he took too long to punch his security code into the computer. "I'm sorry if I freaked you out," I said.

"Sneaking into my building isn't assertive," he said, eyes on the screen. "It's aggressive." He stuck one hand out for the CD and met my stare. "And I don't have a Visa card."

"It's not like I don't understand," I said. "I've been stalked by my fair share of freaks."

I pulled my credit card out of my wallet. The photo of Roger Vasquez was stuck to it. I separated the two, but before I could tuck the photo back in my wallet, Brian Ferrin grabbed my wrist. He plucked the picture from my fingers and took a step back from the counter as he studied it. A look of pained longing came over his face. Then he remembered I was standing there.

"How do you know Roger?" he asked, breathless.

"Roger Vasquez?"

He flinched. "That's his last name? Vasquez?"

"He's missing, Brian."

His eyes shot to mine. I wasn't sure how he didn't know—hadn't he seen the posters all over Boystown?—and then I remembered that he had spent his last two years of high school at an unnamed boarding school on the East Coast.

"He's been missing for two years," I said.

"*What?*"

"Just what I said."

"Why do you have his . . ." He thought better of the question and one of his hands went up as if to hold me in place. His mouth opened and closed several times before he found his words. "You need to go, dude." He stepped out from behind the counter and hurried past me.

"Look, Brian. I shouldn't know what happened to you, but I do."

He spun around to face me. His upper lip was curled. "What are you, like some fucked-up guidance counselor or something? Do you track down all the guys Roger met online and ditched at parties? I bet they're a lot, right?"

I recalled a detail of his story I had forgotten. Brian Ferrin had gone to Spinotta's party with someone he had met in a chat room. I also knew that Roger Vasquez didn't have Internet access, which meant he had used someone else's online service to make Brian's acquaintance. I could feel pieces falling into place, but I didn't want to knock any of them out of alignment by arranging them too soon.

"I'm not stupid, all right?" Brian Ferrin hissed. "I wasn't stupid then. And I'm not stupid now. It just would have been nice if he had called, that's all."

I took note of the confidence he held in his sixteen-year-old self. It told me to proceed with caution. "Why do you think he didn't call?" I asked.

"I don't know," he snapped. "Don't most guys at least try to sleep with you before they screw you over?"

"He didn't try to sleep with you?"

"No," he said. "He was totally . . . nice. We talked on the phone a few times. We even went to the movies once. I didn't have my license yet, so he drove all the way out to my mom's in Santa Clarita."

He turned and headed for the dance section again. I followed him. He started shelving CDs again, with too much speed and too much force.

"And then he ditched you at a party," I said.

"We were chatting online one night and I told him that my date for the prom had bailed on me. Carrie McNey. What a bitch. After she told me she would go with me, she took me aside at lunch and gave some speech about how she couldn't be my date because she thought it would ruin our friendship. Whatever. We didn't have a friendship. I just asked her 'cause I thought she was nice. Boy, was that a fucking mistake. She took me aside in the cafeteria to break the news, with like, all her friends sitting a few feet away. She must have thought I was an idiot. Like I didn't know that someone had told her I used to con my way to the back of the line during PE and wouldn't shower with the other guys."

He had escaped into this high school memory quickly and fully. I got the sense he wanted to hang out in it for a while to avoid facing what came afterward. "What did Roger have to say about that?" I asked.

"He said he knew about this cool party that he could take me to," he answered. "It was the same night as the prom. He said it would be like my own prom."

He forced a smile as he said it.

"Was it, Brian?"

He slammed a CD down into the rack and spun. "Who the *fuck* are you?"

The entry chime sounded and I saw the clerk return from her smoking break. She gave us a bored glance and took up her position behind the counter.

"Why don't you take a break, Brian?" I said. "Let me get you some coffee or something."

"I don't think so," he said in a low voice that he wanted to sound threatening.

"Brian, Roger never called you back because he went missing a few months later," I said. "That's not the same as going on vacation. Missing means you leave all your belongings behind and you don't tell anyone where you're going. The police put your face on a flyer, and when nobody calls about you in a few months, they assume you're dead."

This new information put a dent in his anger. I decided to add to it. "A friend of mine is also missing, Brian. That's why I need to talk to you." It was less than a quarter of an answer to his question.

He looked at the clerk behind the counter as if she might come to rescue him. A terrorist attack couldn't have distracted her from her magazine.

"Brian," I said softly, and his eyes went to mine. "I know what happened to you."

"What happened to me?" he asked in a whisper.

I had painted myself into a corner. For several seconds, I let the silence hang between us. He was waiting for my answer with rigid patience.

"You were raped, Brian."

He let out an irritated-sounding groan and turned to the rack. Then he shook his head as if he were an aspiring musician and I had just told him he had no talent. He had heard my claim before, and as usual, he was determined not to believe it.

"I'm not a fucking girl," he muttered. "I knew what kind of party it was going to be. I knew what it was when I got there, and I didn't want to leave. I wanted to be there, okay. I was fifteen, but I wasn't stupid."

Not only did it sound like he had rehearsed these lines, it sounded like they had been provided for him by someone else. "Who told you that what they did to you was okay?" I asked.

"Not okay," he hissed. "It's just . . . life, all right?"

"You passed out, right?" I asked. He looked at me, startled. "And you woke up in someone's bed with a bunch of guys . . ." I put my hand out for him to finish the sentence, but he didn't. "That's rape, Brian. Who told you it wasn't? Joseph Spinotta?"

At the sound of Spinotta's full name, the breath went out of him. He steadied himself against the rack and looked at me as if I had slapped him. I felt like a monster, but we had passed the point of no return, and I wasn't letting up on him now. I couldn't do my job if I got lost in every story I heard. If I did, I would lose sight of the fact that Brian Ferrin's buried anger and repressed pain were small elements of a larger intrigue that had pulled Corey Howard from visible life.

"Take a coffee break, Brian. Talk to me."

"I don't need a break," he said with wavering defiance.

I nodded as if I thought his fortitude was impressive. "Did Roger know what happened to you at the party?"

"Maybe," he said in a low voice. "I thought that might be why he didn't call. Because I made an ass of myself, you know?"

"How much did you have to drink that night?"

"Too much, obviously," he said. "I was really nervous on the way there. Roger had a flask with him and he let me take some sips from it. I guess I took too many, because I blacked out."

Brian Ferrin had consumed more than alcohol that night, but despite what I had just said to him, he still clung to the conviction that he had brought that night's events upon himself.

"When you woke up," I began carefully, "in bed—was Roger there?"

He shook his head.

"But Joseph Spinotta was?"

He gave me a blazing look. Then he said, "And some other guys. Older. But no, Roger wasn't there. I woke up later and I was alone. Then Roger came in and told me he was worried out of his mind about me because he didn't know where I had gone. He said he had to take me home or else my mom was going to be pissed. I told him it didn't matter because she thought I was sleeping over at a friend's."

"What did Roger say?"

"He said the party was over." Brian's voice grew quavery. "On the drive home, he kept telling me about how I had to learn how to drink like the big boys if I wanted to party with the big boys. I didn't say anything, but I figured he knew what had happened and he was pissed at me for being a jerk and passing out."

I could feel my pulse beating in my temples. I took out my wallet and showed him the pictures of Terrance Davidson and Ben Clamp. "Did you see these guys that night?"

"I've seen them, but . . ."

"But what?"

He furrowed his brow. I realized he wasn't staving me off, just trying to place the two faces. "Online," he said. "The same chat room where I met Roger. They both sent me their photos."

He pushed the pictures at me as if they were on fire. I took them back. "Roger sent you his picture, too?"

"Yeah."

"And Roger was the only one you responded to?"

He chewed on his lower lip and tightened his arms against his chest. "You didn't come forward because you wanted Roger to call you back."

His jaw quivered slightly before he stilled it. The fight was leaving him, but I wasn't sure that was a good thing. If I had not barged in on him, I wondered how much longer his fantasy of a relationship with Roger Vasquez could have protected him from the truth of what had been done to him.

"What happened to you was a crime, Brian," I said. "You didn't deserve it because you had too much to drink. You didn't deserve it because you went to the wrong party. And you didn't deserve it because you were a fag who didn't have a date for the prom."

For a second, I thought he might fall apart, but the moist sheen in his eyes grew to a hard polish.

I took out one of my old cards from *Glitz* magazine. It had my cell phone number on it.

"You don't have to talk to me again if you don't want to," I said. "I can find someone who might be able to help you."

He snatched the card out of my hand and shoved it in his pants pocket. Then he moved ten deliberate steps away from me and went back to shelving CDs. I lingered for a few seconds, then started for the door. I glanced back before I left and saw that Brian Ferrin hadn't turned to shoot me a goodbye look.

As I drove up Laurel Canyon, I imagined myself at fifteen, sitting in front of a computer monitor as one of the Vanished Three downloaded onto my screen. Which one would I have responded to—the pretty boy, the Latin lover, or the jock?

Ben Clamp bore a striking resemblance to the high school football players of my youth, the men I both lusted after and envied. When I was fifteen, an invitation from him would have sent me over the moon. I would have surrendered myself willingly to his late-night phone calls, his movie dates, his promises that I could have my own prom at a sparkling mansion full of men who seemed fully accomplished versions of the creatures I wanted to be. My surrender would have landed me in a stranger's bed, half conscious, aware that I was being raped but powerless to stop it.

My knuckles went white against the steering wheel. The Vanished Three had helped make a horrifying stereotype of gay men a reality. What had been done to Brian Ferrin was more than every parent's nightmare; it was every young gay man's nightmare as well—that any attempt to explore your sexuality would meet with a swift and brutal retribution. And this retribution had been delivered by other gay men not much older than Ferrin himself.

Roger Vasquez's swift removal of Brian from Spinotta's house as soon as the deed was done, along with his prepackaged lines intended to make Brian feel shame about what had taken place, suggested that this member of the Vanished Three had known full well what was going to happen to Brian from the minute Brian responded to the lure of Vasquez's face online.

Yet against my will, I found myself rushing to dismiss Brian Ferrin's story. Maybe Brian was simply lying to explain away some other instance of behavior he wasn't proud of. On too many occasions, I had heard the date rape excuse used by many gay men to cover up for a night of blackout sex with a man they couldn't stand the sight of in the morning—or worse, a night of unsafe sex that had left them with an incurable illness.

I realized what I was doing and felt disgusted with myself. This very line of thinking was exactly what Roger Vasquez and Joseph Spinotta had been counting on with Brian Ferrin, convincing the victim to blame himself. Not to mention that Brian had kept quiet about what had been done to him because he had been waiting for Roger Vasquez to call him back.

I got back to Jimmy's house around six-thirty. He had given me a gate opener, but I still felt like an intruder as I drove down the long gravel path. I glimpsed one of the security guards in the shadows between the eucalyptus trees. I waved at him, but he didn't wave back.

All the lights were on inside Jimmy's office and the doors were wide open. Inside, a tall black woman was tacking a photo of Terrance Davidson to the corkboard wall behind Jimmy's desk. She wore blue nursing scrubs that bagged around her lean body.

She turned and gave me her version of a smile: a slight furrow in her high brow and a tense set to her full glossy lips. Her hazel eyes made a subtle V with the bridge of her long nose. Her dreadlocks were dyed the color of gold dust and held in place by a barrette that matched their color exactly.

Below Terrance Davidson's photograph were several note cards pinned to the board containing pieces of his biographical information. I figured the cards' large sloping cursive was the handiwork of the woman in front of me.

"You looking for Jimmy?" she asked. "He's watching *City Confidential*. That show on A&E where everyone thinks their town is either the nicest or the cutest, and then you find out that the sheriff raped his daughter and left her for dead."

"I've seen it," I said.

"I'm his wife," she said, as if she thought this would relax me.

"I suspected."

"We've got TiVo, and he's got about five episodes on there, so you might want to get comfortable," she said. She turned to the board and tacked a photograph of Roger Vasquez right next to the one of Terrance Davidson. "Let me guess," she said without turning around. "You thought working for James Wilton was going to be more of a thrill ride. It is. But only when he's not working."

I didn't respond. "TiVo's great," she went on. "They'll be shipping it to all the third world countries we invade pretty soon. Mark my words."

I didn't laugh. She was ordering me to leave her husband alone. Jimmy had barely mentioned her, and I wasn't sure how I felt about her setting boundaries in our working relationship. She didn't seem to care how I felt. She handed me a slender file.

"Jimmy asked me to assemble a file on this Martin Cale guy," she said. "He referred to it is a dossier. I call it a file. Anyway, there's not much in it. Cale's a nonentity and he leaves most of the business to his partner, a guy named Irwin Faulkner. Faulkner lives down in Laguna Hills with his wife. They've made the Orange County society pages a few times, and I'm sorry to report that's all that's in the file. Well, that and some press releases about their new subdivisions that mention Cale in passing."

As I shuffled through the file, she crossed her arms over her chest and smiled at me with one corner of her wide mouth. "He told me was hiring an assistant. But you're a lot more than that, aren't you?"

"Is that a compliment?"

"I thought I might be able to help you guys out."

"How does Jimmy feel about that?" I asked.

A curtain fell across her face. "I don't think that's any of your business."

I put two and two together and got marriage counseling. Jimmy was hiding out somewhere in the main house, even though he knew I was on my way back. Meanwhile, his wife had taken over his office, probably so she could meet me at the door and lay down some new ground rules.

She lifted her chin slightly and narrowed her eyes, as if I had just confirmed a dire suspicion she held about me. "Two years ago a homicide detective came to this house and told my husband he had found the killer of a porn star named Jenna Hartt. I stood back and kept my mouth shut, listening to this detective feed my husband a line about how he wanted him to consult on the case. It turned out that this supposed killer was a big James Wilton fan. Maybe he had taken a few pointers from Jimmy's books."

She stopped several feet away from me and knocked one fist lightly against the edge of the desk. "It turned out this supposed killer had a wife who gave him a solid alibi. And it soon became clear, to me at least, that this detective didn't want Jimmy as a consultant. He wanted Jimmy to send this man, this supposed killer, a message. Something along the lines of 'We got you even though we didn't get you.'"

She studied me to see if she had my full attention. She did. I knew the homicide detective in question was Dwight Zachary and I was tempted to tell her that the two of us were hardly buddies. But I didn't think it would temper what she had to say to me.

"Barely a week after that book hit the stores, I came home and saw this supposed killer in my bedroom. My husband's right leg was hanging off the bed as if it didn't belong to him and his face looked like Play-Doh. That's not going to happen again. Do you understand me?"

"Yes," I heard myself whisper.

"You are the only part of this investigation that comes back to this house. No one gets questioned here. No one gets the phone number here, and if anyone asks you who you're working for, you either tell them you're going solo or your benefactor is a mysterious man named Charlie who you talk to once a week on speakerphone. Is that clear?" I was strangely flattered by her comparison of me to one of Charlie's Angels, and I figured she wouldn't make it once she got to know me a little better. "And if I so much as see Detective Jackass turn the corner onto Mulholland Drive, I'll electrify the fence."

I knew she was referring to Dwight Zachary. "Don't worry," I said. "I'm not a big fan of Detective Jackass."

She liked my answer as well as the frightened sound of it. She grasped my shoulder firmly as she moved past me. "I made you a plate. You want me to get it for you?"

"No thanks," I said.

She paused in the doorway as if to appraise my value as an ally in her campaign to ensure her husband kept all his limbs. "Let's try to get along, Mr. Murphy. Just to see what happens."

Once she was gone, I considered breathing again. If Brenda Wilton was going to shoot anyone else, I would be surprised if it wasn't me.

Twenty minutes later, I was reading through the turgid file on Martin Cale when Jimmy came into the office carrying a ceramic plate covered in Saran Wrap. He put it on his desk and took a seat. "Just eat it," he said. "She didn't put anything in it."

"There's no silverware."

"Call Brenda and ask her to bring you some," he said, then guffawed. "Look, I'm sorry she chewed you a new asshole. She has to do it to someone at least once a month. For once, it wasn't me. Thank God!"

"Please tell me what's going on."

He clapped his hands together. "What's going on is that it could have been the Dalai Lama in our bedroom working me over with a tire iron and she *still* would have shot him and she *still* would have found a way to blame me for it."

He pressed his palms against the desk and drew a deep breath. "Samuel Marchand murdered his sister because she was having sex on camera, and his wife gave him an alibi because she knew he'd beat the shit out of her if she didn't. And *Last Daughter* was not supposed to be a message to *him*. It was a message to the higher-ups at the LASD who didn't think the murder of a porn star was worth investigating because they thought anyone in her line of work had it coming, and because the suspect lived in Appleton, Wisconsin, and out of their jurisdiction.

"And *supposedly* I meddled in a real-life case just to compensate for never scoring with the book critics. But the only reason I have any *awareness* of this is because that woman has made me sit through a year of therapy. You would think that would be enough of an admission, wouldn't you? But now that burnt-out Ocean Park hippie of a Brentwood therapist is trying to convince me that I constantly seek out evidence that the world is a brutal and dangerous place because my mother was distracted and inattentive when I was growing up."

He leaned into my face. "Is the air clear yet? Or would you like to hear about our sex life?"

"I'd like to go home and wash my new asshole," I said.

"Sit down!"

I sat down in one of the Eames chairs. Jimmy left the room and returned with silverware and a napkin. I ate my dinner in silence. When I finished, Jimmy was slouched back in his desk chair, his hands folded over his stomach, his face expectant. I took him through the sad story of Brian Ferrin's brief relationship with Roger Vasquez.

"The Vanished Three *all* sent Brian Ferrin their picture in that chat room?" Jimmy asked.

"Yes. I showed Ferrin their pictures and he ID'd all three of them. Roger Vasquez was the only one he responded to."

"And you think if he'd responded to one of the others, he still would have ended up in Spinotta's bed, drugged and assaulted?"

"Yes. You told me these three guys were playing some special role in Spinotta's inner circle," I said. "I think this is it. They were fishermen. Why would they do this shit? They had to know they had turned into everyone's worst nightmare of the predatory fag."

Jimmy didn't answer. "What?" I asked him. "You think they were in it for money? You think Spinotta made them big promises?"

"Yes," he answered. I expected him to say more, but he didn't.

"What, Jimmy?"

"Like I said, I think these guys left behind their old lives to go join a new and better one that Joseph Spinotta provided for them. I think they're probably enjoying it right now."

I got to my feet and went to the office door. The slanting sunlight laced the swimming pool's surface with the shadows of tree branches. Brenda was brushing birdseed off the stone bench at the clearing's edge while Archer waddled eagerly around her feet. If she was so interested in helping us, why was she sitting out one of our major rap sessions?

"You think you're one of these guys, Adam. And you're right that, superficially, their lives resemble yours. They moved to LA in their twenties, just like you did, to leave their difficult histories behind. They were struggling to make lives for themselves, just as you still are. Then they fell under Joseph Spinotta's spell for some reason and started doing this vile shit." He let this sink in for a few seconds. "You're *not* one of them, Adam. You don't have to take responsibility for them, and you don't have to answer for them. You are your own man even when you don't want to be."

Taken aback, I turned to face him. He looked wary, as if I would lace into him. I didn't. Jimmy usually gave compliments on the back of his hand, but the idea that I could investigate the crimes of other gay men without taking responsibility for the criminals themselves flew in the face of every noble fantasy I had held about becoming a crusading journalist. It seemed that Jimmy was trying to strip away my arrogance and judgments, not because he thought I deserved to be punished, but because he liked the person he saw underneath.

"You think Brian Ferrin will go on the record?" he asked.

"I gave him my cell number."

"You don't sound very hopeful."

"I'm not. He's convinced what happened to him was his fault. I tried to make a plea to his inner victim, but I don't think it took."

"Any word from Billy Hatfill?" he asked.

"No," I said. "Maybe he changed his mind about getting me the meeting with Cale. He had some pretty strong words for me the other day."

"Like what?"

"Apparently, I bleed judgments. I leave a trail of them wherever I go. I'm going to drown in them someday." I had delivered Billy's words in a sarcastic tone of voice, but Jimmy didn't seem to get the joke. He furrowed his brow.

"What?" I asked.

"You're right," he said. "Those are strong words."

"You think I should be afraid of him?"

"I want you to remember every single word he says to you," Jimmy said. "If that's too difficult for you, hide a tape recorder in your pocket. I want to know where Billy fits in all of this. I also want to know why he wants you to meet with Martin Cale."

"I'll find out when I meet Martin Cale."

"You'll take Billy out to dinner first."

"What am I going to talk to him about?" I asked. "If I ask him about any of this, I'll lose my meeting with Cale."

"I said dinner, Adam. Billy Hatfill is leading you to Martin Cale for a reason. It would be nice to have some sense of what that reason is before you row yourself out to his yacht."

I could tell he was holding out on me and I stared at him until he broke. "Our working theory is that Corey blackmailed Billy with something he learned from his uncle, right?" I nodded. "Our wild guess is that Corey was using some dirt on Joseph Spinotta. If that's the case, then maybe Billy is pissed about having to take a hit for his sugar daddy. That might explain why he was so helpful the other day."

"You're saying Billy's not trying to help me find out what happened to Corey. He's trying to help me find out what dirt Corey used on him."

Jimmy nodded.

"That's all speculation, Jimmy."

"I know," he said with a wan smile. "That's why you're going to take him out to dinner." I groaned. "I'm your new boss, remember? The other option is that you spend tomorrow morning in a judo class with my wife so you can make sure she doesn't land anyone in a wheelchair. You have three seconds to make your decision."

CHAPTER **8**

Billy Hatfill came out of his front gate wearing a silver dress shirt that had a metallic sheen to it and black pleather pants that were so tight they squeaked like a small bird as he slid into the passenger seat. He directed me down the hill and onto Sunset Boulevard without telling me our destination. It was Thursday, so the traffic on the strip was light. The streetlights winked at me off the face of the silver Rolex on Billy's left wrist.

"Martin Cale is coming to shore Saturday night," Billy said.

"That was fast."

"Well, I didn't tell him Corey was missing. I didn't want to steal your thunder."

"Considering he never told you Corey was his nephew, I guess you two are even," I answered.

"Good point," he said.

"Why does he think I want to meet with him?"

Billy emitted a long, pained sigh. "Martin Cale thinks that you are a very bright and adorable young man who is interested in taking a cruise on his yacht. I'm sending Everett with you just in case Cale gets too persistent."

When I considered the prospect of having to fend off the advances of a wealthy closet case who put miles of ocean between himself and accountability, my forced dinner with Billy suddenly seemed more like a high tea.

"How's it going, by the way?" Billy asked. "Your little investigation, I mean."

"Corey was a private guy when he was still around," I said carefully, my eyes locked on Doheny Boulevard's palm-tree-lined corridor into Beverly Hills. "I'm starting to understand why."

"What do you mean?" he asked.

I shrugged, as if Billy needed some sort of security clearance before I told him anything else. He let out a sharp breath; then I heard his pants squeak as he shifted in his seat. He told me to take a left onto Burton Way, a four-lane thoroughfare that runs smack into downtown Beverly Hills. The wide median held clusters of tall and slender palm trees. Billy directed me to an eight-story concrete building with a row of backlit ficus hedges out front and rows of tiny rounded balconies on each floor. A massive sandstone overhang extended over a set of broad marble steps. The hovering valets wore khaki vests over white dress shirts that made them look like safari guides in search of their hats.

I had read about the place in several magazines. It was an exclusive hotel popular with rap stars and the ten-person entourages that accompanied them. The lobby was an endless sweep of white travertine marble lit by banks of flickering tea candles. The dining room lay behind a series of hanging taffeta curtains that trembled in the breeze from a nearby patio.

The maître d' had a long pale face with pinprick eyes and an artful mess of pinkish-gold hair. He whispered something in Billy's ear as he showed us to a corner table. Billy dismissed him politely, as if the guy had asked him business advice during Billy's off hours. A swarm of fast-talking agents on the patio alternated between checking their watches and looking around in every direction, as if only they knew about the SWAT team that was about to come bursting through the entrance.

I took my seat and tried to lose myself in the menu. It was written in some hotel hybrid of Romance languages. If the restaurant deigned to serve granola, they probably spelled it with an ~.

"What's the look about?" Billy asked me. He was rolling up his sleeves.

"Which one?"

"The one on your face," he said. "What's the matter? They don't have travertine and tea candles back in New Orleans?"

I obliged him and smiled.

"You looked so put out that I thought it might have something to do with Greg," he said.

"Who's Greg?"

"The maître d'." Billy gave me a narrow look. "You blew him."

My eyes shot to the host's stand. The pale-faced host gave me an arch smile and waved at me with the middle three fingers on his right hand. "Oh, dear," Billy whispered. "You really don't remember him, do you? That's okay. He says you weren't the only two guys in the hot tub that night. That's what he was whispering to me, by the way."

There had been a time when I listed every man I had slept with, a record intended to persuade me I was desirable. When it had become more and more difficult to remember those names, the list had shamed me instead of validating me.

"Relax, Adam," he said. "Everyone has a blackout now and then." He returned his attention to the menu.

Had he picked this restaurant solely because he knew I couldn't remember getting nasty with the maitre d'? "I don't get you, Billy. What other people say about you makes more sense than the things you say about yourself."

"Other people don't say anything about *me*, Adam. They say things about Joseph, about the view from his house. You're the only one who's ever shown an interest in what I do once the party is over. You have no idea how much I would like to be flattered by the attention, Adam. But I know full well the two of us would never have seen each other in lighting this good if Corey Howard hadn't come to my house three weeks ago."

He was trying to beg a set of questions I wasn't willing to ask until after my meeting with Martin Cale, so I decided to throw him off. "How did you meet Joseph?" I asked.

He was visibly startled by the directness of the question. "My father set us up," he answered. He gave me a chance to express some kind of disgust or amusement. I didn't. "It's a long story."

I toasted him with my water glass. He took the cue.

"My parents didn't take much of an interest in anything I did. But they were still dead set on having me attend an Ivy League school. Probably because they thought a Yale education would fix everything they hadn't."

He failed to suppress a smug little grin. "So I took the personal essay sections out of the applications for Harvard, Yale, and Brown, and I got some copies of *Stroke* magazine, made a little collage of body parts for each application, and dropped them in the mail. Months went by. Nobody said anything. Then one day my father comes to me and tells me he has a meeting in San Francisco with the IT guy for his investment firm."

"Joseph Spinotta," I said.

Billy nodded and cradled his double scotch in both hands. "My father had never met with an IT guy in his life. He'd certainly never asked me to accompany him on a business trip. Our first night in San Francisco, we had

dinner with Joseph. He wouldn't shut up about this website he was planning to start. *Bam*. I thought it sounded like he was selling cleaning supplies. But he kept running on about all the opportunities it would afford
young people. Suddenly my father was talking about opportunities and
young people as well. Together, they both said those words so many times
I thought I was at a NAMBLA meeting."

He sipped from his scotch. "I never went back to New York." His
eyes betrayed a pain that seemed unrehearsed, a recollection of how it
felt to be traded from one businessman to another like a wholly owned
subsidiary.

"Did you love him?"

He raised his eyebrows at my audacity, but then some other emotion
commandeered his face and he brought one edge of his napkin to his
mouth in a poor attempt to hide it. "I thought he could own the world if
he wanted to," he said. "I thought this made him as happy as it made me.
But it didn't."

"What made him happy?"

"Nothing," he said. "Certain things just made him shut up for a while."

"Like what?"

He met my eyes. "Young people."

I did my best to suppress the thought of the young person whose pain I
had pried my way into that afternoon at Back Beats on Ventura Boulevard.
"How young, Billy?"

"Let me put it this way," he said, resting his elbows on the edge of the
table. "I was never young enough."

I didn't press. I couldn't. Every question I wanted to ask might endan-
ger my meeting with Martin Cale. The fact that Billy had smeared Joseph's
name without much provocation was information enough for now. It supported Jimmy's theory that Billy was trying to cut himself loose from Spinotta's psychic dominion over him. But it didn't confirm it.

"You don't have some informed opinion to offer?"

"I'm trying to work on not bleeding judgments, Billy."

He smiled at the table. "You aren't going to ask me why I stayed with
him?"

"The answer's pretty obvious, Billy. You're wearing it."

He glanced down at the expensive Rolex on his wrist and laughed.

We drove back to his house in silence. Martin Cale was coming to shore on
Saturday night; that meant I had a day or two before I could back Billy to

the wall about the real reason Corey had come to his house, and the magic key Corey had used to get in the front door. After I rolled to a stop in front of his gate, Billy didn't move. He sat with his hands folded in his lap. "I never apologized to you for Everett's behavior," he said.

"Shouldn't Everett do that?"

When he turned his face to mine, the halos from the security lights atop the front gate slid across his pale cheek. "I stayed with Joseph because I thought I could learn from him." His voice had sudden gravity to it. His earlier confession had not gotten the reaction out of me that he wanted, so now he was offering up another answer to a question I hadn't asked. "I thought I could do a better job with his life than he did."

"Have you?"

"Does asking redundant questions like this make you hard?" he whispered. "You think I don't know what you're doing, asking me out to dinner like this?"

"What am I doing?" I asked redundantly, with a redundant smile.

He let out a hiss of breath. I felt his hand enclose my left thigh. He leaned over until our noses were almost touching. In the darkness, I could not make out his face.

"You think Corey's coming here to my house two weeks ago might have something to do with why he's no longer around."

I didn't say anything.

"Is that really the truth, Adam? Or is that just what you've convinced yourself of—because it gives you an excuse to circle me like this? To try to figure me out? Eventually, you would have found a way to write about me, even if Corey still worked at that car wash, and you know it. I see it on your face every time I run into you. But when I give you the story, you reject it. Because it's not the one that you've made up. The kept boy gone wrong."

His hand worked its way to my crotch, and I felt his hot breath against my lips. "You're no better than I was with Joseph. You see my life and you think you can do better with it." He squeezed my groin. "Prove it. Come inside." His eyes fell to my crotch. They were wide and dead, full of something that looked like scientific inquiry instead of lust. He might have spent most of his afternoons polishing and rehearsing every sentence that came out of his mouth until he sounded like a cross between a British playwright and a West Side therapist, but his innate desire to sleep with men who held a cold disdain for him marked him as a spoiled adolescent.

"No thanks."

"How much do you want to meet with Martin Cale?"

"How much do you want me to hear what Cale has to say?"

He loosened his hand, but he didn't turn away from me. The lights that lined the top of his front gate threw him into silhouette.

"Corey was blackmailing you," I said.

I heard the breath go out of him and his next inhalation sounded shockingly like a sob. He turned forward and slumped in his seat, his eyes screwed shut and his chest rising and falling. I had scored a hit. "Blackmail's a crime, Billy."

"And you want to know why I didn't go to the police?"

He had just confirmed Jimmy's initial theory. I was startled silent for a few seconds.

"I want to know what Corey wanted," I said. "Was it money?"

After several agonizing seconds, Billy unsnapped his seat belt and reached for the door handle. I put my hand on his shoulder and he batted my arm away. "I know the time I spent with Corey can't hold a candle to the time you two spent together," he said, his voice trembling. "But I saw someone you refuse to see, Adam. He's full of rage and convinced it's something else. Martin Cale can tell you the rest."

Before I could say another word, he had gotten out and slammed the gate behind him.

"He really wants you to meet with Martin Cale, doesn't he?" Jimmy asked. I was pacing back and forth in my apartment, the poster of Dionysus leering at me.

"Yes."

"The restaurant," Jimmy said. "You think Billy picked it just because you slept with the host while you blacked out."

"I have no idea," I said. "And if I asked Billy about it, I'd get a ten-minute response that evaded the question."

"But Billy basically confirmed that Corey was blackmailing him."

"Yes."

"Don't meet with him again," Jimmy said firmly.

"Fine with me," I said, startled by this sudden about-face.

I counted long seconds while Jimmy said nothing on the other end of the phone. Something about my conversation with Billy was bothering him, and he didn't feel like sharing it with me. "I want something real on this guy," he said. "Something that didn't come out of his mouth."

"I can try to find some witnesses to this meeting he had with Corey. It shouldn't be hard. There was a party going on."

"I doubt the two of them got into it in front of the other guests, but go ahead."

"There's another thing," I said. "Billy went to a famous prep school back in New York called Rappaport. He told me he had an affair with one of his English teachers."

"When did Billy tell you this?"

"The first night I was out asking around about Daniel Brady. I told him I'd gone to college with some of his classmates, and he asked me if they mentioned the guy who had slept with his English teacher."

"So this affair wasn't a secret?" Jimmy asked.

"Apparently not. But Billy said he had no hard feelings about the relationship."

"I wonder if the English teacher feels the same way," he said.

"You want me to find out?"

"I'll look into it first," he said. "Tomorrow I want you to retrace some of Linda Walsh's footsteps. Her file doesn't exactly set my heart racing. But I need you to verify that restaurant manager's story about firing Terrance Davidson."

I sat on my response.

"What?" he finally asked.

"Nothing," I said. "It just feels like a demotion." When he didn't answer, I decided to voice the worry gnawing on me since the ride home. "I went too far, didn't I? Asking Billy if Corey blackmailed him."

For a moment he said nothing, and I assumed that Jimmy agreed with me. "Little man, tonight Billy Hatfill tried to humiliate you and insult you, and you didn't let him do either. He also accused you of having an unnatural obsession with him when it's patently obvious that the opposite is the case. On top of all that, he's withholding information about the disappearance of a man you had deep feelings for. Frankly, I think the fact that you didn't spring across the table and wring his neck is deserving of a Purple Heart."

I was too surprised to speak.

"You are more cut out for this than you think you are," he said. "But you're not a reporter. You're something else."

"What?"

"I'm not sure," he said. "I'm leaning toward infection."

"That's flattering."

"It is," he said. "Look at who you've infected."

"Whatever. Call me when you come up with something better."

After I hung up, I came to terms with the fact that Jimmy and I could do no more than circle our target until I met Martin Cale. Corey had blackmailed Billy Hatfill. Now Billy was leading me to a man who could have provided Corey with the information he had needed to do the job.

Deputy Amy Stahl drove west on Highway 198 into the moun-
tains just west of Coalinga. Her father had been an amateur geologist, and
she distracted herself from the fact that she was carrying stolen evidence
in the trunk of her Ford Escape by thinking about the landscape she was
passing through.

The Coast Ranges had surfaced only a million years earlier. Their interior rested atop a giant platform of granite that had been carried north from
below the Sierra Nevada range by the San Andreas Fault. Before they surfaced, the ocean waters carved them with inlets and bays that were now
home to cattle ranches and grasslands. None of the peaks were high
enough to block out the night sky, but in some places they were rough and
jagged, their granite flanks exposed and flaking. In other places, they were
round and smooth, as if God's hand had favored some parts of the landscape and not others.

Caroline Hughes had given Amy directions to a road that didn't exist
on any map. After twenty minutes on Highway 198, Amy saw the pair of
valley oaks that Caroline had told her about. They were huge trees, their
branches touching the ground as if their crowns had been split down the
center by a giant axe.

Even though she couldn't see the road, Amy made the turn and drove
over a sweep of grassland dotted by tumbles of chaparral. To the west, she
could see the fence of a neighboring cattle ranch. Far ahead, there was a

gentle slope curtained by dense stands of valley oaks with leaves that turned the color of ash in her headlights.

She almost drove right into the fence. It was fifteen feet high and its slender posts were painted black. There was no moon to light the coils of razor wire that ran along the top. Instead of slats or chain link, it had thin strands of something that looked like airplane cable. No sign warned trespassers to keep away.

Amy stepped out of her car and studied the fence. She picked up a stick and hurled it at the thin cables. The collision made a sound like the snap of a giant guitar string. Caroline Hughes had told her that this property used to belong to her father. She had said nothing about why her father had needed the protection of an electrified fence.

Suddenly an entire section of the gate swung inward, just enough for Amy to fit her truck through. The minute she drove through it, the gate swung shut behind her. She kept her Escape at ten miles an hour as she crossed the expanse between the fence and the dense stand of valley oaks that ascended the gentle slope up ahead.

Amy had been a deputy with the Kings County Sheriff's Department for five years. In that time, she had never planted or stolen evidence. The evidence she carried in her truck had lain untouched for over a week, but that did little to stanch her guilt. She knew the reason for her breach of ethics was not a simple one. The Valley was infected by a virus that was being brewed on the stovetops of trailers across the state of California.

The virus was crystal meth, and it killed most of its hosts by setting them ablaze, sometimes igniting explosions so white it looked like heaven had sprung a leak—an explosion that had killed an entire family as well as an innocent schoolteacher who had taken her last breath in Amy's arms.

Two security lights flicked on amid the trees up ahead. The lights guided her into a clearing. The house was a long one-story log cabin with a small front porch. A short chimney rose from the broad sloping roof. From the treetops behind the house, an antenna that looked like it could pick up TV signals from Asia thrust itself into the night sky.

Caroline Hughes was waiting for her on the front porch. She was not the same kind of beauty her mother had been. Janice Hughes had moved through the world with unassuming grace. Everything about her daughter was thick and rigid, from her sculpted arms to her muddy sheen of freckles that almost looked like a coat of war paint, to the way she could make a simple question sound like a command.

Amy opened her trunk and pulled out the box that contained the remains of Tonya McCormick's pit bull. Caroline accepted it in both arms without bending under its weight. "What condition are they in?" she asked.

"Bones, mostly," Amy answered. "There's some skin left too. You going to put them back together?"

"I might not have to," Caroline said.

"You some kind of doctor or something?" Amy asked.

"First-year surgical resident," Caroline answered. She turned and headed toward the cabin. Amy took note of how Caroline's clipped response didn't tell her if she had any plans to return to her studies. Maybe she planned to stay in this cabin forever, hunting the man she believed responsible for her mother's death.

Amy followed her inside. The cabin had a ten-foot ceiling. Vague lamplight came from a loft that extended out from a flimsy plywood wall that separated the galley kitchen from the common room. A giant circular rug displayed the outline of a deer leaping through a yellow egg yolk of sun. In the cast-iron stove, the last embers of a poorly tended fire were dying. A ratty sofa was pushed against one wall, covered with bright, hand-sewn bed quilts. Next to the sofa was an old schoolteacher's desk, its pockmarked wood losing its dark stain. Caroline gathered a mess of what looked like news clippings off it and shoved them inside a drawer. She dropped the cardboard box on top of the desk, angled the desk lamp over it, and peered inside.

"You said this was your father's place," Amy said.

"It was."

"Your father didn't want a place closer to the coast?" Amy asked. Caroline didn't respond. "I'm just curious. Your mother never talked about him."

"Did you have a lot of conversations with my mother?" Caroline asked in a flat voice that sounded somehow accusatory.

"Enough to know that she was a remarkable woman," Amy said.

Caroline removed a pair of salad tongs and several paintbrushes from her desk drawer. Then she squeezed her hands into a pair of latex gloves.

Amy inspected the map of California taped to the wall beside the desk. Thumbtacks had been pushed through several small towns throughout the San Joaquin Valley. They covered an area that went as far south as Bakersfield and as far north as Visalia, the Tulare County seat nestled against the foothills of the Sierra Nevada.

"What are these?" Amy asked.

"Home meth lab accidents," Caroline answered. "Just like the one that

blew apart Tonya McCormick's trailer. Flash fires started all of them. Some
of those flash fires were triggered by the same type of white phosphine
refuse they found under Tonya's trailer."

"What did the Bureau of Narcotics Enforcement have to say about
these accidents?"

"The same thing they said about Tonya McCormick's trailer." She began removing the charred bones from the box and putting them on the
desk. "Meth addicts turn into very bad people who start very bad fires."

"Meth labs go up all the time in this state, Caroline."

"Not like this!" she snapped, jerking her head up to glare at Amy. Amy
bowed her head and raised her palms. Caroline took a deep breath. "There
was a boy involved in all of those as well. Thirteen or fourteen years old.
Less than partial remains found. Just like Caden McCormick."

Amy didn't protest. She trusted the BNE's working theory about the explosion of Tonya McCormick's trailer as little as Caroline did. She couldn't
believe that a thirteen-year-old boy would start a fire that hot, an explosion
that powerful, and then head for the hills out of guilt or shame or whatever
convenient psychological excuse the arson investigators felt like using that
day. In the weeks since the explosion, Amy had done enough research to
know that fires in excess of a thousand degrees still left some human remains, more than those traces of Caden McCormick that had been gathered
from the wreckage of his former home.

Amy turned away from the map as if it was giving off a hot glare.

"Can I trust you?" Caroline asked.

"I don't know what trust means to you, Caroline."

"It means that when you come to me and tell me that my mother's last
words were about a dog, you let me do what I have to with that information."

Amy felt the reflexive maxim of a law enforcement officer forming in
her chest: Civilians, especially the grieving survivors of a crime victim,
should never, ever be allowed to . . .

"Amy, when I told you what Lucy Vernon said to me at the gas station,
you looked like I had busted your kneecap!"

Amy realized her hands were fists and deliberately uncurled them.
"It's a scary story, Caroline. But that's all it is. I've heard it before. Everyone out here who's ever wondered why every Mexican national who tries
to take over the meth trade either goes missing or dies has heard that
story. It still doesn't mean there's some rogue assassin at work."

Caroline squinted at her, then at the bones spread in front of her. "You
wouldn't have brought me this if you didn't believe me."

Amy didn't respond because the other woman was right.

"This is going to take a while," Caroline finally said. Amy stayed put. "There's something else, Caroline." Amy saw that she had her full attention. "I made some calls. Just to see how the task force was doing with its report on the explosion."

"They think he did it on purpose, don't they?"

"Yeah."

"They're going to say Caden McCormick started the fire deliberately," Caroline continued. "A thirteen-year-old boy who couldn't even raise his hand in my mother's classroom. And they're going to say he burned his parents alive. You know that's bullshit." Caroline waved at the map above their heads. "The same bullshit they said about those meth lab accidents, too."

"What do you need me for?" Amy asked. "Sounds like you've got it all figured out on your own."

"I need you because Caden McCormick is alive," she said. "He didn't start that fire. He didn't leave that trailer on his own."

Instead of going home, Amy found a hole-in-the-wall bar in Coalinga where she was the only white face and the jukebox played an endless stream of Marc Anthony and Celia Cruz.

After three beers and a few strange looks from the bartender, Amy closed her eyes and traveled back to the front porch of Janice Hughes's tiny house in Avenal. The night a month before she died when Janice had called to report a prowler, she came to the door with a polite but tense smile on her face, holding the flaps of her robe closed over a V-neck T-shirt. Was Avenal's newest schoolteacher really a lesbian, as Amy had heard? Sometimes one rumor was all your fantasy life needed to get to work.

That night Amy had searched Janice's property and turned up no evidence of a prowler. Janice apologized and gave Amy an apologetic but worried smile, running one hand through her hair in a gesture that Amy watched raptly. When Janice offered her coffee, Amy's heart pounded.

A few moments later, when Janice had squeezed past Amy to get to the kitchen counter, the tip of Amy's nose had brushed against Janice's hair. Janice froze and Amy raised one hand against the woman's side, maybe to steady her if she tripped or maybe so she could slide one arm around Janice's stomach and fold her into an embrace, one slow enough to give Janice time to pull away, if brushing up against Amy's body didn't quicken her breaths the way it seemed to.

The encounter lasted only a second before some imperative of forward motion set in. Before Amy had time to recover, the two of them were sitting at the kitchen table, Janice listening politely as Amy stammered her way through a story about a nature walk she had taken with her father in the Diablo Range just before he passed away. After fifteen minutes, Janice yawned and Amy was on her way, hoping that Janice would report a prowler again some time soon. But the next time Janice Hughes called 911, she reported something far worse.

Amy's cell phone rang in her jeans pocket. She answered it.

"The dog's jaw was crushed." There was a tense energy in the other woman's voice. "Not the kind of fractures you would expect from an explosion. We're talking about an equal upward and downward pressure on the jaw. The only thing I can think of is some kind of animal trap."

The bartender noticed the expression on Amy's face and furrowed his brow.

"The surfaces of the fractures are as badly burned as the rest of the jaw," Caroline continued. "The dog's jaw was crushed before the explosion."

"What does this mean?" Amy whispered.

"It means this guy wanted to sneak up on two meth heads around midnight and he had to get rid of the dog first. How was he supposed to do that? Shoot it and wake up the whole neighborhood? No. He set a trap. He got the fucker by the jaws so it couldn't make a sound."

Amy's racing heartbeat flushed the shivering from her limbs.

"Do you get it, Amy?" Caroline said, her voice rising in pitch. "My mother was trying to tell you that this dog was dead by the time she got to the trailer. She was trying to tell you someone had killed it."

The music in the bar was suddenly piercing. Several feet away, a woman erupted with laughter that sounded tinged with malice. The bartender was still staring at Amy and she saw nothing but evil intent in his narrow eyes.

"She was trying to tell you someone took Caden," Caroline said.

"What are you going to do?" Amy heard herself ask.

The girl took a long time to respond. "Do I really have to tell you?"

CHAPTER 9

When the phone rang, I was dreaming of a marine helicopter pilot named Daniel Brady. I was sitting beside him in the cockpit. The windows filled with blue water rippling with the sun's reflection, and I realized he was flying us straight into the Pacific Ocean. I tried to convince him to pull up, but the words that came out of my mouth were lines from the episode of *Everybody Loves Raymond* that was playing several feet away from my sleeping body.

Suddenly I had the phone to my ear. Nate Bain said my name in a tense voice. I buzzed him in. He walked into my apartment with his head bowed, holding the straps of his backpack. He wore a white tank top that clung to his chest and a pair of baggy gym shorts. He wouldn't look at me directly. The only smell he gave off was the vaguely floral scent of his hair product and the sharp odor of pure sweat. Not the noxious stench associated with crystal meth or the sickly sweet smell of alcohol.

"Were you asleep?" he asked.

"Barely," I said. "What's wrong?"

"Can I hang out here for a while?"

I gestured to the love seat and got him a Diet Coke without asking whether he wanted it. For a while he stared through the flickering television. I studied him. He was a winded and sagging version of the guy who had tracked me down at The Abbey on Friday night. It was late, and he was dressed to get undressed; I was fairly sure he had chosen my apartment over the bathhouse and didn't want to admit it. Now I would do the same thing for him that his sober neighbor had done for me.

He looked up. "Someone's following me."

"Who?"

"I don't know," he said. "I went to a meeting tonight and I saw him sitting in the back. He didn't talk to anyone. I was kind of checking him out."

"Describe him."

"Tall, built, but a young face. He was wearing a baseball cap and sunglasses. In the meeting. Most people don't do that except in movies about AA. He followed me when I was walking home. When he saw I saw him, he disappeared. Then later he was outside my apartment building." He didn't like the look he saw on my face. "I'm not making this up, Adam."

"I didn't say you were. You're kind of high profile around here, Nate. You have fans."

He shook his head. "This guy wasn't a fan."

I thought of the two kids I had seen in Scott Koffler's Jacuzzi the day I had dropped in on him. Hard bodies and young faces. "Why don't you stay here tonight?" I said.

For a second, I thought he might cry. Instead, he said sure and returned his attention to the television.

I didn't think it would be of any use to call Scott Koffler and tell him that I had dropped the Daniel Brady story. If I had wanted to conclude things between us, I should have endured his comments about my mother instead of breaking his nose. I was willing to bet that the guy who had tailed Nate was one of Scott's young charges. If that was the case, Koffler was trying to even a score that would never be settled with lukewarm intimidation. Respond, and I would only crank up the heat.

Nate nodded off after a while. I stayed up another few hours, checking the street outside for any suspicious shadows. There were none. I double-checked the locks, threw a blanket over Nate, turned out the lights, and crawled into bed.

I awoke to the feel of Nate's hands on my bare chest. I opened my eyes and saw that he had shoved my T-shirt up over my chest. He was shirtless, and the sight of his bubble butt in his white underwear did to me what Nate knew it would. His mouth met mine and at first I gave in, ready to use his body to escape my own head.

But Nate's kisses were too urgent and desperate. He rubbed against me with exaggerated movements that seemed more about displaying his body to the rest of my apartment than uniting it with mine. I brought my hands to the sides of his face and gently pulled our mouths apart. "Let's not," I whispered.

"*Why?*" he whispered. He had heard an insult, and his face was scrunched as if in pain. He wanted to give me something, and he believed his body was all he had to offer.

"Because you don't have to," I said.

This didn't please him. He pushed himself off me and got to his feet. "Whatever. I'll just go," he said, his voice shaky with anger and embarrassment.

I got out of the bed and gestured to it. Nate stared at me for a few seconds through the darkness. "Take the bed," I said.

"You think I'm positive, don't you?"

I tried to keep my voice steady. "I think that you're just off crystal and I'm barely a week off alcohol and cocaine. We have enough in common, all right? You don't have to sleep with me to make me your friend."

Nate looked surprised. He cocked his head. "If you're going teach me a lesson, you can at least turn me over your knee first."

He slid into my bed, curled into a fetal position with his back to me, and pulled the covers up over himself. I took his place on the love seat and stared at the ceiling for what felt like several hours.

By now it was a little after midnight and sleep felt futile. Corey's keys were on my kitchen counter. When I saw the tiny gold key on his key ring, I realized there was one part of Corey's apartment that I hadn't searched.

Ten minutes later, I was walking toward Corey's duplex, having parked my car a safe distance away. The lights in the downstairs apartment were off. Corey's mailbox was bolted to the wall right next to the exterior stairway's iron gate.

I opened it with the tiny key and a cardboard box fell to my feet, with several envelopes spilling out after it. I collected them, closed the mailbox, and locked it. Back inside my car, I turned on the dome light. The cardboard box was the size of a videotape and bore the logo of the Life Channel, a cable network that showed nothing but documentaries on things that scared people to death.

I opened it and pulled out a VHS cassette of a documentary entitled *Forming the Corps*. The invoice didn't list a price or a buyer's name or address, but it had a personalized gift message printed at the bottom: "Thought you might like to have a copy of this. Best, M."

Nate was still deep asleep when I returned to my apartment. I slid the tape in my VCR and pressed play without turning on any of the lights. The screen filled with a high-speed montage of Marine Corps recruits crawling through the mud, fighting with pugil sticks, and being shouted down by drill instructors. A voice-over informed me that the Marine Corps brought discipline and integrity to lives that needed both. The music swelled. The title appeared on the screen. So did Corey Howard.

He was identified as "Corey, Recruit." His face was rounder and more boyish and his black hair had been shaved to bristle. In an expressive voice, far more articulate than he had ever been with me, he informed the camera that even though recruits wound up in boot camp for different reasons, none of those reasons mattered in the end. The only thing that mattered was that they did what they were told.

Corey Howard had never mentioned a word to me about being in the Marine Corps. There were no telltale tattoos on his body, no Semper Fi bumper sticker on his truck. And an active-duty marine would never take an apartment and a job in the middle of a gay ghetto. Corey's marine days were over.

Nate hadn't stirred.

A few days ago, the week before, another marine, this one not only active-duty but also married, had paid a visit to West Hollywood. Daniel Brady's marine days were over now, too.

Two disparate threads had come together, and I got the sense they were about to knot tight. Billy Hatfill had not only confirmed that Corey was blackmailing him; he had told me that the Corey he met with that night had been full of rage, and that Billy was convinced it was about something far more infuriating than a boyfriend who wouldn't quit drinking.

I took the portable phone out onto my tiny balcony. After a few rings, Jimmy answered in a sleep-clogged voice. I told him about what I had just discovered. Then I played out the scenario I had come up with: Corey learned something incriminating about Billy from his uncle, Martin Cale. Corey used that information to force Billy Hatfill into blackmailing a marine helicopter pilot named Daniel Brady. To carry out this plan, Billy had enlisted the aid of Scott Koffler.

"Corey never mentioned his time in the corps to me," I said. "And he didn't have any marine tats. I've never seen a marine, even a gay one, who doesn't have some kind of Marine Corps bumper sticker. Corey didn't. I think his time in the marines was short and it ended badly."

"All right," Jimmy said, but I could tell that I hadn't sold him on the connections yet.

"The majority of gay service members are discharged because a former lover or a guy they rejected files a report with their commanding officer. That's a statistic. It's not up for debate."

"So you think Corey was discharged?" he asked. "And Daniel Brady was responsible?"

"It's a guess," I said. "And there's something else, Jimmy," I said, more tentatively now. "I just thought of it tonight. Brady and I look a lot alike. Same hair color, same eyes, same build. Nate commented on it when he first told me about meeting Brady."

"You think Corey fell for you because you reminded him of his old love?"

"Something like that," I muttered.

Jimmy breathed into the phone. I tried to tell if Brenda was stirring beside him, but heard nothing. "It's the second part of your theory I don't like," he said. "I don't believe a guy like Billy Hatfill would hire a loser like Scott Koffler to help him take out the trash."

I thought of how Billy had gone ballistic when I had compared him to Koffler, and how he said he'd ejected Koffler and his young charge from one of his parties. Billy's ire had seemed genuine at the time. I wondered if it had been a show for my benefit.

"Think about it, Adam," Jimmy said. "We're talking about Billy Hatfill here. Loads of money. Lots of connections. Joseph Spinotta out there somewhere, ready to watch out for him if he gets in a jam. Are you asking me to believe that this guy would stoop so low as to hire a two-bit pimp who lives in Palmdale with his mother?"

"They have similar interests, Jimmy. Koffler uses teenagers to get ahead in the social world. Billy's housing a teenager because he wants to turn him into a trophy boy."

"You're putting a streetwalker and a high-priced escort at the same party."

I let this stew for a minute. "I want to go to Oceanside tomorrow," I said. "See if I can find a connection between Corey and Daniel Brady."

"How do you plan to do that?" he asked. I could tell he didn't think I was up for the assignment.

"I've got an hour-long documentary on Corey's days in boot camp. I'll see if I can track down of any of the other guys in his platoon. Maybe some drill sergeants. That's a good place to start, right?"

I was lying to him and he knew it. "Why don't you just tell me how you plan on approaching Daniel Brady's wife?" he asked.

"Very carefully," I said.

"Check in me with every few hours," he said. I agreed.

"What do you think this revenge against Daniel Brady was?" he asked.

"Photographs," I said. "Koffler probably got him in the act with one of his young charges. Maybe he mailed the pictures to his wife."

"So Brady responds by killing himself *and* four crewmates?"

"What do you think they did to him, Jimmy?"

"If Corey needed Billy Hatfill to carry this plan out, that means Billy was bringing something very special to it. Any idea what that might be?"

"No."

"Me neither," he said.

The next morning, I woke up on the love seat to the sound of the shower running. I was waiting for the coffeemaker to let out its thick rattle when Nate emerged from the bathroom with a towel wrapped around his waist and a wary look on his face. I told him he could borrow some clothes and watched his every move as he stepped over my bed and started rooting through my closet.

The towel gaped around his waist, revealing his shaved thighs. "Oh, sorry," he gasped, gathering the towel around him.

"Nate," I said, "I usually never see someone again after I sleep with them, all right? I'd like things between us to go a different way."

"Fine," he answered. "But my sponsor said if you're investigating a murder, I shouldn't hang out with you anyway."

"Who told him I was investigating a murder?"

"I saw your desk, Adam," he said. "The Vanished Three. The West Hollywood Slasher."

"Tell your sponsor I'm not investigating a murder," I said. It was easier than explaining the things he had seen.

"Why?"

"Because I like hanging out with you."

I couldn't tell if my words had affected him. He turned his back to me and slid into my one of my white T-shirts. I had about seven hundred of them. "I don't want you to stay at your place right now. Do you have somewhere else you can go?"

He gave me a blank look. He obviously didn't want to take instructions from me unless they involved various actions performed on my body parts. But Scott Koffler was having him followed, and I now believed that Koffler was acting out something larger than a personal vendetta.

"I can stay at my sponsor's," he finally said.

I drove him there. His sponsor lived in a townhouse condo that took up half of a hunter-green concrete block in the West Hollywood flats, in the blocks just behind 24 Hour Fitness. Its front lawn was crisscrossed by lines of bamboo.

Nate stepped out of my Jeep without saying goodbye. Then he paused and I thought he might apologize for his sour mood. "They've got a dungeon room in there," he said. "I forgot to ask if that was okay with you."

"Knock it off, Nate." He rolled his eyes. "Don't go out by yourself. And if you see that guy again, call me."

He muttered something under his breath and walked off.

CHAPTER 10

San Diego County welcomed me with massive roadside signs advising me to watch out for dust clouds and illegal immigrants attempting to flee the checkpoint station that straddles the interstate's northbound lanes. The hills to the east turned dry and sharp-edged, with power lines riding their ridges and the shadows of fast-moving clouds sliding across their flanks.

A Navy Sea Knight helicopter flew in off the ocean. The sunlight flashed off its dual rotary blades as it came in for a landing on the narrow strip of scrub between the highway and the sea. Camp Pendleton sits on over one hundred thousand acres at the northwest corner of San Diego County, and the stretch of Interstate 5 that passes through it is named for the first marine to win the Congressional Medal of Honor.

The small town of Oceanside sits just to the south of the base. According to the *LA Times*, Daniel and Melissa Brady had lived there for the past four years. They were listed. As I drove in, I didn't see a major chain restaurant on the North Coast Highway. I passed hole-in-the-wall bars, a used car dealership that promised no money down to enlisted men E-1 and higher, and a 1960s movie theater converted into a church. Beneath a neon starburst, the marquee welcomed home the town's marines and sailors and complimented them on a job well done.

I went east on Mission Avenue and found the Bradys' sprawling apartment complex, sitting between two round green hills. It had a spread of duplex units that looked exactly like the one I had seen Melissa Brady being led away from on the eleven o'clock news. The swimming pool in the middle of the complex was full of water the color of a rain cloud and surrounded by a chain-link fence overburdened with warning signs.

I had purchased an orchid on the ride down there. I carried it stiffly in one arm as I walked the steps to Melissa's second-floor apartment. Her windows were heavily curtained and the darkness on the other side was silent. Just as I suspected, she wasn't home.

Her downstairs neighbor came to the door after one knock. She was a pear-shaped woman with a lantern jaw and a long gray ponytail that hung the length of her back. The kittens on her sweater stared at me as if they expected milk. She took one look at the orchid I was holding and narrowed her eyes.

"A little soon for suitors, don't you think?" she asked.

"I'm not a suitor," I said with a sheepish smile. "Let's just say I failed that test a few years ago."

"That's what we're gonna say, huh?"

"I heard what happened to Daniel," I said. "I wanted to pay my respects."

"She hasn't been back here since it happened," the woman said, her eyes wandering over my shoulder. "News was camped out here for a while."

"That must have been a pain."

"So what happened?" she asked brightly. "You break her heart?" I bowed my head as if the answer were too embarrassing to go into. "You look like him, you know? Danny, I mean. That's why I asked."

"I'd like to see her if I could," I said in a funeral-home voice.

"How long's it been?"

"A while."

She frowned, as if my answer had grave implications, then rested her head on the door frame. "She's not doing so well."

"That's understandable."

"She wasn't doing so well before. These days, doctors will give you codeine for a stubbed toe, know what I mean?" I made a sharp sound in my throat to give her the impression that this news about my old friend stung me. "She's staying with a friend of hers. Elena. You know her?"

I summoned an image of the furious friend I had seen leading Melissa down the front lawn behind me on the eleven o'clock news. "Tall, big-boned. Hispanic."

"That's her," the woman said tightly, as if I had identified a murder suspect.

"I'm not a fan," I said.

"Neither am I," she said. "She thinks she's protecting Missy but she's not. She's doing the reverse. What's that called when someone—"

"An enabler," I said.

"That's right," she said. "I dropped the mail off over there yesterday. I knew they were home. I saw that little death trap Elena drives parked out front, but nobody came down when I rang the bell."

"Elena drives a Miata?" I asked.

"Naw, a Celica, I think," she said quickly. "Anyway, I don't know. The newspeople are all gone now. There's no reason to keep Missy under lock and key, but I'm pretty sure that's what she's doing, and it's not going to help anything. Missy's gonna have to get out into the world at some point."

"Sounds like it wasn't that easy being her neighbor," I said sympathetically.

She let out a breath that sputtered her lips. "I've had worse neighbors," she said.

"It would be nice to know what I'm walking into. That's all. And I would like to take Missy out into the world, if I can. Just for lunch at least. You think Elena's going to have a problem with that?"

"She sure will," she said, her face reddening. "Last week I tried to talk to Elena. Missy had some kind of meltdown in the middle of the night and I was . . . scared for her. That's the only way to put it."

"What happened?" I asked breathily.

"She threw her computer out the window. That's what happened." I frowned, wondering what Melissa Brady might have seen on her computer screen that would make her want to eject the entire machine from her home. I had a fairly good idea what it was. "It was about three in the morning and I heard this crash. I went outside and there she was, whaling on that thing with a baseball bat."

"The computer?" I asked as if confused. I wasn't.

"Yeah. She was furious. I asked her what was wrong and she just gave me this crazy look. She told me the thing froze up on her and she got pissed. I know it wasn't the right thing to do, but I laughed. I mean, she was standing right over there on the lawn, her computer in pieces everywhere, apologizing to me for waking me up. Did she really think I was going to sleep through that?"

She looked at me as if she expected me to explain Melissa's behavior. "Does that sound like a meltdown to you?" she asked. "'Cause Elena didn't think so. When I told her about it, she said Missy was under a lot of stress—Danny being in Iraq for so long. I pointed out that Danny had been back for two months, and she just looked at me like I'd called her some kind of name."

"This is unbelievable," I said in a winded tone of voice that sounded somehow naïve, like the one my father always used when he was told of my mother's drunken antics. "When was this?"

"Thursday," she said. "Well, Friday morning, technically."

The night before Daniel Brady's suicide mission. The neighbor seemed to register this fact as well. I spoke again before she could get suspicious. "I should talk to her," I said, as if it were going to take all my nerve.

"Missy? I don't think that's going to do any good."

"No," I said firmly. "Elena."

The woman in front of me almost smiled.

Melissa's neighbor gave me the address of a three-story wood-shingled box that sat wall to wall with its neighbors, just three blocks from the beach. According to the call box, there was an Elena Castillo who lived on the second floor. A white Toyota Celica convertible was parked out front. I figured it was Elena Castillo's death trap and wrote the plate number down on my notepad.

The neighbor had also given me a story that confirmed my theory that Daniel Brady had been blackmailed. Melissa's long-term pill problem suggested that she might have had some idea of her husband's proclivities before she hurled her computer out the window.

I spent an hour sitting in my parked Jeep, hoping that Elena Castillo would leave the apartment so I could pay her new roommate a visit. Another thirty minutes went by before the building's entry door swung open. Elena Castillo emerged, wearing a black halter top, skintight running shorts, and wraparound sunglasses. Her copper-colored hair was pulled back in a ponytail that contrasted sharply with her dark skin. She turned her head in both directions with a look that would have frightened children off the sidewalk.

Melissa Brady emerged from the building a few seconds later. She stood about five-two and looked like she might blow away in a strong wind. A baseball cap was shoved down over her mop of honey blond hair, and huge sunglasses concealed the upper half of her face. She looked like a child star trying to avoid the paparazzi.

I followed them on foot, toward a wooden pier that protruded over the meager surf on a series of spider-thin legs. A miniature amusement park sat at the pier's entrance, with a small Ferris wheel and the kind of transportable rides you find at traveling fairs. Elena was talking a mile a minute. Melissa responded by occasionally brushing flyaway hairs from her forehead.

They took a paved walkway that zigzagged down to the beach. Melissa flounced down on a bench next to a small playground that had a swing set and a rubber-padded jungle gym. Elena launched into a series of stretches that looked more arduous than a ten-mile run, all without diverting her attention from the tiny woman sitting next to her.

Elena said something to Melissa. Melissa didn't respond. Elena waited. Melissa pulled off her hat and her sunglasses and set them on the bench next to her. Elena threw up her hands, then tried to cover for her frustration by running them through her hair. Her charge was showing defiance, and she was losing patience.

Elena shook her head in disgust, then stretched her calves for a second and broke into a sprint, her sneakers spitting up sand as she ran in the direction of the pier. I waited until she was a tiny dot traveling along the distant surf line. Then I descended the path.

I took a seat on the other end of the bench. Melissa didn't seem to notice me. She was too busy watching two toddler-age children scale the jungle gym in front of us. "I don't know why everyone calls it the terrible twos," she said suddenly to no one in particular. "Everything's so new to them at that age. There's nothing terrible about it."

"You have kids?" I asked.

Startled, she looked in my direction. Her hazel eyes were round and hazy. She studied me for several seconds, lines appearing at the corners of her mouth. I figured she could see my resemblance to her husband and I felt guilty for inflicting it on her.

"No," she said as if I had insulted her. Her eyes wandered past me, and her brow wrinkled. "My husband's dead," she said distantly, as if this new thought had just arrived on the wind.

"I'm sorry to hear that," I said. "But you could still have kids. Someday, right?"

"No," she said, shaking her head slowly. "I can't."

"Everything all right with your friend?" I asked.

It took some energy for her to draw her eyes back to mine.

"Sorry. I just noticed that little exchange," I said. "I kinda hung back 'cause I didn't want to intrude."

"This is a public beach," she said flatly.

I gave her a gentle smile. It made her eyes glaze and her lips purse. "You look like my husband," she said.

"Is that a good thing?"

"No."

She returned her attention to the playground. It was empty. The two kids who had been on the jungle gym were being herded down the bike path by their mother. Melissa watched their departure as if a shadow had fallen over us.

"I'm a homeless person," she said.

"Excuse me?"

"I said I talk to strangers now," she said. "Like a homeless person. You know?"

I thought she was more like a woman on several milligrams of Xanax, but I kept this insight to myself. Given how blunt she had been with me, I could have tried to hit her with the hard questions first. Instead, I decided to stick to my original plan.

I pulled out my wallet and removed the only photograph I had of Corey Howard. I had snapped the picture as he was lying on my love seat watching television. He was wearing jeans and a V-neck T-shirt and his typical stony expression made it appear as if he were watching news footage from 9/11.

Instead of telling the woman next to me that I knew her name, instead of doing anything that might make her think I was a reporter who had come to ask about her husband, I slid down the bench and showed her the picture.

"I'm looking for a friend of mine," I said. Her eyes fell to the picture in my hand and froze there. Her face remained blank. "I know he used to live down here, so I've just been asking around."

A slow transformation overtook her tiny face. The shock of recognition sparked there, but it was slowed and blurred by whatever medication was in her system. She closed her eyes, trying to fight off the few painful memories making it through the Xanax haze.

"That's Corey McCormick," she finally said.

"McCormick," I repeated for her. She didn't respond. "You said his last name was McCormick?"

She winced, screwing her eyes shut tighter, her breaths growing more rapid. "He's dead," she whispered.

"What?"

"He died of AIDS," she said quickly and flatly.

"Who told you that?" I asked, even though I thought I knew the answer already.

"Corey McCormick went to West Hollywood and died of AIDS," she said slowly, her head nodding slightly with each word. It sounded like she was mimicking the inflections of the person who had told her this lie.

"Who told you that?" I asked, trying to keep my voice steady.

Her eyes popped open. She saw that I was still leaning toward her and holding the picture up in front of her. "Please put that away," she told me in a hoarse tone.

As soon as I did what she asked, she gripped the back of the bench and pushed herself to her feet. I almost said her name before I remembered she hadn't given it to me.

"I'm sorry your friend is dead," she rasped. Then she hurried past me toward the beach.

I took the cue and jumped to my feet. I found myself standing eye to eye with Elena Castillo. Her chest was heaving, but she had barely broken a sweat on her run. Beyond her, Melissa was heading toward the ocean as if she had no plans for stopping. Her steps quickened and then slowed, then quickened again.

"Keep moving," Elena said. "She's not on the market right now."

"I need to talk to her," I said.

"Did you hear what I said?"

"You first!" I snapped.

She took a step back and raised an arm between us, pointing a trigger finger at my chest. "You better fucking cool it. Right now." Her voice came from her chest and her trigger finger looked stronger than my right arm.

"I'm gay, genius!"

I had hoped this information would get her to drop her guard. It didn't. It seemed to raise her suspicions even higher. Her jaw tensed. She lowered her hand to one side and it looked like she was getting ready to do something else with it. If she didn't know about the trip Daniel Brady had made to West Hollywood the week before, then she had some suspicions about the urges that had led him to make it.

"Get the fuck out of here."

"What's the matter with you?" I asked. "Is it a religious thing? Or maybe you're not that surprised that a gay guy wants to talk to Melissa right now?"

"Are you a reporter?" she demanded.

"No," I said, even though it felt like a lie.

"Is your daddy a reporter?"

"My father's a patent attorney," I said.

She hit me with an uppercut that slammed my bottom teeth into my top teeth. My world became the sky, and it was streaked with something that looked like microscope slides of skin cells. I felt my impact with the pavement several seconds after I knew it had taken place.

Then I felt Elena Castillo tugging at my pants pocket. She dropped my cell phone on my chest. "Call your daddy and tell him you just got hit by a girl."

Both women were gone by the time I got to my feet. I fell into a seat on the bench, my vision blurry, listening to the sound of my own rasping breaths above the dull roar of the nearby surf. I felt eyes on my back and looked up.

A shirtless guy in a backward baseball cap stared down at me from the sidewalk overhead. His eyes were hidden behind expensive Oakley sunglasses, and a battered skateboard rested under his right foot. His skin was the color of sandalwood and his well-defined chest had a sheen of sweat on it that looked camera-ready.

"You all right?" he called down to me.

I tried to smile. It felt like a grimace. "You see which way she went?" I asked.

"Naw. Sorry, dude," the guy said. He kicked the pavement with his left foot and went rolling off down the sidewalk. I watched his departure with an open mouth and a stirring in my chest. Maybe they were just the after-effects of Elena's uppercut, or maybe I was no different from every other gay man on the planet.

I called Jimmy from a chain restaurant next to Interstate 5. Bright sunlight flared off the roofs of cars speeding down the interstate. I had decided to hang back for a few hours to give Elena Castillo the impression that I had left Oceanside. Brenda answered and asked me why I was talking funny. I didn't tell her I had been hit by a girl, because I figured she would want to send the girl flowers. I did tell her what Melissa Brady's neighbor had shared with me.

"Corey went by another last name down here—McCormick," I told her.

"I know Jimmy had Dwight run Corey's name," she said. "Nothing came up. Maybe Mr. McCormick has a more interesting history than Mr. Howard."

"Jimmy didn't tell me he ran Corey's name."

"Yeah. Well. He didn't tell me you were going to Oceanside today either," she said. "Jimmy always gets this way in the middle of a project."

"How's that?"

"Distant," she said. "Jittery."

"So I guess he's being distant and jittery today?"

The waitress delivering my iced tea looked dubiously at the sunglasses I was wearing. I must have looked like an LA poseur calling his friends for directions back home. I went to take a sip of my iced tea and my jaw seized up.

"I thought we were going to try to get along," she said.

"I'd like that," I said.

"I didn't say we should like it. I just said we should try to get along."

Neither one of us said anything for several seconds.

"Feel like hearing the strange tale of Billy Hatfill and his English teacher?" she asked me.

Jimmy had asked for something concrete on Billy Hatfill and I had tossed this out just to appease him—and not only had he given the assignment to his wife, but she had apparently turned something up. "Sure," I said.

"I called the Rappaport School and spoke to their alumni director. When I said Billy's name, the woman sounded like she had passed a stone. I told her I worked for a charity organization and Billy had asked to do some work with us. Given all the controversy around Billy a few years ago, I thought I would check his references."

"Did it work?"

"What do you think? She gave me the name of an old drama teacher who hated Billy's guts."

"I'm listening," I said.

"Since it was pretty clear that nobody at Billy's alma mater liked him very much, I called the teacher and told her I wasn't interested in having Billy involved in my organization, but I gave her the impression that I wanted to feel justified in my decision. That got her talking. It turns out Billy did a lot of theater back in high school, and because his parents were big donors, this woman always had to give him a lead, even though he couldn't act for shit.

"Turns out she also suspected that Billy was trying to put the moves on a colleague of hers. A guy named Dan Braden. He taught English and directed some plays as well. The more she kept an eye on the two of them, the more it looked like they were up to something. Finally she said something to Dan Braden. She made it sound like a warning just to give her colleague the benefit of the doubt."

"And what happened?"

"Dan Braden turned the color of a milk carton and got defensive. Too defensive."

"Something was going on."

"That's what she thinks," Brenda said. "Then a couple of weeks later, Dan Braden was coming out of a gay bar at two in the morning when an *unknown assailant* beat the living shit out of him. He was in a coma for three weeks, and when he came to, he couldn't move the right side of his body."

Suddenly my aching jaw didn't seem like such a mortal injury. But Brenda wasn't finished. "To make matters even more interesting, Dan Braden claimed he couldn't remember a thing and seemed to have no interest in helping the NYPD find his attacker. As soon as he was released from the hospital, he left New York City without speaking to any of his old colleagues and has not set foot inside the Rappaport School to this day."

"So the drama teacher you talked to thinks Billy was behind the attack?" I asked.

"Yes," Brenda answered. "She assumed that Dan Braden broke off the affair after she mentioned it to him, and Billy went ballistic. But Dan Braden wouldn't return her calls, she had no proof, and Billy's parents paid for a new gym."

"Where's Dan Braden now?"

"I'm trying to locate him as we speak," she said. "The teacher had no clue. No one at the school's had contact with him. I've been searching through the archives of every New York newspaper, and I can't find anything about the attack. Looks like everybody thought it was just another gay bashing."

"Because that's what Dan Braden wanted them to think."

She grunted in agreement. I recalled Billy's casual mention of an affair with his English teacher, after I told him I knew some of his former classmates. He'd sounded proud of the affair, said he had no hard feelings about the relationship.

Jimmy was convinced that Billy was using me to free himself from the yoke of Joseph Spinotta. At dinner the night before, Billy had expressed a depth of disdain for his former sugar daddy that seemed to confirm that theory. By telling me that Joseph had been a practicing pedophile, Billy had turned his former sugar daddy from a white-collar criminal to a sexual predator. Had his casual mention of this older affair been an attempt to send me a message—that the older men in Billy's life walk away on Billy's terms?

I tried to picture a teenage Billy Hatfill beating the living shit out of a fully grown man. Even today, Billy didn't seem to have the chops for that kind of job. Like all spoiled brats, he had probably found someone else to do his dirty work.

Billy was determined that I meet with Martin Cale and I had agreed to go. Maybe my pursuit of Corey was just the bait, and Billy really intended for Martin Cale to tell me something about Billy's old sugar daddy that would whet my appetite as a so-called reporter to go after him. If that was the case, then I had already started to do Billy's dirty work for him.

My head was spinning. I was being manipulated by two different men: Corey, who had never told me he was a marine and left behind an empty apartment designed to look like a crime scene, and Billy Hatfill, who shared salacious tidbits of his past as if they were little more than self-deprecating revelations designed to elicit my sympathy.

Brenda had said my name a few times and I had answered with grunts. I told myself to focus and then said to Brenda that I had found a connection between Corey Howard and Daniel Brady.

She congratulated me. I was surprised.

I spent the next few hours circling Elena Castillo's neighborhood. She didn't emerge from her building. Despite the fact that she had tried to realign my facial features, Elena was my new target. She seemed to have firsthand knowledge of what had led Melissa to take comfort in a prescription bottle. She was also playing a role I was unfortunately familiar with: caretaker of a woman who held most of her conversations with the voices in her head.

My going theory was the obvious one. Corey and Daniel Brady had been lovers. Melissa had discovered their affair. Brady had used the threat of a discharge to drive Corey from the Marine Corps in a desperate attempt to please his wife and save his marriage. Flash-forward to an incriminating e-mail, an airborne computer, and a suicide flight that killed four other men as well as Brady. I needed more confirmation of this conjecture before I tried to connect it up with Corey's movements back in West Hollywood.

By three-thirty, there hadn't been a peep from Elena Castillo's apartment building and I was impatient. I parked two blocks from the building and fished a UCLA baseball cap out of my backseat. Clotted clouds moved in off the ocean, their underbellies steel gray with a load of rain they probably wouldn't deliver, but I donned my sunglasses anyway. The neighborhood was desolate. Most of its residents were probably still on base or otherwise at work. It was quiet enough to hear the surf a few blocks away.

I thought it was possible that Elena might have put Melissa to bed after our altercation on the beach. If so, I could knock on the door, tell Elena I had no hard feelings about her attitude or her right fist, and try to convince her that I had information that might salvage her friend's sanity.

I was half a block from the apartment building when I saw a flash of movement behind the gauze curtains in Elena's apartment. I forced myself to keep walking. Several yards ahead of me, a guy descended the front steps of the building directly across the street from Elena's. He clasped his cell phone shut and shoved it in his pocket. There was a skateboard under his right arm. He was wearing a blue polo shirt with the collar turned up, but I caught a glimpse of his Poco shell necklace.

Suddenly he was coming toward me with a determined gait and a toothy smile on his face. Just then I heard a car engine rev behind me. I glanced over my shoulder and saw a white Econoline van speeding toward us. I put two and two together too late to get a sum.

The skateboard's first blow sent me to my knees. I glimpsed a scraped wheel spinning madly in front of my nose as the skateboard was whipped back, then forward again. I kissed a piece of sidewalk lashed with my own blood, heard my agonized groan inside my temples.

My wrists were yanked behind my back. I heard the van screech to a halt and its side door fly open. I heard the driver pop out, sneakers squeaking against asphalt. He whispered fiercely to his comrade. I felt something thin and plastic encircle my linked wrists.

Then I heard a sharp hissing sound followed by a young man's pained cry. There was a scuffle of footsteps behind me. A van door slammed. My captor was yanked from behind my back and I saw only his sneakered feet fly upward as he was thrown to the pavement several feet away, with an impact hard enough to make me wince.

I heard a screech of rubber and managed to roll over onto my back.

Blood plugged my nostrils and greased my lips. I blinked away more blood and saw Elena Castillo holding my skateboard-wielding friend facedown on the pavement by the back of his neck. The plastic cuffs he had tried to tie around my wrists now snared his.

The white van swerved down the street and jumped the curb; then its tires slammed down onto the cross street one block away before it swerved out of sight. There was a can of Mace in Elena's left fist. I realized she must have used it on the driver.

Elena gave me a blazing look over one shoulder. Her ponytail was coming loose. "This guy's a kid!" she hissed. It took me a second to realize she was talking. "You want me to call the police?"

I shook my head and she glowered at me, confused. I tried to summon words and failed. Elena straightened. "Don't move, jackass. I mean it." She lifted the kid by his wrists and slammed him back to the pavement just to emphasize her point.

She knelt down over me, shaking her head and giving me a piteous look. "Who the fuck are you?" she said under her breath, with more concern in her voice than anger.

I coughed, trying to clear my throat of mucus and maybe blood. "That kid's boss is the reason Melissa threw her computer out the window last week," I croaked. "What do you say we take him inside? Ask him a few questions."

Her lips tensed and pulled back from her teeth, and from the look in her eye I could tell she didn't like any of her choices. "Does the name Corey Howard mean anything to you?"

"Corey . . ."

"Corey McCormick," I corrected myself.

She got to her feet, as if she needed to put some distance between herself and the name I had just spoken. "Corey was blackmailing Danny?" she asked.

"Sort of."

"Get up."

Elena's apartment had a large living room with a picture window that, fortunately for me, looked out onto the street. Above a white sectional sofa with torn stitching was a massive portrait depicting a handsome Latina woman reclining on a white chaise longue in a white pants suit with a shock of white in her cascade of black hair.

I walked my skateboard-wielding friend to the butcher-block table, pulled his cuffed wrists behind one of the chairs, and sat him down. Elena was in the kitchen frantically preparing an ice packet. I wasn't sure which one of us it was for. The kid's right eye would be swollen shut in a few hours. His top lip was busted, but the blood had already dried. I hadn't managed to check myself out in a mirror.

Elena returned and thrust a Ziploc bag full of ice cubes at me. I took it and stared at her. She pointed to her right temple and I followed her cue. I heard a dull whir and realized it wasn't coming from my head but from a white noise machine behind the closed door at the end of the apartment's hallway. Melissa Brady's desire to shut out reality included appliances as well as prescriptions.

I reached behind the kid's back and dug in his back pocket for a wallet. He squirmed and groaned in his throat. "Let me see your ID," I said.

He mumbled something, and I asked him to repeat it. "My sock," he muttered, kicking his right foot against the floor. I pulled out a credible-looking ID that told me his name was Philip Percy, that he was twenty-three years old and lived in Westlake Village.

"Your real ID," I said. I squatted in front of the kid. Up close, I could see his soft adolescent facial features: a dull jaw that would harden in a few years, naturally smooth skin, and a small rounded nose. But he was tall and built, just like the guy who had been following Nate the night before.

"Glenn has it."

"Glenn was driving the van?" I asked. Elena tried to cut in. I held up my palm to stop her. "Where is Glenn going right now?"

The kid didn't answer.

"You work for Scott Koffler, don't you?" I asked him.

His eyes drifted shut and he sucked in his lower lip. I sank down into his level. "I know how Scott works, all right?" I said as sympathetically as I could. "I know the minute he gets you in his hot tub he starts feeding you a line about how you need his protection. 'Cause, after all, if the kids back at school find out you've been going to parties in West Hollywood with a bunch of fags, then your life is over, right? Your new friends may be rich, they may even be famous, but they're still fags."

"Fuck you," the kid whispered.

"I need to know what's going on!" Elena shouted. "Right now."

I looked at her. "Daniel Brady made a trip to West Hollywood last week. This kid's boss was his escort, and I think the guy took some photographs that he e-mailed to Melissa on Friday night."

The breath went out of her. "Jesus."

"Does any of this make sense to you?" I asked.

"Not enough."

A portable phone sat in its cradle on the kitchen counter, with a second handset on the end table next to the sofa. I grabbed one and handed it to Elena. Then I turned to the kid, holding the phone up between us as if it were a weapon. "We're going to call your boss right now," I said.

"Oh, yeah?" the kid rasped.

"Or else I'll call the police and everyone back at school will find out why you were arrested and who your new friends are."

His bruised lips sputtered. I gave him another minute for my threat to sink in. When I asked, he said Scott was at home in Palmdale, and I told him what to say when I put the phone to his ear. I dialed the number the kid gave me. I turned and saw that Elena had already brought her handset to her ear, her eyes fixed fiercely on mine.

After two rings, someone answered without speaking. I put the phone to the kid's ear. "I'm so sorry, Scott," the kid whined. "Everything went wrong. I'm so sorry."

I jerked the phone away from the kid's face and brought it to mine. "You sent two teenagers to abduct me in broad daylight," I said.

I heard nothing but silence and maybe breathing from the other end.

"You've fucked up twice now, Scott. Your little stunt with Nate Bain put me right on your fat ass. Now you sent these two kids to abduct me. One of them's right here and ready to wet his pants."

"They were supposed to *escort* you."

"To where?"

"I thought you and I should talk," he said. I said nothing, to lead him to say more. "You've got nothing on me with Philip there. You know what I do, Adam. It's rewarding, but there are risks involved. That's why I make sure I always have an insurance policy. It's very simple. I take pictures. And there are two people in every one. Both people have reputations to protect. Including little Philip."

"You blackmail your own customers?" I said.

"I haven't had to. Yet."

Considering that Koffler furnished his young charges with fake IDs that said they were of age, it wasn't blackmail we were talking about. It was extortion.

"Did you *blackmail* Daniel Brady?" I asked.

Silence. I looked to Elena. She was hunched forward over the table, the phone to her ear. She shoved her bangs up with one palm.

"Why don't we meet?" Koffler asked.

"Give me something first."

"One A.M.," he said flatly. "Plummer Park, just off Fountain."

"Who hired you to bring Daniel Brady to West Hollywood?" I didn't expect him to answer, but I hoped he would say something that would convince Elena Castillo that I was telling her the truth. I was confident that it was Billy Hatfill who had hired him on Corey's behalf.

"You got me fired," I said. "You came to my apartment and said shit about my mother. You're having Nate Bain followed, and today you tried to have these kids beat the shit out of me. Daniel Brady was a special job for you. And you're scared shitless that your boss is going to find out that you exposed him while he was in West Hollywood."

"Let Philip go," he said.

"Who hired you, Scott?"

"You first," he said. "Where the hell is he? I haven't been paid."

My throat closed up and I had to focus on my feet to remind myself where I was. Jimmy's problem with my new theory had been that he didn't believe Billy Hatfill would hire a loser like Scott Koffler. Jimmy was right. I cursed myself for not having seen it sooner.

"Corey hired you," I heard myself say.

"Super Twink, Mr. Star Reporter, scores again," Scott murmured. "But that's just the half of it. Tell Philip to call me in ten minutes, and I'll see you tonight."

I put the phone to the kid's ear and told him to repeat the instruction Koffler had just given me. He did, his voice trembling. I brought the phone to my ear. Koffler had hung up.

Elena held her head in both hands.

I went into the kitchen and got a meat cleaver. Elena Castillo didn't move an inch as I sawed the plastic cuffs from the kid's wrists. It took more work than I expected, and after several minutes I felt like a cross between a psychopath and a jackass.

I replaced the cut cuffs with my own grip and walked the kid to the front door. I kicked it open and shoved him through, the cleaver raised at my side in case he made any sudden moves.

He turned, a stupid confidence returning to him now that he was an inch outside of the apartment. "I would have told them you tried to fuck me," he informed me.

"You're going to be fucked for the rest of your life, Philip."

I closed the door on him. I watched through the peephole as he flew down the front steps and out of the building.

CHAPTER 11

I took a seat across from Elena Castillo at the butcher-block table. She stared expressionlessly at the table as she pulled a pack of cigarettes from her jeans pocket and lit one. There was a small glass ashtray on the kitchen counter. I got it for her.

"She said they had a fight," Elena said. "She said they had a fight the morning he went out. That's all."

I had expected her to lace into me for letting the kid go, but it seemed as if the events Scott Koffler had spoken of had slugged the breath as well as the anger out of her. "You really gonna meet with that guy?"

I needed to steer her back to safer ground if I was going to gain access to Melissa. "How long have you and Melissa been friends?"

"Since high school," she said. "They called us the Stepford Bitches. It was me, Melissa, and this girl Caitlin. Caitlin went off to school in New York, and when she came back she wasn't Caitlin anymore. Missy moved down here to become a marine's wife and I went to Oxnard so I could find out what divorce is like before I hit forty."

She didn't return my smile. "Melissa used to be my rock," she said. "My husband didn't even tell me he was leaving me. I came home one day and the apartment was totally empty. Afterwards I came down here. She was going to support me. Emotionally, I mean."

"How long ago did you move down here?"

"Two years," she said.

"Was Corey McCormick still in their lives then?"

She shook her head. "Missy mentioned him. She said he and Danny used to be friends, but then Corey came out of the closet and left the marines. Then she told me—"

"He went to West Hollywood and died of AIDS," I finished for her.

"Obviously, that didn't happen, right?" she asked. "That guy . . ."

"His name is Scott Koffler."

"He said Corey's missing."

"He went missing the day after Danny came to West Hollywood."

"You're trying to find him?" she asked. "Missy said you showed her his picture."

"I'm trying to find out what he did before he left," I said, averting my eyes. "If that leads to him, then so be it."

I got up from the table and asked her if she wanted anything to drink. She answered by staring at me. "Were you his boyfriend or something?"

"Something. Yeah." I didn't know what else I could say to persuade her. "I need to talk her, Elena."

"You need to, huh?"

"I want to," I said.

She rubbed at her eyelids with a thumb and forefinger. "Don't give me some bullshit about the truth setting you free," she said. "She knows the truth and she's not free. She's been in that bedroom ever since I brought her here. The only way the truth can set you free is if you give it to someone else and they do something with it. Something good."

I heard the challenge. It took me several minutes to decide how I should rise to it. "The Marine Corps is conducting its own investigation into the crash, right?"

"Yeah."

"Has Melissa given a statement yet?"

"Not yet."

"The Armed Services' policy on homosexuality makes gay service members susceptible to blackmail."

"You think she should make this political? Danny killed four men. The other wives turned their backs on Melissa at the memorial service on Monday morning. You think she can change any of that by getting up there and saying that Danny was a—"

I cut her off before the word *fag* could come out of her mouth. "She can't change any of it, Elena. She can only change what she says."

Elena went to the living room window. The slanting sunlight turned the gauze curtains opaque and gave her copper-colored hair a bright halo. "She can also change her prescriptions every now and then, I guess," Elena said bitterly. When she turned to face me, I got the sense that she had settled an argument she was having with herself.

"You have to ask her a question for me, too," she said. "You have to ask her why a perfectly healthy, beautiful twenty-seven-year-old would get her tubes tied."

I waited outside the open door to Melissa's bedroom as Elena went inside. In the milky light, I saw cardboard boxes inside, stacked three high against one wall, their bottoms bulging. Obviously Melissa had no plans to return to the apartment she had shared with her husband. A Vornado fan stood at the foot of the bed, its dull rush accompanying the roar of the white noise machine on the nightstand.

Melissa Brady slept flat on her back beneath a smooth sea of comforter. It was clear that she hadn't moved much during her slumber and didn't plan to start. From the nightstand drawer, Elena pulled out a plastic pill case, the kind with a slot for each day of the week. The slot for that day was almost empty. Elena pulled a red pill from the slot for the next day and the one after.

Elena smoothed Melissa's hair from her forehead. The woman didn't stir. I felt like I was intruding upon a moment between lovers, so I withdrew to the living room. I heard whispers coming from the bedroom. Several minutes later, a shower started running.

Corey had hired Scott Koffler himself. I tried to absorb this fact. Billy Hatfill had not been the go-between, as I had suspected. I remembered Jimmy's assertion from the night before: If Corey had needed Billy Hatfill to carry out his revenge, that meant Billy had provided something essential to the plan.

I heard shuffling behind me. Melissa Brady's damp hair hung flat and straight down the back of her head. She wore a baby-blue bathrobe and matching slippers. She reacted to the sight of me just as she had reacted to Corey's photograph that afternoon.

She screwed her eyes shut and spun away from me. Elena blocked her path. When Elena gripped her right shoulder, Melissa batted her arm away with surprising force. "No!" Elena seized Melissa by both biceps and held her in place. The dam on her anger had burst and I could see it flooding her eyes, filling her throat. "This isn't working, okay?" Elena hissed to her. "It's just not working and I'm tired of it!"

Melissa's entire body quivered. Sobs exploded out of her. Elena pulled the other woman's shaking body to her, but her own stance was rigid; all she was doing was holding Melissa in place.

"Melissa?" I asked.

Her sobs abated.

"How long has it been since you've seen Corey McCormick?"

Melissa muttered something I couldn't make out. "Four years," Elena said.

"Do you know why he left the Marine Corps?"

Melissa turned sharply to face me. Her robe fell open, revealing a pair of men's boxer shorts and a moth-eaten V-neck T-shirt underneath. Her eyes were wild—whatever pills Elena had given her were coursing through her system.

"We were friends, all right?" she yelled at me, her voice thick. "The three of us. Me, Danny, and Corey!

"We used to hang out together all the time. Danny and I were engaged. We used to joke that Corey was like our son, even though he was only two years younger. Still, it was like he was a kid sometimes. And Danny tried to help him out with stuff."

"What kind of stuff?"

"Corey ran away from home when he was sixteen. Danny was a foster kid, but he had managed to make a life for himself. A *good* one! He wanted to show Corey how to do it." Her face wrinkled and her sobs crumpled her mouth.

I gave her a little time to catch her breath. "What happened?" I asked.

"Danny was . . . acting weird, all right? I thought he was just nervous about getting married. But he was . . . disappearing."

"What do you mean?"

"He'd go off by himself and wouldn't come back for, like, a whole day," she said, her words coming out in a rush, without a breath in between. "Corey said it was drugs. Corey's mother, she was a meth addict or something. She went to prison. He said if it was drugs we had to do something. He said we had to save Danny."

I flashed on the tableau of my bloodied drug dealer lying facedown on the floor of his apartment, saw Corey rifling through my bookshelves in the middle of the night as he searched for my stash.

"I was *scared*," Melissa wailed. "I didn't know what to do." She managed to still herself. "I asked Corey to follow him."

"What happened?" I asked, working to keep my voice composed as well.

I watched Melissa travel out of her body and out of the room. She lowered her head and gazed between the toes of her baby-blue slippers.

"Corey followed him for two days," she said, suddenly sounding drowsy.

"He said that Danny got a motel room in San Diego. He said Danny kept going to playgrounds."

I saw where this headed. It was clear from the blank expression on her face that Elena Castillo did not.

"He said that Danny would go in the bathrooms, like he was . . . checking them out, you know? Then he'd go to another playground and do the same thing. Then he'd sit on a bench and watch the kids. He didn't do anything, but Corey said . . ."

Words failed her. Elena brought one hand to her chest as she leaned the back of her head against the wall, her face grim.

"What, Melissa?" I finally asked. "What did Corey say?"

"He said it looked like Danny was *planning* something."

I met Elena's eyes briefly. I wanted to tell Elena that Melissa had just told her why she had her tubes tied at the age of twenty-seven.

"I thought he was lying," Melissa said in a tiny voice.

"Corey?"

She nodded. "I knew Corey wasn't interested in women—that was why he spent so much time with us. I never thought he was in love with Danny. Not until he started saying that shit. I thought Corey was trying to break us up. I didn't think it was true." Her now-wild eyes met mine. "I thought Corey was *lying!*"

Elena flinched, and I had to work not to. The agony in Melissa's voice told me that she had since learned Corey had told her the truth.

"What did you say to Corey?"

Her eyes drifted shut, forcing tears down her flaming cheeks. "I told him he had to leave."

Then her gaze grew suddenly fierce and defiant. "I told him that if he ever came back to Oceanside, I would file a report with his commanding officer. I told him he could either go AWOL or have the words *discharged for homosexual acts* stamped on every piece of paper that had his name on it for the rest of his life."

She had channeled a four-year-old rage and filled the living room with it. She had no idea that for me, she had just damned herself, and for a brief instant I wanted to prove this fact to her by throwing her across the room. Then I realized that I was reacting as Corey must have: He had wanted to punish the woman standing in front of me as much as he had wanted to punish her husband. She was the one who had snatched away what was probably the only stable and meaningful life he'd ever known. "*Did* Corey love him, Melissa?" I asked.

The question threw her. It looked as if she had listened to an echo of what she'd just said and hated the sound of it.

"Did you have any proof that Corey was in love with your husband?" I asked.

"No," she said with what I decided was both petulance and shame.

After having been threatened with a discharge, Corey could have made a preemptive strike against Daniel Brady and filed a complaint of his own. It sounded like Corey didn't have any hard proof that Daniel Brady had molested children, but if the two men had a sexual history together, Corey could have used that to strike back at the woman who had threatened to take his life away. But he hadn't done that.

Daniel Brady had not been Corey's lover. He had been his mentor and his guide. Corey had done nothing more than obey Melissa's instructions; he had followed Daniel Brady and reported back to Melissa on what he had seen. If the relationship among the three of them had been as strong as Melissa said it was, I couldn't see why Corey would have concocted this story.

The sudden surge of sympathy I felt for Corey made me want to run from the room. I felt compelled to choose between Melissa's pain or Corey's vengeful rage. I tried not to choose at all, tried to keep my breaths steady. I had to get to the end of the story.

"You know Corey wasn't lying," I finally said. "You know that now. Don't you, Melissa?"

Melissa crossed her arms over her stomach, her jaw quivering.

"Why did you throw your computer out the window?"

"It was a movie. It started playing the minute I opened it. I couldn't get to it to stop. There was a little boy . . ."

"How little?" I heard myself ask.

"I don't know," she whispered. "Twelve. Thirteen, maybe."

Too young for the boy to have been one of Scott Koffler's young charges. A cold acid roiled my stomach. I tried to absorb the information she was giving me without putting it together too quickly. I didn't want to get distracted.

She continued. "He was drugged . . . the boy. Someone held his face up for the camera by the back of his hair." Melissa went to demonstrate the motion on her own hair, but stopped, screwing her eyes shut, summoning the strength to continue. "There was a white background, a bedsheet, and it was taped to something, I could tell . . . There were some pillows on the floor."

She gestured weakly in the air in front of her and fell silent again. Elena remained leaning against the wall, her back to us, her head bowed; it was clear that she was listening as intently as I was.

"Then Danny came in," she said. "He was wearing a mask, but I could tell it was him. He didn't . . . have any *pants* on. He was wearing this leather jacket . . . It was him. I knew it was him. I could *see* . . ." She didn't have to tell me what part of her husband's body she was referring to.

"What kind of mask?" I asked.

"Uh . . . black. Leather, I think. It had this big smile on it."

Elena turned on her heel. Before I had time to blink, the front door to the apartment had slammed and the hallway behind Melissa was empty. Melissa didn't seem to notice her friend's sudden departure.

"And the boy?" I asked. "What did he look like?"

Her eyes met mine. "He looked like an angel," she gasped.

"What color hair?" I asked sharply. "His eyes?"

"Blond. Bright blond. Like it was bleached. His eyes were closed. I told you. He was drugged. He had a round face. . . . He was *clean*." This last detail seemed to baffle her.

"Was there any message in the e-mail?" I asked, surprised by how steady my voice sounded. "Any words at all?"

She shook her head.

"Where's the computer?" I asked. "What's left of it, I mean."

"I threw it away."

I couldn't hide my reaction to this news.

"I'm sorry," she whispered.

"The morning Danny died," I said. "You guys had a fight."

"I told him," she said weakly. "I told him what I had seen. He didn't say anything. He just left. I knew he wasn't coming back."

She turned away from me and her left leg knocked into one of the dining room chairs. It was a small impact, barely enough to jostle the chair, but it sent her butt-first to the carpet. Now her sobs erupted without sentences to stanch them.

I went over and brought her to her feet, feeling helpless without Elena Castillo to guide me. I walked her down the hallway to her bedroom and pulled the comforter back on the bed. She fell onto the bed without removing her robe, and I brought the comforter up over her.

I stood next to the bed until her sobs subsided, thinking about Nate Bain, wondering if it was my mission to stand at the bedsides of those whose attempts to protect themselves from the truth had left them defenseless.

"Tell him I'm sorry," she finally whispered. "If you find him, tell him I'm sorry."

"The boy?" I asked.

"No," she said, turning to face me. "Corey. Tell him he was right."

She did not have the slightest suspicion that Corey had produced the movie she had been forced to watch part of against her will. I couldn't bring myself to tell her. Elena Castillo knew, and that was enough for the time being.

I left the room.

I found Elena Castillo sitting on the same wooden bench where I'd first met Melissa, staring out at the ocean. Her eyes were dry and her hands rested limply on her lap. A heavy cloudbank on the horizon was making for an early dusk. A few persistent surfers bobbed in the meager whitecaps.

"She needs to go to the police," I said. "I can lead her to Scott Koffler. I've got an eyewitness that puts Danny with Koffler in West Hollywood last Wednesday night. But I can't lead her to Corey. Not yet. I don't have enough."

"She didn't even suspect Corey?" she asked with disgust in her voice.

I couldn't answer; I had been just as surprised by this as she was. "Who's going to believe her?" Elena finally asked.

"I believe her."

"Great," she whispered. "She knew Corey was telling her the truth. She knows she harbored a pedophile for four years. Who knows what Danny was doing to other kids."

She leaned forward, resting her elbows on her knees, and looked abstractedly at the sun vanishing behind a thick line of shadowed clouds.

"She thought they were going to stay together forever. That's why she got her tubes tied. She was afraid of what he'd do to their kids, but she didn't want to leave him."

The disgust in her voice had turned into a kind of breathy amazement.

"That fucking Philip knows where I live," she said suddenly. She got to her feet and brushed herself off. "I've got an uncle down in San Diego. Maybe I'll stay with him for a few weeks."

"Take her with you."

"No thanks."

"Elena, think about this one," I said, trying to put the force of my experience in my words. "Think about this one real hard."

She straightened up and gave me a piercing dismissive look.

"I'm meeting with Scott Koffler tonight," I said. "Let me see what I can get out of him."

Elena Castillo sighed and resignedly gave me her cell phone number. Then she brushed past me without a proper goodbye. I stared after her until I was sure that she was walking in the direction of her apartment building.

CHAPTER 12

I drove for an hour before I noticed that the skateboard's wheel had left me with a navy-blue bruise that extended up the bridge of my nose from just below my right eye. Even as I examined it in the rearview mirror, it seemed to belong to someone else.

It was eight-thirty by the time I made it to Jimmy's house. Brenda was walking toward Jimmy's office as I approached. When she got a good look at my face, she asked me if I wanted some kind of pain pill I had never heard of. I didn't respond. We walked into Jimmy's office together. I was surprised when I felt her hand come to rest on my back, as if she worried I might fall over backward.

The look Jimmy gave me was both fixed and alarmed. I briefed him on everything that had taken place that afternoon, my face aching as I moved my jaw. Brenda sat slouched in the Eames chair next to mine, hanging on my every word.

"Thirteen," Jimmy muttered. "What's the difference between seventeen and thirteen?"

"Puberty," Brenda said.

No one said anything else for a while. It was Jimmy who broke the silence. "A handler displays the kid for the camera, holds him up by the back of the hair, makes it clear that he's been drugged. There's a white backdrop. Brady's been dressed in a leather jacket and a black mask to conceal his identity. According to Melissa, the kid is *clean*. Groomed. Prepared."

He let these details hang in the air. "We're not talking about a night vision camera tucked behind a bookcase. This is not a simple blackmail video. This is a full-on video production—and a production requires an audience. A paying audience."

A paying audience. These words stopped my breath and made Brenda shift in her seat. I waited for Jimmy to comment on how high the stakes had just become if his theory was correct, but he continued in a voice that lacked anything that sounded like fear or disgust. "We know that Corey hired Scott Koffler on his own. We know that Corey went to Billy Hatfill and threatened him. We also know that Scott Koffler provided transport. But he probably didn't get the kid. The kid's too young. So what did Billy Hatfill bring to this whole equation?"

"The kid," I answered.

"Yep," he answered. "What does Billy Hatfill also have in his possession? Somewhere out there."

"Joseph Spinotta," Brenda answered.

"And what did Joseph Spinotta bring to this?" Jimmy asked. "He brought the kid—and he brought the paying customers."

"You think Spinotta's operating a child porn ring from wherever he's hiding?" I asked.

"Yes," he said. "And I think Corey's uncle is one of his paying customers, and that's how Corey found out about this entire operation. Once he did, he decided to use it to his advantage. To get revenge on his old pal Daniel Brady. To broadcast Daniel Brady's disease to the widest audience available."

The three of us pondered this scenario. Then Brenda asked, "How did they get Brady to wear the mask? Isn't that a dead giveaway that he's being filmed?"

"No," Jimmy replied. "Koffler tells Brady that the mask is for his protection in case the drugs wear off and the kid wakes up."

"And the white backdrop?" Brenda asked.

"Who knows what kind of room they were in," Jimmy said. "The whole room could have been white for all we know."

I raised my hand. Jimmy furrowed his brow and pointed at me.

"This isn't it, Jimmy," I said.

"Excuse me?"

"No one would be able to tell who Brady was besides his wife," I said. "What kind of revenge is that?"

"The revenge is that they let Brady know," Jimmy said quickly, defensively. "They tell Brady that his little night with a thirteen-year-old has gone—"

"They didn't let Brady know," I said. "It was sent to Melissa's account and not her husband's. She said the e-mail didn't come with any message attached. There was nothing about a child porn ring. Nothing about anyone else seeing it besides her."

Jimmy reddened and slouched back in his chair.

"I don't even think it was Daniel Brady that Corey wanted to get back at," I said. "I think it was Melissa. Melissa was the one who threatened him. Melissa was the one who forced him to go AWOL. If this video really went out to a wider audience, why would Corey leave out that fact? It would be too good. It would be the ultimate punishment."

Jimmy bowed his head and rubbed at his forehead with the heel of one palm. "It doesn't matter," he said. "We're done."

"*What?*" I shouted.

"You heard me," he said. "Horny teenagers who can't legally consent are one thing. This shit is another. I don't do child molesters. I've never written about them before, and I'm not going to start now."

I realized I was standing. Brenda was giving me a narrow look, but it appeared to contain her muted version of sympathy. She had known this was coming. My mouth moved, but I couldn't summon anything more than a surprised snort.

Jimmy pushed himself to his feet. "I'll go to the goddamn cops myself if Melissa Brady doesn't drag her ass out of that apartment."

"Fine," I said, hating the desperate tone of my voice. "We go to the cops. But, Jimmy, that doesn't mean it's over. We still don't have anything concrete that connects Corey to—"

"Adam, it doesn't matter!" Jimmy barked. "This is over. Tomorrow morning you and I start on something else. Something that doesn't involve one of your friends. Something we don't have to *solve*, for Christ's sake. I need a book, not a medal!"

"This is bullshit!"

He turned a trigger finger on my chest. "You want to know why that kid in the video wasn't masked? Because revealing his identity was not a risk! That means the kid is out of circulation!"

He let this sit. I hadn't thought of murder.

"I'm done! And so are you!"

"So I let Dwight Zachary look for the kid," I said. "That doesn't mean I can't—"

"Yes, it does," he said, in a voice that came from deep in his chest. "This is it. I'm pulling the plug."

"You can't pull the plug, Jimmy. You didn't invent these people!"

"Oh, don't bore me with that Psych 101 shit!" he roared. "For the first time in your life, just shut up and do what you're told—and you might not end up with a hangover and a nosebleed!"

Jimmy charged across the office as fast as his cane would take him. He flung open the door. I listened to Jimmy's hurried footsteps across the flagstones outside. I heard Brenda say my name in a mollifying tone of voice. She said it again louder as I strode out of the office.

I saw Jimmy slip inside the back door of the main house. I went in right after him. For a second, I mistook the sound of my pulse for my own footsteps.

When I entered the living room, he had just taken a seat on the leather sofa. He ignored me and pressed a button on the remote in his hand. The TiVo welcome filled the television's massive screen.

"How dare you talk to me like that, you pompous asshole!" I burst out. "I spent the last week laying my personal shit out for you on a silver platter so you could have another best seller. So you could get yourself out of whatever kind of midlife crisis falls on spoiled, best-selling writers who have too much yard to get lost in!"

"Who said this is going to be a best seller?" he asked.

"You write a novel that lures a murderer to your house, to your bedroom, and then you pull this shit on me about being afraid! I go down to Oceanside and have the kind of day I had today for you and for *your* book, and then I come back here and you talk to me like I'm your fucking D-girl!"

His eyes stayed fixed on the screen behind me. He started flipping through the TiVo menu. Every time he pressed a button, the TV made a sound like a cartoon water drop hitting a piece of cartoon cement.

"Who do you think you are?" I shouted. "No, who do you think *I* am— that I would put up with this bullshit from you? I've slept three hours this week while you kicked back watching *City Confidential* and spinning a bunch of theories. When I have a problem with one of them, you flip out and pull the plug."

I knocked the remote out of his hand. Jimmy and I watched it spin across the tiles into the foyer.

James Wilton's entire body sagged with something that looked like defeat. I felt a cold flood of shame that drowned my anger, the same feeling I would experience when I realized that I was out of cocaine and the sun was up and it was time for me to enter another day as just another drug addict.

Suddenly Jimmy was giving me a frank stare. I could see that I had wounded him, and I had to blink tears from my eyes.

"I was wrong," he finally said. "I thought Billy was using you to free himself of Spinotta. I thought that was why Billy was helping you. But I was wrong."

"How?"

"Christ, Adam. You tell me in exquisite detail how Billy Hatfill says he despises you. Billy Hatfill picks you up off a street corner two days after Corey goes missing. He plants the story in your head that Corey came to his house to talk about *you*. He guarantees that you come to him the minute you find out Corey is missing. He gives you a meeting with Martin Cale five minutes after you get there."

"I know."

"No, you don't," he groaned. "You've been using words like setup, revenge. Blackmail. Rage. Lover. Are you even hearing yourself?" He let this sink in. "*You're* the one being set up, Adam. Whatever this deal was between Corey Howard and Billy Hatfill, it wasn't simple blackmail, and it wasn't just about Daniel Brady. Whatever dirt Corey had on Billy, it got the conversation started. Maybe. But those two men *did* talk about you that night. And they made a deal."

He gave me a few seconds to absorb this.

"It was a trade-off," he said. "Corey got Brady. And Billy got you."

"You're saying Corey gave Billy something on me?" I finally asked.

"I don't know what," he said. "And what really scares the shit out of me is that I don't think you know either. But if you go out to Martin Cale's yacht, you're going to find out."

Jimmy didn't have to get any more specific. I had spent the past year of my life in LA as a blackout drunk. I stared down at the Oriental rug and tried to convince myself that my feet were planted on it. I took a deep breath that my lungs seemed to have no use for.

"So what am I supposed to do, little man?" he asked. "If I ask you not to go to Cale's yacht, you'll lie to me and go anyway. If I tell you not to go to Cale's yacht, you'll quit. So maybe I'm showing you a little more respect than you think."

I barely heard his words. I was too busy running through every blackout, trying to summon the mornings afterward, the surrounding particulars of my shame and degradation. Blackouts like the one I had drunk myself into the previous Wednesday night.

The same night Daniel Brady had been in West Hollywood.

The same night a thirteen-year-old boy had been in West Hollywood. Jimmy broke the silence. "You bleed judgments," he said. I realized he was quoting Billy Hatfill. "You leave a trail of them wherever you go. You're going to *drown* in them someday."

The next thing I knew, the gravel on the side path was spitting out from under my feet as Jimmy called out to me from what sounded like a great distance. Then I was behind the wheel of my Jeep, weaving down Laurel Canyon through low-hanging tree branches turned to dangling skeletons by the pulse of headlights.

Out of the corner of my eye, I glimpsed my mother sitting in the passenger seat next to me. Her purse rested on her lap, and when she said my name, her mild Cajun accent put the emphasis on the second syllable instead of the first. She crossed one leg over the other, and her floral print dress slid back over her thigh, revealing a varicose vein.

I punched the radio on and chased my mother's ghost from the car with a blast of rock music. I didn't hallucinate when I was high; I wasn't going to start doing it sober.

When I was twelve years old, my sister and I were swimming at her friend's pool when, without warning, Candace swam under me and tried to put me on her shoulders. I remember the sudden rush of movement around my legs. I felt her hands trying to find a grip on my thighs as I rocketed up out of the water. I remember hurtling through the air, seeing only oak branches and blue sky and then the flagstone deck rushing up to meet me. I have to take Candace's word on everything that came after.

That afternoon, even though I was as white as an eggshell, I sprang to my feet and started walking toward the house. When Candace tried to block me, I gave her a lazy and bemused smile that sent a chill up her spine, walked a few steps past her, and collapsed. For months afterwards, Candace called me Dead Walker.

Now I felt like Dead Walker again, a creature seeking only to move, without the sense to know that the life had been knocked out of him.

An hour and a half after I got home, I stopped pacing my apartment and pulled my desk chair out onto my tiny balcony. The night was so clear I could make out the winking running lights of jets coming in for a landing at LAX. Every few seconds they disappeared behind the twinkling humpback of Baldwin Hills. At ten to eleven, a familiar-looking Ford Explorer turned onto my street. It pulled to a stop right behind my parked Jeep, and Brenda Wilton stepped out. "You got a parking permit for me?" she called up to me with a smile.

I just stared at her.

"We've got a date tonight," she said. "Plummer Park. One A.M., remember?"

I found my parking permit in my desk drawer and threw it down to her. She thanked me loudly. Soon I was standing in the kitchen as she rooted through my fridge.

"You should really get some juice or something," she said. "All you've got is coffee and water, which cancel each other out." She straightened and turned around, which allowed me to see the strange bulge against her right hip, just above the waistband of her black slacks.

"Got any movies?" she asked.

I made a vague gesture toward the entertainment center. She placed her hands on her hips and frowned at me. "He doesn't think you did what Daniel Brady did. No matter how drunk you were."

I was tempted to tell her that in alcoholic blackouts I had urinated on bars, called members of racial minorities by hateful epithets, and started small fires in other people's apartments. "What makes him so sure?" I asked. "He's known me less than a week."

"He says it's not your truth," she answered.

"What does that mean?"

"He says you go for strong, domineering men. So you can win them over or something. He said you like to be controlled for a little while, and then you get tired of it and move on. Nothing about that fits with . . ." She waved a hand in the air to finish the sentence.

"Maybe I flipped," I said.

Her jaw hardened. "Maybe the fact that you're so willing to believe you did something like that is the real problem, *little man*." Her words settled heavily in my chest. "You only find faith when you need it. You need it, so find some."

She sat down on the love seat and crossed her ankles on the coffee table. "You have TiVo?"

When I just stood there, she gave me her full attention. "He thinks it's something you did in New Orleans, maybe. He says this Scott Koffler character already set you off with something some bartender down in the French Quarter told him. Maybe the guy gave him something else."

I bowed my head, and I heard her let out a long sigh. "On the morning of nine-eleven, Jimmy spent twenty minutes trying to convince me that those planes were flown by white supremacists who wanted to avenge the execution of Timothy McVeigh. He's not right about everything. He's had a run of good luck lately, maybe because you guys are dealing with a bunch of twenty-year-olds who took all their major life lessons from video games and movies. But don't tell him I said that."

"I won't."

"Look, I'm just saying Jimmy's imagination's been burning like a brush fire, and you've been following along, collecting the real stuff out of the debris. Maybe this time it's burning too hot."

"I should have knocked on my neighbors' doors when I got home," I said, my voice thick. "I should have given them a description of Corey and Koffler and asked them if either one of them was here last Wednesday night. Maybe I should have given them a description of the boy, too. But I couldn't."

Brenda Wilton was the last person I wanted to cry in front of, but I didn't have a say in the matter.

"I quit drinking because I hadn't wrapped my car around a tree," I managed to get out. "I hadn't gone to jail. I hadn't run over anyone in a crosswalk. Now Jimmy thinks I might have done something even worse. Forgive me for being callous, but I would have preferred to find out back when I still had something to take the edge off."

"You've still got something to take the edge off," she said. "You always will. You're just not using it anymore. That's all."

She had stumped me.

"Why'd you drink so much?" she asked with what sounded like genuine curiosity.

"Because I didn't know what else to do," I said.

Her brow wrinkled, and I saw a narrow skepticism in her eyes that told me she had never looked at an entire kitchen and seen nothing but a hundred weapons that could be used to kill her in her sleep, that she had never become convinced a plane was going to crash simply because she was on it. I figured I shouldn't bother to say anything more, but I did. She had come to me and not the other way around.

"Because I wake up every morning with a hundred voices in my head telling me I won't make it to the end of the day. Because for some reason, I could look right at my sister's stomach after they cut her open for her

C-section and hold her hand at the same time, but I couldn't bring myself to get the fucking mail."

"And now?" she asked.

"I have something else to do."

"Yeah," she said. "Like convince yourself that you harmed a child."

Brenda got to her feet and stretched. She noticed that I was staring at her. "Those voices you mentioned," she said. "They're all you. Try telling them to fuck off. See what happens."

"You want me to tell myself to fuck off?"

"Something like that," she said. "This is getting too existential for me. Is there a twenty-four-hour grocery store around here?"

"Pavilions," I said. "Why?"

"'Cause you need some juice." Her expression was suddenly grave. "This Koffler guy said he had something to say to you tonight?" she asked. I nodded. "Something you haven't heard before?" I told her she was correct. She leaned forward intently. "Here's the deal. No matter what he says, you come back to the house with me tonight."

When I didn't answer, she said my full name in a tone of voice that made it sound like a threat.

"Deal," I said.

"Good," she said. "'Cause if it wasn't a deal, I was going to use this to shoot you in the fucking leg." She tapped the bulge against her right hip and headed for the door.

I followed her out of the apartment, wondering if she had come to protect me from Scott Koffler or the liquor store just up the street.

At twenty minutes after one, Brenda and I were sitting in my parked Jeep across the street from Plummer Park, a dense rectangle of green space that housed community rooms, several tennis courts, and plenty of space for old Russian men to play chess. In the night darkness, the walls of the tennis courts stole the definition from the low-hanging branches.

Brenda was sitting in the backseat, her breaths loud but even. I was behind the wheel. At my feet sat a brown paper bag with a half-empty bottle of Tropicana orange juice inside.

"Call him again," Brenda said.

"I've called him twice," I said. "No answer."

A pair of headlights turned off Fountain Avenue and headed toward us. My heart skipped. I gripped the steering wheel as the car approached. It was a black Toyota Camry with an elderly woman peering over the wheel. She drove right past us.

"Why did you bring the gun?" I asked.

"Why does anyone bring a gun anywhere?"

"You have a permit for it?"

"Little man," she said, "a homicide detective at the LA sheriff's department is responsible for the fact that I had to kill a man to save my husband's life. If I wanted, I could get a permit to land planes on Mulholland Drive."

I knew now that she was as nervous as I was. Another twenty minutes elapsed. I felt her hand come to rest on my right wrist. "He's a no-show, little man. Let's go."

"I want to go to Palmdale."

"What's in Palmdale?" she asked, even though I was sure she knew.

"His mother's house."

She withdrew her hand. "We had a deal."

Earlier, after we had returned to my apartment from the grocery store, she had insisted that I pack a change of clothes and whatever else I needed from my apartment before we headed over to Plummer Park. "This isn't just about my sanity or safety, is it?"

"I've got something to show you," she said. "Jimmy hasn't seen it."

I guessed that she hadn't shown it to Jimmy because she was convinced he was going to pull the plug and she didn't want him to bury whatever this information was.

"I'm listening," I said.

"McCormick," she said. "Corey's new last name. Old last name. Whatever. All I did was plug it into Google, but I got something. It's interesting."

I turned in my seat. She was staring out the passenger window, her face laced by the fractured light from a nearby street lamp. "Let's go back to the house and I'll show it to you," she said.

"Why do you have so much faith in me all of a sudden?"

"Jimmy's going to write this book whether he likes it or not," she said. "Child molesters. No child molesters. It doesn't matter. He's going to write it. Trust me." She sighed. "And you're the major character, whether he likes it or not. Whether you like it or not too, for that matter."

"Okay," I said, even though I didn't quite have her meaning yet.

"Jimmy says there's always a point where the major character takes over and the author's just a spectator," he said. "It's his least favorite part of the process, but it's gotta happen. That's where we are, little man. It's time for Jimmy to get out of your way."

She gave me a few seconds to absorb this. "But the major character doesn't die. Not in Jimmy's books, at least. That's where I come in."

"Okay," I said.

"You see why we got off on the wrong foot?" she asked.

"Not really. No."

"It was a misunderstanding," she said. "You thought I was trying to protect Jimmy."

I wasn't sure whether to be frightened by her protective instincts or moved by them. After a while, she said, "Spend your life with a man whose life's work consists of nailing nightmares to a bulletin board, and you might sound as crazy as I do."

"Jimmy didn't tell you to come with me tonight, did he?"

She shrugged. I started the car and was just about to turn onto Fountain Avenue when my cell phone rang in my lap. I hit the brake. I answered and no one responded.

"Scott?"

I heard a sharp gasp. "You need to come here." It was Nate Bain's voice, and it had a hollowed-out sound to it. I said his name and several seconds of silence went by. "Just come here," he repeated, emotion swelling under his words.

"Where are you?"

I felt Brenda's hand close on my right shoulder. Nate erupted into hysterical sobs that sounded too much like screams. He stuttered the name of a popular bathhouse that was just west of La Brea Avenue. Then the line went dead.

I turned off Fountain Avenue and saw shadows emerging from the entrance to a dark warehouse several blocks ahead. The shadows walked with bowed heads and quick steps. The neon sign above the front door read Slick. It was one of the area's more popular gay bathhouses. Its patrons were fleeing as if a photographer had started snapping pictures inside.

I pulled to the curb across the street, jumped out, heard Brenda slam the door behind me, grabbed my cell phone, and dialed Nate's number. I heard a chirping ring from in between the parked cars several feet away.

We found Nate sitting on the curb between two car bumpers. He was rocking back and forth, his arms wrapped around his knees, his mouth open as he tried to breathe.

I sank down in front of him and took his face in both hands. His eyes were wild and wet, his spiky hair twisted. "I didn't use," he managed. "I didn't use." He repeated the words over and over again, his voice waning.

"What happened?"

He choked out something that sounded more like anguish than words. Brenda stood behind him on the sidewalk, her eyes probing the entrance of the bathhouse. I turned and saw a tall black woman with Brenda's strong build emerge from the entrance. As the woman passed under the neon sign, I saw that she had a man's strong jawline, wide unblinking eyes, and cheeks caked with glitter. She threw her long braided hair extensions off one shoulder with the back of her hand and hurried off, addressing the sidewalk in front of her in some sort of drug-fueled babble.

As I ran across the street, Brenda shouted my name. I threw the entrance door open to find a wiry guy blocking my path. He wore a backward baseball cap, a T-shirt that bore the bathhouse's logo, and a thousand piercings in his nose and ears. "We're closed!" he shouted. I tried to shove past him and he grabbed my wrists. "We're fucking closed!" he shrieked.

He hit the wall next to me after I shoved him. I threw open the second door and found myself in a narrow corridor lined with half-open doors. Dim industrial lights lined the ceiling overhead, above a metal grate that formed a kind of drop ceiling. The walls and doors were particleboard painted black. They shook with the thumping bass beat of a popular dance song that I had heard in brighter places than this.

I heard the second door fly open behind me and saw Brenda moving toward me through the dim squares of light. "Whatcha doing, little man?" she called, trying to keep her voice hostage-negotiatior-casual but speaking loud enough to be heard above the music. From the expression on her face, I was sure Nate had told her something that had brought her hand to the bulge against her hip. "Police are on their way, Adam."

I moved off down the hallway, pushing open stall doors as I went. The panicked patrons had left behind twisted pairs of underwear, used condoms, and overturned bottles of lube. I turned and found myself facing a stall door that stood all the way open. The cubicle had a single bed in the center and a nautical-style lamp behind a metal cage that had a red bulb in it. It threw a dull glow across a swell of belly and two pork-chop-shaped legs that stuck out from a towel.

I felt tiny pinpricks in my shoulders and upper back. The man on the bed was Scott Koffler. His hands had been posed prayerfully on his bare chest, but his head was twisted to one side. A slick of vomit led from his mouth to the floor. A thin red line gleamed across his throat. The gash was shallow and had emitted barely any blood.

At my feet was a crumpled water bottle. It had no label and looked as if it had been crushed by a fist. But the top of the bottle was mangled in a different way. Scraped. Twisted. Chewed. Suddenly I saw it. I saw the blade being held to Koffler's throat as the bottle was shoved inside his mouth, its contents forced down by his assailant's other hand. Probably GHB. A derivative of body-building products that could induce either a euphoric high or an immediate blockage of blood flow to the brain, especially when it was mixed with alcohol.

Brenda told me I needed to go. I met her eyes. The red semidarkness between us seemed to ripple and shimmer, and she seemed evanescent, distant. I knew what was she was saying to me, knew that she thought Billy Hatfill had something incriminating on me, something I had done in a blackout. Something I would never want the police to know about. But I couldn't react to her, and when she said my name again, there was panic in her voice.

"He set a trap," I said. "He knew I'd be at the park waiting for him. Then he followed Nate."

Brenda pulled me away from the bed, into the narrow corridor outside. I allowed her to guide me without taking my eyes off of Scott Koffler's body. His hands were crossed over his chest, a towel wrapped loosely around his waist. He was posed in the same way as my good friend Paul Martinez, when several months earlier his body had been discovered in a bathhouse just like this one. As Brenda herded me down the corridor, I was thrust back onto a darkened West Hollywood street corner as Billy Hatfill asked me if I still thought about Paul. Paul, whose funeral I had walked out of in a quiet rage over his friends' inappropriateness and disrespect. Paul, one of the first friends I had made after moving to LA.

I heard Billy Hatfill telling me I was going to drown in my judgments one day. Then I saw myself as I had been rendered by Corey Howard's hand, sleeping peacefully and dreaming of steel windmills. The image was replaced by a young boy's face, his eyes heavy, as it was lifted into my vision by a gloved hand. Then I was back in the bathhouse hallway, on my knees, inches from my own vomit, as I heard the sound of approaching sirens.

Brenda's hand was on my back.

"I'm not going anywhere," I told her.

CHAPTER 13

The first officers to respond were Deputies John O'Brien and Frank Murton. They were with the special problems unit of the West Hollywood substation. Several months earlier, they had taken me on a ride-along so they could show me how they politely pushed the transgendered prostitutes and their parolee customers farther toward Highland Avenue with ceaseless questions about the quality of their life choices and talk of recovery programs.

Frank Murton had been the one to give me the tip about Emilio Vargas, the guy who fought back against the fag bashers, the week before. He was about five-eleven, with a broad-shouldered body, a square head, and knife slashes for eyes. He was as straight as they come, but he had confided in me that his brother was a closeted member of the LAPD who drank so heavily to drown the stresses of his double life that he sometimes woke up in a different city and had no idea how he got there.

I was standing outside the entrance when the deputies arrived. Brenda was half a block away, standing watch over Nate, who hadn't moved from the spot he had been in when we first showed up. I told the two cops who they could expect to find inside and what I thought had been done to the guy. O'Brien entered the bathhouse. Something in my face must have told Frank Murton to stay behind. "You know the victim?" he asked.

"Yes, I was supposed to have a meeting with him two hours ago."

"What kind of meeting?"

A second sheriff's cruiser pulled off the boulevard. I tried to focus on the deputy in front of me and not the ones that were advancing toward us. A third cruiser pulled up the street from the other direction.

"What were you doing here tonight?" Murton asked.

"I don't do bathhouses, Deputy. I was supposed to have a meeting with Scott Koffler at one A.M. We were supposed to talk about a story I was working on—"

"What kind of story?" he asked, his voice gaining an edge.

"You're going to want to take me in."

"I am?"

"At ten to two, I got a call from my friend Nate Bain over there. He asked me to come here. I went inside and I found the body."

The radio at Murton's hip crackled. I recognized John O'Brien's voice, confirming that he had just found what I had told him he would find. Two of the deputies returned to their cars and positioned them to block off the street at both ends.

"You'll want to talk to that guy, too," I said, gesturing to Nate. As I did, I saw Brenda lower her cell phone from her ear. Instead of putting it in her pocket, she held it out to one side as two deputies approached her. I couldn't hear what they were saying.

"You want to tell me about this story you were doing," Murton said. It wasn't a question.

I started with Nate's visit to my apartment the previous Friday night and his brief ride with Scott Koffler and a marine helicopter pilot named Daniel Brady. Then I included everything Melissa Brady had told me earlier that day. By the time I was finished, the sheriff's department helicopter was circling overhead, its rotors making a sound like speeding train cars.

"Any idea what kind of relationship there was between Scott Koffler and Daniel Brady?"

I wanted to take a deep breath, but I figured that would show Murton that I was hiding something. I met his eyes. "None."

"Any idea where they went while they were here?"

"No," I said.

Nate and Brenda had both been shepherded off to different sheriff's cruisers, where they sat in the backseat as a deputy stood guard outside the door. When Murton's hand came down on my shoulder, I realized he was about to do the same to me.

They took me to the West Hollywood substation, where I was deposited in a tiny office with an empty desk and blank walls. There was no phone. It was hardly an interrogation room, but Murton locked the door behind him after he left. The laughter of other deputies outside struck me as taunting and irreverent.

As my head began to clear, I ran through what Scott Koffler had told me on the phone earlier that day. Corey had hired him to bring Daniel Brady to West Hollywood and then left town without paying him. I let this fact circle in my mind for a while. It left a vapor trail that stank to high heaven. After all the work he had gone to, I couldn't see Corey skipping town without sewing up this detail. Daniel Brady had died publicly and spectacularly, and Scott Koffler was part of the reason why. For Corey to leave the guy unpaid and unhappy was a phenomenally stupid move.

Another detail nagged at me. Corey had turned the Daniel Brady video into a production. Jimmy was right; it was far more than a simple blackmail video. It was a production that involved brief choreography and costume elements, one of which concealed Brady's identity to anyone who didn't recognize his naked body. Why had Corey gone to all that trouble if the tape wasn't going to be broadcast to a wider audience? Why, in the e-mail sent to Melissa Brady, had there been no mention of such an audience?

The e-mail to Melissa itself struck me as half-assed, given all the work that had gone into making the tape. Not just half-assed. Last-minute. Rushed. Maybe Corey had intended to put the tape to a more elaborate use but couldn't. He didn't have time. Because he knew he was in danger. Because he had given Billy what he wanted, and Billy wanted him out of the way.

The half-assed e-mail to Melissa. Not paying Koffler. They both added up to a theory I had been fighting off since I first set foot in Corey's apartment.

Corey was dead.

I saw his keys, wallet, and cell phone waiting for me on his kitchen counter. Not a message from Corey. It was a different kind of message sent by someone else. Had Billy Hatfill staged Corey's disappearance to look like those of the Vanished Three? Was it another attempt to ensure I came to Billy when I discovered Corey was missing? Maybe it was a backup plan in case Billy's warning about Corey's strange visit to his house didn't have the desired effect on me.

I saw the shallow red line on Scott Koffler's throat. Suddenly I was once again outside of Billy Hatfill's front gate, being pawed by a precocious sex addict with a chunky silver bicycle chain around his neck. When I had rejected young Everett's advances, he had reached for the bicycle chain as if it were a weapon. Maybe Everett had used it tonight, wrapping it around Koffler's throat as he forced the bottle's contents down the guy's throat.

It was almost four A.M., Saturday morning. In a little over twelve hours, I was supposed to meet with Martin Cale. Billy Hatfill was just hours away from providing me with a horrible revelation about myself, and he was cleaning up the wreckage of a deal gone bad.

I felt the kind of nausea that usually followed a half bottle of bourbon. The ticks coming from the fluorescent light overhead seemed to be keeping time to a mad rhythm.

If I mentioned Billy Hatfill's name to anyone from the LA County Sheriff's Department, I could kiss my meeting with Martin Cale goodbye. To say nothing of what Billy Hatfill might do with whatever he had on me.

At ten minutes after five in the morning, the office door opened and Dwight Zachary entered. He was wearing exactly the same outfit he'd had on when we first met, except the polo shirt was dark blue this time.

I felt a small sense of relief. Then I saw the threatening look on his face, remembered the remarks I had made to him the other day, and realized he was going to make this as painful as possible. I decided to make the first strike.

"Where's Brenda?" I asked.

He stuck his thumb in one corner of his mouth, bit at the nail loud enough to make a sound, and sat on the edge of the desk across from me. I figured he had gotten Brenda far away from the sheriff's station as soon as possible. She was evidence of the fact that Dwight had crossed the line years earlier.

"Can I go?" I finally asked.

"I just got here."

"You caught this one?" I asked. There was disbelief in my voice.

"In a manner of speaking."

"I told Murton everything when he got to the scene. You want me to repeat it?"

"Scene," he repeated with a faint smile. "Murton says you did a ride-along with him a few months ago. Already you're speaking the lingo. What other *cool*, official-sounding cop words do you know, Mr. Murphy?"

I kept my mouth shut.

"We had Oceanside PD check on that address you gave us for Elena Castillo. You told Murton the helicopter pilot's wife was staying there?" I nodded. "Looks like no one's home. The car's not there."

"She said she might go stay with her uncle in San Diego," I said. "And she said she might take Melissa with her."

"Might?"

"Melissa was covering up for a pedophile, even if he was her husband. Elena didn't like that." I was relieved that they had not caught up with Melissa Brady or Elena Castillo. If they didn't have Corey's name, they were that much further away from Billy Hatfill.

The cell phone on Dwight's belt rang. He answered, his face tightening when he heard the person on the other end. He grunted something. The person on the other end spoke again. I recognized Jimmy's voice.

"Not a chance," Dwight said.

Jimmy said something that made Dwight rise slowly to his feet, as if he had been told that an angry ex-wife was about to come charging into the office. He turned his back to me and inclined his head. I could see the back of his neck flex with tension. It was obvious that Jimmy had threatened him. But the threat was taking a while. Probably something about what happens to a homicide detective who recruits a private citizen to write a novel about an open case.

Dwight turned, his eyes on the desk between us, and handed me his cell phone.

"Don't tell him shit," Jimmy said. The fear in his voice surprised me. "Okay."

"Nate's here. So's your Jeep," he said. "Brenda's waiting outside the station."

"Okay."

As Jimmy spoke, Dwight threw open the door to the office, then took up a position against it, his arms crossed over his chest.

Jimmy said, "If he doesn't let you out of there, you ask him about the unmarked car he had parked outside of my house three days before Samuel Marchand broke into my house with a tire iron. The car he pulled when his superiors got wind he'd assigned it there. You ask him about the phone call he got from Marchand's wife. The one where she told him that her husband had read my novel, beat the shit out of her, and bought an Amtrak ticket for LA."

"All right," I said, trying to absorb the flood of incrimination.

"That son of a bitch set a trap for Marchand and I was the bait—and he knows it. If Brenda hadn't come early that night, I would be dead." Jimmy wanted me out of Dwight Zachary's custody. He was more afraid of what Billy Hatfill might have on me than I was. That was saying something.

I told him goodbye and hung up. Without another word, I brushed past Dwight and out the open door. I was several steps away when I heard Dwight say my name. I turned. "My phone, please," he said meekly.

I was still holding his cell phone. I gave it back to him, expecting him to get some last dig in. Instead he stared down at the floor, his lips pursed, his eyes vacant, his soul sold.

The Cadillac was idling next to the curb, just outside the substation parking lot. Early-morning light misted the massive glass walls of the Pacific Design Center. Brenda appeared as caffeinated and alert as the other early-morning drivers. This wasn't the first time I had been chased home by the sunrise.

As we pulled down the Wiltons' long gravel path, I noticed that my Jeep was nowhere to be seen. Jimmy was waiting for us in the living room. He hadn't changed clothes since the night before, and his hair was rumpled and sweat-matted. Brenda left us alone.

"The bathhouse didn't have any kind of security system," he said, "and all the eyewitnesses fled when Nate started screaming. There was a back door. It was open, of course. The attendant says it was all regulars who came in. Except for Koffler, who arrived a few minutes after Nate did."

"It was a trap," I said. "Koffler got me to wait for him at Plummer Park, then went after Nate."

Jimmy didn't refute this.

"Corey's dead," I finally said, surprised by the lack of emotion in my voice. "There's no way he would have left town without paying Koffler. And the e-mail to Melissa was last-minute, half-assed. That tape took too much work to fire off in a single e-mail. He and Billy must have agreed to do something else with it. But Billy decided he didn't want to."

"You think Billy killed Corey?" he asked.

"Yes."

"And Scott Koffler? You think Billy killed him, too?"

"Yes."

"Too bad we've got no evidence that Koffler and Billy knew the other was involved."

"We've got no evidence that they didn't."

"True," he said quietly. "And I agree with you. I think Corey leaving town without paying Koffler is stupid. Real stupid." He centered me in his weary gaze. "That's why Corey killed him."

"Bullshit."

"Is it?" he asked. "You just skip over the most relevant questions, don't you? Who stood to profit from Koffler's murder? The guy who had hired him. We know that wasn't Billy Hatfill."

"Koffler's body was posed, Jimmy. He had a towel around his waist and his hands were folded across his chest. Earlier this year, my friend Paul Martinez died of a drug overdose in a bathhouse. They found him flat on his back, with a towel around his waist and his hands folded across his chest.

"Last Saturday, when Billy first came to me, he asked me if I still thought about Paul. Billy knew the guy as well, you see? Billy was at the funeral. Paul's friends were all making inappropriate speeches about what a fabulous drug addict he was, in front of the guy's entire family. None of whom knew he was gay or a drug addict. I walked out. Billy told me that I made a lot of people *angry* when I did that. I got the sense that Billy was one of them."

Jimmy looked at me hard. I could practically hear the gears working in his brain, and then I saw his thoughts clouded by worry or sympathy. "Get some sleep," he said. "There's a bedroom off the living room."

"Where's my Jeep? You said it was here."

Jimmy leaned on his cane so his spine was straight where he sat. "When you wake up, you're going to call Billy Hatfill and ask him to meet you on neutral territory. Brenda and I will follow you. He wants you to find out what he has on you as much as you want to know. You're going to play that. You're going to tell him what you've figured out and see where that gets you."

I glared at him. His gaze didn't waver.

"In the meantime, your Jeep will remain at an undisclosed location and the two security guards will prevent you from leaving this property." He gave me a few seconds to absorb this.

"Until when?" I asked.

"Until I say so!" he snapped. He got to his feet and smoothed the flaps of his shirt as if we had just concluded a routine business meeting. "You are not setting foot on Martin Cale's yacht. I don't care if it ends up in my swimming pool. You're not setting foot on it."

He limped off into the kitchen. I was too exhausted to rebel against the fact that I had been turned into a prisoner. When I looked up, I saw Brenda's shadow retreat from the top of the stairs. I heard the door to the master bedroom close a few seconds later.

The guest bedroom had a queen-size bed with a square black leather headboard. The heavy velvet curtains had been drawn, but a thin sliver of gray light fell across Nate's sleeping form. I stripped down to my under-wear and crawled into bed beside him.

Brenda Wilton had told me that I needed to find faith. I tried to replay her words, in her gentle voice, over and over again, hoping that slumber would follow. It almost did. But then I was roused out of my near sleep by the wet sounds of Nate crying into his pillow. I put an arm around him and pulled his body against mine. He fell asleep again.

I felt my feet hit the floor. I walked into the living room. I opened the door to the liquor cabinet. Less than an hour before, it had been fully stocked. Now it was completely empty. I remembered how Jimmy had gone into the kitchen and waited for me to leave. In the kitchen, I looked in the wastebasket and saw that Jimmy had poured out every bottle so qui-etly that he hadn't made a sound I could hear from just down the hall.

A week earlier, I would have pulled out one of the bottles and tried to shake the last drops down my throat. I might even have hurled the empty bottle through the kitchen window in a blind rage. But now I returned to the bedroom, my limbs as light as if I had downed a stiff drink in one swal-low. Being cared for was starting to feel less new and less frightening.

I feel asleep within minutes.

My cell phone awakened me. It was ringing inside my crumpled jeans, several feet away from the bed. It was a little past noon and Nate was curled into the fetal position with a sheet-covered fist in front of his mouth and a lax expression that told me his dreams were providing him with a nice escape. My keys rested on the nightstand, but my Jeep key had been removed from the ring.

"Did you hear about Scott Koffler?" Billy Hatfill asked me.

I groped for the right response and missed.

"He was murdered," he said mildly, as if being murdered was a minor indignity, like shitting your pants. In the background, I could hear the chirping anchors of some noon news broadcast. I figured Billy was calling me to gloat. "Are you there?" he asked.

"I'm here. Let's meet. How about an hour from now? Lunch, maybe?"

"No."

The curtness of his response set my pulse racing. He hadn't taken the bait because he knew it was bait. It was a small confirmation of Jimmy's theory.

"Everett will be at your place around nine," he said. "Wear that leather jacket of yours. It's colder out on the water."

"I don't think I'm going to be able to make it."

He fell silent. He didn't lower the volume on the television.

"Cale won't be willing to reschedule."

"That's a shame," I said.

I listened for the sound of the receiver cracking in his grip. I heard him lower the volume on the television. Nate rolled over in bed and blinked at me. I turned my back to him.

"Who are you and what have you done with Adam Murphy?" Billy asked. He was struggling to control his voice. I remembered Jimmy's instructions from earlier that morning: Give Billy something. Let him know what I was onto and see how he reacted.

"Ever heard of the Vanished Three?" I asked him.

No response.

"Terrance Davidson. Roger Vasquez. Ben Clamp. I heard they spent some time up at your place. Back when it was Joseph's place."

"They did," Billy said. "For two years I've been waiting for someone to ask me about those guys. I guess I shouldn't be surprised it was you. What would you like to know?"

"Were you aware that they were bringing teenage boys back to the house, then drugging them so Joseph could rape them?"

"I take it one of these *boys* told you this. Did you bother to ask him why he didn't press charges?"

"I can set up a meeting with one of those boys," I retorted. "You can ask him yourself."

Billy breathed into the phone. "You never told me your sister was a schoolteacher," he finally said. "It's Candace, right? I like how she hyphenated her maiden name and her married name. Very New South. Candace Murphy-Bergeron. How old are the kids that she teaches at—"

"Billy—"

"Oh, never mind. It's right here on the website. Fourth and fifth grade math. Does she ever check the e-mail address they have for her on here? I should drop her a line. Tell her what a little investigator you've turned into."

"Corey gave you something on me. What was it?"

He made a small moan in his throat that sounded both piteous and gratified. "You know me, Adam. There aren't many things I can't bring myself to say. This is one of them. Besides, he didn't *give* me anything. That makes it sound like I asked for it."

"What happened?"

"I told you when you came to my house," he said. "He wanted to teach you a lesson. He thought your mother's death wasn't enough."

I made myself wait for him to say more.

"Everett will be at your apartment at nine o'clock." He hung up.

I found Jimmy sitting on the terrace in his robe with a cup of coffee. I recounted my conversation with Billy Hatfill.

"It's a shame you won't be going," he said after I finished. I waited for him to say more. "I've got some new DVDs in there if you and Nate want to watch anything."

Later that afternoon, Nate and I were in the living room working on our fourth hour of daytime television. I had spent most of the time studying the two security guards as they made their rounds outside.

"I need to go," Nate said for the third time that day.

"It's not safe."

"Thanks, Captain Obvious. I'm being held prisoner by a weird old guy with a limp."

"He's a very famous novelist."

"I don't read novels," he said. He got to his feet. "This is stupid. I'm leaving."

I grabbed his arm. "Nate, out of the three people who took a ride in Scott Koffler's BMW last Wednesday, you're the only one who's still alive."

He pulled his arm free and sank down onto the leather sofa. "Last night was a Godshot," he finally said.

"What's that?" I asked.

"It's when your Higher Power intervenes in your life for your own good," he said. "I was going to use. I never got the chance."

I studied him to see if he was for real. He was. "That's a good way to look at it."

Jimmy poked his head in and gave us a strained smile. "You sure you guys don't want to watch one of those movies?" he asked.

"Do hot guys fuck in them?" Nate asked.

"You're charming," Jimmy said.

He left. Nate crossed his arms over his chest and glowered at the television, as if the cast of *General Hospital* needed a stern talking-to.

At five o'clock, the evening news started. Nate changed the channel, probably so we wouldn't have to see Scott Koffler's face. With elaborate casualness, I got to my feet and patted Nate on the back of the head, mumbled something about being back in a minute, and went in the guest bedroom, shutting the door behind me.

The room's window looked out the back of the house, into a curtain of dense foliage. At five-fifteen, one of the guards took a smoke break behind the Cadillac, leaving the other to do rounds along the perimeter of the property by himself. As soon as the active guard was out of sight, I opened the window and dropped to all fours in the dirt.

I crawled through beds of ferns until I was in the canopy of eucalyptus branches. At the fence, I hooked my belt around one of the spikes at the top, pulled on both ends, and tried several vertical steps until I could get my hands around the spikes themselves. Once I did, I pulled myself up—too hard and too fast.

One of the spikes caught between two of my ribs. I thought it might tear my stomach open. Then I lost my left grip. In what seemed like one motion, my ass hit the other side of the fence and I fell headfirst to the gravel shoulder on the other side, thudding directly against the bruises on my face courtesy of Elena Castillo and Philip Percy. Then I was on my feet, limping and struggling for breath as I jogged off in the direction of Outlook Drive, where my friend Rod Peters had agreed to meet me on the condition that I was sober.

Eddie Cairns had made a lot of discoveries about himself in
the week he had been a dishwasher at Atwell's Bar and Grill, a small hang-
out for roughnecks and truck drivers on the outskirts of Bakersfield. If
Eddie ran his hands under scalding hot water for several minutes, the heat
tightened the skin around his fingers and made it easier for him to work
faster. And if he kept his hands in constant motion, the small crawling
things that lived under his skin stopped fucking with him. He suspected
they looked like potato bugs, and the next time one of the fuckers tried
to make an appearance, he planned on opening up his skin so he could
find out.

Earlier that evening, Eddie had made another discovery. If he jabbed
the tip of his tongue up against the canker sore inside his right cheek, he
could make a spiderweb of white flame shoot up the side of his face. He decided to keep this trick a secret from José, the short-order cook he shared
the kitchen with.

The day before, Eddie had made the mistake of telling José his theories about the highways and how the federal government had moved all of
the telephone lines under them without telling anyone. That way the telephone lines above ground could be used for secret transmissions, such as
discussions between high-level defense officials about how Eddie chose to
wear certain colors that keep microscopic insects at bay.

Eddie hadn't meant to include the detail about the microscopic insects, but like most thoughts that entered his head, it had just slipped out. José had just stared at Eddie for a while. Then he said, "You fucked, Eddie. You fucked in the head and everywhere else too, prolly."

Maybe José was the reason Suzanne had been checking on him for most of the evening. She was a nice enough woman, but Eddie was fairly sure she had no idea that the immense folds of fat around her waist were a perfect breeding ground for unidentified organisms that were the true causes of most of the fatal diseases in the world, diseases the government could easily find a cure for if they wanted to. Eddie had yet to write his paper on the origins of cancer and how it was the result of too much of what he had dubbed skin-to-ground contact. He made a mental note to start work on it later that night, after he wrapped the satellite dish in tinfoil.

Suzanne. Now that the woman had entered his head, he couldn't get her out. She'd been in the kitchen four times already, made various wisecracks about how he must have washed each dish ten times in a row. (He did. It was the only way to get them clean. Wasn't that why the bitch had hired him?)

Eddie felt prickles on the back of his neck, and when he looked up he saw Suzanne standing several feet away. Her silver hair was pinned back with a barrette, and her huge glasses made her blue eyes look like marbles she could take out and polish with a dishrag. When she didn't smile at him, Eddie jabbed several times at the canker sore in his right cheek to see if he could scare her. The trick didn't work.

"Take a break, José," Suzanne said.

When the Mexican cook complied, Eddie felt one of the crawly things punch at the skin around his right elbow, and before he knew it, he was holding his right arm to his chest, rubbing the thing into submission with his fingers. Suzanne gave him a long once-over.

Everything was too real all of a sudden. Eddie could hear Faith Hill's voice coming from the jukebox out in the restaurant and the harsh laughter of drunken truck drivers, could smell Suzanne's sickly sweet perfume. For Eddie Cairns, clarity was a beautiful woman that broke your nose the minute you offered to buy her a beer.

Suzanne said, "I went to school with your sister, Eddie. Did you know that?"

Eddie shook his head.

"You should," she said. "I told you the day I hired you."

"Ma'am—"

"How long you been awake, Eddie?"

"Ma'am, I see things that others do not see. It's just that simple."

When Suzanne frowned, Eddie realized he had said the last sentence four times in a row.

"Shit, Eddie," Suzanne whispered. "If jail's not going to do it, what will?"

Eddie thought he could make out a small radio transistor in her gold barrette. This entire conversation was being monitored, and it was obviously a test. How stupid of him to have trusted Suzanne, to have assumed the Highway People had not gotten to her as well.

Suzanne said, "My guys can do whatever the hell they want at home. But I know you've been doin' it at work, Eddie. That just won't do. I'm sorry."

"Could you please take off that barrette?"

"Excuse me?"

"Ma'am, you have underestimated me."

"You need to go, Eddie. I'll pay you for this week—"

When Suzanne's eyes widened, Eddie realized he was closing the distance between them. He saw his hand reach for her barrette, and then she grabbed his wrist and started screaming for José. Eddie was frustrated that there were only a few inches between his fingers and the recording device in Suzanne's silver hair, so he threw his body against hers, driving her against the wall as he bucked his wrist in her grip.

The next thing he knew, José had pulled him off the woman and was dragging him through the kitchen. Eddie hit the gravel parking lot on all fours and heard something break. Betty. His precious Betty. The glass pipe had been with him since he had taken his first toke of meth at sixteen, and now she was shattered. But not beyond repair.

Behind him, José was shouting something, something about how meth came from the devil and turned guys like Eddie into the devil, but Eddie was too distracted to pay attention, too busy trying to collect the tiny pieces of glass from the gravel. He needed something better than his fingers to do it.

"Looks like you need some tweezers, Eddie."

When Eddie looked up, he beheld the most beautiful woman he had ever seen. The security light above the restaurant's back door turned her hair the color of sand in the Sahara Desert, a place where the crawly things under your skin curled up and died, a place where the Highway People had not yet managed to extend their evil empire. This woman was going to take him there. He was sure of it. Her golden freckles seemed to dance and shimmer like those plastic fish scales you sometimes saw on signs and bill-boards, and her full lips were probably the same rosy color you would see if you pulled her thighs apart.

She said something to José that made him go back inside. Then she lifted Eddie to his feet with one arm. "You just got fired, didn't you, Eddie?"

He croaked something. She laughed and said, "Well, whenever I'm having a fucked-up day, I like to cap it off by fucking it up the way I want it fucked up. You get the picture, Eddie?"

"I should warn you about the Highway People," he said.

"Uh-huh. Tell you what, Eddie. Why don't you just come with me so I can slide that big hard cock of yours in my mouth. But first I'll shoot a nice white present up your leg."

"Are you an angel?" Eddie asked her.

"Your angel."

As Eddie tasted his own delighted laughter, the woman pushed him into the backseat of her silver Chevy Tahoe and crawled in on top of him, then pulled the door shut behind her. The tinted window blocked out the security light over the restaurant's back door, but the woman's face continued to shimmer above his.

She smiled at him as she pushed one of his pant legs up past his ankle. Then he felt a sharp stab of pain and prepared himself for the brilliant flow that filled his veins in an instant. It didn't come, and the woman's smile had vanished.

"I changed my mind about the blow job, Eddie."

He felt thorny vines wrapping their way around his leg, tickling his ribs, then wrapping around them as well. Suddenly the woman's arm was against his throat and with a crushing sense of defeat, Eddie Cairns realized that the Highway People had won and that his only option—if he was going to survive—would be to surrender to their evil schemes.

"Sleep well, Eddie. You and I are going to have a long conversation when you wake up."

He grunted something that must have sounded like a question, because the woman brought her mouth to his ear and whispered, "You're going to tell me about the man who killed my mother. You're going to tell me everything, Eddie."

Whatever she had injected him with was dulling the meth he had smoked three hours earlier, and Eddie could hear the dark voices of that great engine of hatred and evil that drove the Highway People and all their emissaries of darkness in the world. Memory.

"No one's ever believed you before now," the woman murmured, "but I do. Maybe I'm not an angel, Eddie. But I'm the best fucking friend you'll ever have."

Before he blacked out, Eddie Cairns was sixteen again and down on all fours, wishing the cattle stall where he cowered would form four prison walls around him. Only that would have protected him from the horror that rained down on him that night. That night's sounds were the worst part, and nothing could have protected him from those. After the crack of the first explosion, the other men hitting the floor like sacks of sod, their furious growls turning to agonized squeals as they were butchered.

CHAPTER 14

At ten minutes to eight o'clock, I was in my apartment standing next to my phone. I was wearing black jeans, a black V-neck T-shirt, and black Doc Martens. The leather motocross jacket Billy had asked me to wear was draped over the back of my desk chair. I was confident that Billy had asked me to wear the jacket for a specific reason. I figured I would find out soon enough.

After one look at the bruise on my face, Rod had driven me back to my apartment without asking me a single question. I was sure he had assumed that I had relapsed and some self-help book had told him it was better not to ask me about it. After Rod dropped me off, I had walked to a hardware store and bought a box cutter with a three-inch blade; then I hit a drugstore, where I bought some base to conceal my bruises from a clerk whose tense smile told me he thought I was in an abusive relationship. Now my bruises were concealed and the box cutter was tucked inside my right sock. The pressure it exerted against my bare ankle made me feel absurd.

At exactly eight o'clock, a pair of viciously bright headlights shaped like a serpent's eyes swung onto my street. Billy's ice-blue Lexus SC430 pulled to the curb outside. Everett was behind the wheel. The kid was wearing a white ribbed tank top, black leather pants, and his chunky silver bicycle chain. Neither of us said a word as I got in. I pondered asking him what it had felt like to wrap the bicycle chain around Scott Koffler's neck, and then I remembered that my sister's e-mail address was viewable to anyone with Internet access. We got stuck in the clot of traffic that always develops around the Beverly Center.

"Where are you from, Everett?" I asked him.

"You're weren't very nice to me last time," he said. "Why should I answer your questions?"

"You were a little forward," I said carefully.

We rode in silence until he merged onto the 10 Freeway, heading west. The West Side became a blur of palm trees and low clouds reflecting the lights of Century City and Westwood.

"You've been to see Martin Cale before?" I asked.

"Many times," he answered, his voice cold.

"You like him?"

He didn't answer. He took the 90 Freeway toward Marina del Rey. Massive beachfront condo complexes rose on the western horizon.

"Any idea what Cale's expecting to happen tonight?" I asked.

"Billy said you asked for this meeting."

"And now I'm asking you a question."

When he glanced at me, it looked as if my anger had sparked something in him that was almost sexual. "Some men like to watch. Some men can't do anything else."

"Which kind is he?"

"The second kind."

He turned into the marina's parking lot. In the harsh floodlights that lined the docks, the masts of over a hundred sailboats looked like trees after a nuclear winter. Everett had a key for the gate in the chain-link fence. He opened it and gestured for me to step through.

He led me down a dock, past the point where the slips ended. The water made a thick and repetitive sound against the dock piles, a sound persuading me the ocean was a hungry thing, impatient to strike beyond its borders. The floodlights turned the rippling water a milky green. I was convinced the ripples were being made by something large and dark waiting for me below the surface.

"Where is he?" I asked.

"Martin Cale lives on his boat."

"I'm aware of that. Where's his boat?"

Everett was standing with his back toward the end of the dock. I counted the number of feet between us. His outfit didn't allow for a concealed weapon. His black leather pants were so tight they left little to the imagination, and his tank top was almost translucent.

"His boat's at sea," Everett said.

"Billy said he was coming to shore," I said.

"He only comes to shore for supplies," Everett said flatly.

Everett pointed down at the water. A metal ladder went down to something that someone somewhere might refer to as a boat. It was a black inflatable dinghy with a small outboard motor and the words *lost at sea* written all over it in invisible ink.

"This is bullshit," I whispered.

Everett heard the tremor in my voice and smiled. "You want me to call Billy? Tell him tonight's off?" He closed the distance between us, his eyes wide and glazed, his lips parted and moist. "Maybe you and I can get a room together."

I gestured to the dinghy floating below. It swung back and forth in the water like a metronome moving through molasses. "You first," I told him.

I sat with my back to the open ocean. The wind in my ears must have sounded similar to what passengers on a jetliner hear after the fuselage comes apart. Everett sat on a bench in front of the outboard motor, his eyes narrowed against the wind but his expression serene.

The temperature dropped by about ten degrees. I pulled up the zipper on my leather jacket. After what felt like an eternity on the water, I glanced over my shoulder and saw Martin Cale's yacht cruising through flat seas. The twinkling strands of light on the southwestern horizon belonged to Catalina Island.

The boat was at least seventy feet long, with a main cabin that ran almost the length of the top deck. The cabin's row of squared-off windows were full of a golden light that looked like it had been stolen from a Rembrandt painting. A canopy flapped wildly over the open back deck. The swollen-looking hull was clad in some kind of dark wood that had deep ridges running through it. Three black portholes stared out at me like a shark's eyes.

The yacht's engine died. The wake collapsed into strands of loose foam that drifted toward us and broke across the dinghy's soft prow. Everett killed the outboard motor, and we drifted toward a foot deck that extended off the back of the boat like Juliet's balcony. As soon as I was within arm's length of the railing, I grabbed it and used it to pull myself up out of the dinghy. I climbed a short metal ladder, which brought me to the open deck. There were three patio chairs and a curved banquette sofa bolted to the floor around a metal table.

A man in a cowboy hat stepped out into the wash of gold light that came from the open cabin door. Martin Cale was over six feet tall. His starched white shirt bagged around an emaciated bantam figure, and his silver belt buckle carried his initials. His sunken face looked as if it had been sand-blasted by years of exposure to the sun. His eyes were round and rheumy, and his shoulder-length gray hair was tucked behind his ears.

Suddenly our noses were practically touching and he was fingering one of the big silver buttons on my leather jacket with familiar affection. He brought his eyes to mine. His razor-thin lips parted slightly, but the only sound he made was a thin prolonged sigh.

I heard Everett jump to the back deck behind me. "Told you I would get him here in one piece," the boy said.

Cale shot the boy a withering look. "What time is it?" he asked. A frog had taken up permanent residence in his throat.

"Ten to eleven," Everett answered.

Cale nodded firmly and made a vague gesture toward the cabin door. Everett brushed past us. "I must say," Cale finally whispered. "This is an unexpected pleasure."

In this man's world, I had somehow become a star. My heart stuttered at the thought. I thought of paying customers and violations like the one Melissa Brady had watched being broadcast to the widest audience possible. Sweat laced my back, and I could feel my sharp breaths on my upper lip.

"Mr. Cale," I managed. "There's something I'd like to discuss with you before . . ."

"Your performance," he whispered.

I told myself he could be expecting Everett and me to put on a show for him. But I knew that wasn't what he really meant.

"Your nephew is missing, Mr. Cale," I heard myself say.

His brow wrinkled. He took a step back. I was not acting out the part he had expected me to. "You know Corey?" he asked suspiciously.

"I do," I said. "And I'm afraid that something's happened to him."

"Corey has a habit of going missing," he said. "How do you know my nephew?"

"We had a relationship," I said. "It didn't work out. He didn't approve of some things." I put the force of a perverse passion behind my words. "Some things that I did. Things that I like to do."

His expression softened. He gave me a wry conspiratorial smile and gestured for me to follow him into the main cabin. Inside, there was a massive poker table ringed by high-backed leather chairs. A banquette sofa sat beneath both rows of windows. A false wall paneled in mahogany chevrons separated the sitting area from the master suite. A large sepia-toned photograph hung from it. Before a horizon of rounded mountains, high clouds cast long shadows over an expanse of golden tule grass.

Martin Cale crossed to a wet bar and offered me a drink. I didn't accept it. A sudden jolt shook the floor and sent vibrations up both of my legs. The twinkling lights of Catalina Island slid south across the cabin's windows.

"Corey and I are not very close," Martin Cale said. "He's a hard young man. His past has toughened him in ways that are no longer of use to him." He sipped his drink and gave me an arch look. "What I'm trying to say, Mr. Murphy, is that we have both been subjected to Corey's *disapproval*."

I nodded and took a seat on one of the banquette sofas. "I wish he could have understood," I whispered, trying to lead him.

He shook his head, as if trying to gain Corey's understanding was like controlling the weather. "I thought the boy looked the other way when it came to my proclivities. But a few weeks ago, he was waiting for me at the dock when I came in. Us, I should say. Everett was with me that night. When Corey saw him come off the boat . . . well, let's just say it looked like he didn't approve."

"How so?" I asked.

"At first it looked like Corey had seen a ghost. Then he gave me this look. I assume he thought the look would have some effect. It didn't. I don't answer to my nephew." But his face had reddened. The simple memory of this exchange had shamed him.

He took a seat on the other end of the banquette sofa, his feet planted firmly on the floor, holding his drink rigidly against one thigh, as if we were teenagers on a first date.

"Why did he come to see you in the first place?" I asked.

"He used to have a room here before I got him that apartment in West Hollywood," Cale answered. "He claimed he left something behind. I let him go on board. By himself. He left quickly, didn't thank me. When I returned to the ship I saw that he had gone through some of my drawers. I figured he was looking for cash. If that was the case, he was out of luck. I don't keep cash lying around."

"When was this again?" I asked.

"Two, three weeks ago," he said.

I tried to engrave this detail in my memory. Just before he had gone to meet with Billy Hatfill, Corey had caught his uncle with a teenage boy and then rifled his drawers. I was curious to know what Corey had found.

My sudden silence made Cale uncomfortable. "Are you the only family he has left?" I asked.

"I'm not sure," he answered. "I don't think Corey's seen his mother for years. Which is just as well, I guess. Where I saw a pile of cow shit, my brother saw an angel with a broken wing. Tonya. Vile bitch." He shook his head, dismissing her. "She probably died with a needle in her ankle. If God is just."

Here was a man who took pleasure in the sexual violation of young boys, casting harsh judgments on drug addicts. I studied the veins in the side of his leathery neck and felt the box cutter burning a hole in my ankle.

"Corey never mentioned you or his mother," I said. "Forgive me for saying this, but I figured he was ashamed of you both." His eyes flashed to mine and he made a small sound in his throat. "But maybe he just didn't mention you because then he would have to tell me where he had come from."

"Hell," he said abruptly. "That's where Corey came from. After my brother died, Tonya took Corey on a little road trip through the underbelly of the Great Central Valley. It ended when she was busted for possession in Fresno. Corey was sent to live with his grandmother in Visalia. Lucinda. An incredible woman. You never would have guessed she had given birth to a vile bitch like Tonya McCormick."

I routed all my energy into focusing on the details he was giving me, tried to push away all thoughts of the revelation to come. I told myself that if Billy Hatfill was about to get what he wanted, I would do my best to get what I wanted as well. But I knew the real reason. I had to gain some understanding of the man who had set me up for this.

"I thought Corey ran away from home when he was sixteen," I said.

"He did," Cale answered. "But he didn't run away from his mother. He ran away from his grandmother."

"Why?" I asked. "If she was such an incredible woman."

"She was dying," he said. "And there was . . . some trouble."

The engines throbbed somewhere below us and the glass decanters in the wet bar rattled together.

"Corey had been in love," he finally said, as if the words made no sense to him, "with a boy named Reynaldo Reyez. He told me Reynaldo was the strongest person he had ever met. Later, after he revealed more to me about his inclinations, he also told me that Reynaldo was the most beautiful person he had ever met. But Corey had no idea that Reynaldo's father was a drug runner.

"Reynaldo's parents had come to Visalia on something they call the Michoacán Trail. It's a pipeline of men and materials that come to the Central Valley from Mexico to work in the meth trade. Reynaldo's father was what they call a spider. He transported goods for a drug lord named Eduardo Velásquez. But nobody in Visalia knew this until after."

"After what?" I asked.

"After Reynaldo's father shot his wife and then turned the gun on himself," he said.

He contemplated his drink. "Reynaldo's father had tried to protect his family, you see. His son knew nothing about what he was doing. But then his wife got hooked on the stuff."

"Meth?"

He nodded. "When Reynaldo's father found out that his work had finally come home to roost, he tried to get out of the business. He wanted to get help for his wife. Eduardo Velásquez suspected that Reynaldo's father was going to cross over and become an informant. So he did what any fine upstanding drug lord does. He located Reynaldo's grandmother back in Mexico and had someone hang her from the rafters of her bedroom. When Reynaldo's father got the news, he snapped. He went home, shot his wife, and then shot himself."

"And Reynaldo?" I asked.

"No one knows for sure," he said. "Some people in Visalia said they saw Reynaldo's father driving him out of town that morning—you know, to give him a last-minute chance to run. But there were only rumors. Hopeful rumors, if you ask me. The police thought it was possible that Reynaldo escaped right after his father shot his mother, but they never found any evidence to confirm it. I, on the other hand, thought that Reynaldo's father probably did drive him out of town, killed him somewhere else, and hid the body because he didn't want to be remembered as a child murderer."

I tried to swallow every detail of this narrative, tried to incorporate it into what I already knew of Corey McCormick. Meth had torn apart his life not once, but twice. It had stolen his mother and his childhood lover. All this had been topped off by the betrayal he had suffered at Melissa Brady's hands in Oceanside. To say nothing of the discoveries he had made about his uncle after he had come to seek his guidance and his aid.

Without meaning to, I had closed my eyes.

"Joseph had the same reaction when I told him the story," Cale said.

When I opened my eyes, I saw Cale had taken a seat on the banquette sofa next to me. His arm rested across the back and he held his drink against his right thigh. The expression on my face startled him.

"Joseph Spinotta?" I asked.

He nodded briefly. Something in my voice had raised his suspicions. "Yes," he said. "Joseph even asked to meet with Corey after I told him about what Corey had gone through in his youth. I think Joseph wanted to take Corey under his wing. I told him I didn't think Corey was ready for Joseph's . . . *world*. But Joseph insisted. They went to lunch."

"When was this?"

"Four years ago," he said. "Right after Corey left the Marines."

"Did Corey meet with him?"

"Oh, yes. But nothing came of it. Corey never said anything about Joseph. Joseph didn't say anything about it either, come to think of it. I assumed he would have some strong opinions about the man." He gave me a knowing smirk. "We can't expect Corey to appreciate a man like Joseph now, can we?"

"Absolutely not," I said, as if this were a great loss for Corey. "Did Billy know about this meeting?"

"Billy," he asked with disdain, as if the young man didn't know arithmetic. "I think Billy was probably too busy shopping."

I envisioned my timeline in my head and added this detail. Corey and Joseph Spinotta had met face-to-face four years earlier. Neither man had said anything about the meeting afterwards.

Martin Cale squeezed my thigh and my stomach twisted at his touch. He got to his feet suddenly and asked me to wait for a second. He walked into the master suite. I closed my eyes and took deep breaths and heard a drawer open.

He returned a few seconds later and handed me a pencil sketch that was as skillfully rendered as the drawing I had found in Corey's apartment. I knew who the subject was without Cale having to tell me. Reynaldo Reyez had a long narrow face and shoulder-length black hair that draped one side of his face. He had slanted eyes that were almost like a cat's and a narrow nose that came to a sharp point.

"Corey had a room here for a while," he said. "He rarely ever used it. After I got him that apartment in West Hollywood, I cleaned it out. But I found this. I don't even know who drew it, but that's Reynaldo. How he described him, at least."

"Corey drew it," I said.

This fact did not seem to interest him much.

"Can I have this?" I asked.

Cale nodded and sipped his drink. "I don't see why not."

I rolled it up carefully and slipped it into the inner breast pocket of my leather jacket. "What did Corey believe?" I asked.

"About what?" he asked. I could hear his impatience.

"Reynaldo," I said. "What did Corey think happened to him?"

"He never said," Cale answered. "I think he wanted to believe the boy was alive somewhere and he was too proud to admit that he was holding on to foolish hope."

He went to the wet bar and refilled his drink. I got the sense that it was his way of closing down the subject.

"When was the last time you spoke to Corey?"

"Almost three weeks ago," he said. "Like I told you. All these questions. Is this an interrogation or is it just nervous chatter? Maybe you've got a case of stage fright, Mr. Murphy? Is that it?" I just smiled. "Why are you so interested in finding my nephew? Truly. Are you trying to win back his approval? Corey will never understand men like you and me. He will never understand that there is no harm in what we do. No harm whatsoever.

"The love of an older man can turn a boy into an angel," he said in hushed tones. "Without it, the boy is never fully realized. That is a truth so profound that people are afraid to speak it."

"Except for Joseph Spinotta," I said.

"Yes," he said. "It's a lesson Joseph taught me, and I will be forever indebted to him for it."

I wanted to ask him why the boys had to be drugged to receive the precious gift that men like Joseph Spinotta had for them. I wanted to tell Martin Cale that no matter what I had done in a blackout, no matter what we were getting ready to watch, I was not like him and never would be. My natural desires were for another man who could think and reason and feel pain the way I did, and those qualities could not be found in a thirteen-year-old boy. The idea of having sex with one was not just repulsive to me; it was preposterous.

I realized I had just listed several good reasons why I could never be convinced to violate a child in a blackout. I felt a small, firm knot form in my chest. I wondered if it was the first sign of what Brenda Wilton had called faith.

Martin Cale glanced down at his watch. "Everett!" he shouted. "It's time!"

The engines died beneath us. Cale gestured toward the master suite. I smiled and gestured for him to go first. He did. As soon as he turned his back on me, I pulled the box cutter from my right boot and slid it inside the right sleeve of my jacket. I pressed my middle three fingers down on the retracted blade.

On the other side of the false wall, a large plasma-screen television stared down at a king-size bed with a chocolate-colored comforter. Two high-backed chairs had been placed in front of the bed. Martin Cale took a seat in one, his eyes already on the television screen. He patted the empty chair next to his.

Everett stood over an art deco desk that sat against one wall of windows. He was watching the seconds tick by on his digital watch. A silver laptop computer sat open on the desk in front of him. Behind it, there was something that looked like a tiny satellite dish. It was angled toward the darkness outside. Joseph Spinotta had been a master at implementing wireless Internet systems, and I figured this was his pièce de résistance. A second cord ran from the computer off the side of the desk. I traced the cord's path to the bottom of the TV on the wall above.

Everett looked from his watch to the desk in front of him. A small white keypad sat in front of the computer. I could just make out a long series of alternating numbers on its LED display. I had seen the device before. Large corporations used it to provide their employees with a unique password every time they logged on to their e-mail accounts. I wondered if Corey had discovered the keypad and the dish when he had searched his uncle's yacht.

The computer monitor's screen went blank. The plasma-screen TV followed suit a few seconds later. A digital countdown appeared, starting at ten and going all the way to two. Then it was replaced by a password entry blank. I heard Everett punching keys on the computer's keyboard and saw small block dots fill the blank on the television screen.

The password entry blank disappeared and the screen went from blank to red, a slow dissolve. A message box appeared. It read *Confirming Authorization.*

"How much longer?" Cale whispered.

"It usually takes about twenty seconds," Everett answered.

Cale closed one hand over mine, the one that had the tip of the box cutter in it. I eased it up inside the sleeve of my jacket. Cale sensed this small motion and responded by adjusting his grip.

"Where does it come from?" I heard myself ask.

"What?" Cale asked.

"The broadcast," I said.

Cale laughed in his throat, amused but distracted by what was to come. "If anyone knew the answer to that question, there wouldn't be another broadcast. We wouldn't want that now, would we?"

I glanced over my shoulder and caught Everett staring at me. My question had brought an unexpected longing to his face. It seemed as if he wanted to know the answer as much as I did. He looked away from me quickly. Maybe he had glimpsed the horror I was trying to conceal and decided he had no use for it.

"How often?" I asked.

"What?" Cale snapped.

"Twice a month," Everett said from behind me.

Cale shifted in his seat. "How much longer, Everett?"

"Ten seconds. Maybe."

Jimmy had been right. Joseph Spinotta was in hiding somewhere, and he was broadcasting his product with a wireless signal that clearly had the strength to travel across a great distance to the computers of his paying customers. The man sitting next to me was one of those customers. He clutched my hand in his as if the two of us were about to witness a birth.

A second password entry blank appeared. Everett responded with a series of keystrokes. The entry blank vanished and Martin Cale interlaced his fingers in mine. I heard a soft sound behind us and realized that Everett had sprawled himself out on the bed.

On the television screen above, the blackness materialized into heavy tree branches shifting in a slight wind at nighttime. The camera tilted down to find a small dirt trail that cut through the dense greenery. The trail was bathed in a viciously bright light, so bright I almost didn't see the young boy stumbling toward us.

The boy gained definition as he approached. He wore a white T-shirt and white boxer shorts. His hair had been cut short and bleached blond. His arms were outstretched in front of him. I saw the white blindfold that covered his eyes.

"Beautiful," Martin Cale whispered.

My vision blurred. I blinked madly and got it back.

The boy reached out toward us, his fingers almost grazing the camera lens. The image faded to black and the words *Bobby is lost* . . . scrolled across the screen. Another few seconds of darkness, then a second set of words appeared. . . . *Bobby is found.*

Then I saw a white backdrop and a spread of pillows. I recognized the drab milk-colored carpeting that lay between the pillows because I walked on it every day.

In the seconds before the camera focused in, I glimpsed the patch of ceiling above my queen-size bed and saw that the white backdrop was a bedsheet taped to the black Oriental screen that I never used, the one that had been opened and placed next to my bed during my blackout.

I made myself breathe.

The same boy we had watched stumble down a dirt path was lifted into the frame gently, by a gloved hand that held the back of his hair. Melissa was right; he had the face of an angel. His full lips parted, his chubby cheeks flushed red with whatever drug had added ten pounds of weight to his eyelids.

A small voice spoke to me through the riot of screams inside my head. It was small and quiet but persistent. It was telling me that the screams were lying to me. I was watching the exact same ritual Melissa Brady had described to me the day before.

The image dissolved. Now the camera shifted back several feet, and the boy lay on his back on the bed of pillows, his head toward the camera. When I saw that he was nude, I closed my eyes and tried to suppress a shudder. I failed. Martin Cale mistook it for desire and squeezed my hand.

Behind us, I heard Everett shifting as he moved in for a closer look.

A man entered the frame. He was wearing the leather jacket I had on at that very moment. There was a black leather mask over his face; it had tiny inverted triangles for eyeholes and a leering grin composed of fat, sculpted lips outlined in gold paint. The man had my height, my build, and my straw-colored hair. He was naked except for the jacket.

I focused on his nudity and not the young boy's. I zeroed in on precisely what Melissa Brady had seen, the very details of anatomy that had led her to throw her computer out the window when she had watched this same video.

The man in the video, the man who had violated a young boy in my apartment, was a marine helicopter pilot named Daniel Brady.

He was my height; he had my build, my hair. Even without a leather mask covering his face, he and I had looked remarkably alike. I had paid too little attention to these similarities between us, seen them as nothing more than proof that Corey had desired both of us at different times.

I was on my feet. Cale's fingers grazed my back, but he was too riveted by the screen to pay much attention to my sudden withdrawal.

I walked toward the cabin windows, listening to my long exhalation of breath, which anyone could have mistaken for a sign of sexual pleasure. The light from the master suite fell across the water outside in a gentle undulating wave.

I could feel the truth behind this scenario revealing itself.

The previous Wednesday night, I had slept in an alcoholic stupor as a marine helicopter pilot named Daniel Brady violated a young boy on the floor of my apartment. I knew Corey could not have filmed the video himself. Daniel Brady would never have agreed to take part if that had been the case. I figured the gloved hand that had lifted the young boy's face into the frame belonged to Scott Koffler.

Martin Cale was riveted. He could not tell that the man on screen was not me. If Melissa Brady had not described the very same video to me the day before, if I had never set out in search of the truth behind Daniel Brady's visit to West Hollywood, would I have mistaken the masked man on the television screen for myself as well?

"They don't move," Cale whispered in paralyzed ecstasy. "They don't arch their backs like a cat. They don't sneer like some little porn star. Their bodies don't know how to resist."

On the bed just behind Martin Cale, Everett sat forward on his knees, his brow furrowed, his eyes squinting, and his lips parted. He had removed the silver bicycle chain from around his neck and crossed his arms over his chest. One end of the chain dangled from his right fist. He was studying the events on screen with a focus I couldn't muster.

His eyes slid to meet mine. "It's not you," Everett whispered. He knew. He had handled the evidence a few days before when he had pawed me outside Billy's front gate.

"You're right, Everett," I said under my breath. "It's not me. But Billy thinks it's me, doesn't he?"

"Quiet!" Cale barked. The man had not heard a single word we said.

"It's really not you," Everett whispered, as if he needed to say the words again to convince himself of their truth. He seemed to be feeling a betrayal as deep as my own.

"Shut up!" Cale roared. "Both of you!"

Everett flinched. Cale shot me a ferocious look, his teeth bared. Behind him, Everett lifted his silver bicycle chain in both fists and spread his knees slightly to steady himself. He jerked both ends of the chain. The spokes shifted and formed a single sharp edge.

Cale settled back into his seat. I watched, dumb and motionless, as Everett brought the chain around the man's throat. "Why don't *you* shut up?" he whispered. He snapped back on both ends of the chain.

I heard my back slam into the window behind me, and then I felt the impact a second later. I watched Martin Cale's mouth fall open and his hands rise to the chain wrapped around his throat. Everett pulled back more on the chain, and the man let out a nasal squeak. Cale's grasping hands fell short of their goal. He pawed at the quilt of red that was sliding down the front of his shirt, summoned some last reserve, and bucked his hips out of the chair.

Everett removed the chain from Martin Cale's neck, holding it out to one side as if it were a piece of wet laundry before he dropped it on the bed. Then he gave the back of Martin Cale's head a gentle shove and Cale fell facefirst to the carpet.

I was whispering a stream of curses into my palms.

Everett was still kneeling on the foot of the bed, his arms at his sides, his fingers slick with blood. He stared down at Martin Cale's body with a wide-eyed intensity and a look of surprised disappointment, like a kid who opens a shiny Christmas present and finds socks inside. Murdering the man had not given him the release he had hoped for.

The movie continued to play. I caught a glimpse of a close-up shot and groped for the back of the laptop computer. I yanked out the cord and the screen went gray. I grabbed the miniature satellite dish and shoved it into my jacket pocket. When I reached for the LED keypad, the box cutter slid out of my sleeve and bounced on the carpet.

Everett gave me a dull look that had madness flickering behind it. I held his eyes as I shoved the keypad into my jacket pocket, then just stood there, my heart roaring. The two of us listened to the water lapping against the boat's hull.

"What was supposed to happen out here tonight, Everett?" I asked him.

"Get off the boat," he said in a voice struggling for aggression. Whatever plan he had been given by Billy had been destroyed by the revelation that I was not a performer in the film we had just watched.

"What did Billy tell you to do?"

"Get off the boat," he said with building anger.

Everett got to his feet and started toward me. He grabbed the bloody chain, strung it between his fists, and raised it in front of him. I stumbled backward into the main cabin.

"Billy told you it was me on that tape," I said. "Billy *believes* it's me on that tape, doesn't he?"

Everett kept advancing toward me across the room, his jaw quivering. My back hit the door to the back deck. It swung open behind me and I had to grab the frame to keep from losing my balance. I heard something hit the floor next to my feet and saw the miniature satellite dish dancing across the carpet away from me. Everett ignored it.

"Were you supposed to kill both of us?" I asked him. He didn't answer, which was an incriminating answer. He was still advancing, the chain level with my throat. I could either get off the boat as he asked or knock the boy off his feet and try to get the answers I wanted out of him.

"Where are you from, Everett?" I asked.

He sprang toward me and I went skittering backward across the deck. The boy worked for Billy Hatfill, and he had just murdered one of Billy's customers. He moved and spoke like a hollowed-out suggestion of a child. He carried a weapon unlike any I had ever seen before. Nothing about the young man computed with what I had just learned about Joseph Spinotta, and I wanted to find out why. But I had just escaped the death of my spirit, and I would not stick around to risk the death of my body.

I climbed into the dinghy and untied the line with fumbling hands. Everett watched at the top of the metal ladder. Once the line was loose, the boat began to drift away from the back of the yacht.

Everett's face went lax. He disappeared inside the main cabin. I pulled the rip cord on the outboard motor and the boat beneath me jerked and shot forward so fast I nearly tumbled out. It took me a minute to steady it, then to angle it toward the dark slopes of the Malibu coastline.

Behind me, I heard a dull roar, as if some creature was rising out of the depths. I glanced back and saw a maelstrom of froth shoot up behind the yacht as it swung to face the open ocean. It headed out to sea, leaving me with only the grating whine of the outboard motor I was struggling to control. The wind tore the tears from my eyes as I watched the shoreline swell before me. Billy Hatfill had been double-crossed and he didn't know it. I planned on telling him.

As I neared the shore, the brutal whitecaps almost threw me from the boat. The near plunge reminded me that I was carrying Martin Cale's keypad and Corey's drawing of a young man named Reynaldo Reyez. I cut the motor and let the surf carry me in like a piece of driftwood. I made landfall on a wide beach lined with post and beam mansions that sat right on the sand, just yards back from the surf line.

From a gas station on the Pacific Coast Highway, I called a cab. I gave the driver the address of a glass and steel house in the Hollywood Hills.

He gave me a helpless look in the rearview mirror. I assured him I would give him more specific directions as soon as we reached the winding hillside streets above the Sunset Strip.

The gate to Billy Hatfill's property buzzed when I was still several feet away from it. He had probably watched my approach on security cameras I couldn't see. The silver shades had been lowered over the house's glass walls, but I could see a vague light beating against them in the foyer and living room. The gate was unlocked. I stepped through it. Buried lights threw interspersed triangles of white across the empty lawn. Beyond the infinity pool, the skyline of Century City loomed in sharp relief. Streetlights twinkled in the expanse of treetops that was Beverly Hills, making the city below look like an inverted night sky.

In the living room, Billy Hatfill stood in front of the flat screen television on the other side of the massive sectional sofa. The security cameras had given Billy time to conceal his reaction to my resurrection. He held a small black pistol in both hands, aimed in my direction. His arms were awkwardly bent. He had adopted a pose he had learned from movies that I doubted he would be able to maintain under assault. His eyes were sharp under his brow, his lips parted. He knew his plan had failed, but he didn't know how.

"Corey came to you and told you he knew Spinotta was operating some kind of child porn ring and that his uncle was a customer," I said.

"Yes," he said in a breathy but controlled voice.

"Then what happened?"

"I told you already. He wanted to teach you a lesson. He said your mother's death wasn't going to be enough. He said he could get me a tape, and if I didn't broadcast it, he would bring the whole operation down."

When I reached for the zipper on my jeans, Billy made a small, frightened sound and jerked the gun up several inches. "Did you watch the tape?" I asked.

"Adam, let's—"

I pulled my jeans and my underwear down past my waist. "*Did you watch it?*" I rounded the corner of the sofa. The answer was on his face. I saw a riot of emotions fighting for control of his eyes as he scrutinized what I was showing him and realized what it meant.

When he saw I was forcing him to back up by several steps, he straightened his arms. I zipped myself back up and he blinked several times. Dazed.

"It wasn't me," I finally said. "*You* asked Corey to make the tape, and he used a body double. A marine helicopter pilot named Daniel Brady. An old friend of his. A pedophile. A real one. Daniel Brady killed himself a week ago, Billy. Corey sent a copy of the video to his wife—the same video I saw on Cale's yacht. She knew it was him, and she confronted him about it. So he flew his helicopter into the Pacific Ocean."

I started approaching him again. Billy backed up into the glass wall behind him. Helpless fury stuttered his breaths.

"Corey duped you," I said.

"Bullshit."

"Come on, Billy, you know it's the truth. Otherwise I'd be dead. See, Everett watched the tape tonight as well, and he knew it wasn't me. He saw the evidence up close and personal the other day, right outside your front gate. That's why he didn't kill me. And you did order him to kill me, didn't you?"

He leaned his head back against the glass. His eyes were filmy, but he kept the pistol aimed at the center of my chest.

"Put the gun away."

"Why?" he asked, a new edge to his voice.

"Because I've got a new boss. And he figured you out before I did. If I turn up dead, all roads will lead to you."

"What if you don't turn up at all?"

"Corey wanted something from you," I said. "He had information that could have sent you to jail for the rest of your life. But you forced him to deal. How?"

"He wanted to know where they were," he said.

"Joseph and the Vanished Three?" I asked.

He gave me a small nod.

"Why?"

"He didn't say," Billy answered. "And I didn't know where they are. I still don't know. I never will. That's how they want it. I said it enough times that he finally believed it." He sounded childishly indignant that the Vanished Three had left him out and that Corey had doubted his truthfulness. "Then I told him that I could think of one person who could find them. One determined little reporter with a big drinking problem. And I knew of a way to send you after them without you going to the authorities."

"Set me up," I said. "Make me believe I had raped a child."

"No," he corrected me. "*Make* you rape a child! He said he could do it. He said all he would have to do is put a few drinks in you and you'd be down on all fours, begging to please him. But I knew what he really wanted. He didn't have to say it. He wanted to teach you a lesson. I could see it in his eyes. I could see that we were both going to teach you a lesson."

"Even you?"

"Yes," he said. "You think you're different, Adam. You think you're better. You think you can live a normal, sober life. You're trying so hard it's almost touching. But you're wrong. We are as sick as everyone else thinks we are. We lose our youth and then we take it from someone else. That is what faggots do, Adam. And you're one of them." A flicker of panic under his hard voice told me that he had been desperate to believe this proclamation for some time now.

"You're just a whore, Billy," I said. "You're just a whore trying to defend your best customer."

His lips pursed.

"If Corey wanted to teach me a lesson, why didn't he use me instead of Brady?" He didn't answer. "Why did he want to know where Spinotta was?"

"He was desperate," he hissed. "He was more of a vigilante than you are. He was going to take us all down in a blaze of glory. That special kind of glory you dream of when you're a white-trash piece of shit from nowhere."

"Bullshit," I whispered. "You never wanted to teach me a lesson. You knew the minute Corey came to you that you would eventually have to get me out of the way, too. You knew the minute he disappeared that I would come looking for him, so you figured out a way to drag me into it. You want to be evil, Billy, but you try too fucking hard."

"That disappoints you, doesn't it?" he asked.

"What happened when he gave you the tape?"

He removed his left hand from the pistol's handle and dug into his pants pocket. He tossed something at me. It thumped against my chest and hit the carpet at my feet.

It was a thin gold chain with a small medallion that had the shape of a scorpion carved into it. This same chain had rubbed against my bare chest every time Corey brought his body down onto mine.

I met Billy's stare and watched the expression on my face bring a twisted smile to his mouth. "I've been carrying it with me the whole time," he said. His voice quivered. He had lost his grip on the cold, smirking malice he had used to bait me into meeting with Martin Cale. "I almost dropped it on the table when we were having dinner. You don't know how tempted I was."

"Which one of you killed him?"

Billy sealed his mouth.

"Not you. Not Joseph. I'm sure he doesn't do his own dirty work. Was it Terrance Davidson? Roger Vasquez? Ben Clamp?"

"Are you out for revenge now, Adam?"

"*Which one of you killed him?*"

There was fear in his eyes. "It was a third party," he said warily.

"Who?" I asked.

He didn't answer.

"Does Joseph know about the game you tried to play with Corey, with me?" I asked.

He shut his eyes briefly.

"He doesn't, does he? You just told him Corey was trying to blackmail you and you needed him out of the way. Joseph has no idea how much you endangered his operation over the past two weeks."

I heard the answer in his rapid breaths. Then I watched a strange energy liven his face. He laughed gently at a joke I hadn't heard, cocking his head to one side as if I had just sung a particularly pleasing note.

"Find them," he urged. "Tell them. Then my bullshit plan will actually become a reality. Adam Murphy will bring down our whole operation. That's only fair, don't you think? It's practically a compromise."

He lowered the gun slightly and straightened his spine against the glass. He was waiting eagerly and happily for me to react. I didn't. "You're going to do it, aren't you?"

"Who killed Corey?"

"Good luck, Adam."

He brought the pistol to his mouth, closed his teeth around the barrel, and fired.

The gunshot knocked me to my knees. I blinked and saw that I had raised both hands on either side of my head, as if the ceiling was about to fall in. When I heard him hit the glass wall, I thought it was a second gunshot.

My ears were ringing. Billy lay in front of me. Blood peppered the carpet around his head and laced the glass wall behind him with what looked like a blossom composed of empty night sky. The window was spider-webbed where the bullet had blown through it after leaving his skull. His gaping mouth was a strange shape. The pistol's kick had knocked his front teeth out of alignment.

I had never seen death before and couldn't see how anyone would think the scene before me would constitute a victory.

I picked Corey's gold chain up off the carpet and left the house.

I walked downhill to Sunset Plaza. It was just after two A.M. Sunday morning, and the Sheriff's Department was closing down the strip. A river of brake lights led me toward my apartment building. A hundred pounding bass beats from a hundred car stereos gave a rhythm to my footsteps that my brain could not. I walked past the darkened high-end retail shops and overpriced restaurants. I heard drunken motorists shout homophobic expressions out their car windows.

When I reached the sudden dip in Sunset Boulevard that housed Tower Records and Book Soup, I saw two motorcycle cops who had been idling on a corner ahead of me go lights and sirens. They swerved out into traffic, weaving through the thwarted cars as they headed off in the direction I had just come from. I figured they were responding to a report of a gunshot up in the hills. I paused to watch them pass.

Billy Hatfill had killed himself rather than give me the identity of Corey's killer. Maybe he knew he would be as good as dead if Joseph Spinotta discovered how Billy had risked his operation. A third party had killed Corey. A hit man of some sort. Someone who could be sent after Billy just as he had been sent after Corey.

I didn't believe that Billy had killed himself out of fear alone. His split-second decision to take his life seemed like an attempt to ensure that I would hunt Spinotta down and get the answers Billy had refused to give me. If I went any further, I would be fulfilling the dying wish of a man who had tried to destroy not just my dignity but my sanity.

I imagined myself sitting in an interrogation room trying to make real what I had seen and heard that night. For all I knew, young Everett was still piloting the scene of Cale's murder across the open seas, leaving me with a drawing of a young man named Reynaldo Reyez and a blinking keypad with a perpetually changing series of numbers on it.

I struggled to remember the things Martin Cale had told me. Four years earlier, Corey and Joseph Spinotta had met face-to-face; neither man had said a word about the meeting afterward. Nothing Billy had said to me indicated that he knew about this meeting.

A few weeks earlier, Corey had been desperate to find Joseph Spinotta. I had to know why.

CHAPTER 15

I rounded the corner onto my street and saw a Toyota 4Runner parked across the street from my building. Behind the wheel was one of the security guards Jimmy had hired to prevent me from leaving the house. Now he was awaiting my return.

I hurried back uphill toward the traffic-clogged strip. I turned my cell phone on. I had fifteen new messages. Nate answered after one ring. "Where the hell are you?" he said in a fierce whisper.

"Are you still at Jimmy's?"

"Yeah. He's freaking out."

"I need my Jeep," I said.

I heard a door open and then Nate let out a small grunt as his cell phone was plucked away from him. Before I could swear, Brenda said my name in a cool voice.

"I need my Jeep."

"Why?"

"Because I need to get out of LA. And you can call the guard who's waiting for me outside of my building and tell him to get lost."

"Jimmy's pissed."

"I don't give a shit. He was wrong."

"How?"

"Corey wanted to know where Joseph Spinotta was. Billy didn't know, but he came up with a plan to find out: he'd get me on tape raping a kid, then use the tape to send me after Spinotta. Corey agreed, but he used a body double—"

"Daniel Brady," she said for me.

"Right," I answered. "The mask allowed him to get away with it."

"Did Corey get away with it?"

"Sort of," I answered. "Billy killed him as soon as he got the tape."

"You're sure of this?"

"Billy confessed," I answered. "He said a third party did the job. Not Spinotta. Not the Vanished Three. Someone else."

"A third party," she mused. I listened to the bleating of car horns from the Strip, watched the luxury sedans and SUVs roll past the intersection one block uphill. "Why do you need to get out of LA?" she asked, but it sounded like she knew the answer.

"Billy's dead. So's Martin Cale."

"Jesus! Did you—"

"I didn't kill either of them. Billy ordered that kid who's living with him to kill Martin Cale and me as soon as we watched the tape. Only problem was, the kid realized it wasn't me and decided not to finish the job. Billy blew his brains out rather than give me the identity of Corey's killer."

"Why?" she asked, baffled.

"I don't know," I said. "I guess it was better to kill himself than have Spinotta do it after he found out the deep shit Billy got him into." Or he was trying to force me into a confrontation with his sugar daddy, because he was convinced I would lose. I kept this thought to myself.

"Brenda, please," I said. "I have no physical evidence for anything I saw or heard tonight. For all I know, Martin Cale's yacht is still heading out to sea with Martin Cale's body in it. If he hasn't been thrown overboard. I could sit in an interrogation room for the rest of my life and I still wouldn't be able to corroborate any of this."

I hoped she was remembering what she had told me the night before— that it was time for Jimmy to get out of my way whether he liked it or not.

"Where are you?" she asked.

"I need a promise, Brenda!"

"Fine. Where are you going to go?"

I didn't answer.

"Dammit," she whispered. "Dwight called here earlier. They caught up with Elena Castillo and Melissa Brady down in San Diego, just like you said. Melissa's not talking, but Elena hasn't shut up. She told them Corey hired Scott Koffler to bring Daniel Brady to LA. Dwight wanted to know why he hadn't heard Corey's name before."

"What did Jimmy say?"

"Nothing," she answered. "But I'm not sure how long that's going to last."

I started walking down a dark side street lined with parked cars, headed away from my building as fast as I could. "Godammit, little man, you better come back with something that makes me feel good about doing this," she said.

She agreed to meet me on an oak-tree–lined street that runs behind the twenty-four-hour Pavilions grocery store on Santa Monica Boulevard. I got there before she did. Across the boulevard, I could see the last drunken revelers dispersing from in front of the gay bars on Robertson.

I heard two cars approach. My Jeep was in the lead, with Brenda behind the wheel. Nate followed in his white Honda Accord. Brenda got out first and started toward me, with the Jeep key in her hand, her mouth opening and preparing to form words. Just then Nate slammed his car door and headed toward us and Brenda said nothing.

"You have my cell phone number?" she asked at last. I shook my head, and she recited the digits, which I programmed into my phone. "You call me every few hours. If you don't, you better switch out the plates on that thing," she said with a nod to my Jeep. "You don't want Joe Ring on your tail."

Nate looked from me to Brenda, desperate for some kind of explanation. "You did a good thing, Nate," I said. "Coming to me about Daniel Brady."

He had done a lot more than that. Nate Bain was the primary reason Billy Hatfill's plan had failed. If I hadn't known about Daniel Brady's trip to West Hollywood, the tape I had watched that night might have affected me the way Billy hoped it would. "Stay with the Wiltons, please," I told him.

"Where are you going?" he asked.

"Stay with the Wiltons and I'll call you."

"If you think Jimmy's so great, why doesn't it make any difference that he thinks you're going to get killed?"

"You got it backward, Nate," Brenda said. Then she grabbed his shoulder and started walking him back toward his car. She steered him into the passenger seat, shut the door, and then gave me a look through the dull glow of leaf-laced streetlights. "I know where you're going," she said at last. "Even if you don't." I figured she was being spiritual again and I didn't have the time for it.

When I drove past my building, the security guard was gone. I went inside and grabbed some changes of clothes, along with the pictures I had of Corey, Spinotta, and the Vanished Three. Then I walked to a cash machine and withdrew all the cash I had: one hundred and twenty dollars.

I took the 405 Freeway clear across the San Fernando Valley to where it met up with Interstate 5, and then I headed north, past Santa Clarita, where the rides at Magic Mountain Amusement Park looked like isolated oil derricks against the dark mountains, and up into the San Gabriel Mountains. Roadside signs advised me to kill my air conditioning to avoid overheating the engine. The few eighteen-wheelers sharing the road with me were lumbering in the inside lane so they could make the ascent without stopping traffic.

The interstate began to undulate through the divide between the Angeles and Los Padres National Forests known as the Grapevine. I became so comfortable and familiar with the feeling of traveling high above sea level that I almost forgot my destination: Visalia, the small town in the Central Valley that Corey had run away from at sixteen. Getting there would require a steep descent.

A wildfire blazed on the near horizon, filling the night sky with something that looked like the trail from a rocket launch. I decided James Wilton had started it to prevent me from leaving LA. I needed sleep.

In the tiny mountain town of Gorman, I pulled into a motel parking lot. When the sodium vapor lights slid across the interior of my car, for the first time I saw the envelope resting on the passenger seat. My first name was written across it in Brenda's sloping cursive.

At first I thought it might be some cash. Then I remembered what she had told me two nights before as we waited for Scott Koffler to meet us outside Plummer Park. She had run Corey's real last name, McCormick, and found something interesting. Jimmy didn't know she had it. I opened the envelope.

It was a printout of an article from the *Bakersfield Californian* dated a little over three weeks earlier. Brenda had retrieved it from the website's archives, so there were no accompanying photographs. The headline read PLEASANT VALLEY MOBILE HOME EXPLOSION KILLS 4. A powerful explosion had ripped apart a trailer owned by forty-seven-year-old Tonya McCormick, just outside the tiny town of Avenal.

Authorities believed that McCormick, who had served time in state prison for possession of an illegal narcotic, had been operating a methamphetamine lab in her trailer, and that toxic by-products from the manufacturing process had ignited the explosion. The article said Tonya McCormick and Kyle Purcell, her boyfriend of three years, and her thirteen-year-old son

Caden were all believed dead in the blast, pending final confirmation from
the state Bureau of Narcotics Enforcement, the law enforcement body in
charge of investigating all meth lab accidents throughout the state of California.

In the story's most bizarre twist, the explosion had also killed a fifty-two-
year-old junior high school English teacher, Janice Hughes. An unnamed
source close to the investigation confirmed that Caden McCormick had
been a student of Janice Hughes, and that the Kings County Sheriff's Department believed the boy gave his teacher some indication that he was being abused.

Janice Hughes had died of her injuries at the scene. A San Francisco
native, she had been a resident of Kings County for less than a year and had
repeatedly expressed concern for Caden McCormick to her colleagues at
Good Hope Junior High, specifically regarding the boy's lack of grooming
and inability to focus during class.

Tonya McCormick, Corey's mother. Caden McCormick, his younger
brother. Both had died the same week Corey had discovered his uncle was
a customer of Joseph Spinotta's. The following week, Corey had gone to
Billy Hatfill asking for Joseph Spinotta's location.

I sat in my parked car, trying to make sense of the article on my lap. But
my breaths rasped like a tired dog's and the text on the paper kept smearing
into an image of Martin Cale's open throat.

I studied my map and found the tiny town of Avenal. It was due east of
Visalia, almost directly across the floor of the Great Central Valley that sat
between the Sierra Nevada and the Coast Ranges.

Brenda Wilton's parting words took on new meaning. She had known
where I was headed, even if I hadn't. I was pretty sure she wouldn't have let
me leave LA otherwise.

Central Coast Ranges
West of Coalinga
Morning

Eddie Cairns awoke to dawn seeping through the slats of the vaulted ceiling above him. He jerked and felt nylon rope securing his ankles and wrists to the bed frame, the exposed metal coils digging into his back.

This much clarity usually meant that he had crashed, but something else had softened the blow. He should have felt like the Holy Ghost had carved his insides out with an ice cream spoon, but he didn't. There was something else in his system. He remembered the golden girl from the night before and her silver needle.

Then she was standing over him. She had lost her luster. Her hair was tangled and her eyes were bagged, and sweat plastered her white tank top to her round breasts. When he tried to form words, her hazel eyes zeroed in on him.

It took him a second to realize the woman had started talking to him. "Eddie, a girl named Lucy Vernon gave me your name. Does the name Vernon ring a bell? Her father was your supervisor back when you worked with that picking crew over in Corcoran. You told him a story, Eddie. Do you remember?"

"What'd you give me?" he asked.

"Something to keep your head clear," she said. "But it's going to wear off soon. Do you remember the story you told Morris Vernon? It was a bad one, Eddie. You scared him shitless."

"My mother sent you, didn't she?"

The girl's face went dead.

"Fuck shit!" Eddie cried. "I fuckin' knew it. You're some kind of crazy herbalist or something."

She cocked one eyebrow. "You think your mother sent an herbalist after you?"

"She was always tryin' to get me to take some herbal shit to get me off the meth. That's what you gave me, right? Where am I? Some goddamn loony bin where they make you pray all day and take out the trash?"

"You're getting distracted, Eddie."

"You tell my mother that I—"

"Your mother's dead, Eddie."

Eddie swallowed. She was wrong. He waited for her to tell him she was wrong, but silence filled the vast space like methane gas. No sound from outside told him where he was. The floor below was concrete. The shafts of light through the ceiling were gaining luminescence, lancing dust motes. He could smell pine and wood rot.

The girl said, "She died last year while you were living up on that tweaker commune outside of Redding. Too bad the place got raided."

"Lying bitch," he muttered.

Eddie Cairns tried to remember his mother's face and came up with next to nothing. Except for her silvery gray hair. Just like Suzanne's, the boss who had fired him the night before. Maybe it was Suzanne's hair he was remembering.

"Your sister's got her things. They're in a storage locker down in Wasco. The will didn't even mention your name, but your sister says you've got a right to some of them. Sounds fair, doesn't it?"

"Let me go."

"We're not at the negotiation stage yet, Eddie."

"I want to see her," he moaned.

"Your sister?"

"My mother!"

The red-haired woman sat down on the edge of the bed frame and patted his thigh gently. That's when he realized that whatever she had injected him with had rendered his legs immobile. She kept patting his thigh, as if to drive this point home. The hard expression on her face, the way her amber eyes bored into his, didn't match her tender gesture.

After a while, the girl said, "You want me to find out where she's buried?"

"Fuck you, cunt!" he roared.

"Stick to bitch, Eddie. Bitch I can handle. Cunt drives me over the edge."

She leaned into his face so close that all he could see were her teeth. "You were half out of your mind when you talked to Morris Vernon. And he'd tracked you down after you missed three days of work, so maybe you were just trying to come up with a good excuse. But your story had a lot of details, Eddie. So many, in fact, that Morris couldn't get the story out of his head."

Tears blurred his vision, and when he blinked, he saw the woman hadn't reacted to them. Then his sobs broke, echoing up to the high ceiling, trying to move parts of his body that wouldn't budge. The woman got to her feet and brushed off her thighs. "Your resistance is boring me, Eddie. You're acting like you've got some life to defend. You don't."

Eddie heard glass bottles knocking together. Then he saw the girl was squatting on the floor several feet away. He saw her lift a syringe above her head and give it a test squirt.

"I'll scream my fucking head off!" he cried.

"Uh-huh," she said.

He began panting uncontrollably as she closed the distance between them, holding the syringe with the needle aimed at the floor as if it were a gun. She twisted one of his arms, ran three fingers over the track marks there, and shook her head.

"Relax, Eddie," she said as she injected him. "At least it's not another spinal."

CHAPTER 16

The motel's bleating alarm clock woke me at nine A.M. from a vague dream of wildfires. After a brief shower, I walked to the gas station next door. The roar of eighteen-wheelers bounced off the granite walls of the mountains that rose on either side of the freeway. They looked poised to unleash a rain of boulders on the gas station. Just a short distance away was Tejon Pass, where Interstate 5 made a sudden northward plummet into the Great Central Valley.

I returned to my motel room with a copy of the *LA Times* and a Styrofoam cup full of rank coffee. The suicide of Billy Hatfill had made the A section. The article was mostly a rehash of the quick rise and quick fall of Broadband Access Media and the sudden flight of the man behind it all, Joseph Spinotta. There were a few quotes from guys whose names I recognized, mostly bitchy asides about how Hatfill hadn't been able to attract the Hollywood and Silicon Valley celebrities and moguls who had flocked to his sugar daddy. I was pretty sure that the tableau of Billy's death would make it clear to the police that he hadn't been alone in his house when he took his life. If that was so, the police had said nothing to the *LA Times* about it.

Next I tore the entire paper apart in search of anything on the fate of a real estate developer named Martin Cale and a seventy-foot yacht piloted by a psychopathic teenager with eyes so blue they each needed their own pool man. I didn't find anything.

I was left with the article from the *Bakersfield Californian* that Brenda had given me the night before. I was desperate to see if there had been any follow-up coverage on the meth lab accident that had killed Corey's mother and younger brother, one week before he had tried to locate Joseph Spinotta. The fact that Brenda hadn't included any told me Jimmy was probably standing several feet away when she discovered the article, and she had known he was about to pull the plug on our investigation.

I read the article again. It was an unnamed source at the Kings County sheriff's department who had given the reporter information about Janice Hughes, the concerned schoolteacher who had gone to check on Corey's younger brother at the worst possible time. This detail struck me as odd, but the reporter hadn't commented on it. The explosion had occurred just a few minutes after midnight. Why had Janice Hughes chosen this time to check on the boy?

Another important fact was missing from the article. There was no mention of Tonya McCormick's other son, the man I had known as Corey Howard.

What I was about to do was stupid. There was a homicide detective for the LA Sheriff's Department looking for me, and it was possible that he would figure out that I had been with Billy Hatfill when he died. But I was confident that I had information that another sheriff's department, miles north of LA, did not yet know. They might be eager to hear it—and that would allow me to deal.

Information gave me the number for the Kings County Sheriff's Department. A man answered.

"Tonya McCormick had a son who ran away from home when he was sixteen" were my first words.

"What's that, sir?"

"He's been living in LA under a different last name. If anyone wants to know anything more about this guy, call me back at this number."

"Your name, please, sir?"

I gave him my cell phone number instead. He didn't ask me to repeat it, so I hung up on him.

I finished the coffee and opened the bag I had packed the night before. I placed Corey's drawing of his boyhood lover on the bed, along with Martin Cale's blinking keypad and my photographs of Spinotta, the Vanished Three, and Corey. Last night had shoved me deeper into Corey's past. I had found the truth behind one strange meeting only to be saddled with another. Four years earlier, Joseph Spinotta and Corey had met face-to-face, and neither man had uttered a word about their meeting afterward. Had Spinotta tried to draw Corey into his circle, recruit him to work alongside the Vanished Three? Ben Clamp, the porn star and prostitute, bore a striking resemblance to Corey. Had he been Spinotta's second choice after Corey turned down the job?

I realized I was leaving out an important detail Martin Cale had shared with me. Joseph Spinotta had asked to meet with Corey after hearing the tragic tale of Reynaldo Reyez, Corey's boyhood lover. Something about the story of Reynaldo Reyez had sparked Joseph Spinotta's interest. I laid the drawing of Reynaldo Reyez, the photograph of Spinotta, and the photograph of Corey out in a row on the bed and let my eyes sweep over them.

I moved Corey's photograph into the middle. He was lying across my love seat in a black V-neck T-shirt. To his left was a detailed pencil sketch of a hauntingly beautiful Latino boy with cat's eyes and lustrous shoulder-length black hair. Reynaldo Reyez was missing, presumed dead, murdered by his father. To his right, a well-coifed man in his forties, with a come-hither grin and a face sculpted by a scalpel, leered into the camera. He was masterminding a high-tech child porn ring from an unknown location.

The longer I stared at this gallery of faces, the more I became convinced that there was a connection among them—a connection forged during a secret meeting four years earlier. Before Spinotta's disappearance. Before Corey's murder. I just didn't have the slightest clue what that connection was.

My cell phone rang. The caller had a blocked number. I answered without saying a word. After a confused pause, a husky-voiced woman said, "You just made a pretty interesting phone call to the Kings County Sheriff's Department. Feel like explaining yourself?"

"Who is this?"

She didn't answer.

"Are you with the Kings County Sheriff's Department?" I asked.

"No. Your call was intercepted."

"Is that a joke?"

"Jokes are funny. Did you call the Kings County Sheriff's Department or not?" The woman's tone bothered me. But she wanted the information I had. I decided to tell her how to get it.

"Learn some manners and I might answer that question. Have a good day."

I hung up. For the next five minutes, I imagined my husky-voiced friend pacing the room. Then my cell phone rang a second time.

"It's hot and sunny here," she said stiffly. "What's it like where you are today?"

"Gray," I answered. "It's the clouds, I think."

"Most clouds are gray."

"Yeah, well, I think I'm in them."

"Like figuratively speaking?" she asked.

"No," I said. "Literally. You ever heard of Gorman?"

"You've got an LA cell phone number and you're in Gorman?" Now it was my turn not to say anything.

"Have you had any recent contact with this long-lost son of Tonya McCormick's?" she asked.

"Not recently, no." It felt like a direct answer, even if I didn't tell her that Corey McCormick was dead.

"What kind of guy is he?"

"Complicated." That flummoxed her for a moment. "You still haven't told me your name," I said.

"Do you think this long-lost son of Tonya McCormick's would be interested in the fact that the BNE is about to release a bullshit report about what caused that explosion?"

I didn't tell her that Tonya McCormick's long-lost son was no longer interested in anything at all.

"I'm interested," I finally said. "I can't speak for Corey."

"That's his name? Corey?"

"Yes."

I had no reason to trust the woman I was talking to. But I needed more details about the explosion that had killed Corey's mother and younger brother. "We should meet," I said.

"Should we?"

"Yes."

My tone seemed to convince her. She gave me directions from Interstate 5 to the tiny town of Avenal, then to a trailer park that sat just north of town on Highway 33. I realized she was directing me to the site of Tonya McCormick's trailer.

"Now can you tell me who you are?" I asked her.

"I'm the schoolteacher's daughter," she said. "That's what they started calling me around here a few weeks ago."

I studied the article in front of me. "Janice Hughes was your mother?"

"Yes." She hung up on me.

She obviously thought there was something more to the fiery explosion that killed her mother than a simple accident caused by careless meth addicts. Maybe she was a grief-driven crackpot. If that was the case, she and I would probably get along just fine.

I let my foot up off the gas as I descended the Tejon Pass. The mountain walls broke, revealing an expanse of golden valley floor that extended to an unbroken line of peaks on the eastern horizon. They were the Sierra Nevadas, and at their feet lay the richest agricultural region in the United States. The Central Valley extended almost the entire length of the state. It was California's heart, but it was a soft and dying one. In some places the soil had turned alkaline, and the cows that grazed on it became sick and died. As I continued north on Interstate 5, massive orchards sprang up out of the dry soil. The Coast Ranges swelled on the western horizon, a smooth counterpoint to the jagged peaks that rose a good distance to the east.

The land I was driving over had once been covered by a massive sheet of water called Tulare Lake, before the cotton interests had strong-armed the federal government into shunting off its tributaries for irrigation. In its day, Tulare Lake had been home to bandits who hid out in its thick beds of tule grass.

After a while, the Kettleman Hills rose off to the left of the interstate, their tule-grass-blanketed slopes shimmering like sand dunes in the afternoon sun. I was driving into the framed photograph I had seen hanging in Martin Cale's yacht.

Highway 269 took me past a squat, rounded water tower with the word *Avenal* painted on its flank.

A few seconds later, I dropped into a valley narrower than the one from which I had just emerged. The Coast Ranges loomed on the near horizon. Avenal was literally the smallest town that I had ever seen. City Hall could have been mistaken for a doctor's office, and the main street ran for only several blocks before it was subsumed by Highway 33's north-south passage through the valley. Its residential blocks were laid out diagonally from the center of town; they were lined with crumbling one-story tract homes, most of which had battered pickup trucks and utility vans parked out front.

When I went north on Highway 33, the town vanished in the blink of an eye. A few minutes later, I came to the trailer park that the daughter of Janice Hughes had described to me. Six trailers were loosely sprawled around a massive dried-out date palm. There had been a seventh trailer, but all that was left of it was a scorched footprint and a chain-link fence missing huge sections. One of the intact fence portions was laced with white ribbons. As I pulled up, a tall woman in a baseball cap dropped a bouquet of white roses onto the small drift of flowers in front of the lone square of chain link.

I approached her slowly. She kept her back to me. Her thick red hair hung down to her shoulders. It was several shades darker than the fields of tule grass extending from behind where Tonya McCormick's trailer had once sat. On the near horizon, a line of power poles crossed the valley floor like giant staples up into the Kettleman Hills.

I allowed the schoolteacher's daughter to have whatever moment she needed. The sweet sayings written on the white ribbons in front of her were all addressed to her mother, Janice. They were parting wishes from the woman's students.

We shared our names but not a handshake. "Do you know what white phosphine is?" she asked.

"No," I answered.

"Tonya McCormick and her boyfriend were running what's called a Beavis and Butt-head lab," she said. "They'd cook about an ounce of meth at a time, then sell it so they could buy more ingredients to make some for themselves. The ingredients are bad enough. The by-products are even worse."

The brim of her cap shadowed her high brow and the sunglasses shielded her eyes. She had a long, expressive mouth and a small, sharp nose with pinched nostrils. Her white T-shirt bore the childish logo of a 10K marathon sponsored by UC Berkeley.

"One of the ingredients in meth is red phosphorous. It's basically the stuff you find on a match head. It gets added during the cooking process. Then you have to filter out the waste and get rid of it. The BNE says Tonya was dumping this stuff under the floor of Caden's room in sealed containers, which was really stupid. Red phosphine is heat sensitive, and when you heat it up, you get white phosphine, which is air reactive. Blast white phosphine with some oxygen, and suddenly you've got a fire so hot the fire department has to stand back and watch it burn. The report's saying Caden started some kind of fire that heated the containers. Then he opened a window or a door to get out and—boom!"

I looked at the blackened plot of land before me and imagined a trailer flare like a match.

"Light before day," she said. "That's how one of the deputies described the explosion. One of the neighbors said they thought an angel was coming."

Now both of us were gazing at the midnight-colored earth before us.

"Tell me about Corey. This long-lost son," she said, her back to me.

There was something she wasn't telling me, but I had no choice but to offer her some facts in the hope of a trade. "Corey's father died when he was a little boy. Tonya took him on the road for a while before she got busted for possession in Fresno. Corey was sent to live with his grandmother in Visalia. He ran away when he was sixteen and ended up in LA. He gave the Marine Corps a try. It didn't work out. He changed his last name to Howard."

Her mouth was a grim line and her thumbs were hooked in the pockets of her jeans. She could tell I was holding out on her. "What was he to you?"

"We had a relationship. You said the BNE report is bullshit. Why?"

"They're blaming Caden McCormick for the explosion," she said.

"A thirteen-year-old?" When I heard myself say the age of Corey's younger brother, I felt my chest tighten. It was the same age Melissa Brady had ascribed to the boy in the movie I had watched the night before.

"They're speculating that Caden started the fire accidentally and then ran for the hills. Out of guilt. Panic. Whatever."

My chest tightened more. "Are you telling me Caden McCormick is alive?"

She looked at me hard. "Yes, that's what I'm telling you."

"I've got an article from the *Bakersfield Californian* that says he's dead."

"Presumed dead," she said. "And they kept presuming it for about a week and a half. They don't exactly move hell and high water for meth addicts around here. Then they found only some hair traces and a chunk of the kid's ear. Not enough to confirm a death." I moved past her to the chain-link fence so she wouldn't see what I knew was happening on my face. "What do you think happened to him?"

"I think he wasn't in the trailer when it went up," she said. "But I don't think he left of his own free will."

"You think he was abducted?" I kept my voice very even.

"Yes," she said. "Caden McCormick told my mother that someone was coming for him."

"Did he say who this person was?"

"A demon."

I didn't say anything for a while. "Does anyone else know this?"

"The Kings County Sheriff's Department knows," she said. "Their response was that Tonya McCormick probably did a lot of talking about things like demons, government conspiracies, and things that go bump in the night. You talk a lot about those things when you spend your life doing a drug that makes a falling leaf sound like a knock on your front door."

"You think somebody was staking out the trailer," I said. "Planning the abduction. And Caden saw this person." She nodded. "And you're looking for this person?"

"Yeah."

A week after his younger brother had been abducted and his mother slaughtered, Corey had tried to find out where Joseph Spinotta was hiding. This couldn't be a coincidence. Joseph Spinotta had somehow taken custody of thirteen-year-old Caden McCormick. I forced myself to summon up the thirteen-year-old face I had seen in the movie I had watched the night before. While Brady's identity was hidden behind a mask, the boy's face was revealed. That meant exposing him was not a risk. Jimmy had said this meant the boy was out of circulation. By out of circulation, he had meant murdered. If Caroline Hughes was to be believed, young Caden McCormick had been abducted in a brief, brutal, and well-thought-out assault. She had described the makings of a vicious ceremony that reminded me of the Vanished Three's departure from Los Angeles, their personal belongings left out for anyone to find. Jimmy had said they were shedding all vestiges of their former lives. Now they were forcing young boys into the same condition. They weren't murdering them. They were taking custody of them.

I had arrived at this conclusion so quickly I didn't want to trust it. I gripped the fence with one hand and watched the white ribbons flap in the wind. Joseph Spinotta had abducted Corey's younger brother and Corey had gone to Billy Hatfill to find out where Spinotta was holding the boy. "Any idea who this demon is?" I asked.

"Some," she said stiffly. She was still holding out on me.

I turned to her. The look on my face made her furrow her brow. "How long have you been out here?" I asked her.

"Since it happened," she said.

"There are others, aren't there?" I asked. "Other accidents like this one. Other boys missing."

Even with her cap and sunglasses she looked shocked. I had scored a direct hit. "How many?"

"Four," she said warily. "Over the past three years."

Three years. The same amount of time that elapsed since Terrance Davidson, the first of the vanished three, had left Los Angeles.

"What are the similarities?"

"The boys were between the ages of thirteen and fifteen," she said. "Only partial remains were found. In Caden's case, very partial. The explosions were ignited by white phosphine refuse and some other type of accelerant. The adults who died in the fires had large traces of Xanax in their systems, which suggested that they were in a crash period after a binge. All of them were operating Beavis and Butt-head labs like this one. Every explosion was ruled an accident—and the boy was given the blame in each one."

"How could they be ruled accidents if the boy was given the blame?"

"Because the boy wasn't around to tell them differently."

"Are there any differences among the explosions?"

"Different counties," she said. "All in the Central Valley."

"How many lab accidents did you have to go through before you came upon these?"

"Three years' worth," she said flatly. "It's your turn."

As much as I wanted to be wrong, I was convinced that one of these young boys Caroline Hughes had just referred to had been in the video I had watched the night before. "Do you have pictures of these boys?"

"I said it's your turn."

I tried to empty my face of my thoughts and emotions. She had researched three years' worth of meth lab accidents for a reason. She had some idea of the identity of the demon who had come for Caden McCormick; otherwise she would have gone home by now. She had a theory of her own, and I wanted her to reveal it to me before I shared mine.

"I want to see their pictures," I said. "Then I'll tell you everything I know. It's a lot."

"Follow me," she said.

CHAPTER 17

Caroline drove a silver Chevy Tahoe that had tinted windows and new-looking all-terrain tires. I followed her past Avenal State Prison, then west on Highway 148. We skirted the edge of a small town called Coalinga and headed directly into the rounded hills.

After almost twenty minutes on the road, the Tahoe turned right off the highway, between a pair of valley oaks whose branches touched the ground on all sides of their thick trunks. I followed her across empty grassland toward a dense thicket of trees that climbed a slope up ahead. We passed through what looked like a giant electrified fence.

In the middle of the trees was a log cabin with a giant barn alongside it. Caroline pulled the nose of her Tahoe right up to the barn's doors. I parked my Jeep in the middle of the clearing and stepped out. She offered me a drink as soon as we stepped inside the cabin. I declined, eyeing the schoolteacher's desk as she walked toward the galley kitchen; I wanted to rifle through its drawers. There was a map of the state on one wall and an old sofa covered in hand-sewn quilts.

"Your mother lived here?"

"No," she said. "My father."

"Were they still together?"

"No," she said. She seemed to hear the sharpness in her response and rested one shoulder against the kitchen doorway, a beer bottle in her right hand. "You sure you don't want one?"

"I don't drink."

She filed away this fact about me and took a slug from the bottle. She had removed her sunglasses. Her eyes looked like frozen amber. In the right light, they would have been beautiful. In the cabin's darkness, they were unnerving. "My parents separated when I was a kid," she said, "after my father chained me to a two-thousand-year-old redwood to keep it from being cut down." She saw my surprise. "His friends were there, too. Chained to the tree, I mean."

"Your father was an activist?"

"Depends on who you ask these days," she said. "Activist. Terrorist. They're practically one and the same now. Whatever. He never let go of the sixties. Back then, people got convictions the way we get e-mails."

A silence fell. I studied the map of California. Five black thumbtacks had been shoved through different towns throughout the Central Valley. I figured they marked the sites of the four abductions she had discovered. A wider spray of red thumbtacks spread out all over the entire map. "What are the red ones for?" I asked.

She opened her desk drawer and dropped a file folder onto her desk, then handed me a child's drawing, a detailed pencil sketch of a trailer surrounded by a chain-link fence topped with razor wire. Behind it, a pit bull had been rendered as a grotesque monster, its gaping jaws twice the size of the rest of its body. In the expanse of open field behind the trailer, there was a small dark figure without a face, its head rounded slightly as if it were wearing a helmet of some kind.

"Caden drew that in my mother's class on the afternoon of the explosion. See the man in the background?"

"Yes."

"Turn the drawing over."

I did. Written there in a schoolboy's raw handwriting were the words: *He's a demon. He comes every night now.*

"Tonya McCormick had a pit bull," Caroline said. "Just like in the drawing. Its jaw was crushed with a steel trap before the trailer blew up. I've got the bones to prove it."

I looked at her. The dog's jaw was the most solid piece of evidence she had that someone had planned to abduct Caden McCormick.

"When they were loading my mother into the ambulance, she was saying something about the dog. But they couldn't understand her. I think she was trying to tell them that the dog was dead when she showed up. She was trying to tell them that what happened wasn't an accident."

She went into the kitchen. I opened the file folder. Each page inside contained a photo assemblage of one of the four boys she had told me about, including Corey's younger brother. Across each one she had written each boy's name and the location and date of the explosion. The photos of the boys were a conspicuous depiction of their retrogression in the care of drug-abusing and drug-cooking parents. As the four got older, their stares grew more vacant and their hair more shaggy and unkempt. Front teeth disappeared, never to grow back. Scars appeared, and eventually the boys' heads were all shaved.

I asked Caroline about it. "Lice," she explained. "They drive tweakers nuts. Most of them see bugs everywhere they look already. Shaving the kid's head is easier than taking him to get a haircut. At least when you're too freaked to go outside."

I picked up the collage of Caden McCormick and studied it. The boy had his brother's high forehead and long eyes. In most of the pictures, his mouth was set into a listless line. I picked up another boy's photos.

Toby Cooper had been abducted in December of the previous year from the town of Taft. I had seen a road sign for it on the way to Avenal that morning.

The night before, I had watched Toby Cooper stumble toward me down a dirt trail bathed in white light, his arms outstretched and a blindfold over his face. Seven months had elapsed between Toby's abduction and the movie filmed in my apartment—seven months in which he had been transformed from a wasted waif to a chubby-cheeked angel. Joseph Spinotta had nursed the boy back to health before violating him on camera. I imagined he had the same plans for the other three boys, and for Corey's younger brother.

"Who do you think took these boys?" I asked Caroline, even though I had my own answer.

"It's your turn, remember?"

"I said I'll tell you everything I know."

I suspected she was just as wary of voicing her theory as I was of relating mine. I eyed the red thumbtacks in the map on the wall next to me. She took a seat on the quilt-covered sofa, held her beer bottle against one knee, and regarded the floor as if she were meditating.

"For the past six years, some individual has been fucking with the Central Valley meth trade," she began. "It's loosely organized to begin with. You can cook the shit anywhere. But any Mexican national who tries to take control, who tries to get things organized, either goes missing or ends up dead in a ditch. Trucks full of supplies have been exploding as soon they cross the border. A super-lab outside of Redding blew sky high last year. There have been so-called accidents at the other end of the Michoacán trail as well. It's the—"

"I know what it is," I said. Martin Cale had used the term with me the night before. It was the pipeline of men and materials that flowed from Mexico into the Central Valley to feed the meth trade. Reynaldo Reyez, Corey's boyhood lover, and his family had traveled it to the small town of Visalia.

"I hear meth cooking is a dangerous business," I remarked.

"It is," she answered. "But there's the type of lab accident where a cigarette ignites a few jars of acetone. Then there's the kind where a vat's worth of white phosphine refuse ignites a fire so hot and toxic that it's the kind of fire they come up with a nickname for." She let this sink in for a few seconds. "The DEA knows what's going on, but their theory is that the Mexican nationals in central California have been targeted by the Colombian cocaine cartels. Meth was a boon for the Mexicans. It was stronger than cocaine and they could make it themselves. They didn't have to rely on the Colombians for the raw ingredients."

"And the Colombians aren't happy about that."

"I haven't asked them, and I don't give a shit," she said. "My guess is they have too much cocaine to worry about to start picking off Mexican meth lords. There's one individual behind this, and he's not a rival drug lord."

"Who is he?"

Her eyes fired into mine. "Some people think he's a hero. Meth is a virus, and this guy is killing the hosts to keep it from spreading. But he still scares the shit out of them." I took note of how she had gone from making statements of fact about this mythical assassin to quoting the beliefs of others, as if she thought expressing her own belief in this urban legend would send me racing from the cabin. She took a slug from her beer and glared at the floor as if she could force the boards to buckle. "They call him El Maricón. You know what that means?" She looked up and me, and I nodded. "I didn't make it up. Don't get offended."

"How did he get the nickname?"

Her eyes dropped. "Not sure," she mumbled. Then she focused on me again. "El Maricón is very fond of white phosphine as an ignition source. I don't know. Maybe it's a symbolic thing—the fact that the resulting fire is so . . . bright."

I looked again at the map's red thumbtacks, the locations of crimes she was attributing to the man called El Maricón. She held him responsible for the death of her mother and was tracking him. Hunting him. "You're sure this guy is a crusader?" I asked. "Maybe he's just a hit man."

She grimaced impatiently at me. She was oddly defensive of the man she held responsible for the death of her mother and the abduction of thirteen-year-old Caden McCormick.

"All right," I said after a brief silence. "So why is he abducting these boys?"

"This is a war," she said. "He's the only one fighting it. He needs soldiers." Her sudden conviction shocked me. "And he's expanding his operations. He's not just blowing up the addicts who make the stuff and deal a little. He's targeting the small-time labs. The everyday users. He's already brought hell to the Mexican nationals out here. Six years ago they found a petty drug lord named Eduardo Velásquez in a ditch. He was missing his head. He was also the strongest fist the Mexican nationals ever had out here. They still haven't replaced him. People think El Maricón did it."

Eduardo Velásquez.

I had heard the name before, but I had to grope to remember where. Then I remembered that I'd heard it the same place I had first heard another term Caroline had just used: the Michoacán trail. Martin Cale's yacht. Corey's boyhood lover, Reynaldo Reyez, had traveled the Michoacán trail to the small town of Visalia, where he and Corey had fallen in love. His father had worked for a drug lord named Eduardo Velásquez. His grandmother's murder had been ordered by a drug lord named Eduardo Velásquez, and the repercussions had torn apart his family.

Reynaldo Reyez. Missing. Presumed dead.

I had studied the faces of Reynaldo Reyez, Corey McCormick, and Joseph Spinotta, convinced of a connection among the three men forged during that secret meeting between Corey and Spinotta. Now I was even more convinced. I didn't have to shoot down Caroline's theory. We were both right. The connections were there, but I still didn't have the first clue why a vigilante like Reynaldo Reyez would end up working for a pedophile. The look on my face brought Caroline to her feet. "Adam?"

"Any idea what El Maricón looks like?"

"He's pretty," she said. "Eyes like a cat's. That's probably why he got the nickname."

I asked her to wait and then walked out of the cabin. My bag was in the Jeep's backseat. I reached in and pulled out the drawing of Reynaldo Reyez.

When I turned, Caroline was standing right behind me. I handed her the drawing. Her eyes consumed it. She turned her back to me as she studied the drawing, probably to hide her reaction.

"Is that him?" I asked her. "Is that El Maricón?"

She looked across the clearing to where the front bumper of her Tahoe rested against the doors to the huge barn, its doors secured by a large silver padlock I hadn't noticed when I drove in. "You ever been to a twelve-step meeting?" Caroline asked.

"No."

"Me neither," she said. "But they use this saying I like. You ready?" I nodded. *"What you see here, what you hear here, let it stay here.* Here here."

She tongued her upper lip. "My mother's scalp came off when they loaded her into the ambulance. She had no skin left on her back. Even then she was trying to tell the cop who was with her that what happened at that trailer was not an accident. I'm going to listen to her, Adam. I'm going to do whatever it takes to listen to her. If you don't approve, you can hit the road."

I looked to the barn doors. Then I gave her a small nod.

She squeezed herself between the Tahoe and the barn doors, unlocked the padlock, and pushed the doors inward. The second she stepped into the darkness, I saw a man lassoed to a metal bed frame with two lengths of nylon rope that met in a thick knot under his back. His long face was skin on bone, and he was asleep or drugged, his slack jaw revealing chipped and blackened teeth. His arms were riddled with track marks. Several looked fresh.

I instinctively pulled the doors shut behind me, plunging the three of us into near darkness lit by wavering shafts of light from slats in the rafters. Caroline lit a Coleman lantern and placed it next to the guy's head. He didn't react. The rest of the barn contained a Skilsaw and a stack of old plywood. "Is he drugged?"

"He's been drugged since he was a kid. Now he's under medical supervision."

With that, she crossed to a small leather bag that sat on the Skilsaw table behind the bed. I watched, stupefied, as she loaded a syringe from a small medicine bottle.

"This is bullshit," I whispered.

"Actually, that's what we're going to find out as soon as Eddie starts talking."

"Some of those track marks are fresh," I said, pointing to Eddie's upturned right arm. "How long have you been at this?"

"A little less than a day," she said.

"You wake him up to see if he'll talk, then you knock him out again?"

"Something like that." She took a seat on the edge of the bed.

"That's torture."

She gripped Eddie's left wrist, just below its cinching of nylon rope, and squeezed, searching for a vein. She didn't find one. She squatted down next to the bed frame, found a vein in the man's ankle, swabbed it with an alcohol pad, and made a quick, clean injection. Then she rose and took a step back from the bed.

"Bigfoot had Roger Paterson and Bob Gimlin," she said. "El Maricón has Eddie Cairns, petty criminal, lifetime meth addict, and teller of tall tales."

The man named Eddie Cairns sputtered. His jaw quivered with the first threat of tears. He made a pained sound in his throat. Caroline rested her hand on Eddie's forehead and regarded me.

"Going or staying?" she asked.

I stayed. She returned her attention to her broken captive. Keeping one hand on his forehead, she raised the drawing of Reynaldo Reyez so he could see it.

Eddie Cairns let out a scream so loud and piercing it blasted me backward. He bucked and writhed against his constraints as if Caroline had dropped a box of snakes on him.

He bucked and yelled for so long that I pulled the drawing out of Caroline's hand so he could catch his breath. She backed away from the bed without a glance at me.

Eddie had twisted his head away from us as he struggled to breathe through his open mouth. Caroline sat down cross-legged on the floor. I saw an old tape recorder in front of her.

"Tell us about him, Eddie," she said.

Eddie flinched. There was no place for me to sit, so I backed up to the nearest wall. Eddie finally turned his head to stare up at the ceiling as if an angel had appeared to him between the rafters. From the sudden wide-eyed expression on his face, it looked like the angel had instructed him to obey Caroline.

He started talking.

Eddie Cairns was sixteen years old when he met the old rancher with a face like a horse. The rancher was sitting in his pickup in back of the diner where Eddie's mother and older sister both waited tables. When Eddie emerged from the back door with a trash bag in each fist, the guy bent forward over his steering wheel, his rheumy eyes wide and chapped lips parted, as if Eddie were as remarkable as the sunset setting fire to the hills.

Eddie was pretty sure the guy was some sort of pervert, so he dropped the trash bags off and headed quickly for the back door. Just then, the guy rolled his window down and asked Eddie if he'd like to make some money.

"You some kinda weirdo?" Eddie asked, even as he approached the truck.

The guy cackled. "I pop wood for a nice set of tits, kid, and from the look of things, you ain't got any. Whaddya say? I betcha your mom don't pay shit for all the work you do trying to cover her ass in there."

The guy's face was almost as long as his mane of wiry silver hair, and his eyes were sunken below the bridge of a nose that resembled an upturned shark's fin. His lips were so cracked it seemed he'd been sucking the exhaust from a tail pipe. The truth was, Eddie bussed a few tables and took the trash out without his mother asking him to, and each time he did it, he hoped she would give him something more than a strained smile.

"Good money, kid," the guy said. "All you gotta do is clean up after a few friends of mine. All cash. None of that IRS bullshit." Eddie heard a tinge of desperation in the guy's voice, knew something wasn't quite right with his manic movements and darting eyes. "Come on, kid. This is a sweet deal I'm offering. Get in and let's discuss the particulars."

Eddie envisioned how the rest of his night would play out if he didn't go with the man. He'd kill time faking his way through his homework in the diner's kitchen. Every now and then his mother would come in, lay her hands on his shoulders, let out a long, pained sigh, and depart, as if her son could offer nothing more than a split-second reprieve from the world outside, including a sister who was always either newly pregnant, recovering from an abortion, or screwing up someone's order. Close to closing time, the pharmacist from down the block would stumble in, a few drinks on his breath, and Eddie would be forced to listen as the guy flirted with his mother, his comments becoming more lewd as the others diners departed. Then on the ride home, his mother and his sister would find something to fight about, something that would leave his sister in hysterical tears and his mother cursing a father Eddie had never met.

"I've got a switchblade in my pocket," Eddie told the wasting rancher. "Try anything fruit and I'll get serious with it."

As Eddie climbed into the truck, the man cackled and clapped his hands together as if he were keeping time to machine gun fire. "That's the spirit, kid. That mouth we'll have to put a muzzle on, but your spirit's A-okay!"

They were speeding west on Highway 198, into the hills on a route that Eddie's mother had forbidden him to take on his bike. The guy's words came out at the same speed his fingers drummed the steering wheel. He'd had a cattle ranch once but lost it, along with his wife, and he'd killed time drinking whiskey and watching his cows die where they stood. Then the rancher had made some new friends. Important friends. Guys who were very good at what they did and needed a nice secluded spot to let off steam.

Eddie knew without asking that the rancher was afraid of these new friends, afraid in the same quiet and supposedly respectful way that his mother was afraid of a God who answered her prayers with a headache or a car accident.

Just as night fell over the inner Coast Ranges, the rancher turned onto a road lined with a rotted cattle fence. Eddie saw a single trailer uphill a little ways from a large barn with a cathedral window over the front door. They jerked to a stop right next to a battered trailer surrounded by the stalks of dead trees. Several yards away lay the burned-out crater where a small house had once stood. Just then the guy's hand brushed Eddie's shoulder, and he jumped a foot off his seat. The guy cackled and reached past Eddie for the glove compartment.

Eddie watched as the guy removed a small glass pipe and a plastic bag full of white rocks stained slightly yellow. Loading the pipe gave the man a sudden focus, and when he spoke, it was with the patient and even voice of a schoolteacher: "You come up here on the weekends and you stay here. Tell your mom you're at a friend's house or something. Come Sunday you get a hundred bucks cash."

"What do I have to do for it?" Eddie asked, his voice shaky and his heart turbocharged.

"The minute you see an empty beer bottle hit a table, you pick it up. One of these guys spits in your direction, you get a rag and start wiping." The guy pressed several white rocks into the glass pipe with one thumb; then he shook it with one wrist. "Every now and then they'll bring in some bitch and get rough with her. If it gets bloody, make sure she's cleaned up after they're done with her. Maybe talk sweet to her or something."

His pipe loaded, the rancher met Eddie's eyes, and Eddie saw there was a strange fire in them fueled by anticipation and fear. "Call 'em all sir.

They're all fucking wetbacks, so they'll love that shit. Especially coming from a little gringo like you. Not señor, 'cause then they'll think you're fucking with 'em."

Before he could stop himself, Eddie said, "These guys aren't really your friends, are they?"

The rancher pressed his feet against the floor and straightened himself, holding his pipe up in one hand as he dug in his pants pocket with the other. He pulled out a lighter and smiled at it. Suddenly the rancher seemed to remember Eddie was sitting next to him.

"And you *don't* sleep," the rancher said. He lit the pipe and gave it a long deep kiss.

When he extended the pipe toward Eddie, Eddie frowned at it. He had some vague notion of what was inside of it, but some cruel instinct in him, as natural as his thirst for water, told him that he couldn't possibly know or judge what was inside the pipe until it was inside his lungs.

During the long nights that would follow, when his fingernails bled because he spent hours on end cleaning the windows, or with his bones trembling as he cowered on the floor of a drunk tank, Eddie Cairns would come up with lots of different reasons for why he took the pipe without asking what was inside it.

He took it because he had buckteeth and chicken legs. Because when his sister came home pregnant by another man, he felt what could only be described as jealousy. Because no matter how tough he tried to be, the sound of a backfiring car made him clutch his heart looking for a bullet hole. Because when his mother moved a piece of furniture several inches to the left, he was overcome by a paralyzing sense of dread and a desperate urge to tell his mother how he felt without having her laugh at him.

Eddie Cairns took the pipe because no matter how hard he tried not to, he still saw things other people did not: fissures, phantoms, and blood. Lately he had started to suspect that all the people around him had trained themselves not to see these things, but for some reason, they had deemed Eddie unworthy of learning their tricks.

When Eddie brought the pipe to his mouth, the rancher took his lighter and applied its guttering flame to the bowl. Eddie saw the white rocks light up around the edges. He inhaled. He watched the orange glow fringe the red rocks inside the glass pipe and then spread to the fields outside and the ridges of the mountains. The strands of low clouds passing high above the truck revealed the strange energy inside themselves by dragging some of it across Eddie's skin.

Then the rancher said, "Suck it in, son. The spiders will be here soon."

At least ten men came to the barn that night: the ringleader, a bald and portly man with cue ball eyes named Eduardo Velásquez, a man who controlled a large chunk of the Central Valley meth trade, and his small posse of meth cooks, runners, and street dealers, the starry-eyed young boys who had come up from Mexico to brew a drug that reduced houses to craters, men to jackals, and mothers to murderers.

The rancher had provided them with enough Corona to keep them singing badly for days on end, and a stereo system with surround speakers mounted on the ceiling. The barn still had some of its cattle stalls, and the men were using one to take turns with an emaciated, groaning prostitute.

Eddie had spent most of the evening doing exactly what the rancher had told him to, but now his teeth felt like they were crumbling in his mouth, and his skin was lacquered with a noxious sweat. He needed a three-hour shower and another hit from the rancher's pipe.

He was about to find the rancher and ask for both when the double doors to the barn rolled open. Right away, Eddie knew the two guys at the entrance didn't belong there. Worse, they had made no attempt to blend in. Both men wore black jeans, black T-shirts, and leather jackets that looked oddly lumpy in the chest and shoulders. Each one had a black motorcycle helmet clipped to the side of his belt.

The first one to step inside the barn had a husky frame, a square head with black steel-wool hair, and a flattened nose. He breathed hard at the scene in front of him like an angry bull. His partner was taller and slender, one of the prettiest guys Eddie had ever seen. His dark hair fell to his shoulders from a part down the middle. He had a dimple in his chin, and his slanted green eyes betrayed no emotion. Neither of them looked old enough to be out of high school.

Right away, Eddie knew there was going to be trouble, so he backed into one of the empty cattle stalls, just several doors down from where the men were going to town on their whore. His first thought was that the strangers had come to use or rescue the prostitute, but Eddie watched in astonishment as the two men moved to the center of the barn, met chest to chest, and started a slow, out-of-synch waltz to the piercing cries of Celia Cruz.

Eduardo Velásquez stepped forward first. Eddie watched him approach the swaying couple like a restaurant manager summoned to a rowdy table.

When Eduardo called out to the men over the music, Eddie heard the steady confidence of a man who was sure his violence could fix any situation in due time. But the two men didn't react to him.

Eddie expected someone to kill the music. No one did. As they stepped forward from the stall, a few of the men started to laugh as if they had figured out the whole thing was a prank and were just waiting for their boss to get the joke.

"El Maricón!" Eduardo shouted.

Suddenly the shorter man spun his dancing partner out, long enough for the pretty boy's slanted green eyes to meet Eduardo's. He gave a sudden smile. That's when Eduardo reached for the pistol on his belt. No one else saw what was coming—no one besides Eddie Cairns. If they had, the two men would have been shot dead on the spot and hell would have stayed where it belonged for at least another night.

Again the shorter man spun his dancing partner out toward Eduardo. Eduardo pulled his gun from its holster just as the pretty boy reached up to the top of his back with his free hand and found a grip on something buried under his leather jacket.

The next thing Eddie knew, Eduardo Velásquez had fired his gun into the air and was stumbling backward, his knees buckling. The pretty boy returned a bloody machete to its hidden holster. Then he and his partner ripped their motorcycle helmets from their belts, put them on, and sank to their knees. Eduardo hit the floor on his back, a gushing red line down the center of his face, between eyes as big as eggs.

Eddie heard the commotion several stalls down as the other men leapt to their feet and crawled over one another. The two strangers stayed right where they were, on their knees, their gloved hands clasped in front of their chests.

Just as the men started to rush them, there was a sound like a giant whip cracking across the roof of the barn. Pieces of glass from the giant cathedral window tore through the air like a swarm of locusts, driving the other men to their stomachs, to their knees, their faces laced with blood and stripped flesh. His ears ringing, Eddie saw shards of glass impaled on the walls of the stall just above his feet. He expected a fire but none came. The explosion had been all sound and force. His back pressed to the rear of the stall, Eddie watched as the two strangers got to their feet and surveyed the bodies all around them. The duo was unscathed, thanks to the helmets and whatever body armor had given their clothes a bad fit.

The strangers went to work. They moved from man to man, lifting each by the back of the head or rolling them over onto their stomachs if they needed to, then swinging their machetes high and leaving long lateral slashes down each man's back. By the time they were finished, the ten men were rag dolls, their limbs twitching, eyes bulging, and jaws quivering. Incapacitated but alive.

Eddie realized that if the strangers weren't killing the men outright, their work was not over. Without a word to his partner, the shorter, thicker man walked out of the barn, ripping his motorcycle helmet off as he went. The pretty boy stayed behind, surveying from behind the visor of his black helmet the writhing limbs all around him.

As soon as the man outside turned his back to Eddie, the boy took off. He could feel the stranger's eyes fall on his back, but he kept running, past the parked cars and past the spot where the old rancher lay, his throat a red grin. Expecting the husky guy to jump out at any minute from behind a fence or truck, Eddie fled up the rutted road in the direction of the highway.

When he was almost to the highway turnoff, Eddie looked back. In the distance, a flickering white glow lit up the interior of the shattered cathedral window. The tall stranger stood in the doorway to the barn, his helmet raised above his head in a gesture of farewell to him. That's when Eddie Cairns realized that they had known he was there all along and had allowed him to run because he had borne witness.

Caroline pressed Stop on the tape recorder and got to her knees. She took one of Eddie's trembling hands in hers and leaned in toward his sobbing face. It sounded like she was saying soothing things to the man.

I stumbled into the clearing, focusing on the leaves that scattered at my feet in the weak wind and the gray-blue luminescence the slanting sunlight gave to the valley oaks all around me. Eddie Cairns had described a slaughter that bled revenge. A young man who answered the description of Reynaldo Reyez had slaughtered the drug lord who had torn apart Reynaldo Reyez's family.

I heard a snap of twigs behind me. Caroline's face was flushed, her freckles almost crimson. "Eduardo Velásquez was found beheaded in an irrigation ditch when Eddie Cairns was sixteen years old," she said.

"Burned?" I asked.

"Eddie didn't say they burned Velásquez's body," she responded. "Eddie said they set fire to the barn after the kid ran for it. Eddie's story has been floating around for years. He just gave us the definitive version."

"Definitive?" I asked. "Directional explosives that don't combust? Body armor under black leather suits? That's not definitive, Caroline. That's illustrative."

"Eddie Cairns just told us that he saw a man who looks just like Reynaldo Reyez murder Eduardo Velásquez. Do you believe him or not?"

"Yes," I answered. "But I think he got the rest of it out of a comic book." Amid all the gory, impossible details, the part of Eddie's story that had affected me the most was his description of his own addictions and the insanity they had visited upon him at such a young age. This, above all else, convinced me that there had been truth in his nightmare.

"Eduardo Velásquez," I said. "How big a story was his murder?"

"I remember it made the nightly news up in San Francisco," she said. "I think there was an article in the *Chronicle*, too."

Joseph Spinotta had lived and worked in California for most of his life. According to the file Jimmy had assembled on the man, Spinotta had been working for tech firms in Silicon Valley six years earlier. It was possible that he had heard the story of Velásquez's murder, maybe even some mention of the killer they called El Maricón. A gay assassin surely would have caught the interest of a man like Joseph Spinotta.

Later, when Martin Cale told Spinotta the tragic tale of his nephew's romance with a young man named Reynaldo Reyez, whose family had been destroyed by the brutally murdered drug lord Eduardo Velásquez, Spinotta had asked to meet with Corey. Had Spinotta made the connection I just had? Had he figured out that Corey's boyhood lover had turned into an assassin visiting a bloody revenge against the drug network that had destroyed his family?

Somehow Reynaldo Reyez had ended up working for Joseph Spinotta, and it was Corey who got him the job. Reynaldo Reyez, also known as El Maricón, had become Joseph's supplier. That might explain why the meeting between Spinotta and Corey had been such a secret. Spinotta would not even give his kept boy the location of their hideout. It made sense that he wouldn't tell Billy about the dangerous assassin he had employed.

"Your boy's been hired out," I finally said. "By a guy named Joseph Spinotta."

She wasn't impressed. It was still my turn. "Let him go and I'll tell you the rest."

"Who?" she asked.

"Eddie!"

She recoiled, then put her hands on her hips. "What did you think I was going to do with him?"

"I didn't ask that question for a reason, Caroline." She rolled her eyes and walked back inside the barn. I felt foolish for having judged her. I was now in pursuit of a man whose operation was larger and bloodier than I had imagined. If Reynaldo Reyez was actually involved in this operation, then someone—either Corey or Spinotta—had lied to him. But if I was going to find him, I needed Caroline Hughes and all her rage.

CHAPTER 18

We left the Coast Ranges behind without saying a word to each other. Caroline turned left on Highway 33 and headed toward Avenal, the reverse of the route I had followed her on. Eddie Cairns lay under a tarp in the cargo bay. He was not a free man yet, which meant I didn't have to tell Caroline squat.

I tried to imagine the lunch between Spinotta and Corey. I tried to write the scene the way James Wilton would.

Corey is still shattered from Melissa Brady's betrayal and his exile from the Marine Corps. Barely out of his twenties, he has returned to Los Angeles a broken man. Suddenly a wealthy and charismatic businessman like Spinotta wants to meet with him in private for no apparent reason. Spinotta starts in gradually on the topic of Reynaldo Reyez, luring the story out of Corey piece by piece. Then Spinotta starts his pitch. He dreams of lifting young children out of the kind of squalor and abuse that Corey was raised in. Does Corey know anyone who can help him make this dream a reality? Corey buys into this lie and agrees to put Spinotta in touch with Reynaldo Reyez.

Reynaldo the assassin and Joseph the pedophile probably communicate entirely by phone, each one unwilling to reveal his identity to the other. Joseph repeats the same lie he gave to Corey: He wants to give kids who are being denied every chance a new shot at life. A new identity.

Reynaldo Reyez believed he was delivering the abused children of meth addicts into a new and better life. But the truth was far different. Joseph Spinotta was taking possession of these young boys and profiting from their sexual violation.

Meanwhile, back in Los Angeles, the man who supplied the connection

that turned Spinotta's mad dream into a reality had started to become suspicious. Over time, Corey had seen things aboard his uncle's yacht, things he
did not approve of. Eventually, Corey discovered that his uncle was a paying
customer of a child porn ring—one that Corey had unwittingly enabled
Spinotta to create four years earlier.

So where did that leave Corey's thirteen-year-old brother?

Suddenly I saw it. Reynaldo Reyez had abducted Corey's brother on
purpose. Reynaldo Reyez thought he was delivering Caden McCormick to
a better life. Corey had been too afraid to tell his old friend that he had
hooked him up with child pornographers, so he had tried to bring down
the operation and get his brother back on his own.

My theory was more sprawling and presumptive than the step-by-step
deductions James Wilton had come up with over the past week. I needed
to establish that Corey and Reynaldo Reyez had remained in contact after
their teenage years.

I needed James Wilton.

A good ways past Avenal, Caroline turned off into a barren field. I watched
her step out of the truck and head around the back. She opened the cargo
door. I couldn't see what she was doing, but it looked like she was trying to
rouse Eddie Cairns from his stupor.

I stepped out of the car just as she was hefting Eddie out of the truck.
His hands were bound and his ankles hobbled together so that he could
take only foot-long steps, and he was blindfolded with a piece of grease-
stained muslin. When Caroline realized she walking him straight toward
me, she stopped, and Eddie leaned back against her, his chin to his chest,
his breaths whistling through clenched teeth.

I took out my wallet and shoved a ten-dollar bill in Eddie's front
pocket.

"He's just going to blow it on meth," Caroline said.

"I hope so," I said. "And I hope he gets a nice big bottle of Crown
Royal to go with it."

I gave her a cheery smile and got back in the car. She walked Eddie a
hundred slow paces from the front of the Tahoe. I saw her give him whispered instructions; then she crouched down and removed a large field
knife from a holster hidden inside the right leg of her jeans. In one motion, she chopped the nylon rope from around Eddie's ankles, then from
around his wrists.

Eddie ripped the blindfold away and took off. Caroline strode to the

Tahoe, slid into the driver's seat, and started the engine. As she turned the car toward the highway, I watched Eddie Cairns turn into a running dot that was almost indistinguishable against the barren mountains in the distance.

"I've got an idea," I said. "The next time you abduct someone, why don't you give some thought to a stocking cap?"

"You think he's going to talk?" she asked. "Who's going to believe him?" She chuckled; I grimaced.

It was time for me to tell her what I knew. "Do we agree that your El Maricón is Reynaldo Reyez?" I asked.

When she said yes, I told her everything I had learned over the past week; then I gave her my new theory. She chewed on it for a while as she drove north on Highway 33. "So El Maricón is working for this Joseph Spinotta," she said. "And your friend Corey got him the job."

"Yes," I answered. "And can we can start calling him Reynaldo Reyez, please?"

I could tell she was skeptical. "Look, you believe Reynaldo Reyez is behind the four abductions you told me about," I began. "I know that one of those boys is being held captive by Joseph Spinotta. Considering that Corey was desperate to find out where Spinotta was, I'm willing to bet that his brother is being held by Joseph Spinotta as well."

She kept her eye on the forlorn horizon. "I think Reynaldo has no idea what Spinotta is actually doing to these boys," I went on. "I bet Spinotta gave him a bullshit cover story about rescuing the kids from methamphetamine hell and giving them a fresh start. Maybe Reynaldo abducted Corey's brother on purpose. Maybe Reynaldo thought he was saving Caden, and he told Corey about it like it was good news. But Corey figured out what Spinotta was really going to do to his brother, so he tried to find out where Spinotta was."

"That's a lot of maybes," she said. "Why didn't Corey tell Reynaldo what Spinotta was really up to?"

"Hi," I said sharply. "Sorry, Reynaldo. Four years earlier I hooked you up with a kiddie-porn ring. I know you're a cold-blooded vigilante, but please go easy on me. It was an honest mistake." She rolled her eyes. I got the sense that she could hear my sarcasm for what it was: defensiveness.

"Okay, fine," she said. "But the one thing you're sure of is that Corey was trying to find out where Joseph Spinotta was. Why didn't he ask his pal Reynaldo?"

"Because Reynaldo Reyez probably doesn't know either," I replied.

"Spinotta didn't even tell his kept boy Billy where they were located. If he's lying to Reynaldo Reyez about what he's really up to, you think he's going to invite the guy to his hideout for tea? I'm willing to bet the two of them have never met face-to-face the whole time Reyez worked for Spinotta. Considering that Reynaldo's abducted only four boys over the past three years, there's not much reason for them to. I bet the kids are exchanged at a drop-off point somewhere. Reynaldo Reyez is an elusive assassin who isn't supposed to exist. I bet that deal works for him just fine."

Now that I had given voice to my new conjecture, I was less sure of it. It took too much explaining and too much defending. There were too many threads, and I had tied them up in too many places. "Look," I said. "If we get to Joseph Spinotta, you're one step closer to the man who killed your mother. I'm sure of that, Caroline."

She made a left turn into the town of Avenal. "Any chance we can run some of this by your friend Corey?"

"No. He's dead."

"You didn't tell me that on the phone this morning."

"I wasn't sure it was any of your business."

She kept driving faster than the town's speed limit. "Fine. Joseph Spinotta. Considering that no one seems to know where he is, where the hell do we start?"

"They're sending out these broadcasts wirelessly," I said. "Maybe Spinotta's got the technology to beam this shit across entire continents. But I seriously doubt it. He's not a corporation. He's one man who stole a big chunk of change. If he's somewhere out here, maybe he's got the reach to hit LA on one side and San Francisco on the other. The abductions were all out here in the Central Valley. Reynaldo Reyez is from here and does most of his work here as well. Spinotta lived in California all of his life."

"California's a big state."

"How long did it take you to find Eddie Cairns?" I asked.

"Good point," she said.

She pursed her lips in thought. "Do we get to have sex?"

"I've got a switchblade in my pocket. Try anything fruit and I'll get serious with it."

When she realized I was quoting her friend Eddie Cairns, the threat of a smile disrupted the hard lines of her face.

*　*　*

She drove us to a rest stop situated between Interstate 5 and the Kettleman Hills. There were no trees, just a stone building that housed bathrooms I wouldn't blow my nose in. The empty parking lot had a view across the valley that was so clear I thought I could make out individual pine trees on the peaks of the Sierra Nevada. "What are we doing here?" I asked her.

"Meeting a friend of mine," she said.

"You have friends?"

She scowled and dialed a number on her cell phone. I remembered that I had agreed to check in with Brenda every few hours. I stepped out of the Tahoe and walked a good distance away to give myself some privacy.

Brenda's cell phone went right to voice mail, which disappointed me more than I expected it to. I left a message telling her that I was fine and that interesting things were happening. Then I hung up. When I tried to shove my cell phone back into my pocket, it caught on something. I pulled out Corey's golden scorpion chain. I saw Billy Hatfill's sprawled body beneath a spider web of cracked glass. The flesh on my palm went hot underneath the medallion, and my vision blurred without warning.

For the first time in days, I doubted my abilities and resolve with a force that was crippling. The dull roar of the passing traffic intensified until it was a ringing in my ears. Without meaning to, I sank on the stone curb in front of me and stared out at the sterile golden expanse before me.

I told myself my grief for the man I had known as Corey Howard was inappropriate and absurd. Even if he had been desperate to find his little brother, he had done terrible things in the process. He had used his deal with Billy Hatfill to visit a retribution upon Melissa Brady that required the violation of a boy in the same situation as his younger brother.

I stared down at the chain in my palm. I had forgotten about one of the most important questions I had left LA to answer. The identity of Corey's killer. Billy had told me the killer was a third party—not Spinotta, not one of his Vanished Three. An obvious candidate was staring me in the face.

Reynaldo Reyez. Surely Spinotta would not have sent Reynaldo after his boyhood lover. Not if Spinotta had been aware of the history between the two men. Not if Corey had been the one to make the connection between Spinotta and Reynaldo four years earlier.

That meant there was another player involved. I didn't like the thought. I knew the conventional wisdom among homicide detectives was that they almost always came into contact with the killer within the first twenty-four hours of their investigation. But I was not a homicide detective.

I spent a few minutes counting the cars that glinted past me on Interstate 5. I reminded myself what day of the week it was. Sunday. A week since Billy Hatfill had tracked me down on a West Hollywood street corner and told me Corey had paid a strange visit to his house. But I had overlooked another anniversary the day before. It had been over a week since I had taken a drink of alcohol. I had not gone that long without an intoxicant in my system since I was fifteen. I was doing something right.

Caroline's shadow fell over me. "You all right?"

"Yes. Why haven't you gone to the authorities?"

"I could ask you the same question."

"You're right. But I asked you first."

She took a seat on the curb beside me and together we watched the traffic thunder by. "My mother asked me not to visit her after she moved here," she said. "She wouldn't tell me why. She left San Francisco without a word to anyone after Dad died. A few months ago, she sent me a letter. She told me that her grief for my father was like a virus, and she didn't want to infect me with it. That's why she left. She said that I was stronger than she had ever meant for me to be. Does that sound like a good thing or a bad thing to you?"

I didn't think it was my place to answer, but it wasn't lost on me that she had described methamphetamine's hold on the surrounding area in the same terms her mother had used to describe her own grief. She turned and rested her butt against the window ledge. "My grief for her feels like everything else, all the time. Nonstop. Everything besides grief."

"My mother died last month," I said.

"How?"

"She was hit by a cab."

She cocked her head at me, and I got the sense that she resented my attempt to make a connection between us, but she didn't want to say anything. Maybe she thought she needed my wild theories as much as I needed her aggressive anger.

"A cab, huh?" she finally said. "Did you try to kill the driver?"

She got to her feet and walked back toward the Tahoe. I didn't tell her that I had never thought about killing anyone. In an alcoholic blackout, I had once confessed understanding for anyone who might hurl my mother in front of a taxicab. Even though I didn't remember saying the words, I knew I had experienced moments of the combined blindness and frenzied motion that people called rage. I was still waiting for some sign that Caroline Hughes was in such a state, but she seemed to see with perfect clarity and moved with graceful determination. She sought murder with a full knowledge of what the end result would be. This I could not understand at all and had no interest in trying.

A red Ford Escape pulled into the rest stop and parked several empty spaces away from the Tahoe. The woman behind the wheel had skin edging from tan to leathery, and her small brown eyes were stamped with crow's-feet. I followed Caroline to the driver's-side window. "Who is she?" I asked.

"Her name's Amy. You have those pictures?"

She had asked me earlier for my photos of the Vanished Three and Joseph Spinotta. I slipped them from my jacket pocket and handed them to her. The woman named Amy rolled down her window instead of getting out of the car. Caroline handed her the photographs without greeting her.

"Truck stops. Gas stations. That kind of thing," Caroline said. Amy studied each picture in turn. "We think they might be staying in an isolated location, but if they're taking any long trips they have to use the 5 or the 101, right?"

"You want to add Nevada to that search area?" Amy asked. "The last time I checked, the 101 doesn't go through my county."

"You have friends in other counties, right?" Caroline asked.

Amy glowered at me. "Who are you?"

"He's the wacko who called the station this morning," Caroline said.

So that was how my call had been intercepted. "Thanks for the fix-up," I told her.

Amy twitched one eyebrow in response, and then went back to inspecting the pictures of the Vanished Three as if they were an apology letter from a boss who had fired her. "If you get anything, call us and we'll follow up on it," Caroline said. Amy gave her a dubious look. "In the most legal and ethical manner possible."

Amy rolled the window up, started her engine, and pulled out of her parking spot.

"She's a cop," I said.

"She had a thing for my mother."

"And you're playing it."

"You're damn right I am."

We watched the red Escape disappear down the slope that led to the interstate.

"Where to?" she asked.

"Visalia," I answered. "We need to find someone who knew Corey and Reynaldo in their younger days. Corey's grandmother is dead. Reynaldo's parents are both dead. But I'm sure there's someone who remembers them."

She kept looking at the interstate.

"I take it you're not excited by this."

"Your approach is a little journalistic for my taste."

"We need to establish the details of their relationship."

"See. You establish things. That's journalistic. Besides, you really think the man who killed my mother still goes by the name Reynaldo Reyez?"

"He sure as hell doesn't go around calling himself the *Homosexual*," I said. "I promise to let you beat the shit out of someone very soon. Let's go."

CHAPTER 19

We went east on Highway 198, across desolate golden fields and past the Lemoore Naval Air Station, which looked like a small regional airport abandoned after a nuclear fallout. She let me drive. Our route took us clear across the Central Valley to the base of the Sierra Nevada. The town of Visalia looked like a suburb without an adjacent city, unless you considered the Sierras a suitable downtown skyline. A canopy of majestic oaks heralded its borders, and the four-lane highway that cut through the center of town was lined with strip malls.

With Corey's grandmother long gone, along with any family Reynaldo had ever known, I was left with one option. After half an hour of searching, we found the place I was looking for.

It was a small single-story building sandwiched between two strip malls, just a few blocks from the spot where Highway 198 left the town behind and started its climb into the foothills. The hardscrabble windowless structure had aluminum siding and a neon sign above the front door that spelled out the word *Budweiser* in all the colors of the rainbow.

Caroline pulled to the curb out front and the two of us listened as Whitney Houston explained to the people inside that she had learned from the best. "You're sure this is a gay bar?" Caroline asked.

Inside was a small empty stage with a dead karaoke machine shoved to one side, black walls with cheap black curtains hung over them in places, and a bar that ran almost the length of the building. The portly bartender was enduring a shrill lecture from a thirtyish guy with seventies-style aviator eyeglasses and carefully sprayed hair. I heard something about his talent and ability not being properly valued.

I gave Caroline a few singles and asked her to go make a selection on the jukebox. To my astonishment, she complied. I took one of the stools. The bartender's eyes brightened when he saw me. Even as he slapped a napkin down in front of me and asked for my order, the guy in the aviator glasses didn't let up.

"I'm talking about the whole thing, Jim. Typing the programs. Making most of the scenery. I do it all. Now wouldn't you think that would earn me some appreciation over there? Even if they are friggin' Methodists, for Christ's sake."

I ordered a Coke from Jim and gave the aviator-glasses guy the kind of look he wasn't used to receiving. He wore a white dress shirt that was too big for him, black slacks, and a name tag that told me he had spent the day waiting tables. "You an actor?" I asked him.

He smiled. "I was supposed to have an audition tonight."

"What's the play?"

"*Steel Magnolias*," he said, taking a step closer. "And I'm not happy about it. First Methodist usually tries to do shows that are half girl parts, half guy parts."

"I still don't see what the big problem is," Jim the bartender grumbled. Suddenly deafening church bells resounded through the bar. I recognized them as the opening of "Hell's Bells" by AC/DC. Caroline backed away from the jukebox and took a seat at the far end of the bar. We glared at each other.

"You might want to tell your friend this isn't a girl bar," my actor friend said.

I read the guy's name tag. "How long have you lived around here, Bailey?"

"I grew up here, unfortunately," he said. "I spent some time in Phoenix, though."

I nodded, as if time spent in Phoenix would earn Bailey his very own A&E Biography. "Does the name Corey McCormick mean anything to you?"

Bailey's eyes turned to slits behind his glasses. His lips widened slightly and I thought his tongue might make an appearance. "It sure does," he said. "I didn't know him very well. We went to high school together. I was three years ahead of him, but I sure did a lot of looking over my shoulder, if you know what I mean."

I grinned. He slid off his stool and tapped his hand on the bar as if he had solved a calculus equation. "A guy like you comes in here asking about Corey McCormick—that's gotta mean something." I let him figure out what it meant. He let out a war whoop that made the bartender jump. "I'm sorry," he said once he'd reassembled himself. "You didn't understand. You coming in here and telling me Corey McCormick was gay. That's like Santa Claus appearing to a six-year-old in the middle of July."

I didn't bother telling him that Corey McCormick was also dead. Caroline looked at me suspiciously from the other end of the bar and ordered a vodka and soda. "What about his friend? Reynaldo Reyez?"

Bailey winced and took a slug of his beer. "I remember him, too. Creepy little kid. He always got made fun of 'cause he was kind of girly. First day of his freshman year, this guy Joe Rogers was picking on him in the lunch line. Joe was a real ass and he wouldn't let up. Joe was about twice the size of Reynaldo, but Reynaldo just hauled off and decked the guy. All of a sudden Joe's bleeding all over the place in front of everyone. Turned out Reynaldo had his keys in his fist."

"Creepy and smart," I agreed. "Did Reynaldo get expelled?"

"No way," Bailey said. "No one was going to rat him out. Every kid they talked to said Joe Rogers was lying through his teeth about the keys. Everyone said he fell 'cause Reynaldo hit him so hard. The guy had it coming. Trust me. Corey was there, actually. I guess he was impressed. After that, he took Reynaldo under his wing." His eyes brightened. "Holy hell. Do you think Corey and Reynaldo were actually—"

"What about Corey's grandmother, Bailey?"

"Lucinda," he said. "She owned a cattle ranch out on 198, just before you hit town." I remembered the area of gnarled tree trunks and stinking mud plots that Caroline and I had passed on the way in.

"Does she have any friends who might still be around?"

"Claire Shipley," he said immediately. "She works over at Linton Realty." He averted his eyes and took a small sip of his beer. "Lucinda was her only friend. She never replaced her."

"Claire's difficult, huh?"

"Look in her oven," he said. "You might find some children."

"But I understand Lucinda was a popular woman," I said. "Any idea why she was friends with a witch?"

"No clue," he said. "Claire used to manage some things out on Lucinda's ranch. The place was about to go under before Lucinda got sick. Claire was bitter about it. One day in the supermarket, she chewed my mother's ear off about how big industry was going to kill the whole valley."

"Sounds like she had a point," I said.

"Maybe," he said. "But Claire had just rear-ended my mother in the parking lot, and the two of them didn't even know each other. It may be a good point, but it's no excuse for running right into someone, is it?"

"No, it isn't, Bailey," I said with a smile he seemed to appreciate. "So she's a real estate agent now?"

"Barely," he said. "Someone had to hire her. She's obviously not going anywhere."

As Bailey gave me directions to Linton Realty, I felt Caroline's hand come to rest on my shoulder. "We better go if we want to watch *Queer Eye for the Straight Guy*," she said.

"That's not on tonight," Bailey said icily.

"It's a rerun," Caroline told him. She walked out of the bar.

"Is that your sister?" Bailey asked.

Once we were back in the Tahoe, Caroline put her sunglasses on and sighed.

"I take it this is boring you," I finally said.

She powered the window down and hooked the heel of one sneaker on the ledge. "Can we have sex later?" she asked. "I hear gay guys give women good oral sex. They get a lot of practice when they're closeted because they can't get it up to do anything else."

"Who told you that? The Fab Five?"

"You're right. I'm bored."

"Well, get ready, 'cause Claire Shipley is all yours. You two sound like the perfect match." More sullenness. "Can you think of any ways we can check out Eddie Cairns's story?"

"Amy's going to follow up on the old rancher he talked about and on any fires in the area," she said.

I didn't point out that Amy wasn't exactly going to be able to get the FBI to run a VICAP search on the term *old rancher*. "Look, Caroline, the only thing that seems real about Reynaldo Reyez is what happened here."

"Fine," she said. "But the abducted boys are next. I want to find witnesses, other family members. Maybe one of the other kids talked to someone, the way Caden did to my mother."

I nodded, but I didn't say anything. What she was asking for could take months, and even if the kids had talked, I didn't think we had any more use for strange tales of demons and government agents appearing to small boys in the night.

The offices of Lily Linton Realty were located in a strip mall that looked exactly like the two squeezing the gay bar building. The front window was plastered with color listings for one-story tract homes and California bunga-lows. Claire Shipley was the listing agent for one property, an empty lot in the southern part of town. I took down her cell phone number.

The receptionist was leafing through a copy of *People* when we walked in. She was not much older than the two of us, but she was under the im-pression that working at a real estate agency meant you had to dress like a matron. When I asked her if Claire Shipley was in, she looked at us with unpleasant surprise. "Are you guys interested in that lot?" she asked.

"We're interested in talking to Claire Shipley," Caroline said.

The receptionist's penciled eyebrows arched. "Why?" she asked, baffled.

I smiled. "Claire's a peach, isn't she?"

The receptionist cackled. I cackled right back. "I tell you. On some days I just want to take that woman by the—"

"The old bitch rear-ended me last week," Caroline interjected. "She gave me bullshit insurance information and I plan on suing her ass. You want to tell me where she lives?"

I stared down at my feet and tried to wish myself out of the office. The receptionist stared at Caroline as if she had just performed a brief soft-shoe in front of her desk. Then she gave us Claire Shipley's address.

Claire Shipley lived in a secluded neighborhood in southwest Visalia that was made up mostly of empty lots and untamed California oaks. Her driveway was empty and her windows were dark. The lot she was trying to sell was two blocks away. Her house was a one-story aluminum-siding box that sat on concrete blocks. The small space between her narrow driveway and her front steps featured every nonblossoming plant known to man. There was a chain-link fence around her entire property and a line of poplar trees in back. Through their shimmering leaves, a large empty field stretched toward a highway. The field had a developer's sign stuck in it.

Caroline and I did not get out of the Tahoe. "Should we call her on her cell phone?"

"She'll probably hang up."

Caroline exhaled loudly, reclined her seat, and shoved the bill of her baseball cap down on her head. Within minutes, her breaths were slow and even, and her head was turned toward the window. Abducting and torturing Eddie Cairns had taken a lot out of her.

The sun went down. Across the field behind Claire Shipley's house, the highway turned into a stream of headlights.

Caroline's jabs about my investigative technique had affected me. I was hoping that Claire Shipley could give us some details about Corey's mental state before he had run away from his grandmother, some indication of whether Corey had believed his best friend was still alive somewhere. All I had to go on was an offhand comment from Corey's uncle about how Corey had refused to speculate on Reynaldo's fate. It was a matchstick supporting a ten-pound theory. A year had elapsed between Corey's meeting with Spinotta and the first abduction in the Central Valley. Maybe that was how long it had taken Corey to track down Reynaldo.

After a while I dozed off. I woke to the ringing of a cell phone that wasn't mine. Caroline was already sitting up behind the wheel, clearing her throat and pulling her cell phone from her jeans pocket.

"It's Amy," she told me. She answered without saying anything and listened. From what I could hear, Amy sounded excited. It was nine-thirty. I had slept for almost two hours. Claire Shipley's house was still dark, the driveway still empty. I wondered what an angry, friendless old woman was doing out at nine-thirty on a Sunday night.

Caroline started the car and pulled away from the curb. When I asked her what was going on, she hung up the cell phone and dropped it to her lap. "Amy got something," she said.

"What?" I asked.

"A sighting," she answered. "A gas station attendant down in Wasco saw the Vanished Three a few weeks ago. She says it wasn't the first time, either."

"Which one did the attendant see?"

"That's what we're going to find out."

She started speeding in the direction of Highway 99, a north-south freeway that parallels Interstate 5, but further to the east. The Vanished Three had been spotted in the Central Valley on more than one occasion. Joseph Spinotta was somewhere close by.

As we drove alongside the barren field, I turned around and located the back of Claire Shipley's tiny house. A mustard-colored corona of light had appeared in the curtain of poplar leaves along her back fence; the security light above her back door had turned on in our wake. Before her house faded from view, I saw the light in Claire Shipley's kitchen had gone on as well.

"She was home," I said.

"What?" Caroline asked.

"Claire Shipley was home the whole time," I said. "She was waiting us out. Someone must have told her we were coming."

I remembered the light that had gone on in the eyes of Bailey the waiter when I had told him Corey McCormick was gay. Maybe he had called Claire Shipley to gloat, and told her we were in town asking questions about her close friend's grandson. Questions she obviously did not want to answer.

The small town of Wasco was only a short drive from where I had come down out of the mountains earlier that day. I glimpsed a sign that informed us that Wasco was the rose capital of the nation, but I didn't see any roses anywhere. We paralleled a set of railroad tracks and passed block after block of one-story tract homes.

We passed out of the town's limits and into an island of sodium vapor lights. Several large service stations ran along either side of the highway. Eighteen-wheelers slumbered in their parking lots. Amy had given Caroline the name of a gas station attendant who worked at a Stop 'N' Go that sat at the end of the strip, close to Interstate 5.

She was a tiny Hispanic woman with a huge mane of black hair that was about to come free of its ponytail. On the counter behind her, I saw faxed versions of the photos we had given Amy earlier that day. Caroline explained to the girl that the men in question had been hanging out with the daughter of a friend of hers, and she was afraid they were a bad influence. It was a cover story Amy had repeated to everyone to whom she had sent pictures of Spinotta and the Vanished Three.

The attendant told us that she had seen Roger Vasquez, the Latin lover, and Ben Clamp, the all-American jock, on three occasions that she could recall over the past few months. All of their visits had been at night—she guessed around eleven o'clock, but she couldn't be sure. No Terrance Davidson. No Joseph Spinotta. Each time, the men had made polite conversation and purchased a full tank of gas and various snack foods. They had come in the same car, a black Chevy Suburban with tinted windows. She didn't know the plate number. She figured they were road trippers from LA, but she had never asked them. She also threw in the fact that she thought they were perfect gentlemen and wouldn't be a bad influence on anyone's daughter.

"Any dents on the Suburban?" Caroline asked.

I had been trying to hide my reaction to the woman's report, but the attendant saw something on my face that made her suspicious. She narrowed her eyes and placed one hand on the edge of the counter in front of her.

"Look," Caroline said in a gentle voice that shocked me. "I'm sorry if this is too much information, but my friend's daughter—she's pregnant. These guys don't seem like the type who pay child support, if you know what I mean. They sure move around a lot."

Her words hit their target. The attendant made a small indignant sound in her throat. Caroline gave the woman her cell phone number and asked her to call if the guys came in again. She agreed.

I walked out into the smell of diesel fumes and the deep drone of idling eighteen-wheelers. I got Caroline's road atlas out of the car and laid it on the hood. The town of Wasco sat on Highway 46, which formed an east-west connection between Highway 99 and Interstate 5, the major north-south arteries of the Central Valley.

Caroline appeared behind me. "What direction do you think they were coming from?"

The map told me that from where we were standing, Highway 46 traveled a westward path through a whole lot of nothing, the town of Paso Robles, then the rolling vineyard country that met the Pacific Ocean. To the east, Highway 46 dead-ended into Highway 99. East of their intersection was the southern terminus of the Sierra Nevada Mountain Range.

"East or west," I said.

"Why not north and south?"

"It's a guess," I said. "LA is south and these guys aren't going anywhere near it. I suspect they're someplace isolated."

"Fine," she said. "East of here, you've got the Greenhorn Mountains. There's a lot of cabins along Highway 155. It goes straight up into the mountains until you hit Lake Isabella. There's not much up there. A few towns. The Kern River Valley. It's pretty isolated."

"And west?" I asked her.

"More nothing, but not much in the way of mountains," she answered. "Forty-six takes you through Paso Robles, then through the Coast Ranges. But the range is different down here. The peaks aren't as high, and the area close to the ocean has a lot of vineyards. Then you hit Cambria. Then you hit the Pacific Ocean."

She was being as patient with me as possible. "So what do you think, Adam? East or west?"

"These guys are stopping here for a reason," I said. "They're either coming down out of the mountains to the east, or through the hills so that they can take the 5 or the 99 to the north. They're traveling at night, and they're driving a black Chevy Suburban with tinted windows. That's not exactly inconspicuous, so I doubt they're sightseeing. Spinotta stole enough money to get them a more inconspicuous car, if they want to take a joyride."

I had her full attention. "They're buying snack foods," I went on. "I bet they get their real provisions closer to home. They're also buying a full tank of gas. That means they're either real close, which I doubt, or they're low on gas by the time they get here."

"So they're close. But not that close."

From the look of the highway on the map, if the Vanished Three were picking this place to get onto Interstate 5, they didn't have a lot of other options close to their home base. From the east, several different freeways flowed down out of the Sierras and toward Highway 99 and Interstate 5. From the west, the options were fewer and far between.

"They're coming from the west," I said.

"A Suburban," she said. Now she was the one thinking out loud. "There's a lot of room in a Suburban, and there's only two of them. You said you thought they were picking up the kids at a drop-off point."

"That might explain one of the trips," I said. "But the attendant saw them several times over the past few weeks. You think those were all pick-ups? You think they've abducted two more kids since Caden McCormick?"

"No, I don't. I would have heard about it."

"These guys are traveling long distances at night," I said. "On a regular basis. I bet if we visited some more gas stations along this stretch we might find someone else who's seen them."

"So what the hell are they doing?" she asked.

"I don't know."

An eighteen-wheeler roared to life several feet away and then blasted past us as it pulled out of the gas station and headed west toward Interstate 5. I watched it depart, its rim lights fading into the night.

"The boys," Caroline said. "They're out picking the boys." She turned to face me. "Maybe these road trips are about finding the boys, picking the right ones."

"You think they tell Reynaldo which kids to abduct?" I asked. "That shoots my whole theory to hell. That means they picked Corey's brother on their own."

"Maybe it was a coincidence," she said.

"I seriously doubt that, Caroline. If they keep ordering Reynaldo to abduct attractive young boys, then he's going to catch on sooner or later that their intentions aren't pure. I bet they give him as few orders as possible. The more requests they make, the more suspicious he might get. And besides, Reynaldo's got to abduct these boys. Reynaldo has to decide whether the circumstances are right."

"You're guessing, Adam."

"We both are."

A silence fell. I got the impression that she was cutting me some slack for the first time that day. A light breeze lifted her hair under the back of her cap.

"Maybe Reynaldo knows," she finally said. "Maybe Reynaldo knows what they're going to do to these kids, and he thinks it's better than what might happen to them if they stayed with their parents."

It was a good explanation for why Corey couldn't go to Reynaldo for help once he discovered what Joseph was really up to, because Reynaldo knew full well what was going to be done to Caden McCormick, and he didn't care.

"My mother did some research," Caroline said, "about what happens to these kids growing up. How they live, how they can die. Their parents keep acetone in the freezer. Sometimes the children drink it by accident. When they die, the parents just get rid of the body. This one woman, she thought her kids were possessed by Satan, so she made them drink bleach every morning. Another one used her daughter—"

"Enough, Caroline."

To my surprise, she stopped giving me the gory details. Yet she had made me question what was a better fate for the four young boys who had been abducted, being abused and killed at home or nursed back to health and molested in a state of near catatonia. I forced myself to recall the video I had seen the night before.

Caroline seemed to be reading my thoughts. "You said the boys are drugged. Maybe they never know what happened to them. Maybe they have no memory of it." Her voice sounded hollow and her eyes fell to the pavement at her feet.

"You think Spinotta doesn't visit them when they're awake?" I asked sharply. "And we still don't have the slightest clue what happens to these boys when they're too old for Spinotta's liking. Billy Hatfill told me he was never young enough for Spinotta, and they met when Billy was eighteen."

"Yeah, well," she whispered, "at least with Spinotta, their parents aren't hogging all the drugs." She grunted, pressed the heels of her palms against her forehead for a few seconds, then ran her hands down her face. "Fine!" she snapped. "So what do we do? We get a room nearby? Wait for them to come back?"

"All their stops have been at night," I said, folding up the map.

"Yeah, so?"

"Tomorrow night, we get a room nearby. Check in with the attendant and wait for them to come back." I grabbed the car door handle, but she didn't move.

"That's your best plan?"

"Until something better comes along."

"I sure fucking hope something better comes along."

"So do I," I replied. "Tomorrow we'll go see Claire Shipley. She obviously doesn't want to talk to us. That means we want to talk to her."

I was chasing a young boy through an endless shimmering field. I jerked awake and felt something heavy fall on my legs. I kicked it to the floor and saw that it was a patchwork quilt. I was in Caroline's cabin, on Caroline's sofa. The only light came from the desk lamp. The photos of the four young boys who had been abducted were spread out on Caroline's desk. I had meant to study them when we had returned, but I had collapsed in exhaustion.

Now I had been awakened by a shrill series of beeps that sounded like they had come from a giant microwave. Caroline's sleeping loft was an empty mess of comforters. The front door of the cabin was open. Caroline was gone.

In the galley kitchen, I opened a cabinet door and found a rack of long-bladed knives just like the one Caroline had used to cut Eddie Cairns's restraints. I pulled one from its sheath and was struck by its light feel. It was perfectly weighted, with a five-fingered rubber grip, perfect for swinging, perfect for striding out into the dark when you didn't have the slightest clue how to wield a knife.

At the front door, I saw Caroline squatting at the entrance to the clearing. At first it looked like she was conversing with a friendly deer, only there was no deer. Her back was rigid, her head still. I approached slowly. She had slipped into a man's shirt and pushed her hair back over her head. In the darkness, it looked like a solid plate against her back. The gun she held in both hands was larger and meaner than the pistol Billy Hatfill used to take his life. It was black with a squared-off barrel and butt. The sinking half moon sent vague light across the empty expanse of field beyond. I could just make out the fence posts in the distance. "This place has a perimeter alarm?" I asked under my breath.

She got to her feet and locked the gun's three safeties with practiced speed.

"Did you see anything?" I asked.

"No," she answered. "Probably just a wayward cow."

My palm had greased the knife handle with sweat. I threw the thing to the dirt as if it had taken a bite out of me.

"That's a Glock field knife, in case you're interested. Strong enough to break a window or an ammunition box," she said. "The gun's a Glock too."

"You feel like telling me why your dad needed a hideout with a perimeter alarm?" I asked.

"I told you," she said. "He was an activist."

"Maybe he got a little too into his work."

Instead of taking the bait, she returned her attention to the moonlit field beyond the tree line.

"You've been asking a lot of questions about Reynaldo Reyez," I said. "Maybe he's onto you."

"You think he's looking for me now?" she asked. She sounded excited by the prospect. I didn't share her enthusiasm. "If that was the case, we would both be dead."

"You really think you know this guy, don't you?" I asked her.

She turned to face me, then slid the Glock into a holster hidden underneath her shirt. I figured she had been wearing it all day, but her baggy T-shirt had concealed it. The open cabin door threw a weak spray of light onto her face.

"What's that supposed to mean?"

"You called Reyez a crusader," I said. "That's the same as an activist, right?"

I saw the insult in her eyes. "Are you judging me?"

"I guess," I said.

Caroline shifted from one foot to another. "Your friend Corey wanted to know where Joseph Spinotta was. He used you to try to find out, and you're still doing his work for him. Even though he's dead. You must have really loved this guy."

"Corey didn't use me," I said. "That's the whole point. He used a body double. He didn't do what Billy asked him to do."

"Yeah," she said. "Have you stopped to think that maybe Corey believed in Billy's plan? That maybe Corey wanted you to believe it was you on that tape, even if it wasn't. That Corey wanted to send you out here to find Spinotta."

"What does it matter?" I asked sharply. "He's dead."

"Exactly," she said. "And you're still doing what he wants. You're going to save his little brother, right?"

She had my mother's special way of pressing words into your chest with the flat of her hand, and I was confident that if I shared that with her she would only press harder.

"You made your point, Caroline," I said.

I walked back inside the cabin. She didn't follow me.

I sat down at Caroline's desk and examined the photo assemblages of the four young boys who had been abducted. I tried to memorize their names and faces. There was no pattern to the dates of the abductions that I could discern.

My eyes kept drifting back to Jim Clark, the first boy to have been abducted. He looked familiar to me. He looked familiar to me because I had seen him before. I picked up the sheet containing his photos. He wore an angry glower in most of his pictures, but his eyes were big. Huge. They looked like each one could use its own pool man.

A little more than twenty-four hours earlier, I had watched Jim Clark cut Martin Cale's throat. His name was Everett now. When I had asked Everett about his parents, where he had come from, rage had flickered in his big blue eyes. He had been fourteen at the time of his abduction, and the physical transformation he had undergone was so total that I hadn't recognized him when I had first looked at this picture. He had ended up in Billy Hatfill's care, following Billy Hatfill's orders even when it meant murder.

Billy had been grooming Everett for a life as a potential trophy boy, he said. Were the other three boys in front of me supposed to meet the same fate?

Everett had been fourteen at the time of his abduction. That made him sixteen now, around the same age as Brian Ferrin, the young man Spinotta had drugged and raped years earlier. Everett was physically beautiful and still of an age to be desirable to Spinotta, but for some reason he had been sent away in his prime.

Had Spinotta rejected Everett because the boy's desires for sex and murder couldn't be controlled? I wondered if the pathologies of the young man I had met were a product of the time he had spent with Joseph Spinotta or of the abuse visited upon him before his abduction.

CHAPTER 20

We made it back to Visalia by ten o'clock the next morning.
The rising temperatures had stretched a layer of brown haze across the
valley that stole the definition from the mountain backdrop. Caroline
pulled to the curb two blocks away from the tiny aluminum box where
Claire Shipley lived.

"You said she was waiting us out last night?" Caroline asked.

"A security light went on over the back door right after we left," I said.
"Then the light in the kitchen went on, too."

"So what are we going to ask this woman?" she said.

I repeated the story Martin Cale had told me, that Reynaldo Reyez's
father had tried to leave the meth-running business behind because his
wife had become addicted to the stuff. When his boss got wind of this, he
ordered the murder of Reynaldo's grandmother down in Mexico. Reynaldo's father had responded to the news by turning a gun on his wife and
then himself. Some people claimed they saw Reynaldo being driven out of
town by his father on the morning of this murder-suicide.

"You think Claire Shipley actually knows something?"

"I think she doesn't want to talk to us."

"You didn't answer my question."

"I don't have an answer."

We got out of the Tahoe. When we were a block away, I saw that Claire
Shipley's driveway was empty, the curtains drawn. I looked for movement
behind them and didn't see any.

Caroline opened the front gate and walked straight through the leafy
plants and down the side of the house. I followed her onto a concrete pa-

tio in back that had no furniture on it. A toolshed sat against the back fence. Caroline opened the screen over the back door and stopped. Her back was to me. She reached under her shirt and removed the Glock from its holster.

I said her name softly. Instead of responding, she gave the back door a gentle shove. It swung open onto a hallway lined with deep shadows. "Miss Shipley?" she called. No response.

Caroline stepped inside. I stood in the doorway, wondering whether or not I should clock her and pull the gun from her grip. She swept the kitchen on her left with a practiced stance and saw nothing of interest. She continued down the hallway. I stepped inside the house.

To my right, the door to Claire Shipley's bedroom was open. A large, unadorned crucifix hung above the bed, and a row of small ceramic statues crowded the windowsill. They were saints.

I turned and saw that Caroline had frozen in the doorway to the living room, the gun held in front of her with rigid arms.

"You want to put that away, honey?" an old woman asked her without the slightest trace of fear in her voice. Caroline didn't move. "Tell your precious little friend to come on in. Is he packing, too?"

Caroline kept the gun level. "No," I answered. "Miss Shipley, we just wanted—"

"Shut up now, honey," said the old woman with vicious politeness. "Your lady friend and I are in an interesting predicament. Come see."

I edged into the room. Sitting in a La-Z-Boy was an ancient-looking woman with a thick wave of wiry gray hair pinned to the back of her head. She had teardrop-shaped eyes that were mostly pupil, and sagging cheeks and jowls. Her fat mouth was an inverted U that stretched from one corner of her square jaw to the other. She held a sawed-off shotgun on us, with one meaty hand above the chamber and the handle resting against her stomach. The hand wrapped around the shotgun's chamber had red scars on it.

The only thing on the wall above her head was a larger version of the plain wooden crucifix in her bedroom. A tiny television was positioned on a shelf across from her that contained books with titles I could see all dealt with government conspiracy theories and imminent apocalypses. An overflowing ashtray and a pack of Chesterfields sat on the end table next to her elbow. "I hear y'all have been asking questions about Corey McCormick," she said. She had a flat southern accent that sounded like it had softened over time spent in California. "I also hear y'all have been going around town telling people Corey was fruit. That true?"

"Watch your language," Caroline said. "Adam's a fruit, too."

Claire Shipley's eyes flicked sideways to meet mine. "Is your lady friend going to put that thing away or not?"

"You first," Caroline said.

"No thanks," she replied.

"Why don't we all count to ten," I said.

"Why don't both you jackasses count to a thousand and get the hell out of my house while you're doing it," Claire Shipley said. "I haven't seen Corey McCormick in years and I'm not real upset about it."

"Good," I said. "You won't see him again. He's dead." The news struck her visibly. I seized the opportunity. "How many years has it been since you've seen him?" I asked.

"Four," she said almost to herself, as if remembering. "Four, I think. He came back here . . ." She realized she was speaking too freely and clammed up.

"Came back here to do what?"

"He was asking questions, just like you guys," she said.

"What kind of questions?"

"None of your business," she retorted. "Corey abandoned his grand-mother on her deathbed. He was tired of watching her die. So was I, but I stuck it out until the end. I don't have much respect for Corey's decision, and I told him so to his face."

"He was sixteen," I reminded her.

"Corey McCormick was *never* sixteen," she said. "He was never ten. He was never eight. There was more of Corey's mother in him than his grandmother ever wanted to believe. I saw it. The boy took what he wanted when he wanted it. If you caught him taking it, he would throw it right at your face."

"Why did he come back here four years ago?" I asked.

Claire Shipley's grip on the shotgun loosened and the barrel fell by a few inches. "He's dead?" she asked. "How? What hap—"

Caroline bolted across the room, her gun raised in both hands. At the very second that Claire Shipley attempted to raise the barrel of her shot-gun, Caroline jammed the barrel of the Glock against the old woman's right temple. I found myself standing in the middle of the room, my hands raised in an attempt to quiet a sudden explosion that had made al-most no sound.

Her shotgun slid to one side of her lap and tipped off her thigh. I sprang forward and grabbed the mouth of the barrel before it could hit the floor.

I was jarred again by laughter—the thick, fluid-filled sound of Claire Shipley's guffaws echoed in the room. "Town witch shot dead," she whispered. "Bobbsey Twins suspected. Film at eleven."

She lifted her eyes to meet Caroline's ferocious look. The old woman's features tensed. "Hand me my glasses, pretty boy," she whispered.

I found them on the nightstand. She slid them on and studied the furious woman standing over her. "Caroline Hughes," she whispered. I felt Caroline tense. "I saw you in the papers. That's a terrible thing that happened to your mother—"

I didn't believe the concern in Claire Shipley's voice was genuine, so I cut her off. "Four years ago, Corey came back here asking questions. What was he asking questions about?"

"An old friend of his," she said. "Reynaldo Reyez. He thought the guy might still be alive. He had heard stories, stories about some assassin they called El Maricón. He thought it was Reynaldo."

In the aftermath of her revelation about Reynaldo Reyez, Caroline and I fought not to exchange a look. The same year Corey had met with Joseph Spinotta, he had returned to Visalia on the hunt for El Maricón. A major piece of my new theory had just been confirmed. Adrenaline quickened my pulse.

"Why did he come to you?" I asked. "What would you know about Reynaldo?"

The old woman seemed to settle a debate within herself; I saw the resistance leave her body. She ordered us to sit. I went to a high-backed chair on the other side of the room; Caroline stepped away from the woman, but she didn't lower the gun and she didn't take a seat.

"Corey came to me because he knew Reynaldo's father and I had a conversation the morning Reynaldo disappeared," she began. She paused, considering. Then she started talking.

Reynaldo's father, José, had been a handsome charmer, one of the most popular men in Visalia. He spent most of his days driving around town, delivering bags full of his wife's authentic Mexican cooking to the women around town whom he wanted to befriend her. Lucinda McCormick, Corey's grandmother, was one of those women. But Ruby Reyez was a recluse who spoke poor English, and even after José Reyez managed to get most of the women in town addicted to her cooking, none of those women was able to draw out his wife.

From the start, Claire Shipley saw José Reyez for who he was: a thug and an operator who used his charm and good looks to distract people from his real profession. When Claire asked him point-blank how he had been able to afford the brand-new pickup truck he drove around town, José told her that he had managed to save up money working various field jobs. In Claire's opinion, his answer lacked even the pretense of deceit.

Claire saw the relationship developing between Corey and Reynaldo's son and warned Lucinda about it. But Lucinda paid no attention. One afternoon, Claire followed Reynaldo and Corey up to Lake Kaweah, where the boys had wandered off into the woods and done things to each other's bodies that boys sometimes did out of simple necessity. This information Claire had not shared with Lucinda.

By then, Lucinda and José Reyez had developed a friendship. José would often stop by the ranch out on Highway 198 and the two of them would sit on the porch watching the sun go down. Sometimes Claire would listen on the other side of the screen door. Lucinda McCormick was already showing signs of the cancer that would eat away her bones, but she listened patiently to José's long orations about the dreams he had for his family and his young son.

Claire was eavesdropping the night José finally came clean to Lucinda about what he really did for a living: running meth and the materials to make it for the Mexican nationals who had managed to organize part of the trade in the Valley. As usual, Lucinda had withheld judgment. She had even offered José work on her ranch. José politely declined.

"See, manual labor—that kind of work was beneath a man like José Reyez," Claire Shipley told us. "Destroying families. Driving perfectly good women out of their minds—that was José's *speed*, if you know what I mean."

José stopped visiting after Lucinda's cancer diagnosis. Then one afternoon word got out that Ruby Reyez, the shy shut-in, had been arrested stumbling down the highway in her slip, trying to explain in fractured English to anyone who would listen that the passing cars were communicating with one another about her. When Claire heard the news, she realized that José Reyez had somehow brought his business home. She wasn't surprised. She had known the chickens would one day come home to roost for the Reyez family, but she had no idea what form God's retribution was going to take.

On an afternoon in February, José Reyez came to Lucinda's ranch. Lucinda had been upstairs in bed, with Corey at her side. Claire Shipley had forbidden José from coming inside even as he pleaded for Lucinda's help.

"He kept telling me over and over again that his family had been destroyed," Claire Shipley said to us. "I asked him what that meant. He told me he had driven Reynaldo that morning up into the woods past Lake Kaweah and told him to run away. He said the boy refused, so he pulled a gun on the kid and threatened him, told him to run into the mountains, to get as far away from Visalia as possible. Then he told me that Reynaldo had finally obeyed him. That Reynaldo had finally run off into the trees."

She gave us a dyspeptic face.

"You didn't believe him," I said.

"Reynaldo would never leave his family behind like that. I didn't care how bad his father scared him." A genuine and belated pain trembled beneath the old woman's words. "I drove up to the lake. I went to the parking lot where José told me he had taken Reynaldo. It took me three hours to find him. Reynaldo Reyez had been shot in the back. He was dead when I got there. José didn't even know that he had killed his own son. He had fired a shot in the air to get the boy to run, and it had killed him."

"What did you do?" I asked the old woman.

"I buried him," she said. "I buried Reynaldo Reyez in the woods and I prayed over him. I even wept, God forbid I should admit that to the two of you."

Caroline let out a sharp breath. I studied the ruined old woman who had described her outpouring of emotion for a death she had concealed with a child's defiance.

"Four years ago," I finally said, "when Corey came to you—"

"I told him!" Claire Shipley snapped. "I told him that I had buried his best friend. He asked me why I had kept it a secret from him. I told him the truth—his grandmother needed him, and I didn't want him grieving for the son of some drug pusher."

"Did it work? Did Corey stick by his grandmother's side until the end?"

Claire Shipley stuck out a furious lower lip.

Caroline cursed under her breath and turned from the room. It was clear that she believed my theory had been shot all to hell. She was wrong. I could feel the pieces realigning themselves into a new theory that was as simple and elegant as the ones James Wilton had come up with over the past week. I wanted to tell her, but I couldn't do it here.

"You be careful, Caroline Hughes," Claire Shipley said. Caroline stopped but didn't turn to face the old woman. "Grief fills the world with shadows, and when the world is full of shadows, it looks like there are no limits at all. All your old rules no longer apply. Isn't that right, missy?"

Caroline turned and gave the old woman a stare that had more pain in it than I had yet to see her display. Claire Shipley seemed to think her words had worked their intended effect. She sank back into her La-Z-Boy and folded her scarred hands across her lap, looking satisfied. The old woman's eyes shifted to me. "What did Corey do when you told him this?" I asked.

"He kicked over that chair you're in and left."

I looked at Caroline.

"Wash your hands in a child's blood and see what color your judgments turn out to be," Claire Shipley said.

As we drove away from the house, Caroline's knuckles were white against the steering wheel. I could see anger, even betrayal in the set of her jaw, and she wouldn't look at me. I reached into the backseat and brought the file on the four abducted young boys onto my lap. Someone had abducted them. Someone who had used the signatures that had been attributed to an assassin they called El Maricón.

"She's lying," Caroline said.

I ignored her. I studied the photos of a boy named Jim Clark and thought back to one of the other stories Martin Cale had told me. Jim Clark had been taken into custody by Joseph Spinotta and then placed in Billy Hatfill's care; two weeks earlier, that same Jim Clark had come off Martin Cale's yacht and Corey had reacted as if he had seen a ghost.

Four years earlier, Spinotta had asked Corey to set him up with Reynaldo Reyez. When Corey had set out looking for Reynaldo, he had discovered that Reynaldo had been dead for years, buried by his grandmother's best friend. But someone abducted the young boys whose pictures were spread across my lap.

I imagined Corey waiting on the dock as his uncle's yacht came into port two weeks earlier, saw his shock when a young man named Everett sauntered toward him. Corey had been stunned to recognize the boy. He had recognized the boy because he had abducted him.

"Corey pretended to be El Maricón," I finally said. "Corey abducted these boys."

Caroline jerked the car to the shoulder and brought us to a stop.

I told her about the incident that Martin Cale had related to me, showed her Jim Clark's picture, and described the reaction Corey had had when he laid eyes on the man. "He knew him because he abducted him, Caroline."

"You're saying Corey abducted his own brother?"

"Yes," I answered. "Corey believed Spinotta's lies. Corey believed he was saving these boys from a childhood just like his. He wanted his own brother to have everything he missed. Then he saw Jim Clark walk off his uncle's yacht and he realized what was going to happen to his brother. He understood what Spinotta was really up to, and three days later he tried to find out where Spinotta was."

I saw my bloodied drug dealer lying facedown on the floor of his apartment, beaten nearly to death by the man I had known as Corey Howard. I saw three other scorched footprints in the earth just like the one left by Tonya McCormick's trailer, saw the parents of the boys incinerated. I had been so eager to cast Corey as the victim that I had overlooked his rage.

"It probably wasn't that hard to trick Spinotta," I said. "He probably never wanted to risk meeting Corey face-to-face. They exchanged four kids over the past three years, probably at a drop-off point. Then Corey gives them his brother, finds out what they're really up to, and realizes he can't blow his cover because they'll probably kill Caden just to get rid of the evidence. So he tries to blackmail Billy Hatfill into giving him Spinotta's location. But everything goes wrong."

"And they kill him," Caroline said. "They killed their own supplier and they don't even know it."

I waited for her to realize another implication of what I was saying: the man she was hunting, the man who had killed her mother, was already dead.

She handed me Jim Clark's picture and turned to face the steering wheel. "Jesus. This whole time—you and I were looking for the same man," she said.

"He's dead, Caroline."

I reached into my pocket and took out the golden scorpion chain. She took it, ran it through her fingers, studied it. Then she closed it in one fist and brought her fist down against the steering wheel loud enough to bleat the horn. She kicked open the driver's-side door and stumbled out into the hazy sunlight. She regained her footing, straightened up, and kept walking away from the car.

I let her go. I thought she might give up right there and go back to whatever life she still had in San Francisco. I could try to convince her that Joseph Spinotta was ultimately responsible for the death of her mother, but I didn't have the energy. As for my own mission, I was not done. I still didn't have the identity of Corey's killer.

Twenty minutes later, Caroline slid behind the wheel. Her eyes were bloodshot but her tears had dried. She tossed the scorpion chain onto my lap and started the engine.

"This video you saw," she said. "Describe it to me."

I did. She showed no reaction.

"How long do you think they keep them before they . . . tape them?"

I pulled out the photos of Toby Cooper, the young boy I had seen in the video, and told her he had been abducted seven months earlier. "So maybe Caden has time," she said. "Maybe we can get to him first."

She glanced at me, then returned her attention to the road. I kept my mouth shut. I did not want her to know how relieved I was. I did not tell her that I thought her mother would be proud.

"So I guess we're heading down to Wasco tonight," she said.

Some seven hours later, as the sun crept behind the Coast Ranges, we left Caroline's cabin and drove south on Interstate 5. We had spent the rest of the day in a state of catatonic exhaustion, speaking to each other in fractured sentences. Caroline was mourning the loss of the crusader she had been hunting, and I was trying to absorb the fact that the man I had known as Corey Howard had slaughtered eight people.

It was dark by the time we got to Wasco. Our helpful gas station attendant was not on duty yet. We bought gas and then got a motel room at an Econo Lodge just down the highway from the Stop 'N' Go where Roger

Vasquez and Ben Clamp had made semiregular visits. Once we settled into the room, I saw our plan for what it was: obsessive and senseless. We could spend the rest of our lives in Wasco, and Vasquez and Clamp might never make another appearance.

Exhausted and depleted, I sat on the foot of the bed and watched television. Caroline went to her car and came back with a large backpack. "Give me your leg," she said.

I did as I was told. She rolled up the right leg of my jeans. Then she pulled out one of her Glock field knives, the gleaming handle visible in its Velcro holster. She wrapped it around my shin, tugging the straps tight. Then she rolled my jeans down over the knife slowly and methodically. I kept watching television. "This is stupid," I said. "I'm sorry." She shrugged and stared out at the window, her face lit by the flares of passing headlights. "We need to regroup. We know they're out here. Maybe there's another way to figure out where they are."

"So Eddie Cairns was lying?"

"You showed him the drawing of Reynaldo before he started talking," I said. "He told you what you wanted to hear."

"Because I tortured him," she said. I thought I could hear a trace of remorse in her voice. "You heard him scream, Adam. I didn't electroshock the guy. I just drugged him a little."

"I think he saw Eduardo Velásquez get murdered," I said. "I think he saw something. He's just too fried to know what the hell it was."

"You know what I'm asking, Adam. He may not be Reynaldo Reyez, but do you think El Maricón is real or did everyone here just make him up? Is it really just some dispute between the Mexican nationals and the Colombians, and everybody wants to believe it's the work of one man?"

"Why do you still care?" I asked her. "Corey McCormick killed your mother."

Three hours later, we were watching an episode of *ER* when Caroline's cell phone rang. She reached for it on the nightstand without taking her eyes off the television. I heard her answer in a bored voice. Then she kicked me in the back and leapt to her feet. "They're here!" she shouted.

At first I didn't believe her. She grabbed her backpack by one strap and headed for the door. "You're kidding, right?" I asked her.

"No!" she shouted. "That was our new friend. She said they just pulled in."

Minutes later, we were rushing into the Stop 'N' Go just as a large black Chevy Suburban swung out onto the highway and headed toward Interstate 5. I glimpsed Roger Vasquez behind the wheel. Ben Clamp was in the passenger seat. The distance between our vehicles robbed the two men of any distinctive characteristics that might make them appear different than the photographs we had used to locate them. They wouldn't seem like flesh and blood until I was staring them in the face.

Ben Clamp and Roger Vasquez went north on Interstate 5. We followed from several car lengths behind them. The Suburban fell into the fast lane and accelerated. They had a long way to go, and it didn't look like they were going to stop anytime soon.

I pulled out my cell phone and dialed Brenda's number. She answered after one ring and managed to say half of my name before I interrupted her. I read her the license plate number of the Suburban. I heard rustling papers and figured she was reaching for a pen.

She asked me to repeat it and I did. Then she asked me what the hell it was.

"It's a plate number for the Chevy Suburban Roger Vasquez and Ben Clamp are driving," I said.

"Holy shit. Well, it's not like I can get Dwight to run it. Not with everything that's going on right now."

"Give it to Jimmy."

"I'll try," she said. I waited for her to continue. "I'm staying at a hotel."

Jimmy had learned she had helped me get out of LA and he was obviously punishing her for it. "I'm sorry, Brenda."

"Whatever. I told you to find something, and it sounds like you did."

I promised to call her back as soon as we found out where Vasquez and Clamp were going. "Adam," she said quietly, "are you armed?"

When I didn't respond, Caroline gave me a brief suspicious glance, the first time she had taken her attention off the Suburban since we had merged onto the Interstate. "Okay," Brenda said. "Whoever's with you— are they armed?"

My lack of a response had told her that I wasn't alone. Moment to moment, Brenda Wilton made for a better detective than her husband, probably because her instincts were to protect the people around her, while her husband was driven by a desire to expose criminals he had never met. "I don't care if they get you by the balls," she said. "You don't pick up a gun, you understand me? You don't have the first clue how to shoot. That means it'll kill you before it kills anyone else."

"I'm just tailing them, Brenda."

She ordered me to call her back as soon as I had followed Roger Vasquez and Ben Clamp to their final destination.

CHAPTER 21

The Suburban turned onto 580 East and suddenly we were heading into the dark rolling hills we had been driving alongside for almost three hours. There weren't that many other cars on the road with us, so Caroline was keeping a long distance. At first I thought I was hallucinating the massive spindly shadows on the hillsides, but after a few blinks, I realized they were wind-powered electric generators, just like the ones Corey had included in his drawing of me.

"I've got a good guess where they're going," Caroline said.

We were on a direct course for the Bay Area. "You ready to go home again?" I asked.

"Ask me when we get there."

At a little after one in the morning, low clouds merged in the sky overhead to threaten fog, and the wind rushing through my cracked-open window dropped by ten degrees. The Suburban joined the thin stream of traffic lined up at the tollbooths for the Bay Bridge. The cloud cover smeared the top of the Transamerica Pyramid and carried the downtown lights away from their sources. It was my first visit to the city. I remembered that it was Jimmy's hometown as well and wondered if he would have wanted to be the one to introduce me to it.

The Suburban crossed Market Street and headed into the heart of downtown. Stone canyons rose all around us, and strong winds made cyclones out of the litter in the gutters. After spending almost forty-eight hours in the rural and small-town Valley, I thought the city looked poised to come tumbling down on us. It took me a few seconds to discern that the dark mounds resting against security gates and freight entrances were homeless people.

From a distance of almost three blocks, we followed the Suburban past Union Square. I recognized the St. Francis Hotel from movies. The dark tracks for its glass elevators made the slender concrete building look as if it had been subjected to a triple bypass.

I rolled the window up, with a new understanding of why people said Southern and Northern California were different countries. The city looked as cold as my hands felt, as if it were afraid to display anything soft or bright because it might lose it to the night winds.

After several anxious minutes of circling blocks on one-way streets, we rounded a corner and saw the Suburban parked at the curb up ahead. The street was lined with low-rise masonry buildings, and the storefronts belonged to pawnshops, electronics stores, and adult video stores that advertised all manner of visual gratification with blinking neon letters.

Caroline braked abruptly, then pulled behind an idling garbage truck. My view was blocked, but she could still see the Suburban a block ahead of us.

"Ben Clamp just got out," she said. "Follow him. I'm on their car."

The minute I stepped onto the curb, the garbage truck started moving forward. Before it blocked my view, I glimpsed a broad-shouldered hulk of a man standing on the far corner. The Suburban turned past him and disappeared.

The Tahoe didn't move an inch. I retreated into a dark doorway and let the garbage truck roll past me. As it rounded the corner, Caroline followed it, then swerved past it in pursuit of the Suburban.

I got a good look at Ben Clamp's face in a storefront's wash of neon four doors down. Excessive prison-style weightlifting and possibly steroids had bloated him past the point of being the all-American jock archetype in the photograph I had carried. His mouth's natural position was slack and dumb-looking, his lips parted as if he were about to take a breath he had been waiting for all his life.

There was a hotel on the corner across the street, the kind of hotel that didn't have security, room service, or optimism of any kind. Ben Clamp was casing it. A few of its windows were shot through with the harsh glow of overhead fluorescent lighting. Some of them spat bedsheets-turned-curtains into the wind.

Ben crossed the street and strolled inside as if he were a guest. I edged in after him, entering the tiny lobby just as he disappeared up a flight of steps. The clerk's station was empty save for a copy of *Wired* magazine and a dismembered copy of the *San Francisco Examiner*.

I mounted the first steps, listening to the sound of Ben's footfalls overhead. The center of the stairway was too small to see anything beyond shadows above. The footsteps stopped, and I started my ascent. I was just below the second floor landing when I heard a knock from one floor above me.

Several steps below the third-floor landing, I stared through the banister and across a sweep of warped hardwood floor. There were about three inches between Ben Clamp's nose and the door to room 3J. His head was bowed, and he had pushed his baseball cap down on his brow.

Ben knocked again, lightly but insistently, and the door cracked open against its chain. He lifted his head and gave the person on the other side a broad, goofy grin. "Dude, I'm sorry," Ben whispered. "I hate to bother you, but I saw that your light was on and . . ." His Tennessee drawl sharpened his I's and put a punch at the end of each word; the routine of a southern buffoon in the big city was so good I almost bought it myself.

All I could see of the man on the other side of the door was disheveled salt-and-pepper hair.

"Listen, my girlfriend and I are staying down the hall and . . . Christ, this is so embarrassing, but it's late and everywhere's closed and . . . uh . . . we don't have any protection. Know what I mean?"

The man muttered something that sounded polite and went to close the door.

"Hey. That's cool," Ben said. "Listen, we've got some beers if you—"

I heard the dead bolt click. The grin dropped from Ben's face. I started backward down the stairs. The second-floor hallway had a large window at the end that looked out onto a rusted fire escape. The fluorescent bulbs overhead banished shadows and allowed me nowhere to hide. I faced the window as I listened to Ben descending the stairs.

A figure loomed in the alleyway below. It wore a baseball cap just like Ben's, a dark sweater, and dark jeans. It seemed to hover in midair against the opposite wall.

One floor below, I heard the hotel's entry door bang shut behind Ben.

Headlights strobed the alleyway's entrance as Roger Vasquez stepped down off the top of a trash can, holding something in both hands. It was too dark for me to see what it was.

He walked down the alley and into the glow of a security light illuminating an iron door and a trash-bag-swollen Dumpster. He lifted a trash can with both arms and brought it to the edge of the security light's glow, setting it down so gently it barely made a sound. Then he stepped up onto it, removed the security light's casing, and unscrewed the bulb, plunging the alleyway into near-total darkness. I realized he had repeated this routine up and down the entire length of the alley.

His head bowed, Roger walked in the direction of the streets with tiny careful footsteps, heel to toe, heel to toe. He was measuring the distance between the fire escape and the alley's mouth. At the end, he stopped and glanced back.

I threw myself back against the wall, waited a few seconds, and then risked another look. Roger Vasquez was gone.

I looked down the length of the hallway. The walls were painted a dark gray that had a black grain mixed in to give it the illusion of texture. The heavy doors to each room were chipped, and the knobs didn't match. I could practically hear the groans of now-dead prostitutes, pissed to have moved on to the afterlife without someone having made a musical about their lives. I was sure that Roger or Ben or both were about to make a second appearance. If I didn't get out of the hotel, I would be trapped.

I stepped out of the hotel and walked right into her. Her expression and her stance had no urgency to them, and she gave me a slight smile. She had put on her baseball cap and threaded her hair into a ponytail hanging out the back. I tried to hide my relief. But the truth was, now that I had Caroline Hughes, I didn't like going solo.

I told her what I had seen, and she nodded and studied the windows overhead. "These guys are good," she said. "Ben goes in to pay his visit. Roger disables all the lights in the alley in about three minutes. They don't meet up on the sidewalk. Instead, Ben goes straight to where Roger parked the Suburban. Then Roger follows about a minute later. They don't meet up, so no one sees them together."

She looked down the empty street. "What do you want to bet Roger's the one who goes in tomorrow night?"

"Tomorrow?" I said.

"They're gone," she said. "And I didn't feel like driving anymore tonight." She looked away from me so she wouldn't have to see my frustration. "They're coming back, Adam, and soon. This was just a site visit."

We were waiting for the clerk to return to his desk when I noticed the lockbox on the wall above his empty chair. It was unlocked. A wire-reinforced sheet of glass came down to eye level between the clerk's desk and the lobby. I felt a cold draft.

"He's out back," I whispered. "Probably on a smoke break."

Caroline reached for the tiny bell on the desk, but I grabbed her wrist. I pointed to the lockbox on the wall. "We want to find out why they're so interested in the guy in room 3J, right? Maybe there's an extra key."

"Why don't we just go to room 3J, then?"

"His room will tell me more than he does," I said. "And he pretty much slammed the door in Ben Clamp's face, which means he's not open to visitors." I tried the knob on the door in the wall next to the desk. It was locked. "Grab my waist," I said to Caroline. She looked as me as if I were crazy. "If the clerk comes back, we'll just tell him we were sick of waiting."

I crawled over the top of the desk, my back scraping against the edge of the glass as I slithered through the narrow space between the edge of the window, feeling grateful for the first time in my life that I didn't have the kind of muscle-bound gym body I always desired in other men. Caroline made no attempt to help me. I made the mistake of gripping the chair with both hands. It rolled out from under my grip and I fell headfirst to the linoleum.

"Jesus," Caroline hissed, "at least let me go distract the guy!"

Caroline raced out of the doors of the lobby as I got to my feet. I listened for the sound of approaching footsteps, heard none, and opened the lockbox. There were seven rows of keys inside with labels above each ring. Most rings had two sets hanging from them. The one for 3J only had one. I felt a little too proud of myself.

I unlocked the side door and went through it into the lobby, shutting it quietly behind me, then dashed out of the hotel. No Caroline. I had programmed her number earlier that day. She answered after four rings.

"You find the clerk?" I asked.

"No," she said. "I'm by the alley."

"I got the key."

The lobby door swung open behind me and I spun around. The man who emerged had disheveled salt-and-pepper hair and a prematurely wrinkled face with a nose like a bird's beak. He buttoned a puffy 49ers jacket that was too large for him and hurried past me down the sidewalk, shooting paranoid glances in every direction. It looked like the surprise visit from Ben Clamp had frightened the man from 3J out of the hotel.

"Look back toward the hotel," I whispered into the phone. "You see him?"

"Yep."

"Follow him," I said. "I'm going into his room. Call me back if he starts to head this way." I hung up before she could protest.

*   *   *

Room 3J was situated above the entrance to the hotel. The mint-green walls were spiderwebbed with cracks in the plaster. The queen-size bed had no box spring, and the elderly television had rabbit ear antennae and a bulging screen that made for a good mirror. Everything else in the room was too nice to belong there. The navy-blue curtains looked new, with a faint luster to them. The bedside lamp had a round deep-blue shade and a thick rounded base made out of dark wood. A three-tiered Ikea desk station was positioned next to the window, with a row of framed photographs along the top shelf. In the closet, which had a pull curtain instead of a door, was a row of expensive suits from Brooks Brothers and Armani, wrinkled and badly in need of dry cleaning.

I flipped through a stack of mail on the man's desk and found past-due notices from just about every credit card company in existence, and envelopes with letterheads of multiply-named law firms, all addressed to a local PO box for one Cameron Davis. He hadn't seen fit to open any of them. The photos on the shelf told how in happier days a well-groomed Cameron Davis had worn country club outerwear and gone on bike rides through Golden Gate Park with his chubby-cheeked children. Now he was living in a downtown flophouse.

The small bathroom had a shower stall, an overhead bulb, and two drawers under the sink. Remembering the man's paranoid glances, I looked for drug paraphernalia. I pulled out a Gucci toiletry bag from under the sink, unzipped it, and found nothing stronger than Paxil.

My cell phone rang. "He's heading through Union Square," Caroline said. "He's moving fast, but he's wandering. It looks like their little visit freaked him out."

"Maybe he thought they were debt collectors," I whispered. "This guy has past-due notices from every credit card under the sun." I returned to the desk station. "He's also got pictures of his family in here. They don't look like the kind of people who would visit him in a place like this."

I opened the nightstand drawer and saw pawn slips. "And he's pawning stuff," I said.

Caroline grunted. There was something else in the nightstand drawer, something that struck me silent. I pulled out a blinking keypad that had a perpetually changing series of numbers on its thin LED screen.

"Adam?"

I knelt and saw a thin laptop computer resting on the floor under the bed. Behind the desk on the windowsill was a row of hardcover novels by Tom Clancy and John Grisham. I pulled out two of them and saw a tiny satellite dish angled out the window.

"He's a customer," I said.

"You think he didn't pay his bill?" she asked me.

The room was exhibit A of a life falling apart. Now that Roger Vasquez had disabled all of the lights in the alley, I wondered if he was coming back to deliver the final blow.

Caroline said my name several times, but I didn't answer.

Ben Clamp had knocked on the door of the room I was now standing in, checking to see if their target was where they expected him to be. Roger Vasquez had created a cover of darkness they could use. They were planning an abduction, not of a young boy, but of one of their own customers.

Caroline had told me tonight was just a site visit. If that was the case, I couldn't see why they had darkened the alleyway now, only to give someone the chance to replace the bulbs the following evening. I said Caroline's name and was answered by deep silence. I said her name again. She didn't answer. No one did. Someone had ended the call.

I reached under the right leg of my jeans and removed the Glock field knife Caroline had strapped there earlier that night. I held it out in front of me and opened the door to the hallway. It was long and empty.

We had driven right into a trap. One man had gone after Caroline; the other was after me. I holstered the knife and raced down the stairs.

I was several steps from the bottom when I saw that the tiny lobby was dark. I stopped, almost lost my footing, and gripped the railing.

A tall shadow rushed toward me out of the dark lobby. I hit the stairs ass-first, reached for the holster on my right leg, and felt cold steel wedge its way under my jaw. It was too dark to see the man's face, and I didn't know which one he was.

"Stand up," the man said.

"Where's Caroline?"

"Stand the *fuck* up," he hissed.

I stood. He pulled the back of my shirt out of my jeans, wrapped one arm across my back, and wedged the barrel of his gun into my armpit. Then he walked me down the stairs and into the dark lobby. The clerk had still not returned to his desk. I wondered if he ever would.

We hit the sidewalk. "Why are you abducting one of your own customers?" I asked.

Roger Vasquez jabbed the gun harder into my rib cage and walked me briskly down the side of the hotel and into the alley. The Suburban was waiting for us. He held the gun on me and opened the rear cargo doors without taking his eyes off me. There was nothing like madness in his eyes, no wild and uncontrollable emotion that I could try to turn on him.

The Suburban's rear seat had been removed and replaced by a solid plywood wall that turned the cargo space into a traveling prison cell. He ordered me inside and crawled in after me, pulling the doors shut. He was familiar with the darkness inside.

I felt his fingers go for the holster on my leg. I kicked wildly, felt my foot meet his chin, saw him tilt back. Then the butt of the gun smashed across my jaw, sending white streaks across my vision. The pain almost distracted me from the pinprick in my forearm and the hot wave that flooded up my arm.

He pinned my forearm to the wall above my head. I felt the cuff click around my right wrist. He did the same to my left arm. As the drug took effect, ten pounds of weight were added to my legs and suddenly my wrists were dangling limp in the steel cuffs without any pain or cramping.

"I heard you were looking for us, Adam Murphy," he said. "I heard you had one night in heaven with a sweet *young* thing and you regret it. Is that right? It seems you're saying you were too drunk to remember it."

"Billy Hatfill told you I was coming."

I thought I heard him unlock a door. Whatever he had injected me with was taking its effect.

"It wasn't me," I slurred.

Roger Vasquez laughed and caressed the side of my face. "That's what they all say, Adam Murphy."

I heard the rear doors slam. Roger's footsteps on the pavement outside sounded like he was retreating down a long dark hallway.

I felt the floor of the cargo bay swaying beneath me. I opened my eyes in darkness. The rear windows were painted black. The steel cuffs were digging into my wrists. I tried adjusting my hands but couldn't. Muffled sobs came from the dark shadow cuffed to the wall next to me.

"Cameron Davis," I whispered.

The sobs stopped. "All I did was watch," he rasped. He had forced brave resolve into his voice. "That's all I did. I just watched. I didn't even know it was real."

He was lying. I had seen one of the videos he had paid money for, and there was no doubt that the subjects were live humans and not digital creations.

"How'd you end up in that hotel?" I whispered.

"I thought it was someone who knew . . ."

"Knew what?"

"Knew that I was . . . watching," he gasped. "I didn't think it was *them.*"

"Someone who knew that you were a customer?"

"Yes," he answered. "They found drugs in my desk. At work. I've never even smoked pot, for Christ's sake. Then someone started calling my wife. They pretended they were a little boy and asked for me, said I had shown them a good time. She went crazy. She wanted me to call the police. I told her I had never touched a boy in my life. It's the truth."

"But you didn't call the police."

That shut him up. He hadn't called the police because he didn't want anyone to know that he was just watching.

"She left me," he said. "Took the kids. I haven't seen them in months."

"What else did these people do?"

"Someone started fucking with my credit," he said. "They got all my account numbers somehow. I used to shred everything—"

"Did you have that information on your computer?" I asked.

"I keep everything on my computer," he whispered. "I'm a fucking systems analyst for Christ's sake." He sobbed. "I *was* a systems analyst. They fired me."

We were traveling a winding, swelling road. I couldn't tell the Suburban's speed.

"What about you?" Cameron Davis asked. "What did they do to you?"

Davis would have to earn the right to that answer, and I seriously doubted he would be able to do that. The cuffs that pinned both of our wrists above our heads were the wrong height to constrain a child. Roger Vasquez and Ben Clamp had been making regular late-night trips in a vehicle outfitted to confine two grown men at a time. I wondered how many other customers of this operation had ended up in the back of this Suburban. This was not just a child porn ring; it involved the abduction of young boys and the systematic destruction of the men for whom the boys were violated. My new captors believed that I was even worse than their customers. Thanks to Billy Hatfill, they believed that I had not just watched a child but violated a child myself. I remembered the strange light sparking in Billy's eyes when he realized I was going to hunt down the men he worked for. He had taken his own life to guarantee I would do so. He had guaranteed that the very men I was looking for would try to punish me for a crime I had not committed.

"How did they get to you back there?" I asked Davis.

"He got me when I came back to the hotel."

"Just one."

"The Latin guy."

I was sure that Ben Clamp had gone after Caroline while Vasquez had subdued me. Caroline had been right on Cameron Davis's tail. Why hadn't Ben Clamp caught both of them? Why had Roger been forced to work double duty?

The Suburban rolled to a stop. Cameron Davis cursed under his breath. I heard footsteps crunching gravel.

The back doors flew open. Over Roger's shoulders I glimpsed a terraced cliff descending toward a two-lane blacktop and saw rolling white-caps in the near distance. We were on Pacific Coast Highway.

Roger yanked Davis's right ankle toward him and drove a syringe into the skin. Then he seized mine.

"There's been a problem, right, Roger?" I said. He gave me a look that blazed in the dark. His jaw had a thin coat of black stubble. I couldn't imagine his face forming the bright smile he displayed in the picture I had carried with me for a week.

"You haven't heard from Ben, have you?" I asked. "He ran into some trouble with my girlfriend, didn't he?"

Roger grimaced and drove the syringe into my ankle.

CHAPTER 22

I awoke to the smell of wood rot and a damp chill that told me I was below ground. I struggled to assemble the sensations I had experienced in my stupor: footsteps creaking the boards overhead, Cameron Davis whispering the Lord's Prayer over and over from somewhere close by, his muffled cries as he was torn from the room.

A dim light seemed to come from miles away. I tried to focus on it. I was in a long narrow cellar. There was a cube of exposed drywall at one end. A half-open door revealed a prison-issue toilet and a single overhead bulb. I managed to get myself off the cot I'd been lying on and backed up toward the bathroom so that I could use its light to see the rest of the cellar. It was almost fifteen feet long and seven feet wide. There was a large bookshelf against one wall.

Once my eyes adjusted, I moved to it and read some of the titles on the spines: *If It Doesn't Feel Right, No More Little Secrets, Journey Into Healing.* The topic remained the same for all of them. Some were books intended for children dealing with sexual abuse, featuring drawings of round-faced kids and their parents engaged in conversation. Others were thick psychiatric tomes.

In the bathroom, I gulped from the faucet. When I straightened up, I saw there was handwriting on the wall. It started in ink, but then the pen had obviously run dry, and the author had used its ballpoint tip to scratch into the drywall. First there was a ledger of days, six vertical lines crossed through by a seventh. Then the writer started to lose count. Daylight obviously didn't penetrate down here. There were nonsensical fragments of words: *First Account. Empty . . . Maybe Just a Punishment . . . First Broken Promise: NO WALKS!* When I turned around, I saw that words were scribbled all around me, above the doorway and down the opposite wall. In the mess of etchings on the inside of the door, I saw the phrase *I am not quality material!* It was followed by the letters NQM, scrawled in a sloping column all the way down to the floor, the acronym that Joseph Spinotta had written atop project proposals.

Joseph Spinotta had been held in this cellar. After a while, his ledger of days had run out. Joseph Spinotta was gone.

I returned to the bed and tried to make sense of this. In our final conversation, Billy Hatfill had never uttered Spinotta's name. But at dinner several days before, he had told me that Spinotta was a pedophile and had expressed a hatred for the man that shocked me. I thought of the drama teacher Billy had arranged to have beaten nearly to death, his hatred for the older gay men he had manipulated. Spinotta's operation had been hijacked by the men who worked for him. Now it served a far different purpose from the one Spinotta had intended.

Footsteps shook the ceiling overhead. A few seconds later, a section of wall swung inward and Roger Vasquez entered the cellar. He was wearing a supply belt that held a two-way radio, a large pager, a Bowie knife, and an empty holster for the pistol he was aiming at my face.

"How long?" I asked.

He approached me.

"How long did you keep Spinotta alive?"

Without any change in his face to warn me, he hit me across the forehead with the butt of his pistol. He waited for me to right myself and then slammed the pistol across my jaw.

"Billy told us you ask a lot of questions," he said. "He said it's a defense mechanism. You use it to hide things like the fact that you're a disgusting drunk who likes to rape little boys." His voice was prim and matter-of-fact. Here in his controlled world, there was not a question he did not have an answer for.

He watched as I lay on the damp floor, feeling at my bleeding head and trying to work my mouth. I didn't tell him that I had never laid a hand on a young boy. I figured it would get me a shattered jaw. He ordered me to my feet. He walked me up the stairs out of the cellar, holding my wrists with one hand and keeping the pistol between my shoulder blades with the other. When I realized he wasn't going to restrain me in any way, I figured that meant he was walking me toward my death. I tried to control my panic.

On the top step, he shoved me too hard and I fell to my knees on the floor of a massive barn lined with rotting wine barrels. He jerked me up and walked me out of the barn and into weak gray light. I couldn't tell if it was dawn or dusk. Low, wind-driven fog blew through a stand of squat oak trees up ahead, smaller than the ones I'd seen on Caroline's property.

He walked me into the trees. I wanted to plead for my life, but another blow to the head would knock me unconscious, and I didn't want to meet death in a blackout.

We stepped over the twisted roots of giant sycamores. The foliage thickened around us. Then we entered a clearing where a ghost was waiting for us. Cameron Davis had been suspended by his ankles from a high branch. His bare chest was heaving with labored breaths. He was stripped naked, and his face was covered by the same black leather mask Daniel Brady had worn in my apartment: two tiny inverted triangles for eyeholes, a leering grin with fat lips painted gold. Off to the right was a wooden platform with a high pole in the back. It was missing a rope, but I could tell that it was a gallows. Two chairs were positioned side by side, each with metal spikes covering the seat and the wooden slats in the back and steel cuffs at the ends of the arms. Cameron Davis was situated so that he could survey all the different forms of torture that awaited him.

Roger Vasquez slammed me against the trunk of a giant sycamore. There were two steel cuffs nailed into the trunk, just like the ones I had been confined by on the ride there. I dropped my eyes to the dirt to avoid the sights before me, but Vasquez seized my chin and brought my eyes to his. I worked to keep my body from shaking.

"Calm down," he whispered. "It's not your turn yet." My vision blurred. My mouth had turned to sandpaper, but I could feel bile in my throat. Roger's eyes took on an almost sympathetic cast and he patted me lightly on the cheek. Then he went to Cameron Davis's suspended body and pulled his Bowie knife from its leather holster.

I looked back in the direction we had come. Beyond the barn, a sea of withering grapevines stretched toward a low hill, with what looked like a one-story Italian villa at the top. The house was surrounded by a dense stand of Monterey pines, and the golden light in its front windows was gaining luminescence. Night was falling. An entire day had come and gone while I had lain unconscious in Joseph Spinotta's prison cell.

Roger Vasquez put one arm around Cameron Davis's bare chest, then dragged the knife blade down Cameron Davis's abdomen too gently to break the skin.

"Let me tell you what makes me angry, Adam Murphy," he called back to me. "A man like this, a man with wife and kids, will stop off at a children's restroom or some other secret place and inflict his disease upon an innocent young boy. Now what if that boy turns out to be gay, Adam Murphy? Eventually he might talk about the abuse he suffered at the hands of a diseased, liar like this man. Maybe the boy tells a family member, or a therapist."

He checked my face to make sure I was still with him. "And what happens? What happens when that young man finally decides to seek help? When he tells the truth about what happened to him? For one thing, people assume that his abuse *made* him gay. And then, as if that's not enough, they assume that his abuser was gay as well."

He let this hang in the air as he studied his victim.

"Do you see what that means, Adam Murphy?" I didn't answer. "Thanks to men like Cameron Davis here, gay men everywhere are given the blame for the crimes of the deceitful, the diseased. Those gay men have risked everything to come out to their families, to themselves, and then they're blamed for the crimes of liars!"

With a flick of the wrist, Roger opened up a small wound above Cameron Davis's left nipple. The man let out a muffled cry into his leather mask as blood streaked down his chest. I dropped my eyes and heard Roger's footsteps coming toward me.

"Let me tell you something about our customers," he said. "Not one of them lives in West Hollywood or the Castro or Chelsea. They live in Los Gatos. Simi Valley. Daly City. They have wives, children, and respectable lives they hide behind while they commit crimes that are blamed on men who have done nothing more than be honest about who they are."

He studied me as if he were mildly concerned that I might not be getting his point. He was speaking from a well of personal experience that had driven him to the point of madness, and for the first time in a week, I was too terrified to utter a word. I was tempted to try to use the sexual abuse in his past in an attempt to connect with him, but I doubted this would yield anything more than the choice between a noose and a bed of spikes.

"And then," he said, "here I am, doing all I can to rid the world of the men who abuse us and demonize us, and then I hear about someone like *you*. One of our own. A traitor within our own ranks. Disappointment doesn't even begin to describe it, Adam Murphy."

He must have felt the same fury toward Joseph Spinotta, the man he had served. I recalled Billy Hatfill's hatred of the man and realized that the Vanished Three had shared that loathing while they fed him boys, keeping him happy until they could get their hands on his money and his operation.

He brought the bloody knife blade to my throat. I closed my eyes but felt it against my Adam's apple. Then the blade left my throat. When I opened my eyes, Roger was standing next to Cameron Davis's body as the blood jetted out of the man's throat from a fresh gash.

"Collect your thoughts," Roger said. "You're next."

"I can prove to you that it wasn't me on that tape," I said. "But it doesn't matter, does it? You're going to kill me anyway. Now that I've seen what you do."

"You never should have tried to find us," he said. "Besides, we would have found you soon enough."

We had just emerged from the trees when I saw a figure running toward us across the vineyard. Roger stopped and tightened his grip on the back of my neck. Terrance Davidson raced toward us. His blond hair was cut short and he had added bulk to his small frame. His white T-shirt was sweat-stained, and his round blue eyes were wide with panic. I recognized my cell phone in his right hand. "It's her!" he gasped. He handed the phone to Roger, then regarded me as if I were an alien being. He lacked Roger's supply belt and weaponry.

"What does she want?" Roger asked.

"She says she wants to talk," Terrance gasped. "To all of us. She's hurting him, Roger. I can hear—"

"It's Caroline, isn't it?" I asked.

"Shut up!" Terrance roared.

"She's got your friend Ben," I said.

I felt something warm and wet hit the side of my face. Terrance Davidson had spit on me. When he saw the expression on my face, his eyes widened and he took a step backward. He lacked his friend's controlled rage. From behind me, I heard Roger ask Caroline what she wanted. The answer came in the form of a bloodcurdling male scream that was so loud it turned to static in the cell phone's speaker. Terrance Davidson's hands flew to his ears and he spun away from us. "Do something, Roger!" he screamed. "Do something!" It was clear he had deep feelings for the man Caroline held captive.

I couldn't make out Caroline's words, but her voice sounded calm and controlled.

"Not a chance," Roger replied.

Caroline spoke again. Roger frowned. Terrance was hunched over at the waist, his eyes wide and moist. If Roger Vasquez was their ringleader and Ben Clamp was their muscle, then the pretty boy in front of me was their hand-wringer and well of raw emotion.

"Fine," Roger said. Then he clicked off the phone.

"What does she want?" Terrance asked.

"She wants to talk," Roger said. "To you and me, and him." He jerked his chin toward me.

"You wouldn't give her our location," I said.

"I believe Terrance told you to shut up," Roger said.

The three of us started across the vineyard. The withering grapevines clung to their metal poles with what looked like desperation. The villa at the top of the hill had a flat slate roof and a series of slender columns down the front porch. It looked like a palace for a Roman senator who had long since departed. The slender stone columns along the front porch were cracked and weathered, and their vines had outgrown their ornamental boundaries. The thick interlocking branches of the Monterey pines that surrounded the villa formed a kind of perimeter wall that also shielded a squat smaller out-building with a rounded roof and a single barred window.

"Got a thing for Ben, huh, Terrance?" I asked.

Terrance just looked at me, his face anxious and pouty. I could have sung him a sad song about what happened to skinny pretty boys who got involved with towering hulks of muscle that reminded them of the guys who used to make fun of them in high school, but I was too busy wondering where they were taking me and what I could hope for from Caroline.

We moved up the villa's front steps. Across the sea of trees that surrounded the vineyard below, I glimpsed green, rounded hills blurred by a low and fast-moving fog. It was impossible to see where the property ended, but I figured it was vast.

The walls inside were eggshell white, the texture of the plaster visible. The floors were concrete. Floor-to-ceiling windows surrounded a central courtyard with a large dry fountain crowned by a reproduction of Donatello's *David*. The statue's head had been cut off. A window in the far wall revealed a dark hallway that danced sporadically with a television's flicker. I figured the boys were being entertained while their abusers were tormented and slaughtered by the men who had taken them into their care.

I thought of the young man I had known as Everett and how coolly he had tightened his silver bicycle chain around Martin Cale's throat. His behavior made more sense if he had been exposed to the type of violent retribution I had seen visited on Cameron Davis. But so far I had not encountered a single boy. They were being shielded from the events that were unfolding on other parts of the property.

Terrance Davidson sat me down in a large wooden chair that bore a frightening resemblance to the torture devices I had seen out in the clearing. He raised two wooden boxes that hung from the end of the chair, placed them over my wrists, and slid wooden pins through them. There were instruments of confinement even in the main house that told me that Joseph Spinotta or the men they abducted were sometimes brought here. I thought of all the markings Joseph Spinotta had made on the walls in the bathroom of his prison cell. His captors had kept him alive for a long time, and I wanted to know why.

Roger Vasquez moved to the massive fireplace, lifted a phone off the floor, and placed it on the fireplace's empty mantel. He pressed Speakerphone and dialed a number. Terrance stepped back against the wall and folded his arms over his chest. His hysteria had turned into fury, but it was directed at his comrade, who took a seat in a chair angled toward mine. I figured that Terrance blamed Roger for Ben's current predicament.

The rings stopped. "Adam?" It was Caroline's voice. The sound of it brought tears to my eyes, made real the horror I just had witnessed outdoors. She said my name again.

"Answer her," Roger Vasquez ordered.

"I'm here."

She was silent. Then, "Are you okay?"

"I'm in one piece," I said.

"East or west?" she asked me. I remembered our moment at the Stop 'N' Go in Wasco when we had studied the map. But Roger Vasquez stiffened.

"East or west, Adam?"

"If he gives you our location, I will kill him and then you'll have no reason to come here," Roger said.

"West," I said fast.

Terrance shot forward. "Did you hear what he fucking said?"

"Hey!" Caroline shouted. "Yeah, that's it, pretty boy. You keep your fucking mouth shut. Your boyfriend here's been crying for you—and he's only got seven fingers left!"

Terrance's growl turned into a shriek. He spun around, gripping the back of his head with both hands. Roger rolled his eyes and rubbed at the bridge of his nose with his thumb and forefinger.

I waited for the two of them to collect themselves.

"What did Joseph Spinotta want to do out here?" I asked.

Terrance answered. "Joseph said he was going to rescue boys from meth homes and make new lives for them. He said he was going to create a family for them."

I had assumed that this had been Spinotta's cover story. But it had actually been his real mission, even if his obscene motivations lay close to the surface. "Was he lying?" I asked.

Roger Vasquez said, "We all knew what he was really going to do to the boys once he had them."

"So you took him prisoner," I said. "You held him down in that cellar. You held him for a long time. Why did you keep Spinotta alive for so long?"

A man's gasping breaths came through the speakerphone on the mantle. Caroline was holding the phone down to Ben Clamp's mouth so we could hear his fear.

"He had to show us how to use the technology," Terrance Davidson spat out.

"The technology," I repeated. I waited for one of them to elaborate. Then I saw it. "You're saying Spinotta never wanted to create a child porn ring. That was all you guys."

Roger bolted up. "How dare you—"

Terrance shot forward and placed a hand on Roger's shoulder to quiet him. "The boys have no memory of what's done to them. None! We've made sure of that! We take them out of hell and we give them a chance at a new life."

"You use them," I said. "You rape them on camera and use it as bait for men like Cameron Davis."

"*We* don't touch them," Roger said through clenched teeth. "We leave that to men like you." Terrance's mouth snapped shut. Roger's denial brought an icy glare from his comrade.

"So the whole thing," I said, "it's just a giant trap. It's just an excuse for you to kill your customers." Neither man answered. "How many men like Cameron Davis have you killed?"

Caroline broke the silence. "I heard a question, gentlemen. One of you better fucking answer it."

"Five," Terrance answered.

"How many customers are there?"

"Twenty," he said. "And growing."

The image of Cameron Davis dangling by his ankles as he bled to death was still fresh in my mind. But I had also seen one of the movies that men like Cameron Davis enjoyed. I had seen the helpless victim laid out, in a production designed and choreographed by men who felt their own innocence had been taken from them. The abused were catering to the abusers. For a few terrifying seconds, I saw their logic, felt the hot pulse of rage that had fed their madness over the past three years.

Roger Vasquez was trembling with rage. Terrance Davidson still seemed panicked over the fact that Caroline had his lover in custody. I needed to calm them if I was going to get any more answers out of them. "Where was Billy Hatfill in all of this?" I asked.

"You didn't ask him before you killed him?" Roger demanded. Terrance looked fearfully at the phone on the mantel. "Joseph needed guys like us to bring him the boys he wanted. Billy handpicked us for the job. But we were supposed to keep track of everything Joseph did. Take pictures. That kind of thing."

"You were supposed to set Spinotta up?" I asked.

Terrance gave a sidelong look at Roger and continued. "Billy knew his days were numbered. He wanted an insurance policy, especially if Broadband Access Media was a success. He wanted our help to make sure Spinotta didn't get rid of him. But then Spinotta told us about his plan. To come out here. To *save* boys. Broadband Access Media was just a front to get money for this place. So Billy came up with a plan that made everyone happy. We convinced Joseph to let us come with him and help. And before we left, we convinced him to sign everything over to Billy."

A young boy's peal of laughter rang from somewhere deep within the house. This place was not the perverse sexual playground that I had imagined. The boys had no memory of the sexual abuse they suffered. They had not been present for the murder I had witnessed earlier. Whatever panic and dislocation they felt from being ripped from their families, they were not destined to grow up to be Everett, furiously sexual, murderously violent. Yet the young man I knew as Everett had lived here as well. He had been sent to live with Billy at the age of sixteen, and I couldn't figure out why.

"What's supposed to happen to these boys when they grow up?" I asked.

It was Roger Vasquez who answered. "We set up accounts for them," he said with evident pride. "With the money we steal from our customers."

Behind Roger, Terrance Davidson had gone white, his blazing eyes fixed on my face. The topic of the young boys' fate had rattled him. "They're allowed to leave at a time of their own choosing," Roger went on. "We won't force them. When the time comes, they can reenter the world as new men."

His answer baffled me. Terrance took a step forward, his jaw quivering.

"What about Everett?" I asked.

Now it was Roger's turn to go white.

"Jim Clark," I said.

Roger got to his feet, glaring at me as if I had grown another head. Terrance shot forward and pulled the pistol from the supply belt on Roger's hip. The breath went out of me. I braced myself for a gunshot, even though I wasn't sure how I had earned it.

But it was Roger who was staring at the barrel of his own pistol. "I'm sorry, Roger," Terrance Davidson whispered. "We couldn't do it."

"What the hell's going on?" Caroline demanded.

"It's all right!" I shouted. A pleading look had risen in Terrance Davidson's eyes, even as he aimed the pistol at Roger's face.

"Everett was a problem." Terrance sighed. His eyes were boring into Roger's as he spoke. "He'd been abused so bad before he came here. He was a bad influence on the other boys. We had to get rid of him."

"Right, asshole," Roger said, "but you weren't supposed—"

"Ben and I sent him to live with Billy," Terrance said quickly. He wasn't addressing me. He was explaining himself to Roger Vasquez. "Billy said he could handle him."

"You fucking idiots," Roger whispered.

"We couldn't do it, Roger!" Terrance cried. "We couldn't kill him just because you fucked him!"

Roger lunged at the pistol. Then the pistol went off.

I heard Caroline screaming my name. I called out to her to show I was alive.

Roger Vasquez lay on his back across the Oriental rug. The bullet had torn through his right shoulder, and his lips were trying to form words. Terrance stood over him, panting.

A strange knocking echoed through the house. I twisted in my seat. The sound was coming from across the courtyard. A small shadow blocked out the television's blue flicker. It was a young boy, slapping his hand against the glass. I couldn't tell which one he was. He had obviously been terrified by the gunshot and wanted to know what was going on.

Roger Vasquez took rasping breaths through clenched teeth. By sleeping with Everett, he had set into motion the chain of events that had brought me to their compound and led to the bleeding wound now darkening the carpet. If Corey had not seen Everett come off his uncle's yacht, had not recognized the young man as one of the boys he had abducted, I would never have met the two men in front of me.

Terrance Davidson regained his composure and stepped toward Roger's prone body. "You're a liar, Roger," he whispered. "You're a liar and a hypocrite. Just like Joseph. You said we could break the cycle."

Terrance shot Roger through the forehead.

"Terrance?" The young man didn't respond to the sound of my voice. He backed away from Roger Vasquez's body. His grip on the pistol remained tight, but his eyes were stunned with shock. Terrance Davidson made for a more unpredictable captor than Roger Vasquez and I wasn't relieved that he was now in charge.

There was still one question I needed an answer to. I had left LA to discover the identity of Corey's killer.

"Terrance!" This time it was Caroline who called out to the man. "Terrance, let's assess the situation here, all right?" Terrance turned to face the phone on the mantel as if it were a human being. "You want to be reunited with your friend Ben here?" Caroline asked him.

"Yes," Terrance said in a trembling voice.

"Okay, then," she responded. "Let's talk. There's one of you now, Terrance. I'm sorry. But that's not our fault. Now let's—"

A shrill series of beeps filled the room. Terrance twisted around. The sound was coming from Roger's supply belt, from the large pager I had noticed earlier. The sequence and the volume reminded me of a sound I had heard a night earlier: Caroline's perimeter alarm.

"You bitch!" Terrance roared. "You lying bitch! You knew where we were this whole time!" I heard Caroline's voice protesting, but Terrance's shouting drowned out her words. "He told you, didn't he? Ben gave you our location! You fucking tortured it out of him!"

I knew it couldn't be true. If Ben had given Caroline our location, she would have been here by now.

I felt the truth moving in from the edges of my vision. I felt four years' worth of strange meetings, secret deals, and abductions coalesce into a single act that explained the past week of my life in a way that nothing else I had learned ever could.

As Terrance screamed invectives at Caroline and waved the pistol, I fought to keep my breathing even and my mind clear, pulling facts from the timeline in my head and placing them side by side. Four years earlier, Joseph Spinotta had asked Corey to set him up with a man named Reynaldo Reyez. Corey had tried to locate Reynaldo only to discover that he was dead. Corey had impersonated Reynaldo and abducted young boys for Joseph Spinotta.

And now Joseph Spinotta was dead.

"Terrance, listen to me!" I called out in a firm voice that got the man's attention.

The perimeter alarm on Roger's belt went silent for a few seconds. Then it started again. I ignored it.

"Who abducted the boys, Terrance?" I shouted over the beeping.

He looked from the speakerphone to me, torn, totally lost.

"Answer me and you'll find out who just broke through your fence!" I screamed.

"Reynaldo Reyez!" Terrance gasped.

"Have you ever laid eyes on Reynaldo Reyez?"

"No!" he gasped, leveling the gun on me. "Reynaldo still thinks Spinotta is in charge. We let him. Spinotta hired him."

"Did Joseph ever tell you how he met Reynaldo Reyez?" I asked.

Terrance just stared at me.

"Answer him!" Caroline shouted.

"No!" Terrance cried.

I heard Caroline mutter something in shock. She had already figured out where I was headed.

"A week ago," I said, struggling to control my voice, "Billy Hatfill called you and told you to kill a man named Corey Howard."

"Yes," Terrance said instantly. "He said Corey was trying to blackmail him."

"Did the name Corey Howard mean anything to you?" I asked.

"No!" he spat.

He was telling the truth. Joseph Spinotta never told his three companions who had hooked him up with an assassin named Reynaldo Reyez. Maybe he had kept this secret on purpose, in the hope that it would someday bring down the young men who had taken him prisoner.

"Who killed Corey Howard?" I asked.

Terrance didn't answer. He could tell that Caroline and I were already a hundred steps ahead of him, and that seemed to terrify him more than the shrill summons of the perimeter alarm.

"Who killed Corey Howard?" I asked.

I saw Scott Koffler's naked body, wrapped in a towel, murdered before he could tell me what Corey had hired him to do. I heard James Wilton telling me that Corey was the only one with the motive to kill the man, even as I had insisted that Billy Hatfill had done the job. I heard another perimeter alarm, the one on Caroline's property that had gone off the night before, suggesting that we were being followed. I saw a golden chain with a scorpion on the end, tossed at my feet, solid evidence that the man I had known as Corey Howard was dead. If it hadn't been removed from his neck by his killer, then who could have possibly handed it over to the Vanished Three?

"Answer the question, Terrance!" I said. "Who killed Corey Howard?"

"Reynaldo Reyez."

For a long while, the three of us listened to the perimeter alarm. Then Caroline spoke up. "You fucking idiots," she said. "You called Corey and asked him to kill himself."

CHAPTER 23

Terrance Davidson ripped the phone off the mantelpiece and sent it flying across the room. Then he thrust the gun under my jaw and undid the wooden cuffs around my wrists. He forced me to my feet, turned me around, and jammed the gun into my lower back.

"What the fuck was she talking about?" Terrance screamed in my ear.

"You heard her."

He forced me through the front door of the villa and out onto the porch. The vineyard below us was silent and empty. A vague light came from the barn beyond it. Inside the villa, the perimeter alarm was still howling.

"Where's Caden McCormick?" I asked.

"Why?"

"Because that's who he wants," I said.

I lifted one foot off the edge of the porch and rested it lightly on the top step. I listened to Terrance's ragged breathing. Then I kicked myself backward and felt the barrel of the pistol slide up my spine. Terrance lost his footing, and the two of us stumbled backward through the front door.

We hit the concrete floor and I rolled off him, scrambling to my feet just as he raised the gun at me. I flew out the front door as a gunshot tore through the frame above my head. I hit the bottom of the steps and started running for the cover of the Monterey pines along the side of the house. Corey was on the property and Terrance had just given away his location by firing a shot at me. My only instinct was to get as far away from Terrance as possible.

I saw the squat, rounded building hidden in the trees that I had noticed earlier and ran for it, expecting to find a locked door. But it was open, and I stepped inside and locked it behind me.

Inside was a long wooden table with a flat-screen computer monitor on it and a row of blinking CPUs underneath. There was an open can of Diet Coke next to the keyboard along with a set of keys. I pocketed the keys. Terrance Davidson must have been sitting at this desk when he received the phone call from Caroline Hughes. He had dashed out in a panic. On the computer monitor's screen, I saw an Excel file. It was a customer list. Five of the customers' names were in red, including that of Cameron Davis.

On the wall overhead was a bank of video monitors, three of them showing silent images of the property's distant perimeter fence. Beyond the fence were low, rolling hills dotted by sparse stands of oak trees. The three monitors below them gave interior views of the villa. Another monitor showed a garage buried in the oak trees that ran alongside the vineyard. The Suburban was parked outside.

Terrance Davidson appeared on one monitor at a heavy wooden door somewhere inside the villa. He punched numbers on a keypad in the wall next to the door. I figured he was trying to get to the boys. But I could see the boys' living quarters; a camera was angled down the length of a hallway that had dormitory-style rooms. The doors were open, giving me glimpses of rumpled twin beds. In a central living area, the big screen television flickered. No one was watching it. The boys were gone. They had either been set free or Corey had them in custody. Considering that they were evidence of his crimes, I didn't want to think about what he might to do to them.

A series of soft beeps came from the wall next to me. I saw a keypad just like the one Terrance Davidson was using inside the villa. Next to the keypad was the almost invisible outline of a door in the black-painted wall.

The lock clicked. Whatever code Terrance had entered into the keypad had unlocked the door right next to me. I drew it open slowly and saw a tiny cell with dark-blue walls and a twin bed with white plush bedding. A flat-screen television was broadcasting a succession of pristine landscape photographs designed to soothe the prisoner.

Caden McCormick sat on the floor, his knees against his chest. His head had been shaved, and his cheeks were sunken. He had been in this new home for almost four weeks. Obviously, he had not been ready to play with others. A plate of food lay overturned on the floor in front of him.

"Caden?"

His gaunt, glazed eyes stared at my legs. "I need to see my mom," he said quietly and determinedly.

"We need to go, Caden."

"I *need* to see my mom," he repeated. "She knows about the demon! She wants me to be safe!"

Whatever life had been offered in this place, Caden McCormick had fought it. Maybe that would have changed over time.

"I'll take you to see your mom," I said. "Just come with me, okay?"

He brought his deadened eyes to mine. "Are you lying?"

I turned and looked behind me through the doorway. On one of the interior monitors, I saw Terrance Davidson lying facedown in front of the door he had been trying to open moments earlier. Corey had entered the house and killed him, just like the eight meth addicts whose sons he had taken. Just like his own mother. Now Corey knew that his brother was not among the other boys.

"The demon's back, Caden," I said. "We need to go before he finds us."

The boy tensed, assessing my face with what seemed like desperate calculation. Then he mustered some reserve of courage that I would have never expected to find in a thirteen-year-old and got to his feet, his chin held high. I took his hand. Corey was nowhere to be seen on the video monitors. I studied the image of the Suburban and the garage and mapped our course.

The boy's legs gave way as we started to move. He was skin and bones. I squatted and told him to get onto my back. He climbed on. When his hands met in front of my chest, I got to my feet, opened the door, and ran.

I ran through the Monterey pines, down the hill, and into the oaks that ran alongside the vineyard. The oak branches were low, and I felt Caden tuck his face to my left shoulder as we went. We reached the barn. On the other side of it, I could see the garage and the Suburban in the distance. Getting there meant a long run through open space.

I didn't stop to doubt myself. Caden let out a small wail when he realized we were out in the open. I kept running. The barn shielded us from the villa for a few seconds, and then we were out in the open again. I was running so fast that I slammed into the side of the Suburban. Caden dropped from my back and fell to the dirt on his side. In one motion, I opened the driver's-side door. Caden crawled over the gearshift and into the passenger seat. I stabbed Terrance's key into the ignition, started the engine, and slammed on the gas, ripping the steering wheel to one side so I could accelerate and avoid hitting the garage at the same time.

We rocketed forward and plummeted down a long grassy hill. The trees broke and I saw an expanse of hills before us offering no sign of civilization. I glanced at Caden and told him to put his seat belt on. Instead of obeying, he pulled an oily black pistol out of the armrest by the handle.

"Put your seat belt on!" I shouted.

He had seen stronger anger than mine. Without so much as blinking, he turned forward, buckled his seat belt, and held the barrel of the gun in both hands. I swerved to avoid a gnarled oak tree and felt the impact of a large rock against the front tires. The land bucked underneath us like ocean waves.

Finally the perimeter fence rose in front of us, yards of moonlit chain link topped by coils of razor wire. Beyond it, more grassy hills like the ones we had just traveled. No dirt road. No highway. No lights in the distance. I had to drive right through the fence and keep going.

Then I saw the headlights behind us, cresting the hills we had traveled, disappearing from view only to reemerge again. At the top of a hill, when the front tire of the Suburban exploded, I assumed we had been shot at. Then the entire carriage jerked and screamed beneath us. In the rearview mirror, I saw a dark shape fly backward away from the car. The tire. The Suburban had been sabotaged before we set foot in it.

The entire nose of the carriage dropped. I slammed on the brakes too late. Speed and gravity formed a deadly union. My stomach rose into my throat. I realized we had left the ground. I heard Caden scream, saw the rocky slope slide beneath us across the windshield.

I tasted something coppery. I felt fingers stroking my face and a powerful arm encircling my lower back. I felt my shoulders scraping against the mangled frame of the Suburban's driver's-side window; then I was lifted into open air. When I opened my eyes, the man I had known as Corey Howard didn't smile. He lowered me to the earth and set my back against the side of the black Lincoln Navigator he had pursued us in. Several yards away, the Suburban lay on its roof, the weight of its carriage resting forward on its crushed nose. The driver's-side headlight shot a mangled beam across the wind-rippled grass.

Corey held my face in both hands to make sure I could keep my head steady. He was clean-shaven, his long dark eyes unblinking, and there was nothing in them to suggest that he had almost driven me to my death.

"They told you to kill yourself," I said.

"Yes."

"You pretended to be Reynaldo Reyez," I said. "You abducted those boys. You killed those people."

"I saved them. You know that," he said. "That's what Joseph Spinotta said he wanted to do."

"It was Everett, wasn't it?" I asked him. "You saw Everett come off of your uncle's yacht, and you thought that's what your brother was going to turn into. So you tried to get your brother back."

He nodded emphatically. Too emphatically. I realized I was giving him his story, taking the burden off him. He had been alive the entire time. He had known what Billy Hatfill was going to do to me and he had done nothing to stop it.

"I made a mistake, Adam," Corey said. "You're right. I saw Everett. I had to go to Billy. I wasn't scheduled to deliver another kid to them, so I wouldn't have a chance to follow them afterward. But Billy said he didn't know where Spinotta was."

So far his story matched the one Billy Hatfill had given me. I stayed silent. There was still something he wanted from me, and if I kept him talking I would find out what it was.

"But Billy had a plan," he said. "He said we could get you to go after them."

"And you did," I said. "You set me up. You used Daniel Brady to do it."

"You're right. As soon as I gave Billy the tape, I got a phone call. It was Roger Vasquez. He asked me to kill a man named Corey Howard." He sneered at the damp earth between us and shook his head, as if the two of us had been snared in a practical joke without real consequence. "He said I needed to do it to protect the operation and all the good work they were doing. Billy thought it was you on that tape, and I knew he'd show it to you."

He squeezed my shoulder. "But I knew you were stronger than Billy thought you were."

He seemed to sense my skepticism. He grabbed me by both shoulders and brought his face an inch from mine. "I believed in Billy's plan, Adam.

I knew you would find Spinotta. So I waited. I watched you become the kind of man you always wanted to be, the kind who never gave up. Most of the time I had tears in my eyes, watching you . . . grow."

"You killed Scott Koffler."

"I was protecting you."

"You killed him before he could tell me anything."

"He wasn't going to tell you shit! He went after your friend Nate!"

He took my face in his hands. "I *chose* you, Adam. I knew you could do it. Come on, Adam. Look at all the things you've done."

"I can't. I'm too busy looking at the things I've seen."

"They paid me six hundred thousand dollars for each boy," he said. "I saved it all. We could have a life together. The three of us. You, me, and Caden. I want my brother to see your courage. I already made one terrible mistake with him. You can keep me from making another."

I turned my face away from him. He seized my chin with a sudden power that didn't match the trembling emotion in his voice. He forced my eyes back to his.

"You failed me once, Adam. You were sick. But I gave you a second chance. And you didn't fail me this time. You found my brother, just like I knew you would."

"I *was* sick?" I asked him. "I'm not sick anymore? You cured me, is that it?"

"Where is my brother, Adam?" he said in a low voice with nothing I would call love or admiration in it.

"You knew what Billy was going to do, and you left town without warning me," I said. "*Maybe* you thought I was going to find your brother. But if that didn't happen, you still would have taught me a lesson."

He took a step back. As soon as I got to my feet, he placed one hand on my chest to hold me in place. I wasn't surprised to see him level a mean-looking gun on me with his other hand. Both motions told me that I had hit on the truth beneath his exaggerated emotions.

"Billy said you liked his plan," I said. "He was right, wasn't he? You knew Billy wasn't just going to show me that tape. You knew he was going to put me through hell first. You knew that maybe just for a day or a few hours, I would believe that I had harmed a child. And then you would have taught me a lesson. The same lesson you taught Melissa Brady.

"You wanted me to think you used Daniel Brady as my body double to spare me? Bullshit. You just saw another chance for revenge." He didn't respond. "You didn't follow me out here to ask me to live with you," I said. "You followed me here because I know you killed eight people. You followed me here because I know what you did to Daniel Brady and his wife. Because I know you killed your own mother. But you couldn't kill *me* until I led you here."

Whatever spark existed in his eyes went out.

"Did you really want to give Caden a new life?" I asked him. "Or did you just want to get paid to kill your mother?"

"Where is he?" Corey asked. There was no concern in his voice. He had asked for the whereabouts of his younger brother as if the boy were simply the next in a long line of targets.

That was why, after breaching the perimeter of the compound, Corey had gone straight for the boys' quarters before pursuing Terrance Davidson. Even when it was clear that his younger brother was not among them, he had taken the two other boys from the compound. He had removed the living evidence of his crimes. Caden and I were living evidence as well.

"You didn't want to save your brother from this place," I said. "You saw Everett. You realized who you were really working for. And you wanted the exact same thing you wanted against everyone else who ever wronged you. Revenge."

He brought the barrel of the gun to my forehead and pressed it gently against the skin.

"You don't save people. You only punish them," I said. I saw a blur of movement in the darkness behind him, approaching fast down the slope of the hill. Corey took a step back and leveled the gun on my face.

"Every life I ever tried to make for myself was stolen from me," he said.

I said his name in a voice that I wanted to sound pleading. His face went taut and he shook his head in a slow denial of what he thought was a plea for my life. It was not a plea. It was a distraction. There was a crunch of grass from behind him. He heard it and pivoted toward it.

Caden McCormick raised a pistol in his hands. Corey froze. "Mom was right," the boy said. "You're a demon."

Caden fired. I hit the dirt, saw Corey's body jerk. He tumbled in front of me, and when he rolled onto his back I saw the bullet hole in his throat. For a few seconds, the wound was black and bloodless. Then it filled.

The kickback had knocked Caden off his feet, and the pistol was lying in the grass between us. Stunned by the shock of gunfire, the boy was down on all fours, his back heaving, his neck lax. I sank to my knees in the grass next to him and placed my hand firmly on the small of his back, whispering hollow assurances under my breath to blot out the sound of Corey's blood-filled wheezing, holding the boy in place so that he could not lift his head and see the full effect of what he had done.

Corey went silent, and then I heard the sharp sounds of restrained movement from the back of the Lincoln Navigator. The other boys. I would never know what Corey had planned to do with them.

CHAPTER 24

James Wilton was sitting on the stone bench at the edge of his
property as I arrived at his house. I took a seat beside him. Neither one of
us said anything for a while. I had spent the last forty-eight hours in the
custody of the Paso Robles police department. I eventually lost track of
how many hours they spent interrogating me.

During my interrogation, the Paso Robles police got a call from a
sheriff's deputy out in the Central Valley who told them she had a man in
her custody. An anonymous 911 call had tipped the deputy to the man's location, a barren field just south of Highway 198's passage across the floor
of the Central Valley. The deputy had discovered an audiotape in the
man's front pocket. The conversation on it was not for the faint of heart.
The man was also missing three fingers. The reporting deputy's name was
Amy Stahl. She made no mention of a woman named Caroline Hughes.

I wanted to believe that Caroline had set out in search of me as soon
as we got disconnected, and that she had turned back as soon as the story
of what I had discovered broke across every radio station in the country. I
figured she didn't want to explain the torture of Ben Clamp and the abduction of Eddie Cairns.

Now I told Jimmy everything. My voice sounded like it belonged to
someone else. As I talked, he kept his attention focused on the San Fernando Valley's expanse, a view he had earned by creating contained versions of the nightmare I had just been through. He didn't interrupt or ask
questions.

When I was done, he got to his feet and walked up to the line of hedges.
"I'm going to start work soon," he said.

"On this?"

"A novel," he said. "It's about this young man who's so desperate for intrigue and escape that he ends up with blood on his hands. So he starts hanging with this group of black militants from the other side of the Bay. It's the early sixties, so that's not exactly the best choice. It doesn't go so well for him." He gave me a look. "In the end, the only stories I have are my own, little man."

"I'm sorry, Jimmy."

"Nate tells me he's been going to a lot of AA meetings. Have you thought about tagging along?"

"A little."

"So what do you think?" he asked. "Was he right?"

"Who?"

"Corey," he answered. "Did you grow into the man you always wanted to be? Were you cured?"

"Corey didn't even know who I was."

He looked out over the valley and shifted his weight painfully from one leg to another. I heard footsteps on the grass behind me. Jimmy turned and glared at someone over my shoulder. It was the first time Brenda had been back to the house since Jimmy had asked her to leave.

"Adam's going to be staying in the guest bedroom for a while," she said. "I was thinking of cooking something, probably eightish." Jimmy turned his back to her. "Yeah, I let you have your moment, *big* man, but I'm sick of room service and you always get tired of playing God after a day or two, probably because you can't even keep a date book, much less keep Saturn spinning on its axis. So you can stomp around as much as you want and slam that overpriced cane down on your desk. But it won't change the fact that Adam's not dead and he didn't kill anyone, and as usual, you forgot about the most important part of playing God."

"What's that?" he asked without turning.

"You can't be wrong. Ever."

She walked off without another word. He returned to the bench.

"If you hadn't believed you were diseased, Corey wouldn't have believed it either, and he wouldn't have been able to do what he did to you."

I blinked and decided not to cry.

"Shell shock is about going blind, little man. Not having your vision expanded." He put an arm around my back and walked me toward the main house. "Stay awhile for real, this time."

*   *   *

Ben Clamp confessed to the extent of the operation he had been part of, and all twenty of the operation's paying customers were arrested. Clamp was going to be tried for the murders of five men, and there was little doubt that I would have to testify against him.

Brenda helped me move my things out of my studio apartment in West Hollywood. Some of them went into storage, and the rest of them went into their guest bedroom. They hadn't set a time for how long I was going to stay with them. I made a weak stab at organizing Jimmy's library as he disappeared into his office to begin work on a novel that he considered to be all his own.

I placed several calls to a Kings County Sheriff's Deputy named Amy Stahl. She did not return any of them. I did a little digging and found no evidence that Caroline Hughes had returned to her life in San Francisco. Ben Clamp had apparently described his abduction and torture at her hands in enough detail to make her a person of interest. I was sure Caroline had left the state. I was curious to know how well she did on the run when she didn't have someone to hunt.

Martin Cale's yacht had not been discovered, and the young man who had piloted it out to sea was still at large. Pictures of fifteen-year-old Jim Clark had been plastered all over the news. Not even in the desk or files of the late Billy Hatfill had anyone been able to locate a recent picture of the young man I had known as Everett, whose chance encounter with Corey Howard had triggered a series of suicides and murders. He was the one missing piece of a story that continued to make national headlines weeks after it broke.

Jimmy and I both pressed Dwight Zachary as hard as we could for any information on Caden McCormick and learned nothing more than the fact that Caden, along with the two other boys Corey had abducted, were all being held at a psychological facility different from the one named in the news reports about them. Visitors were not welcome.

Thirty-four days after I had stopped drinking, I met Nate Bain at a newly opened recovery center just off Santa Monica Boulevard. The place had steel wool carpeting, folding chairs with thick cushions attached to the seats, and strident sayings in cheap frames hanging on the walls. There must have been a hundred other gay men in the room with us, and all of them looked so bright-eyed and fresh-faced that I couldn't imagine them ever having set foot inside a bar or a bathhouse.

The speaker was a small-framed raven-haired woman in a black pants suit. When she announced she had been clean and sober since January 1983, there was a torrent of applause so loud it hurt my ears. She spent a good twenty minutes detailing the most depraved episodes from her days of drinking and using. Every shocking detail she shared was met with an explosion of laughter that made my own sense of shame over my numerous blackouts seem childish and melodramatic.

After she was done, Nate Bain was one of the five people who accepted a small token celebrating his thirty days of continuous sobriety. The changes in him were evident. Weight had returned to his face, and he took careful pauses between his sentences.

After the meeting let out, a group of us walked up Santa Monica Boulevard. It was a clear July evening, and I could see all the way to the spot where the San Gabriels collided with the San Bernardinos under a purple sky. Nate slid his arm through mine and leaned his weight against me as he walked inside the halo of energetic conversation from his sober friends.

We were about to cross San Vicente Boulevard when I realized we were being followed by a tall, big-boned man in a baseball cap, sunglasses that were not necessary for the hour, and a rumpled blue shirt. After another block, I realized that it was not a man who was following us. The knot in my chest softened.

I watched the person cross Santa Monica Boulevard and head in the direction of West Hollywood Park, a small square of green space that sits across the street from the Pacific Design Center. I kissed Nate on the cheek and I told him I would meet him in a few minutes at Starbucks. There was a pull of worry around his eyes and it took him several seconds to release my hand.

I found Caroline Hughes sitting on a bench next to the empty playground. I hovered next to it instead of taking a seat. She was a wanted woman, and it was clear she was afraid that we were being watched. Under the back of her baseball cap, I saw her signature red hair had been replaced by thin black bristle.

"You're a hero now, Adam Murphy."

"Only because you didn't step forward to take any of the credit."

"Credit for what?" she asked. "Kidnapping a crazy meth addict?" She made no mention of the things she had done to Ben Clamp. "Eddie Cairns is doing just fine, by the way. We managed to find him a place in a nice recovery home up near Sacramento."

"We?"

She ignored the question. "Corey," she prompted softly.

I scanned our surroundings and saw one homeless guy wandering at the park's edge and a muscle bunny walking his poodle. I took a seat on the bench. "After they told him to kill himself, he started following me. He knew what Billy was going to do, and he let it happen."

"He followed you to his brother," she said.

"Right," I said. "So he could kill us. He wasn't interested in saving Caden. He wanted to get rid of all the evidence."

"On the news. They said . . ."

"Caden shot him."

I was surprised to feel her fingers close around my hand. She brought my hand to her chest and held it there for several seconds, her head bowed. I figured it was her way of thanking me for facing the man who had killed her mother.

"Who's *we*, Caroline?"

She got to her feet and pulled a pack of Marlboro Lights from her pocket. In the forty-eight hours we had spent together, I had not seen her smoke one cigarette. She had applied a coat of base that concealed her freckles and it made her face appear oddly masklike.

"Don't worry about Everett," she said. "Or should I say Jim Clark? We caught up with him outside your apartment building last week. I almost lost a finger to that crazy bicycle chain he was wearing. Turns out Billy Hatfill had promised to send him back to the compound as long as he followed orders to kill you and Cale. Everett said those guys were the only family he ever had." She bowed her head respectfully. "I felt sad for him," she whispered.

"Where is he now?" I asked.

She reached into her pocket and extended one closed fist in my direction. She dropped a chunky silver bicycle chain into my open palm. If there had been any blood on it when she tore it from the kid's neck, she had wiped it clean.

"He was sixteen," I whispered.

"Really?" she said. "He went for my throat like a man."

I wasn't surprised Everett had decided he was wrong not to kill me on Cale's yacht and had tried again. I had destroyed the place that must have felt like a fresh Eden for him. I realized that I was holding a murder weapon and pushed it into my front pocket.

The park was enfolded in night darkness. Caroline removed her sunglasses, and in the light from a nearby streetlight I could see that she was wearing contact lenses that darkened her unnervingly amber eyes to brown. She surveyed the urban landscape with the curiosity of a hunter. On the near horizon, the Sierra Tower apartment building rose fourteen stories against the twinkling hillside. Somewhere up there was the house in which Billy Hatfill had taken his life. I knew that it was for sale, but that buyers shied away.

"People always say bad shit about LA," she said. "It's nice here."

"This is West Hollywood," I said. "It's a different city."

"How long have you lived here?"

"A year."

"You plan on staying for a while?" she asked.

"I'm staying with friends," I said. She reached into the front pocket of her jeans and handed me a matchbook for a place called Atwell's Bar and Grill that had a Bakersfield address. I flipped it open and saw a strange series of numbers written on the inside flap.

"Since I know where you're going to be," she said quietly, "you can get me at that number."

My stare forced her to continue. "Claire Shipley lied. Reynaldo Reyez was alive when she got there that day. He's alive today."

I remembered how the old woman had told Caroline that grief made you forget the rules you used to play by, and how her words had formed a strange and sudden connection between the two of them.

"I told him everything you did," she said. "I told him we had to watch out for you. He said that's fine. He thinks you're a brave man. As for Corey, he said we are not the product of what is done to us—we are the product of our response to it. A little spiritual for an assassin, don't you think?"

"Corey never made contact with him?"

"No," she answered. "Claire made sure of that. When I told him what Corey had done, he wasn't pleased."

I noted her use of the old woman's first name as if she had become a friend. I had not doubted Claire Shipley's story for a second. I had believed that she had buried Reynaldo Reyez to keep Corey's attention on his dying grandmother.

"She raised him," I said. "She trained him."

Caroline gave me a faint smile and a nod. "She says an eye for an eye leaves everyone blind. That's why she taught him to cut off their legs." A hard edge had crept into her voice. It sent a chill through me. "You going to keep that number, or are you going to throw it away as soon as I'm gone?" she asked. "If you keep doing what you're doing, you're going to need it."

I slid the matchbook in my front pocket and felt her lips brush against my cheek. When I looked up, she was already heading across the park. Her head was bowed and her shoulders were hunched as she merged with the shadows.

Later that night, Nate and I drove up Laurel Canyon beneath a sky cleared of its stars by the city's glare. I had dropped Everett's chain in a trash can on Santa Monica Boulevard, but the matchbook with Caroline's phone number was still in my pants pocket. It pressed against the inside of my thigh like a small finger, an invitation to violence and bloodshed like the kind that still tortured my sleep.

As we entered the backyard, I saw the door to Jimmy's office standing open, heard the cadence of his fingers flying across the keyboard. I clutched the matchbook advertising a place called Atwell's Bar and Grill in my fist and waited for him to notice my presence. He didn't, so I didn't tell him about my strange visit from a woman named Caroline Hughes. I wasn't sure if I would ever tell him.

According to Jimmy, my memory could drive me blind, so as I walked back toward the main house I took in every quiet detail as if it had been rendered by an artist who was desperate for my approval. In the guest bedroom, I found Nate sitting on the foot of the bed, his arms bent behind him, his breaths heavy and slightly strained, his lips parted and his brow furrowed in an expression of vulnerability that was surprising given his history.

"Can I stay?" he asked.

He arched his back beneath my weight and I tried to study every part of his body I touched as he wrapped his legs around my back and I accepted an invitation to assume a role with which I was not familiar. But when I parted his hairless thighs, my vision expanded to include a redhaired woman driving up a rutted mountain road beneath a canopy of fanned pine boughs. With a certainty I possess only in dreams, I knew that there were shadows awaiting her arrival at the road's end, and that as soon as she got there, they would step forward and repeat their promise to guide her through the pulsing radiance that continued to strobe her vision long after the flash of light before day that had stolen her mother.

Before Caroline Hughes could reach her destination, I pulled Nate's body against mine with the force of one arm and drove sounds out of him that lost all traces of human will or resistance. I whispered words in his ear that Corey McCormick could never have spoken to me.

Acknowledgments

Light Before Day was initially inspired by a special report by the McClatchy Company's California Newspapers on the methamphetamine trade in California's Central Valley. Journalists writing for the *Fresno, Modesto, and Sacramento Bee* have compiled their outstanding reporting into one of the most authoritative and brutally compelling documents we have on the scope and horror of this epidemic. As of this writing, their brilliant work can be found at *www.valleymeth.org*. Additional insight into the experiences of children raised in meth homes was provided by Deputy Tom Salisbury at the Riverside County Sheriff's Department. Deputy Salisbury coordinates the Drug Endangered Children program in Riverside County and is just one shining example of the great strides being made by the State of California in caring for the children affected by this epidemic. Thanks also go to Julie Garza, MSW, with the Riverside Child Assessment Team.

Dr. Michael Chernoff helped to deepen my understanding of meth's toll on the gay community. He is a leader among the gay psychotherapists who are helping to find roads to recovery for the shockingly large number of gay men trapped in the grip of this drug. In his trail-blazing first person account, *Life vs. Meth*, writer and editor Kevin Koffler gave gay men everywhere an invaluable testimonial about what this drug is capable of doing to certain members of our community. As of this writing, Koffler's piece can be found at *www.poz.com*, where I hope it remains until further strides in battling this side of the epidemic have been made. (The fact that its author shares a last name with one of the novel's more unsavory characters is pure coincidence.)

Generous members of the Los Angeles County Sheriff's Department assisted me in other areas of this novel. As always, any deviations from reality belong solely to the author. Homicide Detective Elizabeth Smith gently advised me on issues of jurisdiction and procedure, as well as which storylines were too implausible to include. (I did not heed all of her advice on the latter.) At the West Hollywood substation, Sergeant Lewis of the Crime Impact Team along with Deputy Mosquera and Deputy Van Leeuwen provided invaluable insight into the inner workings of what is probably one of the most progressive law enforcement agencies in the country. Sergeant Donald Mueller was also of valuable assistance. None of these individuals bear even the slightest resemblance to Dwight Zachary.

David Biancardi, at Audio, Video & Controls in New York City, endured ceaseless questions about wireless technologies. I hope he forgives me for being unable to include most of the invaluable information he provided. *Light Before Day* grew in part out of a short story I originally published in *Genre* magazine. Thanks go to then-editor Andy Towle for giving me the outlet to start growing this one. Some historical insight into the Great Central Valley came from an outstanding book called *The King of California: JG Boswell and the Making of a Secret American Empire* by Mark Arak and Rick Wartzman (Public Affairs Press).

For the third time, the outstanding team at Miramax Books gave me their absolute best, enduring a drastic last-minute change in projects and many extended deadlines due to my father's illness. Jonathan Burnham puts the class in class act and David Groff remains a master wordsmith and gentle guide. Kristin Powers and Kathy Schneider continue to rock. Claire McKinney is a much welcome addition. Sad goodbyes go to Bruce Mason and the divine Hilary Bass. Thanks also go to Mitchell Ivers and Louise Burke at Pocket Books. Over at *The Advocate,* Bruce Steele was generous and understanding about my column deadlines when the pedal wasn't quite hitting the metal.

Blessed is Lynn Nesbit, even though an early draft of this novel almost landed her in a coma. There are not enough thanks for Richard Green, my man at CAA. Both provided generous feedback on early drafts and continue to foot the bill at nice places, even though a Southern gentleman is always supposed to pay.

My writer pals provided various forms of support along the way they might not be aware of. Thanks to John Morgan Wilson, Jan Burke, Denise Hamilton, Paula Woods, and DeLaune Michel. During my father's illness, my mother's support staff became family. Thanks to Ross Tafaro, Sue Q, Lucky Tebbe, Sandra, Yancy, both Joes, Scott Z., Linda—

and yes—even you, Amy. A big kiss to my tireless web mistress Heidi Mack. A moment of silence for Nicholai, probably the greatest Siberian cat to ever saunter across the earth.

As for the personals, I would be lost without my close friend, colleague, and confidante, Eric Shaw Quinn, who responded to my dark moments of doubt by advising me to shut the hell up and finish the damn novel so we could go out to lunch.

My mother has blessed me with a life of love, abundance, and clarity of heart that bears no resemblance to the one experienced by my fictional alter ego.

There is not enough gratitude in the world for my gifted and adorable partner in life, Brian David Orter. I will start by refraining from sharing his pet name with my readers.

Dad, your chant remains loud and clear.